Sign up for our newsletter to hear
about new and upcoming releases.

www.ylva-publishing.com

Other Books by Jess Lea

The Taste of Her
The Taste of Her - Vol 1 (e-book)
The Taste of Her - Vol 2 (e-book)
The Taste of Her – A Collection of Ten Erotic Short Stories (paperback)

A Curious Woman

Jess Lea

This book is for Sam.

Chapter 1

MARGARET LOOKED AROUND THE DARKENED museum, and weighed the harpoon between her hands. She shut her eyes for a moment, the blackness deepening and settling around her like a cloak. The chill air, the silence, the weapon in her grasp... For a moment, things were as they should be, and she was almost at peace.

Opening her eyes again, she shook her head. No, that was an illusion. Nothing was settled here, and she had work to do. She stepped out into the main display area, her shoes striking the stone floor with a hollow clunking sound.

A key jangled in the front door, and a young woman's voice sounded, nervous and tentative. "Hello?"

Her assistant.

Margaret didn't reply.

From outside came a creaking noise as the wind bent the trees. The windows rattled in their tiny frames. This old stone building wasn't designed for letting in light or fresh air. It squatted close to the earth, huddling down against the icy gusts that came screeching in off the bay, straight from Antarctica.

It had been built as a watch house in the nineteenth century. The small, dim rooms now used for storage and office space had once housed bushrangers, pickpockets, drunks, and poisoners on their way to the chain gang or the gallows. Rumour had it, some nights in those rooms you could hear things: a hammering on the doors, a scrabbling of fingernails against the stone.

Margaret had never heard them herself, but perhaps the ghosts were afraid to disturb her.

The main display room, once the old courthouse, lay in silent gloom. Another power cut, thanks to the storm, and the sun was late to rise at this time of year. The main switch was all the way over by the front door, but it didn't matter. She knew every inch of this place, and the darkness never troubled her.

Her eyes adjusted, and she could make out the crouching forms of long-dead animals: a team of stuffed huskies, their eighty-year-old fur dull and patchy, pulling a sleigh. On it sat a dummy dressed in explorer gear from the Scott era, his body shapeless in canvas trousers and a hooded smock, his eyes hidden behind slitted leather goggles.

Margaret returned his blank gaze for a moment then glanced to the right to meet the reproachful glass eyes of a fur seal, its relatives long since hunted to extinction in these parts.

"Moth-eaten old monsters," she'd heard Kelly, her assistant, describing them to a friend with a shudder, when she thought Margaret wasn't observing her. A mistake; Margaret was always observing. "Why can't we be a proper, modern museum?"

Margaret assumed that meant a place full of touch screens, flashing lights, and cheerful recordings explaining how gravity worked. A glorified childcare centre: a place that never showed people anything they didn't wish to see. Well, Margaret had not come back to this little map smudge of a town to make people happy.

She caught a flash of movement and swung around. But it was only her reflection in a glass cabinet. The cabinet's contents—miniature replicas of the Erebus and Terror—would have looked harmless by daylight. But here in the shadows there was something eerie about the ships, as if they had been shrunk by witchcraft along with their human crew, to be frozen behind glass for eternity.

"Hello there?" Kelly's voice had grown plaintive; she must have forgotten the location of the main switch.

Margaret's mouth tightened in distaste. Incompetence irritated her, and so did obvious fear. She did not answer or pick up her pace as she made for the entrance, her heels beating a slow rhythm against the stone. In the shadows, an alien figure loomed beside her, its arms and legs swollen, its domed head enormous, faceless, made of gleaming metal: an antique diving suit. Margaret acknowledged it with a glance. Then she stepped out into the vestibule and flicked the main light switch to the building.

Kelly screamed.

The lights flickered and blinked bluish-white. Their flash illuminated Margaret's reflection in the front window, gleaming against the semi-darkness of the outside world. Tall, lean and angular, clad entirely in black. Her short dark hair was slicked close to her skull; her ivory face seemed disembodied, surrounded by darkness. The shadows and flashes of harsh light exaggerated her high cheekbones, firm jaw, Roman nose, and shadowed eyes. Her feet ended in towering heels; her fingers were clad in black gloves. They flexed like spiders. She held the harpoon in a practiced grip.

Kelly's shriek—choking, bubbling, spanning several octaves—would have made a Hammer Horror heroine proud. Then the lights came on properly.

Things steadied, and Margaret saw her usual reflection this time, standing calmly before the reception desk. She wore her black work suit, plain but elegantly cut, with a high Mandarin collar and silver cufflinks, along with the black cotton gloves she always used when handling exhibits. Like this harpoon from an old whaling ship, now under restoration here.

"Calm yourself, Ms Petrovich." Margaret kept her voice deadpan, her expression composed. She had not put down the harpoon.

"Oh, Ms Gale! I didn't know you were here. I forgot where the light switch was, and I… I got a scare."

"Please, Ms Petrovich, show some self-control." Margaret sniffed in disdain. "This is a small coastal maritime museum. What is there to alarm you here? We only deal with shipwrecks, scurvy, snow-blindness, mutiny, rum, sodomy, and the lash." She drew the last word out with a long, sibilant hiss.

"Sorry, Ms Gale." Kelly swallowed and made a desperate attempt to look professional. "I was just about to get things set up for the school tour this morning." She shifted from foot to foot. "I thought… I thought I could lead the tour, if that's okay, Ms Gale? I could use the practice and, well, after last time…" Kelly flapped a helpless hand.

Perhaps she did not like to refer in detail to what had happened the previous time Margaret had hosted a school group here. In Margaret's opinion, her management of the situation had been perfectly appropriate, but that meek little rabbit of a teacher had looked rather shaken.

"Certainly." Margaret laid the harpoon back in its cabinet in the front display. Then she pulled off her black gloves, finger by finger, and tucked them reverently away. She could sense Kelly watching, wide-eyed.

Margaret locked the cabinet, clipped her key chain back in place, and straightened up slowly. She turned her head with a predator's lazy grace.

"Have you nothing to do, Ms Petrovich? I do hope we are not boring you here?"

"Oh! No, I'll get on with…" Kelly scuttled away, her expression equal parts resentment and fear. A reaction Margaret was used to. A reaction she welcomed. She could almost hear Kelly berating herself for studying museology in the first place, when she would have been much happier with a nice job in a bank.

When she was alone again, Margaret Gale permitted herself to smile.

Chapter 2

BESS WOKE WITH A JOLT. Through the window the dawn sky was pale grey, but the room was still dim and huddled with shadows. Someone was watching her.

Adrenaline pounded through her. Her heart hammered, her limbs jerked. Her right hand shot out to grab the full, metal water bottle she kept on the windowsill. She gripped it tight. She would not be helpless this time.

Flinging off the blankets, Bess sat up—and gasped as the crown of her head thudded into the sloped wooden ceiling. Eyes watering, she swung around to face the intruder.

There was a scratching sound of claws against wood, then a triumphant, warbling shriek.

Her vision cleared, and she found herself looking down into the bright amber and black eyes of a rooster.

Russet and scarlet coloured, with a great plume of white tail feathers, Bess's housemate stood on the top step of the ladder that led up to the loft bed. He chortled to himself, his wattles quivering. He was waiting for breakfast.

"Oh, you little..." Bess dropped the bottle and flopped back onto the mattress. She rubbed her aching skull, then let out her tension in a hoot of laughter. "Oh, Genghis." She scooped him up into the crook of her arm. "Where would I be without my brave defender?"

Bess clambered down the ladder and into the main room of her tiny house. The pot-bellied wood heater had burned itself out and the chilly air nipped at her ankles. Still, as she looked around her, she felt a surge of warmth. The room smelled deliciously of wood-smoke and last night's homemade apple crumble.

There was the kitchen ledge and barstools she'd sanded and varnished herself. A fold-down couch with bright cushions she'd embroidered, the rainbow rug she'd knotted together from scraps of old clothing, and a fruit-bat mobile she'd made dangling above her head. It had been a year, and Bess wasn't missing television at all.

There was the little gas-bottle stove, the kitchen chopping-block, and the bookshelves that covered the eastern wall, holding everything from Virginia Woolf to Pippi Longstocking. Not to mention the tiny camping fridge, containing nothing but milk, yoghurt, and a few beers. Everything else kept fine in the outdoor pantry at this time of year. Why had she ever thought she needed to pay huge energy bills to keep a big fridge full of crusty old pickle jars and withered vegetables? She'd been such a sheep back then.

Bess nodded to her belongings as if greeting old friends. She reminded herself to pay attention. *Every moment is unique.* This was home, all twenty square metres of it, and it was all hers.

She glanced over at the chickens' corner. On the cold winter nights, Genghis, Charlotte, Emily, and Anne would settle down there in an open drawer, wearing the paisley chook-nappies that Bess had made for them. She recalled where her pets had been living before being rescued: the garbage-filled yard of a squat behind Bess's flat in the city. Some hippie housemate had brought them there as chicks and forgotten about them. After weeks of looking out the window and seeing their distress—left without water for days on end, their hutch filthy, Genghis bleeding from a dog attack—Bess had finally had enough. The night before she left Melbourne for Port Bannir, she'd jumped the fence under cover of darkness, like a plump, angry ninja, and stolen them all.

She reached down to scratch her companion behind his comb.

"All in the past, mate," Bess murmured, remembering her counsellor's advice. "Acknowledge the memory, then place it gently onto a pretty little raft full of flowers, and let it float out to sea." She swept back her tangle of red hair and remembered to smile. *You are in charge of your emotions. So choose joy.* "Breakfast?"

Her feet crammed into gumboots and with a coat over her pyjamas, Bess stepped outside. Out here, the air was so cold it made her cheeks ache, but the sunshine was dazzling. She smelled damp foliage, possum droppings, and crisp, clean air. Dew glinted on the grass and on the small granite water feature Bess had installed (recycled water, of course). It was designed to promote tranquillity. The gum leaves above her seemed to have been brushed with silver; the paddocks stretched as far as she could see. Magpies were warbling, and the chooks hopped down the steps behind her to peck around in the dirt. Bess hugged herself and breathed deep.

"I am fully present," she repeated, as she did every morning. She wriggled her fingers and toes, anchoring herself inside her solid, freckled body. "I am grateful. I am valid. And I deserve to be happy."

She sat down on the steps, reached for her ukulele, and picked out a few verses of *Botany Bay*. Soon she would go back inside and eat the fruit muesli she'd made for herself—with a handful of Coco Pops thrown in because Coco Pops were okay as long as you ate them mindfully. Then she would get on her pushbike and head into Port Bannir for another day at the best job she'd ever had.

What did a few nightmares matter when she was living the dream?

She hummed along to the cheerful ukulele melody of a song about exile. How could she not be happy? Everything she loved was right here.

⁀〜〜∽

Bess was still humming to herself as she cycled into Port Bannir. She passed the bakery, the Country Fire Authority shed, the town hall, and the charity shop, waving to a few locals on the way. Some waved back; some didn't. Not everyone in town was a fan of Bess's workplace, but she assured herself that they would come around in time.

Turning off the main road, she puffed her way up a sloping gravel track. The thick scrub and banksias hid the coastline from view, but she could smell the cold, salty sea-spray and hear the whoosh of the waves. Then she rounded the corner. The vegetation thinned away, the wind whipped her hair around her face, and there it was: the bright azure of the harbour, the white beach, and at the end of a rocky promontory, her destination.

The Cabinet of Curiosities.

On the outside, the building was stark: great, dark concrete slabs that made it look like a Soviet missile silo. Bess didn't like that, but her boss Leon insisted it was perfect. He said it gave visitors no inkling of what they would discover inside. *They come in expecting to be disappointed*, he said. *And then we blow their minds.*

"Morning, Christos." She nodded to the security guard as she chained up her bike and changed her shoes.

"Bess. Nice day for it."

She checked her appearance in the glass sliding doors. The polka-dot rockabilly dress was her own creation, cut to flatter her heavy breasts and hips and her plump, shapely arms, their skin creamy beneath the freckles. Teamed with cat's eye spectacles and glossy red sling-backs, the effect was eye-catching.

Back in the city, Bess had spent years hiding in the frumpy, overpriced clothes that were sold begrudgingly to fat girls, and enough was enough. Nowadays, she was determined to make an impression.

"Is his royal highness around, Christos? I've got something for him."

"Try the vampire room." Christos yawned. Then he sauntered down the path to deal with the first busload of tourists, who were already craning their necks and pressing their noses to the coach windows, desperate to have their minds blown.

～

"Bess!" Leon waved with his free hand. With his other hand, he snapped a picture of himself inside the coffin. "One for the social media feed?"

"Why not?" Bess glanced around. Inside the Cabinet of Curiosities, the lighting was kept low. Leon wanted to create place of mystery, he said, not some sterile museum or gallery.

The vampire room featured half a dozen upright coffins, which members of the public were encouraged to try for size and comfort.

Satisfied with the shot, Leon hopped nimbly out of the coffin. He brushed down his mustard three-piece suit and twiddled his waxed ringmaster-moustache.

"So, Bess! My right-hand woman, my consigliere, my fairy godmother— what have you got for me today?"

"Well…" Bess returned his smile. Leon might be a bit pretentious and pleased with himself, but this place was special. "I know where we can get our hands on a moa egg."

"Not the great prehistoric monster-birds of New Zealand?" Leon's eyes widened.

"The very ones." She showed him the photo. "Nine hundred years old, ninety percent intact, beautifully preserved. I thought we could exhibit it inside one of those Victorian gilded birdcages, hung from the ceiling."

"Brilliant!" The newspapers said Leon was Australia's most successful cynic, but the promise of a new exhibit made him bounce and beam like a child at Christmas. "Put a cuttlefish in the cage, yeah? And one of those little mirrors with bells."

Bess nodded and made a note.

"Any news on the Andean mummy?"

"They're still holding out for the original price. But I'll beat them down."

"I know you will." Her boss grinned and rubbed his hands together. He set off on one last check of the building before the tourists were admitted. Bess hurried along at his side. "Anything else I need to know?"

"Well, I've been going through the visitor feedback." Bess consulted her notes. "The forty-foot tapeworm is a winner, and the schoolkids love posing for photos with their heads in that set of diprotodon jaws. But I should tell you, the wall of Edwardian cock rings has had quite a few complaints."

"I see." Leon fondled his moustache. "Did you get them in writing?"

"Yep."

"Excellent. Pick the most outraged ones, and post them on the website."

"Already done." Bess flipped through her to-do list, as they walked past a cabinet labelled "Rubber Chickens Down the Ages." It was right next door to the Bearded Ladies' Hall of Fame.

Bess said, "Now, that news crew will be here at ten for your interview."

"Great!"

"Are you sure you want to film it inside the bouncy castle made of blow-up sex dolls?" She chewed her lip. "The lighting in there is not flattering."

"Of course! I chose this suit to coordinate with it."

"All right, it's your funeral. Hey, speaking of suits, what do you think of this? The artist is keen for a quick sale." She pulled up photo. "It's a suit made entirely from the labels cut from hundreds of other suits."

"Love it!" Leon whooped. "You totally get me, Bess. You get what I'm trying to do here." He opened his arms wide. "When I was a kid, I used to get so excited by school trips to the museum or the art gallery, but they always turned out to be rubbish. Cabinets full of rocks, paintings of gloomy old people, and cranky grown-ups telling us to *shush*." He groaned. "Dreary, elitist nonsense—intellectual child abuse! For twenty years, I refused to set foot in one of those places. I became a successful restaurateur instead; my cookbooks topped the bestseller list and people flew all the way from Tokyo just to taste my birthday cakes made entirely of sashimi."

"I'm a vegetarian myself," Bess reminded him.

"But when my Sydney restaurant burned down, I had a crisis of faith. Did I really want to rebuild and do the same thing for the next twenty years? Or did I have the guts to start something really fresh?" Leon nodded to himself. "So I took the insurance money, and I took one hell of a risk. I started this place—and not in a wealthy, culturally literate big city, but in a little coastal town where I used to come for holidays as a kid. People said I was out of my mind. Who would travel all the way from Melbourne just to look at a crazy gallery full of the weirdest, most amazing shit I could get my hands on?" He narrowed his eyes. "And you know what I told them?"

"That the public would love to drive four hours to see an exhibit of historic condoms?"

"Ex-actly!" Leon grinned. "And I was right. Look at this place—it's buzzing! In the past five years, we have transformed this town into a hub for regional tourism, and all those stuffy big-city museums are struggling to imitate *our* style. We've proved it's possible to show remarkable things in a way that entertains the public instead of boring them into a coma. Do we tell people to shush? No, we do not; our staff go up to visitors and engage them in conversation. Do we say 'Don't touch'? Hell no—we encourage it! Do we post long, tedious essays next to every exhibit and make people feel like they're obliged to read everything before they're allowed to look at the object itself? Fuck, no! Instead of plaques, we have screens beside the exhibits with a rolling Twitter feed, where visitors can post their own thoughts on what they're looking at while they're looking at it!"

"Some of them do post 'this is shit', though," Bess cautioned him.

Leon waved that away. "Yeah, but they say it *ironically*." He let out a happy sigh. "I'm so bloody proud of this place and of my team. You all took a risk working here, but boy is it paying off, right?"

"It's the most interesting job I've ever had," Bess said truthfully.

Leon took a little leap in the air and clicked his heels together. "And in light of that… Bess, there's an item I'd really, really love you to secure for me."

Bess wrinkled her brow, waiting. Then realisation dawned. "Oh, Leon… I don't think that's going to happen."

"Come on, Bess! It'd be epic!"

"I've called the Maritime Museum about that item three times, Leon. She refuses to sell. She wouldn't even come to the phone; she made her assistant take the call."

"So, go there in person. You can persuade her, Bess; I have faith in you."

"She's meant to be a tough character, Leon. I've never met her, but she's got quite a reputation in town."

"Sure, for running the world's most boring museum." Leon rolled his eyes. "Small-town local museums—is there anything more dire? Open one afternoon a week and run by a historical society whose members belong in a fossil display themselves." He grimaced. "Model ships? Coins? Foghorns? Jesus wept. Then the bloody woman gets her hands on one truly fabulous item and she keeps it in storage! It's positively criminal."

"Maybe. But…"

"Anyway, she must be in need of the money. I'm sure no one visits her place any longer, not since we arrived in town. Offer her double if you have to. I want that item, Bess!"

Bess sighed in defeat.

"I'll do my best."

"You're a star." Leon paused to enjoy one of their new displays—a wall of television sets showing people soulfully performing one-hit wonders in sign language. (To judge from the performer's expression, "Tainted Love" was especially moving.) "And can you block out some time in my diary today? I need to do some focused thinking about next year's headline exhibit."

"Sure." Bess made another note. "What's it going to be?"

"Well, so far I've only confirmed the title," said Leon. "I'm thinking of calling it *Blood Is Thicker*. What do you reckon?" Bess gave a half-hearted nod and hoped it would not involve any abattoir photos. "And hey, Bess, about that suit made of labels. Is there any chance of getting it here in time for my interview? Maybe I could model it for the cameras."

"I'll get Mikiel onto it."

"Wicked. Thanks." Leon hesitated. For the first time that morning, a look of uncertainty crossed his face. "Unless… You don't think it might make me look like…well, like a bit of a hipster, do you?"

"No." Bess did her best to look shocked. "Of course not."

"Thank God." Leon's expression cleared. "You know me, Bess. If there's one thing I can't fucking *stand*, it's a hipster."

He twirled his moustache, lit up his pipe, and hurried away.

⁓

Bess coasted back into the town centre, conscious of a few odd looks from the locals she passed; cyclists were rare in Port Bannir. As she dismounted and chained up her bike, she had to admit that Margaret Gale's Maritime Museum might turn out to be boring on the inside, but it was certainly housed in a more handsome building than Bess's own workplace. The old colonial courthouse was beautifully maintained, and it had a dour grandeur about it, like a haunted house that only accepted ghosts of historical significance.

Contrary to Leon's prediction, this local museum kept normal business hours, and the doors were already open. A large noticeboard was propped up outside. It read:

> *Welcome to the Port Bannir Maritime Museum, guardian of this*
> *district's rich and colourful past. We trust you will enjoy your visit.*
> *No food or drink.*
> *No flash photography.*
> *No mobile phones.*
> *No backpacks.*
> *No touching the exhibits.*
> *No running in the display area.*
> *No refunds.*

"No diving in the shallow end," Bess murmured to herself. She read on.

Toilets are for staff and visitors only.
Visitors making excessive noise will be asked to leave.
Visitors changing children's nappies in the display area will be asked to leave.
Pirate impressions in a Maritime Museum are NOT
ORIGINAL, and may result in visitors being—

"—asked to leave," Bess finished under her breath. How horrible, to think that a museum curator could resent her own visitors so much. She could imagine Margaret Gale now: ancient, crabby, crusty, and shrill, the sort of mad old biddy who terrorised local councillors and wrote letters to the newspaper complaining about her neighbours who didn't bring in their rubbish bins on time.

Although… Bess hated to admit it, but part of her was a tiny bit envious of anyone who felt free to enforce the rules so rigorously and without apology. Bess had been pretty appalled the first time she'd seen parents changing their baby right on the table at the café at Leon's gallery. They hadn't reacted well when she'd asked them to use the bathrooms instead. "We thought this was a family-friendly place!" the woman had hollered, from underneath Leon's signed photograph of Betty Page.

Following Margaret Gale's list of rules, the noticeboard concluded:

This museum covers Australasian and Antarctic history exclusively. To avoid
embarrassment, kindly refrain from asking questions about polar bears.
Please note: the 18th century cat-o'-nine-tails in Room 3 is a DISPLAY ITEM ONLY.

Bess blinked several times. Then she straightened her polka-dot dress and stepped through the doors.

Inside Margaret Gale's museum, the lights were operating-theatre white. The air held a faint tang of disinfectant. Bess's footsteps rang against the stone floor.

"Full fee or concession?" asked the jumpy-looking kid behind the information desk. His nametag read Kenneth.

Bess explained that she was here to see Ms Gale, and no, she didn't have an appointment.

The colour drained from his face. "Did you call ahead of time, Miss, or…?"

"No. Is your boss in?"

"She's… she's in." His Adam's apple seemed to be trying to leap to safety. "But she doesn't really like it when people drop by without a booking—"

"Won't take a minute." Bess smiled and brushed past him, sensing she could be here all day otherwise. For goodness sake, she knew jobs were hard to find in Port Bannir, but the young man's cringing manner seemed a bit over the top. He was working for a museum curator, not a Disney villain. Surely.

Inside the main display area, a woman whose nametag read Kelly was lecturing a group of school children about what it was like to travel in a convict ship. They were the only visitors in the room, apart from a couple of bewildered Chinese tourists, who had probably gotten lost on the way to Leon's museum. They were examining a cabinet of sextant's tools, which were in beautiful condition. Leon would have laughed at her, but Bess found that stuff kind of amazing. To think people had travelled right across the globe using nothing but longhand sums. Bess could barely make it home from the supermarket without her well-thumbed map of Port Bannir and Surrounds.

Still, Leon had been right about the museum in general, she decided. Ships' logbooks and travelling trunks—snore. And so much writing! Plaques everywhere; surely no one had the patience to read them? And all those stuffed animals gave Bess the creeps.

One display made her feel quite queasy: a life-sized dummy dressed in oilskins brandished a harpoon gun, while another hung from the deck by a monkey belt, about to skin a fibreglass whale, which was liberally spattered with red paint. Beside them, another model whaler sat, scraping flesh from blubber with a large knife. Was it really ethical to show that stuff to kids? Bess didn't mind her own gallery's exhibits of occult paintings and surgical leeches, but there were limits.

She glanced around in search of Margaret Gale. Bess could picture her: just like the cranky old substitute teachers they used to have at Bess's school. Wearing wrinkled stockings and a droopy cardigan and false teeth that would shoot out of her mouth when she yelled at you.

Seeing no one fitting that description, Bess wandered over to a cabinet against the far wall. The lid was unlocked and open, and inside lay the most marvellous old flintlock revolver. It was a battered thing, but splendidly engraved, and Bess could imagine it being waved around by Ben Hall as the bushranger held up the mail coach at Jugiong. Although she knew she shouldn't, she couldn't resist reaching into the cabinet to run an admiring fingertip over the barrel.

She felt a rush of air and saw a flash of silver. Out of nowhere, a sword came swishing down to halt in mid-air, half an inch above her wandering fingers.

Bess froze. The weapon looked old but viciously sharp. Not an actual sword, she realised—the shape was wrong—but just as alarming. It must have been heavy but it hung in the air perfectly still. Slowly, Bess's gaze slid up the long blade and handle, to a black-gloved hand and a dark sleeve, then higher still, to gaze into the eyes of her opponent.

The woman was a good foot taller than Bess. Her face was white, her black gaze narrow and focused, her hair lying close to her head like a sleek dark cap. Her perfume was faint but spicy.

The woman glanced down at her blade, poised over Bess's knuckles. When she spoke, her voice was deep and resonant. "Hands. Off."

Bess eyes widened. Very carefully, she drew away from the antique gun.

Her assailant waited until Bess had stepped back, before laying her weapon down in the cabinet next to the revolver.

According to the plaque on the wall—which Bess felt keen to read all of a sudden—the weapon that had just been brandished at her was a boarding knife from an old whaling ship.

Bess swallowed hard, composing herself. That perfume drifted around her.

Margaret Gale was not what she had expected.

⁓

Bess Campbell was *exactly* what Margaret had expected.

As she peeled the black cotton from her fingers and extended a reluctant hand to be shaken, Margaret reflected that the so-called wacky individualists who worked for Leon Powell all looked as if they'd come out of the same inner-city sausage machine.

It wasn't just their preposterous dress sense—although at least this one wasn't wearing roller skates and a monocle. And it wasn't just that they lacked any appreciation for history or museology. No, it was their arrogance that grated on Margaret, their sense of entitlement. Who were they, after all, but a bunch of failed graphic designers who had been in this town all of five minutes? Look at this one—she'd barely set foot in the museum and she was already trying to steal things!

Margaret fixed her guest with a look that would have frozen the beak off a penguin.

"Ms Campbell, I presume. If you've come about the matter you discussed with my assistant last week, I'm afraid you have had a wasted journey. Do feel free to take in the exhibits before you leave." Margaret gave a thin smile. "Our gift shop has a charming picture book about a ship's cat which you might enjoy."

To her surprise, Bess Campbell did not crush easily. In fact, she seemed to have recovered from the boarding knife incident remarkably quickly. She had the nerve to smile and say "Actually, Ms Gale, I came by to apologise. We went in too hard before, trying to persuade you to sell."

"Indeed?" Margaret's eyes narrowed.

"Of course. The artefact we discussed is unique and precious; I'm not surprised you won't part with it. Something that unusual must be the centrepiece of your collection." Bess looked around with an innocent expression, as if searching for the item.

Margaret growled inwardly. The little pest knew full well the thing wasn't on display to the public. "It's under restoration," she snapped.

"Well, we at the Cabinet of Curiosities were wondering if we might come to a mutually beneficial arrangement."

Margaret turned away, snapped the cabinet shut, and locked it. "No."

"A lease system…."

Unbelievable—the woman was still talking!

"We would pay a substantial premium to host the item, with full acknowledgement of its ownership here." Bess had the nerve to step between Margaret and the cabinet, obliging Margaret to look at her. She had light freckles all over her face and throat, and pale pink lips. There was a delicate tattoo of a drifting dandelion peeking out from beneath the strap of her dress.

"The exposure of your item in our gallery might benefit your business here." Bess was rude enough to glance around the almost empty room.

Margaret scowled. "I doubt that. The sort of people who enjoy your exhibits of exotic lavatories are unlikely to take much interest in our district's seafaring heritage."

"Actually, we've got a toilet seat from an old sailing ship," Bess enthused.

She seemed on the verge of describing it, before Margaret's look made her halt.

"We'd be more than happy to set up an exchange exhibit," she said, changing track. "If there's anything in our collection—"

"There is nothing," Margaret said, "in that junk shop of Mr Powell's that would be of the slightest use to us here. Now, if that is all…"

"Could I look at it?"

Dear God, this Bess Campbell was nothing if not hopeful. Hopeful in that bouncy, perky way that Margaret had always found intensely irritating.

"Before I leave?"

"No."

"It's just that my boss is so keen," Bess urged. "But if I could tell him that I'd seen the item and it was rubbish—"

"It's a masterpiece!" Margaret could have slapped herself for getting sucked in by such an obvious ploy. But she was sick of this—sick of her precious collection being dismissed and ignored by the world's teeming population of imbeciles.

Margaret's phone buzzed in her pocket. She glanced down; it was the chair of the historical society. Calling, no doubt, to pester her again about hosting his grandfather's collection of polished cow horns. Despite Margaret having explained to him in no uncertain terms that dairy farming had not played a significant part in this district's colonial history, and that she was not running a council rubbish collection.

That decided things. She thrust the phone back into her pocket and beckoned Bess after her. "Two minutes, then."

The item was kept under lock and key in the secure storage area. As Margaret unfastened the drawer and eased it open, she sensed Bess leaning in, craning to get a closer look. The pose caused the strap of Bess's polka-dot dress to slip halfway off her smooth, freckled shoulder. Margaret fought the urge to reach out and snap it back into place. She did not like disorder.

"Oh…" Bess breathed. A delicate pink flooded into her cheeks. "Oh, it's *wonderful.*"

Margaret couldn't help relenting just a little at the woman's obvious delight. It was rare to find anyone who really appreciated the artefacts here. And this one was unique all right. Encased in a leather travelling case lined with midnight blue silk and inset with a glass panel, it had clearly been treasured once. It was carved from the tusk of an elephant, decorated with the most exquisite designs—in China, most likely—and finished with the word *Diana* engraved in dainty cursive into the wings at the base.

"It was found in the estate of an Anglo-Indian military family, who migrated here after the Gold Rush to run a shipping line." When Margaret spoke about her exhibits, her naturally commanding tone dropped to a gentle murmur, as if soothing the precious things back to sleep. "It's been dated to 1880 or thereabouts. It sat forgotten in an attic for over a century—it was very nearly tossed out when the house was sold." She ran a caressing hand through the air above the treasure. "Handcrafted. Unique."

"Stunning," Bess agreed. "And how amazing, to think some liberated woman was playing with sex toys back in 1880."

Margaret froze. Her spine stiffened. So this was why the ghastly Mr Powell was interested in the item. She might have known. "It is a Roman-style fertility symbol." Margaret's voice turned steely-cold. "The Victorians were fascinated with pagan iconography. This was clearly based on the Roman *fascinus*, an effigy used to summon divine protection against the Evil Eye and guard the *sacra Romana*, the safety of the Roman state. Such symbols were found all over the ancient Mediterranean."

From behind her cats-eye glasses, Bess gave an incredulous stare. "You're joking, right?"

She did not dignify that with a response.

"Margaret. It's a dildo."

Margaret's nostrils flared. "I should be grateful if you would refrain from addressing me in a familiar way, Ms Campbell. I'm aware that Mr Powell's employees have, at best, a passing acquaintance with history, but I can assure you the item is an imitation Roman symbol. Admittedly the size differs somewhat from actual pagan artefacts, being—" Margaret cleared her throat "—significantly larger, and the reference to the goddess Diana is anachronistic in this context, but nevertheless—"

"You're taking the piss, aren't you?" Bess was still smiling, as if hopeful she might have missed a joke. "Mar—Ms Gale, this is clearly…" Bess appeared to search for another way of phrasing it, before giving up. "A great big cock. And don't you think it's likely that Diana was the name of the woman who…"

"No, I do not, Ms Campbell." Margaret closed the drawer so hard the item rattled inside it. "I realise some people would prefer a tawdry, fictional explanation. But this artefact happens to be part of the rich cultural heritage of our region."

"Well, I'm not arguing with that."

"And the fact you would exploit it for cheap, historically inaccurate laughs demonstrates to me once again that your…place of business has nothing of value to contribute to this town." Margaret's eyes narrowed as she folded her arms.

Bess blinked. "Excuse me?"

Margaret made no move to relent or apologise.

"What's your problem?" Bess demanded.

"At present? Inefficient use of my time." Margaret brushed an imaginary speck of dust from her gloves. "Now, if there's nothing more…" She gave her best stare, the one that terrified tourists, cowed her staff, and sent tradesmen scuttling back to their vans to adjust the invoice.

To her aggravation, Bess did not flinch. Instead, she let out an incredulous laugh. "I came here offering an excellent deal," she said. "It would have benefitted you more than us. Hell, we've already got our own display of historical sex toys."

Margaret glowered. "It's a faux-Roman—"

"—and you act like this," Bess finished. "I can't believe you're so rude. No wonder no one wants to come here! It's bad enough paying to look at old tin cans, without having Cruella de Vil taking your ticket." She hoisted her handbag onto her shoulder and pushed her red hair back. "I'll see myself out. If you come to your senses, you know where to find us. Just follow the crowd."

Margaret lifted her chin. "That is not something I've ever made a habit of doing."

The view from behind as Bess swept out might have been worth looking at, but Margaret didn't. Instead she returned to the display room, took out her microfibre cloths, and set about rubbing finger-marks from a glass cabinet with more force than was necessary.

Inside the cabinet were the tin cans Bess had sneered at. They were leftovers, originally part of a stash earmarked for the Franklin expedition. Technically not Australian history, but the unfortunate Franklin's record as lieutenant-governor of Van Diemen's Land made the inclusion permissible in Margaret's eyes. If you knew where to look, you could still see the lead sealant. Those tins had been a wonder of technology at the time, a means of preserving food and keeping men alive for months in the frozen sea. Instead, so the theory went, the tins had poisoned the crew and sent them wandering off, mad, to their deaths on the ice.

Margaret scrubbed until her wiry arms ached and her face grew warm. These things *were* interesting. They were real, and they mattered. Why couldn't people see that?

By the time she'd finished, the glass was sparkling. She put away her rags and rubbed her hands with sanitiser until everything was clean again.

Outside, Bess straddled her pushbike and took some slow, angry breaths. Then she refreshed her lipstick, shut her eyes, and did another affirmation. As she murmured "I am grateful", she heard sniggers from the kids in the school group. They had left the museum and were lining up for the bus.

Bess's eyes snapped open. *"What?"*

Her voice was loud enough to turn heads. She reminded herself to calm down and be in the moment—but just at this moment, she didn't feel very grateful or valid at all.

Chapter 3

"Bess!" Kylie looked up as the plastic ribbons stirred in the doorway. Bess struggled through. Her face still felt flushed as she stomped up to the counter. The recollection of Margaret's sneer made her long to pedal back to the Maritime Museum and throw an authentic sailing ship's toilet seat through the window.

"Your place of business has nothing of value to contribute to this town." Who the hell did that woman think she was?

It took an effort for Bess to remind herself to be present, to hear the slap of worn linoleum under her feet, and breathe in the warm air, enticingly scented with baking bread, fresh croissants, and golden-brown scones fresh from the oven. McKenzie's Bakery was a Port Bannir institution. Tourists made day trips from Melbourne to stock up on rhubarb and white chocolate muffins, and truck drivers took the wrong turn-off on purpose so they could saunter innocently out of McKenzie's with a steak and mushroom pie in each hand.

Kylie leaned her fleshy arms on the counter. "Bad day, Bessie?"

Bess breathed slowly. "Well, *'bad day'* is just a meaning we humans assign to a random series of events over a twenty-four hour period," she explained, remembering how her self-help books had phrased it. "Did you know that most of our unhappiness comes from attaching meaning to things, instead of just practising acceptance?" She caught Kylie's eye. "Pretty bad. And it's barely lunchtime."

"Speaking of which…" Kylie flourished her tongs. "The usual?"

"That'd be great." Bess watched as Kylie packed up warm spanakopita and Greek salad for her, a jumbo egg and lettuce roll for Christos, a mini cheese and bacon quiche for Leon, and a selection of cakes for the staff afternoon tea. "Red velvet lamingtons? Is that innovation or sacrilege?"

"Only one way to find out." Kylie added a couple to Bess's order. "On the house."

Some Port Bannir residents resented the Cabinet of Curiosities, complaining that the place had made traffic a nightmare, ruined the view of the peninsula, and attracted weirdos to the area—but most local businesses were all in favour. Kylie's only complaint was that the tourists demanded her coffee and cinnamon rolls faster than she could make them.

"What's been ruffling your feathers, then?"

"Oh, just a difficult meeting." Bess shook her head. "Down the street, at the Maritime Museum."

Kylie's eyebrows shot up. "Not with Morticia Addams?"

"Ms Gale, yes." Bess counted out her money. "Do you know her?"

"Oh, yeah. Her bloody security firm keeps ticketing my suppliers for parking in her driveway. I've complained, but it's a waste of time. No one knows the bylaws better than her, and no one is better at scaring the mayor into doing what he's told." Kylie snorted. "I've seen him sneaking out of council chambers through the bin bay to avoid running into her."

"She did seem a bit…confrontational."

"She's a witch with a capital B," Kylie said. "Always has been. My cousin Gill was at school with her forty years ago. Just around the corner, at Port Bannir primary. And Gill reckons she was a piece of work even then."

"Really?"

"Yeah. When she was ten, Margaret got banned from netball after a fight on the court, so she broke into the PE store cupboard and punctured every single ball." Kylie, a lifetime member of the Port Bannir Football Netball Club, sucked her teeth in horror at this outrage.

"I didn't realise she was from here." Bess was surprised. Port Bannir had produced wool barons, conservative National Party MPs, and a few footballers, but somehow it was hard to imagine this town producing Margaret Gale.

"She left after school, of course." Kylie nodded. "Melbourne, I think, or Sydney. Couldn't believe it ten years ago when she came back. I walked past her in High Street and my jaw just dropped. Course, she pretended like she didn't recognise me. Lots of young ones go away saying they'll come home after uni, but not many of them do."

"Why did she come back, then?" Bess reached for the warm package and tucked it under her arm.

Kylie shrugged. "Who knows? So she could lord it over the rest of us, I suppose. Or maybe she just couldn't hack it in the city. After all, she might act like she's the Queen of Sheba, but underneath you can tell she's a bit, you know…"

"What?"

Kylie looked surprised that Bess hadn't caught on.

"Nutty," she said. "Mark my words, there's something there that's not right."

⌒⌒

"Bessie!" Leon gave a deafening groan down the phone. Bess shifted it away from her ear. "You are killing me here!"

"Sorry, Leon, but she wouldn't budge." Bess clamped the phone between her chin and her shoulder as she strapped the food package to her bike.

"Come on, Bess, you're better than this! What happened to the woman who got me that set of Rita Hayworth's fake eyelashes for half the asking price?"

"I can't work miracles, Leon." Bess picked up her helmet. "If it's any consolation, there was hardly anyone in there. Her museum is very… old-fashioned."

"Obsolete, you mean." Leon gave a grunt of contempt. "Well, let the records show I tried to do this the nice way. But the rate that woman's going, it won't be long till she comes crawling to us begging for a quick sale. Then I might not be so generous."

As Bess peddled back to the gallery, even the smell of Kylie's baked treats wasn't enough to lift her spirits. She hated screwing up at work.

Really, she shouldn't have got the job in the first place. As if a fine arts degree and three years of working in an alternative gallery the size of a shoebox qualified her for a curator role at Australia's newest and funkiest tourist destination! But her brother had been urging her to get out of Melbourne and stop brooding over the things that had happened there. So, she'd sent in her résumé, and after the most peculiar job interview of her life—Leon's questions had included "What's your favourite palindrome?" and "If you were a crayon, what colour would you be?"—she'd found herself employed. Her new boss told her he was less interested in qualifications than potential, and that a candidate's "vibe" was more important than their references.

The shock of actually getting the job had acted on her like a jolt of adrenaline. It had given her the nerve to get out of her funk and start afresh: build a new home, new habits, and a new attitude. *Fake it till you make it*, she'd told herself, as she worked harder than any of her colleagues. And to her own surprise, she'd done well. Today's clash at the Maritime Museum had been her first real failure in months.

She glowered to herself as she puffed her way up the drive. Who was this Margaret Gale, anyway?

***

"Miss Gale?" Christos the security guard munched his egg and lettuce roll. "Big scary butch one, right? Looks like the Trunchbull from *Matilda*?"

"What? No, she's very—" Bess stopped herself. After her confrontation with Margaret, she was not about to say that Margaret had looked striking and regal—beautiful in the way that a frozen clifftop or a medieval fortress is beautiful.

Instead, she settled for saying, "A woman's worth has nothing to do with her appearance."

"Aw, sorry," Christos said, through a mouthful of shredded lettuce and Kylie's homemade mayonnaise. "Yeah, my little brother had to do work experience at her museum—after he got banned from the supermarket, and the garage, and the funeral home. He said she was mean as."

"How so?" Bess sifted through her salad, picked out an olive and bit into it, relishing the firm flesh giving way to an oily, salty squish.

"Well, he was there one week, and she did not smile at him the entire time." Christos swallowed solemnly. "She reported him to the school for getting in fifteen minutes late, and when he borrowed one pencil from the stationary cupboard without asking, she said it was a criminal offence! Can you believe that?"

Bess thought back to the woman she'd met that morning. "Yes."

"Scary," Christos confirmed. "My brother, he doesn't even like walking past the building anymore."

"If you don't mind me asking," Bess said, "why was he banned from those other places?"

"Oh." Christos finished his roll in one mammoth gulp. "Just for cracking his knuckles when he got bored. Unbelievable!"

"Seems a bit harsh."

"I know. And he was good at it too; he could play 'Colonel Bogey' on them. And 'She'll Be Coming Round the Mountain'." Christos crumpled his sandwich wrapper and scored a perfect hit into the bin. "Yeah, apparently Miss Gale was really mean about that, too."

❦

"Mad Margaret?" It was nearly five and the ticket desk at the Cabinet of Curiosities was quietening down at last. Irene was sorting through the receipts with one hand and adjusting the dial to the easy-listening station with the other. "Heavens, everyone remembers her. My next-door neighbour Candice was at high school with her." Irene shook her head and whistled silently. Her lips were pleated from decades of smoking. "Not nice at all."

"How do you mean?" Bess sorted through Leon's mail. It was the usual: requests for media interviews and threats from copyright lawyers.

"Oh, you know. She was one of *those* women." Irene gave a meaningful look.

Bess had been subjected to her views on the decline of traditional family values before. Either Irene had never noticed that she was working at what one newspaper had dubbed the Smithsonian for Sickos, or else she was hoping to convert people from the inside.

"Soon as Margaret arrived at school, the teachers and the other children knew she wasn't right," Irene continued. "Still, they tried to be kind to her. But then she became obsessed with this other girl. Amy, her name was. Amy had a boyfriend—I think he was called Jacob?—but that didn't stop Margaret from following her around and writing her crazy letters. Candice saw one once. She said it was obscene."

Bess blinked, trying to imagine Margaret Gale writing smut.

Irene's eyes were bright with the thrill of exposing other people's bad behaviour. "In the end, poor Amy had to leave town—that was how bad it got. Absolutely sick! And no one could do a thing. Course, you're not allowed to say anything against them nowadays, are you?"

"Wasn't this back in the eighties?" Bess asked, but Irene ignored that. Just as she'd been ignoring Bess's rainbow pin all year.

"I'll tell you one thing." Irene slammed the cash box closed. "I wouldn't let my daughter work there. Not for a million dollars."

"Your daughter's looking for work now?" Bess heard herself snap. "What happened—did they stop screening midday television?"

Then she apologised to Irene, because Margaret Gale probably didn't deserve defending. And besides, it had not been a compassionate thing to say, even if Bess had enjoyed it for a second.

༄

"Malcolm Gale's eldest?" Hilda cleaned the toilets and the café at the Cabinet of Curiosities. She put her bucket down and gave Bess a dark look over her squeegee. "That girl was always a wrong 'un. You can tell—it's in the eyes."

"People said she stalked a young woman and punctured some netballs," said Bess.

This won a snort from Hilda. "I'm not talking about all that. I'm talking about the murders."

Bess stared.

Hilda sprayed the glass front of the cakes cabinet with detergent and gave it a cursory wipe, just to build anticipation. Then she said, "When Malcolm's daughter was at school, she started hanging around another girl."

"Amy," Bess prompted. "Who had a boyfriend called —"

"Jacob, yes. I used to babysit him when he was little." Hilda craned forward until Bess could see the milky cataract in her left eye. "And do you know what happened to Jacob? He went around to the Gales' one night to tell Margaret to leave young Amy alone." Hilda lowered her voice to a death-rattle. "And he never came back."

"You mean…?"

"Postman found him lying by the front gate the next morning. Dead as a doornail." Hilda shook her head. "Seventeen years old."

"That's terrible. But why would you think…?"

26

"Everyone thought the same thing. Margaret was alone at the property that night; her father was away. And before the week was out, she'd gone too! Packed a bag and scarpered, and no one knew where. Do you think that's how an innocent person behaves?"

"Well—"

"Then twenty years later, she had the nerve to show up here again like nothing had happened." Hilda whistled through her long front teeth. "Moved back in with her father, and wouldn't say a word about where she'd gone or what she'd done. Why Malcolm took her back I've no idea. She'd never come home to visit once in all that time." Hilda paused. "Not that you could blame her much for that, I suppose. Her old man was hard on his kids. A bit of a bastard, really. But after his daughter came home, Malcolm stopped going out. My Gus hardly ever saw him down the pub anymore; he even skipped the regatta and the footy club awards night. We started to wonder if she was keeping him locked in the house. Then one morning Malcolm walked down the drive to pick up his newspaper—and he just dropped dead! Nothing the matter with him; he'd always been strong as an ox. I know; I used to clean the doctor's surgery."

Hilda gave the dangerous smile of a woman who'd once known every bunion and haemorrhoid in Port Bannir. "Malcolm was found in his pyjamas by his front gate, with the newspaper still in his hand." Hilda paused for effect. "In the exact same spot where poor young Jacob had died!"

"Maybe he took offence at a headline," Bess suggested "the *Port Bannir Advertiser* does love a bad pun." This won a glare from the old woman. "Well, come on, Hilda. It's a sad story, but it doesn't mean anything. People do die."

"Hmph." Hilda wrung out her mop with such vigour that slimy water splattered across Bess's shoes. "Especially people who get on the wrong side of Margaret Gale."

⌒～૭

The road out of town was dark and empty by the time Margaret turned her immaculate black sedan into the driveway of the old Gale property. Tall pines lined the path, shivering in the wind and casting jagged shadows.

The car purred up the concrete drive. It had been dirt and potholes when she'd first come back here. She'd paid for the repairs herself, keeping a close eye on the labour and querying every item on the invoice. Still Dad had complained—that it wasn't needed, that she was getting ripped off, that the work was shoddy, that she was only doing this so people would think he had dutiful children, when in fact....

She slammed the car door, the sound ringing across the yard and the empty paddocks beyond.

Margaret unlocked the security door and the deadlock. She wiped her feet on the outside doormat, then the inside one. After closing and relocking the door, she stepped out of her shoes and hung her keys on the plain metal hook.

Standing by the hall table, she slid the old ivory letter opener into the first of the envelopes she'd pulled from the mailbox. The paper sliced open with a soft crackle. She couldn't stand raggedy edges.

Gas bill. Water bill. A statement showing that the pharmaceutical shares she'd chosen had tripled in value. A grovelling letter from an antique dealer apologising for the delay in delivering a map she'd ordered and promising to knock ten per cent off the price. They'd learned their lesson last time. Oh, and there was another letter from that development company.

Margaret took out her phone and paid the invoices. Then she switched on the shredder and fed the mail into it, watching old debts and deals turn into confetti with a satisfying whirr. Never put personal papers in the garbage intact. You never knew who might go through them.

The house was cold, but she never used the heater until after dinner. Walking towards her bedroom, she saw the red light blinking on the landline phone's answering machine. Almost no one called that line any longer. Just wrong numbers, or people trying to sell her a different phone deal. Or...

"Margaret?" The voice on the answering machine was hushed and hiccupping, like someone calling secretly for help in a hostage situation. The red light flashed: five new messages.

"Margaret? So I was thinking, do you suppose I might have gallstones? The doctor says not, but I didn't describe my symptoms very well. I don't know why, I get so nervy in there. Or am I being silly? I know I'm silly, I'm very silly, but could you call me anyway?"

"Margaret, next door's been doing it again—they've been putting rubbish in my bins! It's disgusting, it smells, and no one believes me, but they're doing it on purpose to make me upset, it's all because I complained about that dog of theirs, and, and..."

"Margaret, someone's broken into my house again. The coffee cups are in the wrong places and the light's on in the laundry..."

"Margaret, you're not coming around tonight, are you? You didn't say you were, but I thought I'd call. Someone might see you and say something. It's not—it's just not a good idea, Margaret..."

"Margaret, can you call me, please? Sheila next door said someone in the bakery was asking questions today. About you. Margaret? This isn't good for me. I'm supposed to take things quietly. Can you call?"

There was no change to Margaret's expression. She hit "Delete" five times, her finger holding the button down on the fifth occasion until the machine screeched in protest.

After replacing the phone, she ran a hand over her sleek hair, and continued on down the corridor.

❧

Bess was still frowning as she locked the back door to the gallery, retrieved her bike, and coasted down the empty driveway. The crowds had gone, and the street leading back into town was silent.

There was only one person in sight: a young woman Bess didn't recognise. Not a local. She had short, feathery, white-blonde hair and a fluttering sundress that looked completely inadequate for Port Bannir's climate. Her features were delicate and there was a wistful look about her, like a pre-Raphaelite maiden waiting by a tower window. Except this woman was leaning against a baby-blue hatchback.

When she saw Bess approaching, she gave a limp wave. "Excuse me?" She had a thin, whispery voice.

As Bess pedalled nearer, the woman looked at her properly and flinched. The sight of a plump woman doing physical exercise seemed downright obscene to some people; Bess had noticed that before. She reminded herself to practice Buddhist nonchalance and avoid assigning meaning to the moment. Otherwise she might have been tempted to run over that breathy-voiced bimbo's toes. "Can I help you?"

"Is this...?" The woman craned forward and lowered her voice even more, which seemed weird to Bess, since there was no one around. "Is this where Leon works?"

"Leon Powell?" Bess nodded. "Yes, this is the Cabinet of Curiosities. But I'm afraid it's closed for the night. Are you with a tour group?" She wondered if the woman might be lost. Her pale blue eyes had a way of glazing over every few seconds that made Bess think she wouldn't be much good as a navigator.

"Oh no." The woman gave a tiny giggle. "I'm Arwyn. Arwyn Ross."

She seemed to think the news would amaze Bess, but Bess had never heard her name before.

"Did he not tell you I was coming?"

"Um, no." Was this woman a dealer or a critic? Or one of the eccentric artists who showed up here sometimes, trying to spruik their works? Bess would have put her money on the latter. "If you had a meeting scheduled with him, I'm afraid he's gone home for the night."

"Oh!" Arwyn Ross covered her mouth. "Oh, I am *useless*, I didn't realise! How stupid of me not to check."

"We open at ten tomorrow." Bess thought about asking who Arwyn was and why Bess should have heard of her. But it was getting chilly, and she didn't want to get trapped out here chatting to a conceptual artist. "Good night, then."

"Good night."

But as Bess pedalled away, she noticed that Arwyn was making no move to leave. She stayed leaning against her car and gazing up the drive, towards the locked and empty gallery.

A bit odd, but they got all sorts of visitors here. Riding back into town, Bess soon put it out of her mind. She was more troubled by the encounters she'd had earlier this afternoon.

It wasn't just the accusations against Margaret Gale, she decided, as she reached the old post office. It was the fact that she, Bess, was gossiping, swapping stories behind another person's back—stories that were outlandish and nasty, and probably untrue.

Bess didn't snoop into other people's lives. It was unethical and bad for her karma. Was she turning into a judgemental mean girl, like the other women in her family? Or was she just turning into a local?

She glanced up and down the deserted High Street before unlocking her letterbox. Night had settled over Port Bannir, and the traffic had faded to the occasional rattling cough of a farmer's ute. The only other sound was the muffled din of voices in the pub. The sky was stunningly clear. She had never seen stars like these in the city.

Bess checked her mail once a week. Thanks to her solar panel, she had nothing much in the way of power bills now. She'd ditched the credit card last year, and she paid rent to the farmer in cash. No subscriptions apart from her crafting magazines, and no junk mail. No car insurance or registration. She would never have those things again.

Sometimes a friend sent a postcard from Bangkok or Berlin or Barcelona, always ending with a promise to catch up when they got home. And sometimes they did, but it always involved Bess catching the bus to Melbourne. After their first visit, her friends hadn't been keen to drive out here a second time.

"It's so *far!*" they'd grimaced, as if the distance was shorter from the opposite direction.

Bess felt her mouth tighten. Maybe they just didn't want to see her again. To be reminded…

She shook the thought away, wiggling her shoulders until they loosened. Guilt was pointless and resentment was toxic. Those emotions probably gave you cancer, or back pain, or thrush.

The letterbox turned out to be empty except for a square cream envelope. The cardboard felt heavy and embossed; her name was printed in an elegant copperplate font. She turned it over, imagining a communiqué from a mysterious benefactor, or an invitation to attend a school for wizards.

Then she realised what it must actually be. She sighed, and ripped it open.

You are cordially invited to the wedding of Richard
James Horner and Melanie Ruth Campbell

Why did they always include the middle names, Bess wondered? In case she might have another sister called Melanie? One was plenty.

The thought of cramming herself into some taffeta monstrosity and following Melanie very slowly down the aisle caused Bess to feel a little queasy. So did the invitation's words "and partner".

Her family had never liked any of the partners Bess had brought home before. Not the tattooist or the animal rights blogger. Not even the one who was running for parliament and had been on the news and everything. All those women had got a similar reception from Bess's folks.

Her sister had stared like she was watching America's Skankiest Dance Moms, and her mother had pulled the same face she'd pulled when Bess had been sent home from school with nits. (Stoical, yet repulsed.) Her dad had excused himself to check on the barbecue, even though they were going to a restaurant.

She shook her head. Admittedly it might have helped if the tattooist hadn't spoken in Monty Python quotations most of the time, a quirk Bess had tried to find adorable at first. And yes, it would have been better if the political candidate hadn't been running for the Outlaw Party and worn her Mad Max costume to Bess's parents' anniversary dinner. And okay, she would have preferred it if the animal rights blogger hadn't been an hour late to dinner after getting arrested at a petting zoo and then asked Bess's parents for a loan....

Bess sighed. Girlfriends. Well, at least she wouldn't have that problem this time around.

She was busy reminding herself that self-pity played no part in her life now and that she was grateful for every one of life's experiences, even going solo to her sister's wedding—when she heard it.

The screech of brakes ripped through the evening silence. She spun around, her insides plummeting with dread. A second later came the crash and hailstone sound of breaking glass. Then the roar of an engine speeding away into the night.

Bess found herself hunched over, one hand clamped across her mouth. Her neck and shoulders were tensed for impact. Her bag, keys, and wedding invitation were scattered around her feet.

Shaking, she bent to pick them up. Up and down the street, lights were going on and people were spilling out the pub doors in search of the commotion. Bess got unsteadily to her feet and followed. She traced the noise halfway along the street until she reached... Oh.

Above the front door, a blue security light was flashing. It reflected off the pebbles of glass that lay scattered across the footpath and the reception area. So much glass—it crunched under her feet and lay in a carpet inside the building. Fragments were sprayed across the reception desk and the window ledge. The instrument of this destruction had skidded all the way across the marble floor. Bess stared.

Someone had hurled a brick through the door of the Maritime Museum, and it wasn't even her.

Chapter 4

THE TOWN HALL WAS BUZZING by the time Bess arrived. Crowds of older residents were milling about, swapping greetings and queuing at the tea urn. A sign out front read *Getting Tough on Teen Thugs: A Community Safety Forum.*

Bess was surprised that the vandalism of an unpopular local museum a week ago could have caused such a kerfuffle. But that broken door at the Maritime Museum had prompted the *Port Bannir Advertiser* to run a bunch of articles about youth crime in the town centre getting out of control, hinting at gang activity and meth labs—which was news to Bess. She wouldn't have thought there were enough young people in Port Bannir to make up a gang.

Still, when the public meeting was announced, she'd decided to go. It felt like something a proper local would do.

Up on the stage sat the police sergeant, looking grumpily resigned to being blamed for everything, and a man whom Bess recognised as the editor of the *Advertiser*. Next to them sat a woman in a powder-blue suit that must have cost more than Bess's whole wardrobe and a blonde bob that could have survived a cyclone. To her right was a greying man wearing faded jeans, a jersey from the local football club, and a nametag reading *Paul Baker*. Bess gathered that he was the youth worker from the shire council. He was explaining patiently to a local pensioner that no, the council could not send someone to arrest her neighbour's grandson for wearing an offensive T-shirt.

The hall was packed. Bess had to sidle all the way up to the front row, where there were still some empty chairs. Which might have been because people hated sitting right up front—or it might have been because no one wanted to sit next to Margaret Gale.

Bess hadn't seen Margaret since she'd stomped out of her museum in a huff a week before. Now Margaret looked tense and paler than ever, dressed in a dark suit, high-heeled boots, and a black full-length coat with a high military collar. She was ramrod straight, refusing to acknowledge the empty seats on either side of her. It might have been damage to her property that had led to this meeting, but Margaret didn't seem to want sympathy.

Bess couldn't pretend to be pleased to see her. But ignoring Margaret or leaving a space between them would have felt childish and rude. So she cleared her throat and managed a polite smile.

"Anyone sitting here?"

When Margaret turned and recognised Bess, her rigid expression gave way to surprise. Then she composed herself. "Evidently not."

Bess sat down. The plastic folding chairs had not been built with the voluptuous woman in mind, and she was conscious of being far too close to Margaret. Bess's green-spangled skirt brushed against the hem of Margaret's coat, and when Bess moved to put her bag down, their elbows bumped together.

"Um, I was sorry to hear about the broken door," Bess ventured. "I hope nothing else was damaged."

"No, everything's back in order now," came Margaret's curt reply.

"You must have had quite a job the next morning. Glass is a bastard to sweep up. If I break a cup, I find bits of it up the other end of my tiny house a month later."

"Hmph. Well, perhaps it will discourage those backpackers from wandering into my premises in their filthy bare feet."

Margaret's manner still wasn't what Bess could call sociable. But since she wasn't snarling insults this time, Bess figured she may as well keep talking. "I didn't like that sign out front very much, did you? I mean, 'teen thugs' is so divisive. I'm really hoping we can use this session to come up with some good ideas for community strengthening. If kids around here had something to do, they'd be less likely to get involved in vandalism, right?"

Margaret didn't seem to be paying attention. Her black gaze was fixed on the stage and its four occupants. Bess could have sworn Margaret Gale didn't blink as often as a regular person.

"*So,*" Bess persisted, raising her voice in the hopes of piquing the interest of other people nearby, "I came up with a bunch of ideas for cool stuff we could organise for young people in town. You know, to show them you can have fun without smashing things. I thought that youth worker from the council might be interested." Bess pulled out her notebook. "What about holding a circus skills workshop? Or a beatboxing tournament?" She frowned. "Do kids still do that?"

"I don't know what that is," was Margaret's reply. She was still glaring at the people on the stage.

"Never mind, I have other ideas." Bess flipped over a page. "What about getting the kids to make gigantic papier-mâché sculptures, then set them on fire?"

"What?" Margaret turned, distracted.

"You know, in a parade! Like at Las Fallas." Bess consulted her list. "Or how about hosting a poetry slam? Or knitting hats for the town statues? Or adopting a community donkey?"

Margaret muttered something which sounded like "I think we already have".

"I also have ideas for 'Dress Like An Ewok' Day, and a new sport I invented called Unicycle Polo," Bess said. "But maybe that's a little too out there. What do you think?"

"I think it's a waste of time." Margaret exhaled hard. Then she glanced over and seemed to notice the hurt look on Bess's face. "Oh, not your ideas. If you want to keep the teenagers out of trouble by making hats for donkeys, go ahead. Perhaps it will stop them from throwing their burger boxes in my gutter. But it won't make a difference here tonight."

"Why not?" Bess asked, as the newspaper editor rang a bell and called out to everyone to please take their seats. In the noisy shuffle, she had to lean closer to hear Margaret's answer.

"It wasn't a bored teenager who broke my door."

The meeting was called to order. Paul Baker spoke first, in a gentle, laconic drawl that made him sound like everyone's favourite uncle.

"No point in beating around the bush," he said, stretching out his lanky legs under the table. "We all know there's a handful of local kids who are in trouble more often than they're out of it. Gary here—" nodding towards the sergeant "—has known their families for years and so have I. Sometimes the apple doesn't fall far from the tree." The youth worker sighed and rubbed the back of his neck. "Now, I know some of you have been upset by what's been going on lately. But I'll ask you to think about things from the kids' point of view. There's nothing much for them to do around here. Some of them have been labelled troublemakers ever since they were little tackers. They've got no good role models, and some of them are just plain bored. Now, I'm not excusing what they've been up to. But I think it's fair to say we could have done better by them. That's why I've started a youth club in town, to give the kids somewhere to go in the evenings, get them off the streets, and help them make better choices."

"He's quite good, isn't he?" Bess whispered.

Margaret didn't answer.

The police sergeant seemed to agree, though. He reiterated that they weren't here to profile anybody or encourage bad feeling, but rather to work together to keep Port Bannir a welcoming place for everybody. He was sure everyone here tonight would go along with that.

Then the accusations started.

Two other businesses in High Street had had windows smashed in the past month—which was news to Bess. Four places had had their mail stolen. Three properties had had rubbish bins set on fire, and one had had a garden hose shoved under their door on the weekend, ruining everything inside.

"That's terrible," Bess whispered.

Margaret murmured back, "Hm, and all within a five-minute radius. Funny, that."

"What do you mean?" But any answer Bess might have received was drowned out by the rising tide of voices.

"And the littering—it's getting worse!"

"The language I hear around the bus stop!"

"Twice I've had shopping trolleys dumped outside my house."

"Teenagers wearing pyjama pants in the supermarket…"

"The canteen at the station has stopped selling coffee scrolls!"

At that point, Margaret mumbled, "We have lift-off…"

"Well, I want to know when something is going to be done about Norm the butcher. The sausage cartoons in his window are not funny; they're offensive."

"Well, *I* want something done about my neighbours' cats. They keep doing number twos in my garden, and they broke my gnome."

"I left my denture behind in a glass at the coffee shop, and they threw it away!"

"We seem to be getting a bit off topic," Bess muttered.

Margaret glanced at her watch. "Hm, twenty minutes in. Quite restrained for this lot."

"We won't get anything done if people keep complaining about random nonsense."

"Really, Ms Campbell." Margaret rolled her eyes. "If you want to get things done, you don't gather people together and ask for their opinions."

"That's a bit negative. All these people turned out to support you, didn't they?"

Margaret gave her a look that could have spoiled milk. "They turned out," she said, "because it's a Tuesday night in Port Bannir, everyone has already seen both of this month's movies, and there are free scones."

The newspaper editor was struggling to make himself heard above the din. "Well, it's obvious this is an issue people feel passionately about," he was saying. "But now we are delighted to welcome Georgina Harper of the Victoria Development Initiative, who has come along tonight with a bold new solution to the challenge of township regeneration. Let's make her welcome."

There was a smattering of confused applause. A stagehand scuttled over and began fiddling around with a laptop and projector.

In the half-silence, Bess stole looks sideways. She was struck by the black gleam of Margaret's hair, shot through with silver at her temples, and by the fine, neat lines in the corners of her eyes and mouth. What would it feel like to touch that skin of hers?

Jesus! Bess blinked. She did *not* just think that. Not about Maritime Margaret.

Definitely not. Put it down to a moment's distraction and going to bed alone in a loft for too long.

Still, Bess let her gaze drift over to Margaret's foot in its high-heeled boot, just an inch or two away from Bess's ankle. The laces, threaded tightly through metal hooks, criss-crossed all the way up Margaret's shin. Bess fancied she could smell the leather.

"Ladies and gentlemen of Port Bannir." Georgina Harper's voice cut through Bess's unsettling thoughts. "What a pleasure it is to be here tonight."

Georgina Harper was well past forty, but there was something about her manner that told Bess she'd once been the captain of a private-school hockey team.

"Tonight it is my privilege to unveil for the very first time an initiative that I believe will revive a neglected and unsafe town centre and bring jobs and growth to a depressed regional area." Her voice rang out through the hall, easily reaching the back rows and beyond.

Georgina pressed the clicker in her hand, and up on the screen came an artist's impression of what looked to Bess like an outsized apartment block. It was surrounded by cherry blossom trees (which didn't grow in Port Bannir) and cartoon people who looked a lot younger and fitter than anyone in this hall.

"What's going on?" Bess whispered to Margaret. "I thought we were here to talk about community safety?"

"Ladies and gentlemen." Georgina flashed an expensive-looking smile. "I give you the Incursium Estate—the community of the future!" She clicked the PowerPoint again, showing the same building at different angles. "A complete solution to Port Bannir's housing, tourism, and cultural needs."

"What *is* this?" Bess hissed again.

Margaret flashed her a dark look and growled, "The real purpose of this evening's meeting."

"Conveniently located in the heart of town, but set in its very own tranquil gardens, Incursium Estate is a little slice of peace and freedom," Georgina Harper was reciting. "The estate offers luxury, serviced apartments, five-star hotel accommodation, and an elegant, fully serviced retirement community. With ground-floor space ideal for boutique shops, restaurants, and supermarkets, this is a unique opportunity to restore a run-down coastal town to its former glory."

"You're the local history expert," Bess said under her breath. "But did Port Bannir's former glory involve a really humongous block of flats that no one here could afford to live in?" To her surprise, she saw the corners of Margaret's mouth twitch into a faint smile. "Seriously, though, that thing looks awful. I left Melbourne to get away from stuff like that. Is that six storeys?"

"Seven." Margaret raised her shapely eyebrows. "And take a look at where it's going to be located."

The images on the screen looked so unlike Port Bannir that it took Bess a few moments to spot a familiar landmark: the library clock tower.

"But that's… that's High Street, isn't it?" Bess screwed up her face. "And if the beach is on that side, then the place they want to put the Incursium Estate is…" Her mouth fell open.

Margaret nodded. "Right on top of my museum."

"No way!" It came out too loud.

Heads turned.

Margaret sat taller, glaring straight ahead as if Bess were nothing to do with her.

Which was true. Why was Bess gasping with outrage on behalf of a museum she'd found so boring, and run by the rudest woman she'd ever met? A woman who was rumoured to be something worse?

Still, since she seemed to have the floor, Bess couldn't resist raising her hand and calling out towards the stage, "Excuse me? Is this just a proposal, or have contracts been signed? Because it looks like you're planning to buy up a chunk of the main street and tear down some heritage buildings, and I think the community should have been consulted."

"Which is what we're delighted to be doing here tonight." Georgina Harper's smile had grown steely. She exchanged a look with the editor, as if urging him to take note of who was asking the irksome questions.

"No, you're not—none of us even knew you would be here! And you're talking as if it's already happening." Bess leaned sideways to Margaret and hissed, "Is it already happening?"

"It's complicated." Margaret, it seemed, could speak without moving her lips. "I own the building and it's heritage listed. But money's like water; pour out enough of it, and it gets around everything."

"What's the starting price for these apartments?" someone called from two rows back. Georgina replied with a figure that won snorts and sniggers from the crowd.

"Bullshit!"

"Who's going to buy that?"

"Yuppies and foreign investors."

There were angry rumblings.

"Well, I don't know what you lot are whingeing about," someone else interjected. "It'll mean new jobs, more tourist dollars..."

"Somewhere to go for dinner besides Porky's Pizza Palace..."

"They might even fix the potholes."

"As head of the Port Bannir Residents' Association," called a white-bearded man in a beanie, "I demand to know why we weren't consulted beforehand. And we will require the full tender documents and heritage assessment before we make our decision—"

"Oh, sit down, Clem!"

"I must ask everyone to remain civil..." The editor of the *Port Bannir Advertiser* was still smiling, but he had a sheen of sweat across his face.

Bess waved to get his attention, then stood up. "As someone who's lived in a bunch of places, I can testify that Port Bannir has a very special character. Its eccentric old buildings are part of its charm. In my workplace, I meet tourists every day who come here because this town is *not* like everywhere else. If we lose that character, why should anyone come here at all?"

Bess took a quick breath, then went on, "I hope you didn't call us here tonight so you could tick some box to say you'd consulted people. And I think it's really disrespectful to run a presentation like this without even acknowledging the people who live and work in the buildings you're trying to flatten, when they're sitting right here."

As she sat down, blushing a little, she caught a look from Margaret that was almost...mollified.

"Look, obviously this is still in the planning stage," the editor said, "and nothing is off the table..."

He was distracted by a scone bouncing off his head. It had been thrown by an elderly woman from the breakaway Port Bannir Residents' Action Group, who was shouting "And how much are these crooks paying your paper in advertising, then?"

Up the back of the hall, a scuffle was breaking out.

"Thank you for saying that." Margaret spoke quietly. She was still looking ahead, her hands locked in her lap. "Your comments were ineffectual, of course. But...appreciated."

"Can they really force you out?" Bess was surprised by her own dismay. But then, why shouldn't she be concerned? She liked this town, even if the town hadn't always embraced her. And as for Margaret—well, she might be unfriendly and weird, and Bess wouldn't be paying to visit her museum any time soon, but Bess recognised a woman devoted to her job. Bess could imagine how she'd feel if her own work was ripped out from underneath her.

"Don't worry." Margaret managed a thin smile. "It's not over yet. And it's not often I lose a fight."

The meeting seemed to be breaking up. Members of the rival residents' groups were shouting at each other, and Georgina Harper was being hustled protectively off the stage.

As she stood up, she heard a voice hiss from across the hall. "Bess!" Someone was beckoning her, someone in a baseball cap, an ugly brown nylon jacket, and supermarket jeans.

"*Leon?*" Bess gaped at her fashion-conscious boss.

He pressed a frantic finger to his lips. "Shush! I'm incognito."

"Is that what that brand's called?" Bess couldn't repress a snigger. "Leon, you look ridiculous."

"Can't I be a private citizen for one night?" He looked sheepish as he pulled his cap lower. "Listen, Bess, that was a compelling little spiel you gave there. I didn't realise you were such a strong public speaker."

"Thanks, I—"

"Please don't ever do it again." For once, Leon wasn't smiling. "Totally respect your opinion and all that, but Incursium has got enough hassles without you winding up the locals."

"What are you talking about?" Bess stared. "You can't think this development is a good idea?"

"Jobs, tourists, and rich retirees, Bess. It's a no-brainer. Exactly what we need."

"It'll wreck the town!" She goggled at him. "It'll push house prices up, squash the little local businesses… And what happened to keeping Port Bannir kooky and special?"

"Don't be so dramatic." Leon rolled his eyes. "It's just a few apartments."

"A few hundred! And you know that's just the thin end of the wedge."

"Bess, I didn't come to this town to watch it stagnate."

"I can't believe you're not opposing this!"

"Opposing it?" Leon stared. "Bess, I'm their biggest shareholder. When Incursium Estate goes up—and trust me, it will go up—the hotel section will basically be owned by the Cabinet of Curiosities. Special room rates for our visitors. We'll get honeymooners from China, luxury hens' nights from Sydney, Russian art dealers and their entire families. It'll triple our profits in five years." He glanced around nervously. "So please, for the love of God, and I mean this in the nicest possible way—*shut up.*" Leon tugged on the brim of his baseball cap and hurried off into the crowd.

Bess stood there stunned. Then she cursed under her breath and dashed back to her seat to grab her bag and coat, determined to give chase.

But when she turned around, Leon had vanished. Instead, Bess found herself staring into the face of Margaret Gale. And from the set of the other woman's jaw and the cold fury in her eyes, Bess realised Margaret had been listening to every word.

❧

Margaret pulled her car into the drive and switched off the engine. She sat staring out across the darkened paddocks. There was no sound of traffic from the highway; no crackle of leaves. Everything seemed to be holding its breath.

Her gloved hands clenched around the steering wheel. A wisp of cloud drifted across the moon.

It had been thirty years since Margaret had been frightened by anything. In the decade she'd been back in this miserable glue-trap of a town, she had never backed down to anyone. There had been the local supermarket owner who'd tried to seize her museum's car park, the neighbours who claimed they had a right of way through her land, the journalist who'd come around

43

muck-raking… She'd seen them all off. And she'd enjoyed doing it, enjoyed securing a small measure of revenge against this place.

But now…

The pressure from the developers had been growing for months, but tonight had amounted to a declaration of war. These enemies weren't going away, and she had a sickening feeling that they were out of her league.

Could she bear to be defeated again?

Her phone buzzed, its bluish light illuminating the interior of the car.

She picked it up and read the text message. She paused, turning its contents over in her mind. Then she put the phone down on the passenger seat and turned the key. The engine growled, the headlights flashed, showing the black dancing skeletons of trees.

Margaret swung the wheel hard and headed back down the drive.

⌒〜◗

Bess awoke to the joyous trill of magpies, but for once she couldn't bring herself to be present and relish the moment. She was thinking about last night.

Leon. How could her boss, a man who insisted that even his sandwich fillings had to be edgy and radical, be supporting this greedy new development? No, not supporting it—leading it! How could he not see the damage it would cause, how it would be the first step to turning this scruffy oddball town into Anywhere, Planet Earth?

Bess had come to Port Bannir to lead a distinctive life. The thought of waking up every day to a place just like the city she'd left was appalling.

And then there was Margaret. Bess recalled the look on Margaret's face when she discovered that the Cabinet of Curiosities was not just her rival, but was leading the charge to evict her. Despite her mistrust of the woman, Bess felt ashamed. If the Maritime Museum were forced out of its home, where would it go? Bess couldn't think of any other suitable buildings in town, and it didn't seem as though the locals would put themselves out to help. Would Margaret have to break up her collection and sell it off? All those maps and steamer trunks and figureheads that Bess found boring but that Margaret clearly cherished?

Bess dressed in a hurry, feeling icy breezes flitting into the tiny house and raising goosebumps across her skin. She gave the chickens their vegetable scraps and watched while Genghis picked out the best bits for the hens and called them over.

Then Bess made up her mind. She would speak to Leon again. Probably he hadn't realised what a bad idea this was. Maybe the developers had spiked his beetroot latte or something. Bess had talked him out of some terrible ideas in the past. She remembered the gorilla-hand ashtray, the Inuit skull, the double-headed foetus in a jar, and grimaced. Yes, Leon did make mistakes. But she could sort him out again.

As she pedalled into town, Bess repeated affirmations under her breath: *"There is always a choice", "I am always enough."* By the time she puffed along the path to the Cabinet of Curiosities, she was smiling.

Her smile faded as she reached the building and took in the scene. Police cars. Ambulance. Blue lights. The crackle of radios. Christos the guard slumped against his car, clutching a thermos of tea like an oxygen mask.

Bess dropped her bike and rushed forward.

"Stay behind the tape, please." Jacs, the local constable, had always been friendly and flirty with Bess when they'd met down the shops. But now she looked grim as she hustled Bess away.

"Jacs, what's up?"

"Just stay over here, please. We'll need to speak to you shortly."

Bess found herself ushered over to stand next to Irene, who was clasping her handbag and relishing the drama.

"Irene, what's happened?" Bess craned her neck. The doors to the gallery were open, and people in white paper suits were moving about inside.

"Haven't you heard?" Irene's eyes lit up. Whatever the bad news in town, she always had it first.

Bess couldn't understand why the newspaper had never offered Irene a job. "I haven't heard anything. I live in a paddock, remember—I've got no phone reception." Bess felt an icy weight drop into her stomach. "What's going on?"

Irene leaned in closer until Bess could see the grey roots of her hair and smell the instant coffee on her breath.

She said, "It's Leon. He's been killed."

Chapter 5

BESS SHIFTED BACK AND FORTH in the creaking plastic chair and wrapped her cardigan tight around herself. The air smelled of sickly orange disinfectant. In her peripheral vision she caught a flash of blue light reflected in the glass.

"Sorry to have to do this now," said the detective, who'd introduced himself as Gavin. "But the sooner we get it all down, the better."

"Happy to help," Bess heard herself say, then wondered if that was insensitive. What words were you meant to use when talking about your murdered boss? Not that anyone here was talking about murder yet; the police "couldn't confirm anything". But the main point was clear.

Leon was dead.

Bess tried the words out again in her head, but it still sounded like a mistake. Or like a piece of performance art staged by Leon himself to make an absurdist point, like he might pop out from behind the furniture with a video camera at any moment.

Gavin had already quizzed her about her job at the gallery, her movements for the past few days, the security system, the exhibits, and how Leon got on with his staff. Then he asked about that meeting at the town hall. "So, you were seated next to Margaret Gale…"

"Yes," Bess whispered. Her stomach plummeted. She'd assumed that the local gossip about Margaret was exaggerated nonsense. But if the police were bringing up that town hall meeting, did that mean they thought…?

Gavin made notes while Bess went over the revelation about Incursium Estate, Leon's involvement, and the threat it posed to the Maritime Museum. He queried every detail but gave nothing away.

"Do you think...?" Bess swallowed. "Do you think Margaret had something to do with Leon's death?"

"As I've explained, Ms Campbell, we're just making inquiries." Gavin put his pen down. "We'll need a sample of your fingerprints before you go. To distinguish them from any others in his office."

Bess swallowed. "His office? Is that where...?"

"We'll be making a full statement shortly," Gavin said.

Bess's stomach lurched. She found herself remembering the first time she'd been in Leon's office, for that crazy job interview. He'd posed his last question ever so earnestly: "Finally, Ms Campbell, in your opinion... who would win in a fight between Batman and Spiderman?" She had replied that Jill Trent, Science Sleuth, could kick both their arses, causing Leon to break into a grin and extend his hand. He wore a nineties mood ring. "Bess Campbell, I think you're going to fit right in here."

Now Bess stared up at the Crimestoppers poster on the wall and blinked back a tear. God, the difference it had made to her, moving to this town. And now to realise that it was all an illusion, that Port Bannir was really no safer than anywhere else...

"Ms Campbell," Gavin interrupted her thoughts. "Do you recognise this woman?" He passed a photograph across. It showed an elderly woman in a ratty fur hat and a raincoat with a cabbage rose drooping from the lapel. Her orange hair might have been a wig; her eye shadow was electric blue and thick. She was holding a sign reading *FAITH*.

"No." Bess squinted at the setting behind the woman. "Was that taken outside the Cabinet of Curiosities?"

"Yes, February last year. Sure you don't recognise her?"

"No, I wasn't working there then." Bess shook her head. "Who is she?"

"Hermione Morris," Gavin supplied. "She used to stand outside your gallery every Thursday, holding that sign. Last year, Mr Powell took out an intervention order against her; nowadays she has to keep her distance."

"I never heard anyone mention her." Bess shrugged. "Was she a religious nut—sorry, enthusiast? Some of our exhibits attract them; Leon likes to be controversial. I mean, he liked to be..." She covered her mouth in dismay.

"We're still putting all the pieces together," Gavin said. "Did Miss Morris ever threaten Mr Powell, to your knowledge?"

"No, I've told you, he never mentioned her. Why, you're not saying…?" Bess stared at the picture. Hermione Morris looked tiny and frail, dwarfed by her own sign. "She's just a little old lady, isn't she?"

"Like I say, Ms Campbell, we're just trying to piece together the fullest picture possible." Gavin heaved himself up, signalling the end of the interview.

Out in the reception area, Jacs gave Bess a nod. "Need a ride home, Bessie? I'm headed out that way."

"Someone will have to deal with things at the gallery…"

"Mr Powell's got a brother travelling in," Jacs said, lowering her voice. "I expect he'll make the arrangements, as well as the ID."

"I never asked Leon about his family." Bess sniffed. All of a sudden her body felt limp. She longed to be back in her warm loft bed with Genghis snoozing in the crook of her arm. "Jacs, how did he die?"

"You know I can't talk about it, Bess." Jacs held the door open. "But it would have been pretty fast."

That response made Bess feel sick. She stepped outside, flinching as a fierce wind stung her eyes. Jacs ushered her down to the car park. The constable was unlocking her car door and gesturing for Bess to get in, when a taxi came to a halt nearby. From behind Bess came the fast staccato rap of high-heeled boots against the concrete. Someone else was leaving the police station. Bess turned and found herself looking at Margaret Gale.

Bess's lips trembled. But before she could form a single question, Margaret had already opened the cab door and slid into her seat.

Margaret stared straight ahead as the cab drove away.

❦

Jacs pulled out into the street. Bess switched her phone back on and winced as it exploded: texts, missed calls, emails, tweets, news alerts… All saying the same thing: *What happened to Leon?*

The police were keeping tight-lipped for now. But someone—Christos the guard maybe, or the gossipy Irene?—had been talking to the media. Leon had been discovered in his office first thing this morning, dead from a fatal stab wound to the chest. The weapon had not been found.

News anchors described Leon as a "maverick star of the arts world, now the victim of a crime so bizarre it could have come from one of his own exhibits". Celebrity chefs posted tearful tributes to Leon's culinary genius. Painters, actors, and fashion designers described him as a visionary and a personal friend. The Minister for the Arts praised what Leon's gallery had done for the state's economy, while the Shadow Minister said his death was proof that this government was soft on crime.

There was no mention of Margaret's name or of the other woman Gavin had mentioned: Hermione Morris. Of course, Margaret might have been at the police station for some other reason altogether—her vandalised door, maybe? Bess shook her head and switched her phone off again.

Jacs stopped by the Cabinet of Curiosities to allow Bess to pick up her house keys on her way to taking her home. Bess had dropped them in shock when she'd arrived there earlier. Already cars were backed up the length of the drive. She could see microphones and cameras, and locals jostling for a good view.

The building itself—massive expanses of dark concrete, all straight lines and corners—had been starkly modern in Leon's designs, but today it seemed to have taken on a sinister air.

"Where did the news crews come from?" Bess asked. "We're hours from anywhere."

Jacs shrugged. "I reckon this lot can teleport."

As she stepped out to find her keys, Bess saw brightly coloured objects piled up beside the gallery doors: flowers and cards, and other things that people obviously thought more appropriate for Leon, like kitsch Jesus statuettes and pink flamingos.

Nearby, a young woman was being interviewed. She was exquisitely pretty, with rose petal cheeks and blonde hair in a feathered pixie-cut. Bess squinted. She'd seen this woman before, waiting in the street the other night. Arwyn something?

Whoever Arwyn was, she seemed devastated. She wrapped her arms around herself and shook with emotion as she told the reporter, "Leon was a very special soul..." She broke into tears, but somehow still managed to look demure, with no snorting or nose-dribbling.

Bess could never work out how some women managed that. She wondered who this woman was.

She found her keys in the gutter and hurried back to the car.

"Get a move on," Jacs grumbled. "It's a bloody circus here."

As Jacs turned the car around, Bess looked at the crowd. At the back, behind all the jostling bodies, she caught a glimpse of a raggedy fur hat and a large white sign held high.

FAITH

It was a relief to get back to the paddock, where there was no phone reception and no one to ask her questions. Genghis came bounding over to greet her, while the hens pecked away at bugs in the soil. Bess picked up the rooster and carried him inside. Then she stoked up the heater, sank down, and buried her face in his crisp feathers. She squeezed her eyes shut, trying to clear her mind of roadside memorials, blue lights, and news bulletins hinting at horrors to come.

She listened to her own breathing, like the counsellor had taught her, and wondered when it, too, would stop.

❦

There was no need for Margaret to venture back into town.

The Maritime Museum was closed today, and her solicitor had advised her to "keep a low profile". She wasn't charged with anything, but no doubt someone had already spread the word that she'd been talking to the police. Until things got sorted, she was supposed to be "sensible", which was to say cowardly, and stay out of sight.

Except that she needed milk, and no local gossip was going to make her drink her coffee black.

When the supermarket doors snapped open and she stepped inside, she could have sworn every conversation stopped. Even the screech of trolley wheels seemed to cease as she headed for the refrigeration section down the back. The only sounds remaining were the jingles on the speaker system and the echo of her shoes. Locals yanked their baskets and children out of her way.

After her dad's death there had been stares and whispering. Old acquaintances would cross the road to avoid her; shopkeepers would miraculously run out of the products she was after. Neighbours had hurried past with their eyes averted or glared sideways at her with baffled hatred. And after Jacob's death…well, she hadn't stayed around for that.

Today, though, the wind seemed to be changing. This seemed like more than suspicion, more than dislike. She yanked open the fridge door and felt the blast of freezing air.

Self-service checkouts hadn't made it to Port Bannir yet. Margaret placed the plastic bottle on the conveyor and wiped her hand discreetly on her jacket to rub away the condensation. Her neck ached from looking straight ahead. If she turned around, how many pairs of eyes would be fixed on her?

"Hi, how are you today?" came the robotic greeting, followed by a gasp as the checkout operator recognised her customer. The girl's chapsticked lips opened and closed in dismay; her eyes bulged.

She was far too young to actually remember the events of Margaret's youth, and Margaret wondered what sort of local legends this girl had been raised on. Tales of blood and gore and witchcraft, of men found dead from fright?

"I'm very well, thank you," Margaret replied, her tone poisonously polite. "Such a fine day, isn't it?"

The checkout operator dropped her head, as if ashamed on Margaret's behalf. She swiped the milk and Margaret's card, and almost threw them back at her.

As she stepped out into the fresh air and heard the doors close behind her, Margaret's breath released in a rough burst. If she turned and walked back inside, would she hear a dozen voices raised in horror, outrage, and delighted disgust? For a second, she was tempted.

Instead, she hurried back to her car. Once inside, she checked that all four doors were locked, before pulling out of the car park.

She drove home carefully, double-checking every corner, slowing dutifully at every amber light. This morning she was not certain she could trust her own judgement.

Chapter 6

"BESS CAMPBELL?"

Steven Powell ("whatever you do, don't call him Steve", Christos had warned her) was as unlike his brother Leon as Bess could imagine. His grey suit was conservative and probably expensive, but it looked like he'd bought it without trying it on first. It was too long in the legs, too short in the arms. He had kept his remaining hair in a brown rim around the base of his skull, accentuating the gleaming dome of his head. In Bess's absence, he had commandeered her office and covered her desk with spreadsheets.

If he was devastated by his brother's death, he did a good job of hiding it.

"Yes, I'm Bess." Coming back to work had not been easy. The Cabinet of Curiosities was closed today, but Bess had heard Steven wanted it open again tomorrow. The crowds had drifted away, but the memorial was still there, the flowers now tattered and limp.

Steven Powell blew his nose with a honk, then offered his right hand. "Nice of you to join us at last, Miss Campbell."

Bess shook it, trying not to grimace. "Well, I usually start late on Thursdays because—"

"Now you can tell me: who manages HR here? My brother's records are a mess."

"Um…" Bess glanced at her desk and saw Steven's coffee mug resting there. His name was written in marker on one side. The other side read "You don't have to be crazy to work here but it helps!"

Which was such a cliché it was almost ironic, Bess thought. Leon would have bought that mug and turned it into a postmodern goldfish bowl or something. The thought made her eyes sting with tears. She composed herself and said, "We don't have an HR manager."

"You don't *have* one?" Steven's jaw dropped. "Who conducts your quarterly performance reviews?"

"Well… I've never really done those."

"Then how was my brother assessing your outcomes?"

"We generally just go to the café and have a chat." Bess faltered. "I mean, we used to…"

"This explains a lot," Steven Powell muttered.

"Is there some concern about my work?"

"No, no, I'm sure you've been doing your best." Steven paused. He was staring past Bess to the label on a large box that had been delivered last week for an exhibit.

Alien Autopsy: THIS SIDE UP

Steven shook his head with an expression of distaste. "But in the wake of the recent, ah, tragedy, we will be implementing some structural and operational changes to the business model."

"Are you…?" Bess squirmed. She didn't know how to speak to this new Powell brother. "Are you in charge here now?"

"As a member of the Board of governance, it is my sad duty to step in as acting CEO, until things can be…finalised."

"I didn't know you were on our Board," Bess ventured. "To be honest, I didn't know Leon had a brother."

Steven gave a humourless smile. "I was elected to the Board last month. My brother always did need all the help he could get."

Bess blinked and wondered if she should jump to Leon's defence.

But Steven was speaking again. "You can start by bringing me everyone's job descriptions. And when you've done that, perhaps you could pick up some carpet samples? Something…quiet."

"Carpet samples?" Bess was starting to feel helpless and panicked.

"For the CEO's office," Steven explained. "The cleaners have finished in there, but the, ah, damage has been significant."

Bess's eyes widened with horror.

Steven droned on, apparently oblivious to what he was implying. "The walls will need a fresh coat of paint too. Perhaps it's for the best. Why my brother chose that orange colour, I can't imagine."

"Tangerine," said Bess in a small, sad voice.

"Well, get something neutral this time, will you?" Steven sat back down at Bess's desk, apparently dismissing her.

Eager to escape, she didn't argue.

As she reached the door, Steven called out "Oh, and Jess? Another coffee in here. And could you call Georgina Harper's office?"

Bess paused. "That developer? The one in charge of Incursium Estate?"

"That's the one." Steven was hunched over his pocket calculator. "I need to arrange a meeting with her."

Outside Leon's office, Bess paused. The door was open, the furniture piled up in the corridor. The room smelled strongly of cleaning products. In the middle of the carpet was a stain the colour of rust. Bess covered her mouth and hurried away.

Probably there was no fun way to spend a day like this. But phoning the Karpet King from a corner of Irene's office while Irene filed her nails and complained about her daughter, wasn't it. Bess gritted her teeth and reminded herself that it was a few hours of her life and that she would have her own desk back eventually. The portable TV in the corner played one of Irene's soaps on mute.

"Hold on," she told the sales representative on the end of the phone. Glancing up, Bess saw the program give way to a news bulletin, leading with a photograph of Leon. From the eager expression on the announcer's face, there seemed to be some new information. Bess put her hand over the receiver and fumbled for the volume button.

"...in the hunt for the killer of art world mogul Leon Powell," the announcer was saying. "We can now reveal, exclusively, the security footage taken at Mr Powell's gallery on the night of his death, which may prove a crucial piece of the puzzle."

The screen gave way to grainy black-and-white imagery clearly taken by one of the security cameras above the main doors at the Cabinet of

Curiosities. The footage showed the entrance area darkened and empty. A figure appeared, walking towards the building.

"As you can see, the footage shows a woman approaching the gallery and appearing to enter," the announcer said. "Five minutes later, here she is again leaving the gallery. We understand police have already tracked down the mystery woman, who was the only person seen entering the premises on the night of Leon Powell's violent death. Could this footage hold the answer to the case that has shocked this sleepy seaside town?"

Bess stared. The phone receiver twittered in her hand. She put it down.

The footage had been taken from above, but she recognised that glossy dark head, that military coat. Anyone else in this town could have recognised it too.

"*Well!*" Irene was sitting upright. "Didn't I tell you? Didn't I say?"

"Yeah," Bess whispered. "You did." On the TV screen, an advertisement for cat food flashed up, replacing the picture of Margaret Gale.

Bess leaned on the desk. This was the woman she'd defended at the town meeting, the woman she'd thought might turn out to be all right. The woman who'd sat next to her, smelling of leather and perfume, and left her breathless.

"Who released the footage?" Bess heard herself ask. "They didn't say it was the police."

"The police went right over our office at the time," Irene said. "I'm sure they got those security tapes. I showed them everything myself."

From the smug smile on her face, Bess thought she knew who had copied and leaked that footage.

"I said that woman wasn't right in the head." Irene folded her arms. "I always knew."

"Now the whole world is going to know," Bess murmured. Had Margaret really done it? Come in here and stabbed Leon—zany, greedy, fun-loving Leon—to death?

It looked like she had done it. And blurry footage wouldn't protect her identity for five minutes around here.

Was it anger or fear that sent Bess racing out of the office to grab her bike, leap aboard, and go pedalling back to the centre of town?

She wasn't the first one there. The lights were on in the Maritime Museum and the *Open* sandwich board was out front. Someone had kicked it into the gutter.

A small crowd had gathered: gawking locals, kids with their phones out, reporters with microphones… And Arwyn Ross, the young woman with the elvish blonde hair whom Bess had seen outside the Cabinet of Curiosities. Back then, Arwyn had looked dainty and ethereal, as if she might sprout fairy wings at any moment. Now she was screeching obscenities and swinging a baseball bat.

"You fucking evil witch! This is your fault!" Arwyn took a wild swipe at the lock on the museum door, which someone inside had sensibly fastened. "I'm going to kill you!"

Another swing, then a crash and a cascade of broken glass as the panel on the door shattered.

Bess flinched. Margaret's museum must be providing a good income for the local glazier.

"Where are the police?" Bess grabbed the person next to her, who turned out to be Kylie from the bakery.

"Oh, hiya Bess." Kylie shrugged. "I dunno. Someone will've called them."

"Who is she?" Bess struggled to make herself heard above the din.

Arwyn was doing a thorough job on the remains of the door, hammering away madly and hollering, "You bitch! You *monster!*"

"Leon's girlfriend from the city, apparently," Kylie said. "Sad, hey?"

"Leon never mentioned a girlfriend." Bess frowned, but was distracted by the appearance of people inside the museum.

Kelly the guide was there, her phone pressed to her ear, yelling for the police. The kid, Kenneth, who sold the tickets was crouched behind the desk and calling out, "I wanna go home! It wasn't my fault! She's just my boss!"

And marching towards the battered door with an expression of cold rage and no fear whatsoever was Margaret Gale.

"Can you believe she's here?" Kylie sounded quite thrilled. "She's got a lot of nerve."

"She does," Bess agreed.

Margaret raised her voice loud enough to be heard above the crowd, "The police have been called and you are being filmed. If you want to add assault and battery to your list of charges, feel free to try."

"You did this!" Arwyn's face had turned a murderous shade of hot-pink. "You evil hag!" She swung the bat through the space where the window had been.

Margaret caught the end, wrenched it out of her grip and tossed it away.

Arwyn swore, reached through, and started fumbling with the catch on the inside of the door, oblivious to the fragments of glass that stuck to her wrist and embedded themselves in her fingers.

"This is nuts!" Bess could hear a siren, but it had to be many blocks away. The locals were yelping with excitement, and three TV cameramen almost came to blows trying to get the best shot.

Margaret's face was a mask of anger as she surveyed the crowd—all the people she'd known for years who were doing nothing to help her. Were they leaving her in danger because she'd killed Leon, Bess wondered? Or had some of them always hoped for a moment like this?

Bess's hands were shaking. Was she about to see someone get beaten up in front of an audience of dozens of people? Were these her nice neighbours—was this her friendly little town?

Arwyn was wrenching at the lock now, her teeth bared, blood streaming down her wrist. A long shard of glass had snapped off the door; she grasped it in her free hand as a weapon.

Kelly and the ticket boy had fled to the back room, but Margaret didn't budge. "Listen to me, you lunatic," she shouted. "Unless you want your face to match your arm, you *stand down!*"

The lock snapped open; Arwyn gave a screech of triumph. She kicked the door open and surged forward. The light flashed off the glass shard in her hand.

Bess didn't stop to think. She sprinted towards the museum, shoving past the cameras. Crossing the threshold, she took a flying leap at Arwyn, catching her around the middle and sending them both crashing to the floor.

Arwyn yowled and swiped, but she was no match for Bess's heavier weight. Bess bore down on her captive, then shuffled forward until she was sitting on the young woman's shoulders. She caught a movement out the corner of her eye; Margaret was darting behind them. Bess turned her head in time to see Margaret drop a knee into Arwyn's back and wrestle her wrists into a pair of hefty iron shackles.

Bess stared. Her elbows and knees were stinging from the particles of glass that littered the floor. Her face was hot; her heart was thumping with shock.

Arwyn was hollering threats and insults, and the crowd outside were surging forward, their phones held high.

Bess wondered how many YouTube hits she would have by this evening.

"Margaret, are those…?"

"Original blacksmith-forged nineteenth-century manacles, yes." Margaret was breathing hard. "Rumoured to have been worn by Black Douglas after his gang were captured at the Alma goldfields. They were part of the original watch house here."

"And you just…carry them around with you?" Bess's voice came out in a squeak.

Margaret arched one impeccable eyebrow. "Only when the occasion demands it."

The police didn't keep them waiting long. In a daze, Bess was aware of being pulled off Arwyn and half-ushered, half-shoved out of the building. The crowd had grown to fifty or so, but in this usually quiet street it seemed like thousands. The noise and heat, the blue and red lights, and gaping faces made Bess tremble. She was being pushed into the back of a police car. Margaret was already in there.

Through the window, she could see the screaming Arwyn being bundled into another car. Arwyn's wrists were still cuffed behind her.

"Goodness," Margaret said. "I believe I forgot to bring the key."

Her voice was light. But when she turned her head, Bess could see the lines deepening in her face and the look of shock in her eyes.

"Bess," said Margaret. "I didn't do it."

Chapter 7

THERE WERE ONLY TWO INTERVIEW rooms at the police station in Port Bannir. There wasn't much call for more. Margaret knew that local crime rarely went beyond underage drinking and the odd Saturday night punch-up. Arwyn had been placed in one room. Margaret and Bess were in the other.

"I can't believe it!" Bess was flushed in the face, pacing back and forth. She smelled sweaty from the fight. "They're bloody *charging* us?"

"They said it was a possibility, that's all. Common assault, unlawful imprisonment…" Margaret sat very still, watching her companion with interest. Her own pulse was still racing from the scuffle and the police questioning, but her head was cool as she observed the woman next to her. Bess's red hair had come unravelled; her tights were ripped at the knees from where she had wrestled Arwyn to the ground. She was breathing hard.

"That is just…" Bess clutched at the air. "How *dare* they? Everyone saw what happened! How many people were filming it, for God's sake?"

"Let's find out." Margaret unzipped one calf-high black boot and withdrew something that had been strapped to her leg.

Bess stopped pacing. "They let you keep your phone?"

"No, I handed it over yesterday to assist with their investigation." Margaret arched an eyebrow. "This is my spare." She tapped in a search. "Oh, my."

"What?" Bess hurried over. Margaret showed her the wobbling footage: disjointed shots of Bess shoulder-charging a cameraman, then chasing a screaming, bleeding Arwyn and hurling her to the ground.

"*Country Catfight Turns Deadly*," Margaret read out in a deadpan voice. "*Bizarre twist in Leon Powell murder case. Police called as three former girlfriends of Mr Powell turn on each other in a shocking main street brawl.*"

Bess choked. "Excuse me?"

"Yes, that comes as news to me, too," Margaret said calmly. "Oh, and look: according to this one, *Onlookers were aghast as Mr Powell's personal assistant launched a savage physical attack on his grieving fiancée...*"

"She was attacking you!" Bess spluttered. "And she's his fiancée now?"

"This one speculates that Mr Powell was killed in a satanic ritual by a rural lesbian coven," Margaret went on. "Oh, but here's one praising you for *rushing to the aid of a distressed young girl being held hostage by the woman considered the prime suspect in the Leon Powell murder case...*" Margaret shrugged and flicked the phone off again.

"This is crazy!" Bess ran her hands through her hair.

Nice hands, Margaret considered; plump and shapely, with short, polished nails. There was strength in those hands, too. Margaret recalled Bess's fearless tackle of Arwyn and felt a flicker of admiration. As Bess shook the tangles out of her hair, Margaret caught of whiff of her shampoo, something cucumber scented. A clean smell.

Bess's face was pink as she said, "This is so unfair! I'm a positive person; there's no violent energy in my life. I was stopping that woman from ripping your face off, that's all!"

"Hm." Margaret studied her. "Yes. Why did you do that?"

"What do you mean, why?" Bess glared. "She was dangerous. I had to step in."

"Well." Margaret paused. "That's not quite true, is it? No one else did."

Bess swung around, her hands clenched by her sides. Then she pulled out the chair opposite Margaret and sat down hard. "I saw the footage on the news," she said. "Of you going into our gallery."

"Perhaps by now you've learned not to trust film footage," Margaret said.

Bess folded her arms and leaned back in her chair. "Did you kill Leon?"

Margaret lifted her chin. "No. I did not."

"You had reason to," Bess said. Her brow was furrowed with concentration. "And you were there."

"So the police were good enough to point out." Margaret kept her tone even. "And yet the search of my house turned up nothing, and I was released without charge. Why do you think that was?"

Bess was watching every twitch of Margaret's face, every slight movement of her hands.

Margaret found herself impressed by her focus, the intensity of her gaze. She would not have thought Bess had it in her. Margaret had thought at first that Bess Campbell was just another of Leon Powell's glib little followers. All that wittering on about Victorian sex toys and unicycle polo; all that tedious talk of community strengthening. Margaret had been surprised when Bess stood up to those developers at the town hall, and astonished when Bess came rushing to her aid today. No one had come running to help Margaret before. Was it possible Margaret had underestimated this woman?

Was it possible that Margaret needed Bess now?

"I don't know," Bess said. "Why didn't the police lock you up?"

"Three reasons," Margaret said. "I'm surprised you haven't spotted the first already. There are two ways into your gallery—the main front entrance, where I went in, and a back door for the staff. I glimpsed it as I was driving in. For reasons I'm not privy to, there is no security footage available from that back staff entrance. My solicitor requested it and was told it didn't exist."

"There's a camera over the back door." Bess hesitated. "That's weird there's no footage."

"Secondly, there was the lack of forensic evidence," Margaret continued. "I daresay if that detective Gavin had found any prints of mine in Mr Powell's office, or blood on my clothing, he would have said so by now. He has not. Because I was never in there."

Bess chewed her lip and said nothing.

"And finally," said Margaret, "there's this." She turned her phone on again and brought up a file. Turning it around, she explained, "Before my regular phone was confiscated, I took a screenshot. I received this text message shortly after the town hall meeting on the night Mr Powell died."

The text read *Drop by my office on your way home. Got something that might change your mind.*

"This is from Leon," Bess murmured.

"Well spotted."

"He had your number?"

Margaret shrugged. "Anyone could find it. It's on our website for auctioneers and dealers to contact me."

"And Leon messaged you?" Bess was frowning over the text.

"No, *please* or *sorry*, you'll notice."

"Why did he want to see you?"

"I never found out. I entered the gallery—the front doors were open—and made my way to the staff-only corridor. But the security entrance to the staff section was locked and the place was in darkness." Margaret shrugged. "I knocked, waited five minutes and then decided that Mr Powell had been wasting my time yet again. So I turned around and drove home." Margaret worked hard to keep her tone natural. After hours of questioning by police, even the most straightforward story began to sound like a lie.

Bess said slowly, "There are no security cameras inside the staff-only section."

"So I gather."

"So I've got no way of knowing if what you've just told me is true."

"You think I slaughtered a man for being irritating?" Margaret asked. "For wearing an offensive moustache?"

"He threatened your livelihood." Bess was not smiling.

"Incursium Estate threatens my livelihood," Margaret corrected her. "The removal of Mr Powell won't change that."

"Leon had a controlling interest in the project, and it's his gallery the tourists would have been coming to Incursium to see. Without him…" Bess broke off, biting her lip.

Rather appealing lips they were, too, Margaret realised. The colour of pink daisies.

But Bess was frowning again as she said, "You really expect me to believe that Leon just happened to text you to come over right before somebody else went there and killed him? That's a pretty huge coincidence."

"No coincidence at all," Margaret said. "I'd wager the killer was there at the time. Either they knew Mr Powell was summoning me—or they were the one who sent the message. Did Mr Powell have a lock on his phone, do you know?"

"He had one of those screens that recognises your thumbprint." Bess paused and the colour drained from her face. "God, you're not suggesting…"

Margaret looked away tactfully.

"Jesus, that's disgusting."

"The whole town knew that Mr Powell and I had a...difference of opinion," Margaret said. "To anyone who wanted him gone, I would have been the perfect patsy." She grimaced at the last word. She didn't enjoy describing herself as anyone else's puppet.

"So you're saying someone else hated Leon too?" Bess folded her arms. She did not look convinced.

"He was rich, powerful, and obnoxious," Margaret said. "I'd say it's just possible."

"Maybe. But no one else in this town..." Bess trailed off.

"I see where you're heading." Margaret paused. Was it going to be necessary to talk about this? Was it worth raking up the past to win over Bess Campbell? Bess, who had nothing much in the way of power or prestige, but who had been close to Mr Powell and who might, just possibly, decide to help Margaret?

Margaret made a decision. "You're referring to my reputation as Port Bannir's very own Lizzie Borden?"

"Well." Bess had the decency to blush. "People around here like to talk."

"As you've seen today." Margaret arched an eyebrow. "But if you've heard the rumours concerning my father's passing, I'm sorry to tell you there was nothing mysterious or interesting about it. Malcolm Gale had late-stage melanoma after a lifetime of working outdoors. He refused to go to the local doctor. I drove him to Melbourne to see the specialist." Margaret paused. "Not that there was much they could do for him by then. He didn't tell his neighbours or former workmates, and he wouldn't let me tell them either. He didn't want people feeling sorry for him. He was a hard man who intended to stay that way. I nursed him at home, and then he died." She shrugged. "End of story."

Bess had listened with a frown on her face. "If that's what happened, why didn't you tell people the truth afterwards?"

"Well, there's some blue-sky thinking." Margaret rolled her eyes. "No wonder your gallery has a reputation for being cutting edge. As it happens, Ms Campbell, I did tell people the truth afterwards. But many of them chose not to believe me."

Bess was silent, apparently pondering what she had just heard. At last, she said, "And what about that kid who died? Jacob?"

Margaret's face hardened. So they'd been filling Bess's head with that business too. She felt an unexpected sting. Couldn't there be one person in Port Bannir who didn't know that wretched story? Was that so much to ask?

"That young man's death happened thirty years ago," Margaret made herself reply. "It was a tragedy. And a mystery to me."

"Like Leon's death is a mystery to you as well?" Bess's eyebrows lifted. She sounded far from convinced, but at least she had remained calm. Respectful, even.

"Indeed," Margaret said. "And on the topic of Mr Powell's passing, I trust you can account for your own movements on the night in question?"

"You...what?" Bess stared.

Margaret glanced down at her nails. "Well, with all this media publicity, people are bound to pay you more attention than previously. And as Mr Powell's second-in-command, some might assume you stood to benefit from his...absence."

"That's—" Bess gaped. "That's insane! I would never hurt anyone. And I haven't inherited Leon's job, have I?"

"Of course not," Margaret purred. "Not yet. I'm just talking about how the situation might be viewed from the outside by stupid people—which is to say, most of them. And I couldn't help seeing you squabbling with Mr Powell at that town hall meeting an hour or so before he died."

"That was nothing!" Bess shook her head. "You think I'd kill a man over a planning dispute?"

"No." Margaret looked her up and down. "No, I don't think you would. It would be nice if you could extend the same courtesy to me. In the meantime..." Margaret reached into her breast pocket and drew out a business card. "Should you require legal representation in relation to this assault accusation or—" Margaret coughed politely "—anything else, I can recommend this firm. Mention my name; I once sent them quite a bit of business in relation to a case of artefact fraud." She paused, then pulled out a fountain pen and wrote the number of her spare phone on the back of the card in her neat, even hand. She held it out.

Bess hesitated, then took it. Her eyes lingered not on the law firm's details, but on the handwritten number.

"Should you need me." Margaret weighed up the risks and benefits, then reached over to touch Bess's wrist. Her fingertips lingered against Bess's warm skin. "After today, I am in your debt."

Bess bit her lip, looking between Margaret and the number. She said nothing more until Constable Jacs came to let them out.

Margaret stepped out into the reception area. She dusted down her black jacket, as if to remove any residue of the police station, and tugged it until it hung straight. Then she heard a muffled sob.

A woman sprang up from the row of chairs and rushed towards her. "Margaret..." The woman was small, with a shrunken, colourless look. Her greying brown hair was held back with an Alice band; her fingers had swollen around her engagement and wedding rings so she couldn't pull them off. She was forty-six and looked sixty.

"Oh, Margaret!" She flung her arms around the released prisoner. She barely came up to Margaret's shoulder. "I saw you on TV! Everyone saw you, Margaret!"

With reluctance, Margaret patted her and felt her trembling. "It's quite all right, Deirdre. Don't get upset."

"They were saying...saying he was *murdered*." Deirdre fluttered in Margaret's arms.

"Don't worry about it. It was a mistake, that's all." Up close, Deirdre smelled of talcum powder. Like an old lady, Margaret thought, or a very young child. But her fingers were unexpectedly strong as she gripped Margaret's arms, digging into the elegant blazer and the flesh underneath.

"Margaret..." Deirdre beckoned her down to hiss in her ear. "Do you need me to say something to the police? To say you were with me?" Her fingers tightened. "We had dinner together," she recited in a whisper. "Then we went to bed."

"No, Deirdre." Margaret shut her eyes, blocking out the urgent expression on the other woman's face. "No, there's no need for that. You don't tell them anything." As if poor Deirdre could have covered for her. Even if Margaret hadn't been caught on tape at Mr Powell's gallery, Deirdre couldn't get a story straight to save her life.

She would have tried, though. Deidre would have lied, desperately, badly, on Margaret's behalf without hesitation. Without asking Margaret whether the accusations were true. The thought sparked a flicker of emotion in the cool hollow of Margaret Gale's chest.

Margaret forced a smile. "Everything's fine now. See, I'm not being dragged off to prison, am I? It was just a mistake. Shall I take you home?"

"Paul drove me." Deirdre released Margaret reluctantly, stepped back and blew her nose. "He said I was being silly." She gave a tearful laugh. "I'm always being silly, aren't I, Margaret? I can't seem to stop."

Margaret's jaw tightened. "Come on," she said. "Let's get your things." As she ushered Deirdre back towards the waiting area, Margaret felt Bess Campbell's eyes on her.

Bess stood behind her in the doorway, watching them both with surprise.

Margaret turned to meet her gaze. "My sister," she explained, before leading the quaking Deirdre away.

<hr />

"Tess. You took your time." Steven Powell straightened up from his spreadsheets to scowl at her.

"Sorry." Bess cleared her throat. "I was just—"

"Getting arrested and bringing this place even deeper into disrepute?" Before she could answer, he continued, "When did you book my meeting with Georgina Harper? We need to progress this."

"I—I'll do that now."

"I see." He leaned back in his chair, his shirt buttons straining over his stomach. Bess could smell his stale breath from across the room. "I don't suppose you got that new carpet sorted, at least?"

"I did get some quotes," Bess fumbled. "And then I saw the TV news, and…"

"Well, get on with it, will you? I can't use that room the way it looks now. God knows how my brother ran this place, but if you want to work for me, you'll need to pull your socks up." He turned back to his calculator, stuck a pinkie finger in his ear and twiddled it. "And I'll be docking today from your annual leave."

Bess stood in the doorway for a moment, staring, but Steven Powell did not look up again.

⌒∽

Bess had missed lunch and her head was thumping. The events at the Maritime Museum had caught up with her at last; her scrapes and bruises throbbed and her brain was trapped on a ghastly merry-go-round of memories. Arwyn screeching, the crowds gawking, blue lights whirling, footage of herself being shared and laughed at by countless strangers. The lawyer telling her she would probably be all right, but that the incident might come up on her record when she went for future jobs.

It wasn't wise to sneak off work again, but she was too hungry to care. The gallery itself might be closed, but the café overlooking the beach was open every day. And there was a Persian fetta, pine nut, and edamame salad there with her name on it. Protein and salt were calling to her.

She stepped through the door and realised her mistake. The people at the tables fell silent, elbowing each other. One man whipped out his phone and snapped her picture. Hilda, wiping down the benches, froze at the sight of Bess, her washcloth dripping onto the floor.

Christos passed her, coffee in hand, and his mouth fell open. "Bess! What the fuck? I just saw this video—"

"Yeah, I know." Bess ground her teeth. "Maybe it will get me a spot on *Celebrity Big Brother*."

"What were you doing over there?" he demanded. "You can't go near that woman, Bess; she's a bloody psycho."

"Well, she was certainly carrying on," Bess said. "And whoever gave her that baseball bat didn't help. But as you saw, I stopped her from doing too much damage, so—"

"Not the little blonde chick." Christos shook his head. "I meant Miss Gale." His voice dropped to a whisper.

Bess could sense the entire café craning to listen in.

"You heard she killed Leon, right? And they let her out to do it again! What the hell is that about?"

"Well…"

"You gotta stay away from her, Bessie." He leaned in, his swarthy face crumpling in concern. "Seriously, Bess, you didn't see what she did to Leon.

I was the one who found him." Christos lifted his coffee to his lips and took a shaky sip. "It was bad."

The silence in the café was excruciating. Bess patted his arm, knowing she should be supportive, but wishing she could just get out of here. "I'm sorry, Christos."

"Never mind sorry," he said. "Just stay out of her way, mate. I don't want to find you next."

⁓

Bess left the café empty-handed. Her stomach gave a gurgle of protest. She thought about raiding the staff room fridge; hadn't she left some Greek yoghurt and fresh blueberries in there? But she found Irene in the staff room, whispering with the new intern—a conversation that halted as soon as Bess walked in. Their horrified stares were enough to send her edging away again.

She ended up outside in a clump of bushland behind the sculpture garden, seated under a big ghost gum and lunching on a bag of chips from the vending machine. On the fence nearby, hidden from view of the main building, was a small graffiti caricature of Leon, drawn by a visiting artist. Leon had enjoyed adding little touches like that to the gallery, things most visitors would not even see.

Shutting her eyes, she tried to anchor herself in her surroundings: the sea breeze caressing her face, the whisper of the gum leaves, the taste of processed potato and more salt than she was supposed to eat in a month. But instead, her mind kept sliding back to Margaret—Margaret who could have been savagely attacked today; Margaret who claimed to have been falsely accused; Margaret who kept vintage handcuffs at the ready, who had called Bess by her first name just the once, and who was persuasive in making her arguments. Maybe too persuasive.

Bess groaned in frustration and knocked her head gently against the tree trunk. Whatever was going on, she should not let herself get dragged into it. Maybe Margaret had nothing to do with Leon's death. Well, Bess should leave that to the system to sort out.

Except that her faith in the system was not strong. And she didn't like the idea of leaving Margaret at its mercy.

"Leave it alone," Bess muttered to herself. But even as she said it, she was taking out her phone. She got online and typed in a name.

Predictably, Arwyn had also achieved overnight stardom, with some sources portraying her as a grieving widow and some as a whiny attention seeker who'd probably been after Leon's money. Bess found Arwyn's Facebook page and perused the posts. They were full of extravagant eulogies for Leon, making him sound like a superhero who did a lot of charity work. She paused on one post.

I will never forget the first time we met. It was at Leon's restaurant in Sydney, the legendary Posutomodan. No one has created cuisine like that before or since. I will always remember his first words to me: 'I recommend the red algae and sea vegetable platter with a turmeric shot...'

Bess scrolled down. Past messages of love, loss, rage, revenge...and some photos.

Some rather surprising photos.

◠◡

Hiding in the house did not suit Margaret's temperament, but right now she had little choice. She'd arrived home to find a small mob of reporters waiting by her front gate.

Dad had always taught her that any sign of fear was fatal: *"Act like prey, and that's how they'll treat you."* So she'd kept going up the drive, her eyes fixed on the horizon, as if she couldn't hear the shouts on the other side of the glass and see their hands leaving sweaty prints on her car.

"Margaret, any response to the shocking allegations?"

"Margaret, did you do it?"

"Margaret, do you have anything to say?"

What she wanted to say was *"Who said you could call me by my first name, you repellent little insects?"* Her foot pushed down on the accelerator and the car shot forward, scattering cameramen in her wake. She was "Ms Gale" to everyone in this fleabitten town. Over the past decade since Dad had forced her back here, she'd made sure of that.

All those years spent winning people's grudging respect—had it all been for nothing?

She'd locked herself in, pulled the blinds, and busied herself getting the house in order. Vacuuming the floors, scrubbing the shower, disinfecting the sinks. Now she was removing and dusting every book in her collection. Histories of admiralty and exploration, biographies of Sir Francis Drake, Matthew Flinders, and Marcus Agrippa. Accounts of the slaughter of seals, whales, and mutton birds that had once taken place on the windswept beaches of Port Bannir… She was dusting a volume on the extraordinary career of the pirate queen Ching Shih and her Red Flag Fleet, when the phone rang.

"Margaret?" The voice on the other end was sharp with excitement. "Hey, it's Bess."

"Ms Campbell." Margaret put the book back in its correct place and straightened up. She strove for a correct and formal tone; her earlier lapse—"Bess, I didn't do it…"—seemed embarrassingly gauche now. "To what do I owe the pleasure?"

"Arwyn Ross." Bess's words tumbled out. "I've just discovered she's not Leon's fiancée."

"Slow down, Ms Campbell." Margaret stepped closer to the kitchen window and lifted the blind.

"Margaret, I don't think Arwyn was ever Leon's girlfriend. I've been going through her Facebook page, and there are all these pictures of the two of them together."

Margaret frowned. "Explain more clearly, please."

"Those pictures never had Arwyn in them!" Bess's tone was elated. "Margaret, I know those pictures because I took lots of them. There's one shot where Leon is standing under a pine tree in our gallery's grounds. He's wearing a green suit. It looks like he's got his arm around Arwyn, but I remember taking that shot. He was really hugging a six-foot garden gnome we'd just imported from Germany. And in the next picture, he's kissing Arwyn's cheek—but that picture was originally printed in our annual report. Leon was actually kissing a mummified crocodile on loan from the Egyptian Museum."

"Was he?" Margaret pinched the bridge of her nose. Was *this* the man who had nearly ruined her?

"And in another picture," Bess said, "Arwyn is flashing an engagement ring while Leon holds up a bottle of champagne. But I recognise his red bowtie in the photo; he decided he didn't like it, so he only wore it once.

He was toasting the arrival of a preserved walrus penis from the Icelandic Phallological Museum."

"I see." Margaret closed her eyes. "You realise you're providing me with some very real motives for wanting him dead?"

Silence fell at the other end.

"That's not funny." Bess's voice was flat.

"My apologies." Margaret tried to sound contrite. "Being falsely accused doesn't agree with me. You're saying Ms Ross has doctored the photographs?"

"Definitely."

Margaret got the sense Bess was starting to wish she'd called someone else instead—but it would seem Bess had no one else to confide in.

"Arwyn's done a good job," Bess continued, "but I've no doubt the photos are faked."

"Interesting." Margaret ran a fingertip along the spotless countertop. Bess was observant, it seemed, and thorough. Margaret appreciated that. "This certainly puts a different slant on her performance at my museum. Not so much the grieving widow as the raging—"

"—fantasist," Bess supplied.

"I was about to use a different word, but please yourself." Margaret chewed the inside of her cheek. "Although I'm not sure it gets us much further. By all means take this to the police, but you'll have to work harder than that to prove Mr Powell was killed by a crazed fan."

"I'm not trying to prove anything." Bess spoke slowly.

Margaret could almost picture her frown.

"I'm trying to work out what happened."

"And that matters to you?" Margaret looked out the window. The backyard was covered with paving and bare earth. After Dad's death, she had ripped out the weeds, creepers, and dying shrubbery, but she'd never replaced them. Now she remembered this yard as it had been thirty years ago: tall red gums, dripping with globules of golden sap, and morning glory dragging the old fence halfway to the ground. And deep tyre tracks in the dirt.

"Why would you ask that?" Bess sounded incredulous. "Of course the truth matters. Leon deserves justice."

"Justice." Margaret's voice caught. "Yes."

"And there's something else," Bess said. "Leon's brother, Steven, has taken over from him at the museum. He's a patronising sexist dick—and I get the feeling he didn't like Leon much."

"How inexplicable."

"I'm serious." Bess ignored Margaret's sarcasm. "There's something weird about Steven. He's pissed off with me about pretty much everything: my work hours, the exhibits, his calendar, the carpets…"

"Carpets?"

"Never mind. But you know the one thing that doesn't seem to bother Steven at all? The fact that I rescued the woman whom everyone thinks murdered his brother." Bess halted for breath. "Weird, huh?"

"Somewhat weird," Margaret conceded. "Yes." She stood taller. "Ms Campbell, thank you for telling me all this. Does this mean you no longer suspect me of this dreadful crime?"

Silence stretched out between them.

"I don't know how Leon died," Bess replied at last. "When I heard what happened to him…" She drew a breath. "I couldn't believe something like that could happen here. That this lovely little town was no safer than anywhere else. You know?"

"Yes. I know."

"But then I realised." Bess's voice settled, grew stronger. "If this place is really no safer than anywhere else, then there's no point in running and hiding. I may as well do the right thing by Leon and try to find out what happened to him. So that's what I'm going to do."

"Admirable." Margaret paused. "Perhaps you'll permit me to help you, Ms Campbell."

"Maybe." Another hesitation. "I'm due back at work; I have to go." Bess rang off without saying goodbye.

Margaret entered Bess's details into her phone. Then she laid it down on the bench and gazed at her own face, eyes narrowed with concentration, reflected in the black screen.

Chapter 8

THE WOMAN BEHIND INCURSIUM ESTATE knew how to make an entrance. Georgina Harper swept up the drive to the Cabinet of Curiosities in a dove-grey Audi. Bess could not see a single finger mark or speck of dust anywhere on its gleaming paintwork. Behind the wheel sat Georgina's driver, a mountain of a man in a tight dark suit, with a shaved head and an earpiece. Did he think he was guarding a president? Bess was tempted to snigger, but was put off by the cold gleam in his eyes.

Georgina alighted from the car. She lifted her sunglasses to survey the gallery then dropped them again. Her tailored grey suit matched the car and her blonde hair was flawless. She moved in a cloud of perfume.

"Georgina Harper." She thrust her right hand out for Bess to shake. Her grip was firm, her skin cold. Gold bangles knocked together. "Mr Powell is expecting me."

Ms Harper stalked through the gallery without glancing left or right. She passed sculptures, water features, and a mobile made from hearing aids, but she might as well have been passing a brick wall for all the interest she showed.

As she ushered Georgina inside, Steven leapt to his feet and knocked over a jar of pens. "Ms Harper! Welcome."

"A pleasure, Steven." She shook his hand, then waited until he pulled his chair out for her to sit on. "A shame this had to happen under such tragic circumstances."

"Yes. Tragic. Yes." Steven hesitated, glancing around the office. "Betsy, we need another chair in here. Hurry up, will you?"

As Bess trudged off to fetch one, she listened in.

Georgina's well-modulated voice carried down the corridor. "Steven, I don't need to tell you how unfortunate this situation is proving to be. Your brother's, ah, passing has created some highly negative publicity around this town and your gallery." Georgina placed an emphasis on the word "your".

"It is unfortunate," Steven rushed to agree. "Very…unfortunate."

Ms Harper's presence seemed to render him tongue-tied.

"As you'll be aware, one of the biggest demographics we hope to attract to Incursium are retirees," Georgina said. "You know what elderly people are like; they jump at their own shadows. If they get the impression this town is an unsafe place to live—"

"The gallery is cooperating fully with the police investigation," Steven assured her.

Bess located a chair, lifted it, and shuffled back down the hall.

"Well, I suggest you cooperate a bit harder." Georgina's voice had developed an edge. "I saw that peculiar woman from the Maritime Museum on the news. Haven't they charged her yet?"

"Apparently not." Steven looked up as Bess entered the doorway. "About time, Betsy. Did you stop for a snack on the way?" He flashed a toadying smile in Georgina's direction, but she was tapping instructions into her phone.

"Now," Georgina said. "What you need is a distraction. Something to take people's minds off this very sad event. What about a new exhibit? I believe your brother was planning a show before he died. I forget the title—something to do with blood?" Georgina spoke dispassionately.

Bess got the sense she wouldn't have minded if Leon had been planning to slaughter cattle in the main gallery, as long as it brought the tourists in.

Steven, on the other hand, winced at the word.

"Yes, well, I don't know what that was about." He hesitated. "But I'm all for a new exhibit. What about a celebrity portrait competition? They do one every year in Ballarat and the public seems to love it."

Bess could barely restrain herself from snorting with scorn. Celebrity portraits? Leon would have laughed in his brother's face.

Georgina, on the other hand, seemed happy to leave artistic sensibilities to other people. "Good. Let us know how you get on."

"And how are you getting on with the—acquisitions?" Steven noticed Bess still hovering in the doorway. "All right, dear, you can get back to work now."

Bess resisted the impulse to throw something at him. Instead she pulled the door shut as gradually as she could, listening as Georgina explained "Pretty well. Lots of interest from local property owners; they know they won't get offered prices like these again. Of course, a few diehards are making trouble, just to get their pictures in the paper, but in my experience…"

The door clicked shut; Bess didn't hear the rest. She retreated down the corridor, reflecting that Georgina Harper might know less about art than Genghis the rooster, but at least this was one person who could not have wanted Leon gone.

Bess went to work on the invoices, but it was hard to concentrate. Now that she had a boss who didn't respect her, she found she no longer cared as much about doing a good job. When Irene left the office to make a cup of tea, Bess picked up the phone.

"Good morning," she said to the desk clerk at the Port Bannir Motor Inn. "Do you have an Arwyn Ross staying there?"

⌒〜৭

Bess knew it was risky, going to McKenzie's Bakery after work. As she wrestled her way through the plastic strips hanging in the doorway, she half expected to find a news crew lying in wait for her.

Still, she'd decided a public place would be safest.

"Bess!" Kylie called out a friendly greeting from habit. Then her face fell. Clearly she was recalling what had happened last time she and Bess saw each other. "Um… How is everything?"

"Not bad." Bess's lips tightened. Was this how Margaret felt, being suspected and gossiped about by everyone? "I'll have a slice of the leek and mushroom quiche and a warm bean salad, please."

"To take away?" Kylie said hopefully, as if keen to get Bess's new notoriety out of her shop.

Her smile faded when Bess replied, "No, thanks. I'm meeting someone here."

Bess was seated at a table in the back corner, relishing Kylie's shortcrust pastry, when Arwyn appeared in the doorway.

75

The young woman wore a thin baby-pink cardigan over a flimsy dress printed with rosebuds. Her feet were clad in little sequined ballet pumps. Bess wondered how she hadn't frozen to death yet. Arwyn's right hand was bandaged, her translucent skin marred with bruising. She took two wary steps towards Bess's table.

"Arwyn." Bess made herself smile. She wasn't here to project any aggressive energy into the world, she reminded herself. She just wanted to get to the truth. "Thanks for agreeing to meet me. We've never actually been introduced; I'm Bess Campbell." She held out a hand.

Arwyn stared at it, as if at a live jellyfish. Then she took it and gave the limpest shake Bess had ever experienced.

"You said this place was nice." Arwyn looked around at Kylie's battered furniture and framed football jerseys, and gave a pout of distaste.

"Let me get you a snack." Bess got up. "Have a seat. What would you like?"

Over at the counter, Kylie was watching her new customer in dismay.

"Don't worry," Bess whispered. "She didn't bring her bat. Can we get a small skinny frappuccino and a lavender cupcake, please?"

As she seated herself back at the table, Bess said to Arwyn, "Listen, I hope I didn't hurt you yesterday. I had to take action to stop the violence, but I didn't mean to injure anyone."

Arwyn's eyes were a very pale blue. They flitted aimlessly around the bakery before focussing at last on Bess. She stared at Bess's bright woollen dress, her thick red hair, her glasses and her solid, rounded body. The sight seemed too much for Arwyn, who shuddered and looked away again.

"I'm all right. You said you had something to tell me about Leon." As she uttered his name, Arwyn's eyes lit up at last.

"In a minute. Listen, it's none of my business, but you probably shouldn't take calls from anyone who rings your motel room. You're becoming famous; you might get harassed."

"That doesn't matter." Arwyn's coffee arrived; she wrapped her hands around it. "I don't mind talking to people. They have to know the truth."

"About you and Leon?" Bess kept her tone neutral.

Arwyn nodded, her eyes welling up. "He was… We were so much in love." She steadied herself and continued, "I was in a bad way when I met him. My mum had died the year before, and I'd dropped out of art school.

My best friend turned out to be a back-stabbing bitch, and my boyfriend wasn't…wasn't nice. And I tried to make new friends, but it's hard, you know?" She gulped. "I used to watch Leon on his cooking show, and I saved up for months to eat at his restaurant. I needed something to look forward to."

Arwyn gave a painful smile. "It was lovely in there. He'd done the place up in this crazy Japanese steampunk style, and the dishes were works of art. Ever since I was a little girl, I'd always loved pretty things. Things that made me feel special." She looked down into her coffee. "Mum wouldn't even let me hang pictures on the wall, because we were renting and it might leave a mark. And we could never afford nice clothes or—or anything." She shook her head. "When I saw Leon in person…" Her eyes shone with tears. "Well, sometimes you just know, don't you?"

"Arwyn." Bess finished her quiche and put down her fork. She placed it out of reach, just in case. "I've seen your Facebook page. I know you altered those photos. You and Leon weren't really together, were you?"

She tensed, wondering how Arwyn would react. Would there be tears? Violence? What she didn't expect was for Arwyn to give a small, smug smile.

"I knew you'd say something like that."

"Did you?" Bess frowned.

"Oh, yes." Arwyn cut a tiny piece of lavender icing from her cupcake and nibbled it. She swallowed, patted her lips with a napkin, and said, "I'm used to ignorant people refusing to validate our relationship. People have always tried to keep us apart."

"Keep you apart?"

"Yes." Arwyn's smile grew compassionate. "Don't worry, I'm not mad at you. Even though you attacked me yesterday and I could press charges if I wanted to." She paused, apparently relishing this scrap of power. "But I understand. You were Leon's assistant, weren't you? So you knew what he was like."

"I—"

"It's okay; you don't have to say anything."

To Bess's astonishment, Arwyn reached over to pat her hand.

"I get it: you were in love with him too. I don't blame you. Leon was…" She looked up to heaven, her eyes misting over. "He was too special for this world."

77

"Um…yes." Bess edged her hand away. "Listen, Arwyn, it's obvious you're going through a hard time. But here's the thing, and I'm really not trying to be unkind: I know you weren't engaged to Leon. He never mentioned you to any of us at the gallery."

"Well, of course he didn't." Arwyn sniffed. "He knew that fame was a burden. He didn't want me being victimised by the media and all those evil, envious women."

Bess willed herself to stay calm. "Arwyn, I've looked at your photos. I know they're manips. And if I've figured that out, it won't be long before somebody else works it out too." Bess shifted in her seat. Telling someone they were lying was oddly embarrassing. "Arwyn, did you go to see Leon, maybe? Did he reject you? Hurt your feelings?"

"Hurt—?" Arwyn's eyes flew open. "Of course not! Leon would never hurt me; he loves me."

"Arwyn, I'm sorry." Bess grimaced. "But I don't think he even knew you. You showed up in this town just before he died, and…"

"I know what you're trying to do." Arwyn's girlish voice hardened.

"You do?"

"Of course I do. Jealous women have always tried to come between us. Like I say, I don't mind you loving him. I feel sorry for you." She cast another glance up and down Bess's figure. "It must have been really hard, knowing he would never love you back. But if you think you can deny my identity as his fiancée, that's just offensive."

"Deny your…?" Bess's head was starting to ache.

"And if you think making up lies about me is going to help you get closer to him—"

"If I wanted to get closer to him, I'd have to get a job at the morgue!" Bess caught Kylie staring and lowered her voice. "Arwyn, you do understand that he's dead, right?"

Arwyn's lip wobbled. "Yes. If I could get my hands on that disgusting hag…"

"You mean Margaret Gale?"

"I saw her." Arwyn's voice dropped to a rasp. "She just walked out of the gallery like nothing had happened. Right after she'd—" Arwyn gave a hiccup of horror. "She's pure evil!"

"Yes, we've all seen that footage," Bess said. "But—"

Arwyn lifted her frothy drink and buried her nose in the cup. Suddenly she wouldn't meet Bess's gaze.

Bess looked hard at her. "Arwyn? You were talking about the security footage of Margaret that was on the news, weren't you?" There was no reply. Bess's eyes narrowed. "Arwyn, did you go to the Cabinet of Curiosities the night Leon died?"

Warily, Arwyn lowered her cup.

"You did, didn't you?"

"No..." She sounded like a child caught in a lie.

Bess leaned forward. "Tell me the truth. Did you go into the building? Did you see Leon in there?"

"No." Arwyn's voice had faded to a whimper. "No, I stood in the trees and waited for him to come outside. I waited and—"a muffled sob—"he never came out!" She tried to lift her cup but it clattered against the saucer, spilling foam across the table. "If I'd known—if I'd had any idea what was happening in there..." Arwyn drew a shuddering breath. "I would have torn that bitch apart with my bare hands!" Her voice had risen to a howl.

Over at the counter, Kylie and two of her regulars were staring.

Cautiously, Bess got her companion's attention. "Arwyn, if you saw Margaret there, why didn't you say so at the time?"

"I..." Arwyn hesitated. "I didn't want to get into trouble." Seeing Bess's quizzical gaze, she added, "Oh, I wasn't really meant to go to the gallery. See, Leon had this stupid, mean, ugly lawyer. She literally wanted to kill me! She made him take out one of those things against me."

"An intervention order?" Bess hazarded.

Arwyn blotted her eyes and nose with a pink tissue. "It's okay, I know it wasn't Leon's idea. He loves me. And no one else has the right to tell us what to feel about our relationship. Only we know what it's really about."

"Arwyn." Bess tried to take deep, cleansing breaths. "He's dead."

"I know that, all right?" Suddenly Arwyn's voice was loud enough to stop passers-by in the street. "That monster killed him! And you, you bitch, even now you can't leave us alone! You have to spoil everything, because—because you're jealous and spiteful and *fat!* You wouldn't even let me avenge him; you had to get on TV instead and make it all about you."

"That was the last thing I wanted."

"Then go away and leave us alone!" Arwyn's fingers were clamped so tight around the coffee cup that Bess feared the handle would snap off. Her pale eyes were gleaming. "That Gale woman walked right past me, close enough to touch. She never knew I was there in the trees. I could have got revenge for Leon right then, if I'd only known…"

Arwyn got to her feet. Her posture was steady. Her little-girl voice was had grown eerily cold. "Margaret Gale won't get away with what she did," she said. "And if you try to get between us again…" Her eyes bored into Bess. "I will *incinerate* you."

She slung her pastel handbag over one narrow shoulder and walked out, leaving Bess to pay the bill.

⁓

"I'm telling you, she's dangerous." Bess leaned on the reception desk and pointed at the items she'd printed from Arwyn's Facebook page.

Constable Jacs was studying the printouts too, but with less excitement.

"They're faked, right?" Bess insisted. "And she said she would 'incinerate' me. Jacs, I want her investigated."

"Really? Would you also like fries with that?" Jacs yawned. She took a sip of what appeared to be cold coffee, and pulled a face.

"Look, she told me she went to our gallery the night Leon died. She admitted to hiding outside and seeing Margaret Gale there. And she's obsessed with Leon. What if the fire at his Sydney restaurant was arson? And what if she went to our gallery to finish the job?"

"What if my uncle had tits—would he be my auntie?" Jacs sighed. "Bess, I know you're upset about what happened, but you're barking up the wrong tree. I saw what happened to poor Leon, and trust me there was no way that anorexic little princess could have done it." She lowered her voice. "Whatever the killer used, it went clean through his ribcage and out the other side. It was brutal. Whoever did it had muscles and nerve."

Bess flinched. But she persisted, "I know Arwyn's small, but I've seen her in a rage. And she's crazy about Leon. If he'd rejected her, who knows how she might have reacted? Please, you need to look into this."

"All right, all right. Thank you for bringing it to our attention." Jacs took the printouts and placed them under the counter.

Bess stared. "Are you even going to show them to anyone?" Her face was growing hot with frustration.

"As a matter of fact, yes." Jacs leaned on her elbows. "But Gavin's out at present. And Bessie, seeing as how you may have to face court over that palaver at the Maritime Museum, you might want to use your best manners here in the future." She jerked her chin, making clear it was time for Bess to go.

Reluctantly, Bess turned away—and nearly crashed into someone queuing behind her. "Sorry!" She had to crane her neck back to look into his face. It was a face pitted with old acne scars and topped with a shaved head and an earpiece. Georgina Harper's driver. "Oh, hello. We didn't quite meet earlier. I'm Bess."

"Vince." He'd waited a full three seconds before saying it, as if assessing whether speaking to Bess was really worth his time.

She felt the urge to mutter "Stuff you too", but reminded herself that it always took conscious effort to make the world a gentler place. "What brings you here, Vince? I hope you didn't have an accident in that beautiful car?"

"Security matter," he said. "Defacement of property belonging to the Victoria Development Initiative."

"Oh." Bess thought back. "I think I saw that on my ride into town. Someone wrote *Piss off, you greedy bastards* on your billboard? I don't mean to do the police's job for them, but I'm guessing that was the Port Bannir Residents' Action Group. They're all quite old, so they have lovely neat handwriting, and they put the comma in the right place."

"Yes." Vince scowled. "Our security firm sighted them fleeing the scene, but those mobility scooters can reach high speeds, and they managed to evade us."

"Well, that's... that must have been very upsetting for you..." Bess ran out of steam and sympathy. "Anyhow, nice meeting you. Say hi to your boss for me."

As she stepped out the door, she could hear Vince saying to Jacs, "Who was that?"

Margaret's eyes narrowed to black slits as she pored over security footage from her Maritime Museum. There were weeks' worth of recordings here, and while the museum often seemed virtually empty, it was surprising how many people did visit, when you were forced to look at every single one.

If only she knew when, or who…

"Ms Gale?" There was a meek knock on the door frame. Kelly was standing there, fidgeting. "The new front door's been fitted. And the security firm said to tell you the place is all clear and they'll leave a bloke on the front door."

"Thank you, Kelly." Margaret swivelled around in her chair. "How does it seem out there?"

"Well…" Kelly bit her lip. "There were a few guys lurking around the front earlier; I think they were hoping for pictures of…well, you." A pink rash was spreading up Kelly's neck. "And we had a bunch of visitors this morning who just hung around whispering to each other. I guess they were hoping that something would, you know, happen."

"And they had to look at shell necklaces and convicts' hammocks instead." Margaret raised an eyebrow. "At least it's given our business a boost. I should arrange to be falsely accused more often."

"Um…yeah." Kelly seemed eager to flee.

Margaret held up a hand to stay her. "You seem nervous, Kelly. I hope the distressing events of the past few days haven't been too much for you?"

"Uh, no. No, I'm fine."

"Because if there was something preying on your mind, I'd like to think you would come to me. I take a keen interest in the wellbeing of my staff." Margaret leaned forward, holding Kelly in the searchlight of her gaze. "Nothing escapes me."

"Truly, I'm all right." Kelly's eyes slid around in desperation, before fixing on Margaret's computer screen. "Is…is that our CCTV?"

"It is." Margaret folded her hands. "Kelly. Are you sure there isn't something you'd like to tell me?"

Kelly's lips trembled; the tip of her tongue darted out to wet them. She shook her head, then leaped like a rabbit when someone behind her cleared his throat.

"Excuse me, Ms Gale?"

Margaret's eyes flashed with annoyance.

"Did I not say 'no interruptions', Kenneth?"

The kid from the reception desk winced, the acne on his neck blushing a deeper red.

Kelly took her chance and slipped away.

"Sorry, miss. But there's a lady to see you. She says it's important?" He wriggled with embarrassment. "I recognised her from…well, you know. It's Bess Campbell."

"Ah." Margaret paused. "Send her in."

But when he began to leave, Margaret beckoned him back. "Kenneth. Before you run away." He froze, his eyes widening. "I've been meaning to ask you: how are your family members doing?"

"My…family?"

"Your dear mother—I heard she's not been well. MS, wasn't it? And there's your brother, of course. How old is he now…ten?" Margaret's eyes narrowed. "You work hard for them, don't you? To take on such responsibility at such a young age. It's admirable."

"I…" Kenneth swallowed. "Well, you know how it is."

"I do." Margaret watched him. "Are you still at the house on Ivy Street? That old place must need an awful lot of upkeep. Gets costly, I imagine."

"No, we…" Kenneth's voice cracked; he coughed and forced it down again. "We sold up and moved. A few months ago."

"And you forgot to update it in your HR file?" Margaret clicked her tongue. "You'd better get on with that, hadn't you, Kenneth?" Her smile widened, showing a hint of teeth. "I have to know where to find you." Abruptly, she glanced away, dismissing him from her notice. "You can send Ms Campbell in now."

Bess looked rather fetching, Margaret thought, in her green and white checked dress and her coat the colour of moss. It brought out the colour of her eyes. "Ms Campbell. What can I do for you?"

"Actually, it's something I need to do for you." Bess was frowning. "Listen, I had coffee with Arwyn today."

"Our assailant?" Margaret's eyebrows flew up.

"Yeah. I told you I suspected she was stalking Leon. And that maybe—well, you know."

"So, you…had coffee with her?"

"Well, I thought I should ask her to her face." Bess looked earnest and ethical.

Margaret blinked. "Absolutely. It would have been rude not to."

"Well, I don't know for sure if she did anything to Leon, but she's as deluded as we thought and I reckon she could turn dangerous."

"Yes, I had the same thought when she smashed my front door in." Margaret's lips tightened. "But please continue."

"Margaret, Arwyn saw you at the gallery that night. She was hiding in the trees near the building and she watched you. I don't think she's told anyone else yet, because she was banned from going near Leon, but I didn't exactly have to waterboard her. She can't stop talking about him."

"What if she does talk?" Margaret shook her head. "I've never denied I went there, and they've got me on tape."

"Yeah, but what if she starts editorialising a little? Saying she heard a struggle inside, or saw you hiding a weapon, or..."

Margaret nodded. "Fair point. I'll speak to my solicitor."

"You might want to speak to your security guard, too." Bess hurried forward, pulled out the chair opposite Margaret's desk, and sat down without asking. "That's the main reason I came here. I tried telling the police, but they're not taking it seriously. Margaret, Arwyn really hates you."

"I'm not warmly disposed towards her. That door wasn't cheap."

"No, I mean she keeps talking about how she was close enough to kill you at the Cabinet of Curiosities and how she's going to make you pay. Seriously, I know she's tiny, but you've seen what she can do."

"Yes."

"Maybe you should...I don't know, leave town for a few days?"

"Run away?" Margaret blinked, incredulous. "Because of a hysterical girl and a five-second news report? Don't be absurd."

"Well, it's up to you." Bess sighed, looking around Margaret's neat office. "Hey, I meant to ask, is your sister okay? Back at the police station, she seemed pretty upset."

"Hm? Oh no, by Deirdre's standards that was a good day." Margaret halted herself, regretting the words. "She's...she's a vulnerable woman."

"It seems like she really loves you, though."

Margaret glanced up sharply, but Bess's expression was open, without guile. "That's gratifying to hear." Margaret paused, then heard herself add, "She's the main reason I stayed on in this town after our father died."

"Do you two have other family?"

"Deirdre is married," Margaret conceded. "But her husband has never impressed me much. Very good at saving the world's problems, not so inspiring in his own home. There is no one else."

"That's sad."

Normally Margaret despised pity, but for some reason it didn't bother her as much coming from Bess.

Bess added: "Well, *my* sister is getting married to a guy called Dick Horner and keeps posting about how hard it is to choose between eighteen shades of peach wedding napkin, so count yourself lucky." She smiled.

Margaret permitted herself a half-smile in return. Bess Campbell wasn't such objectionable company, really. Compared to most people, she was almost acceptable.

"So…" Bess nodded towards Margaret's computer screen. "Is this about your broken door? The first one, I mean?"

"I'd hoped to catch sight of someone lurking around, plotting the attack," Margaret said. "A suspicious character, as it were. But security footage has a way of making everyone look suspicious."

"That's a pain. Since Leon died, I guess everyone's lost interest in all that vandalism, even the police."

"Perhaps the people behind the vandalism decided they'd made their point." Margaret tapped today's copy of the *Port Bannir Advertiser*, which lay on her desk. Underneath the headline about Leon's death was a smaller article: *Feasibility study gives new estate the green light.* An accompanying picture showed Georgina Harper flashing her pearly smile and shaking hands with the mayor.

"What do you mean?"

Margaret rolled her eyes. "Come along, Ms Campbell. The businesses and houses targeted for defacement were all on or near the proposed site for the new estate. Not everyone wanted to sell, so…"

"No way!" Bess burst out laughing. "Margaret, I've met Georgina Harper. I can't see her throwing bricks through your window. Her manicure looks like it cost more than my tiny house!"

"You may be correct." Margaret curled her lip. "But I expect she knows a thing or two about outsourcing."

"Well, I think you're being a little paranoid." Bess was still smiling. Then something seemed to distract her. "Hey, is that the new *Antiquities Quarterly*?" She nodded towards a magazine on Margaret's shelf, sitting underneath three hefty leather-bound histories of Victoria.

Margaret glanced up in surprise. "You take *Antiquities Quarterly*?"

"Yes, but I haven't seen the latest one yet," said Bess. "I arranged a bunch of subscriptions like that for the gallery, so we could keep up with auctions. In January, we picked up a tea set that once belonged to Tilly Devine."

"Of course you did." But Margaret was pleased to learn that Bess attended auctions, at least. She would not have been surprised if Leon Powell's staff just scavenged their exhibits off the street during hard rubbish night. "I'll be putting a few items for sale in the magazine in August."

"Not that antique dildo?" Bess risked a grin.

Margaret narrowed her eyes. "As I've explained, it's no such thing." She paused, then could not resist adding with a raised eyebrow, "Do you think I don't know what I've got my hands on?"

Bess's lips quivered—seemingly half embarrassed, half delighted.

Margaret asked, "Do you want it?"

"I…"

"The magazine," Margaret deadpanned, enjoying the blush creeping into Bess's cheeks.

Bess flicked back her hair. "If you're done with it. Thanks."

Margaret lifted the three heavy volumes easily in one hand, retrieved the magazine from underneath, and handed it over. "Bring it back when you're done," she said. "At this rate, I'll probably still be sitting here."

"Good luck finding your vandal." Bess gathered up her things. "Hey, if the footage doesn't help, why not set up a stakeout? Cruise the mean streets of Port Bannir after midnight, keep a look out for Georgina Harper loitering around with some spray cans…"

"You could trail her on your bicycle," Margaret said. "Tackle her to the ground…"

The two women smiled at each other.

"Well, anyway." Bess cleared her throat. She seemed to be waiting, expecting something.

Margaret hesitated. She wasn't used to wanting people to stay in her office; usually she was eager to kick them out. Should she keep talking? Ask what Bess was doing tonight?

But before she could decide, Bess spoke. "I'd better go."

This time as Bess left the room, Margaret remembered to look. But while the view from behind was very agreeable, Margaret was conscious of a pang of disappointment.

⚬⚬⚬

That night Bess sat out on the steps of the tiny house, a cold beer open beside her, the chickens scratching around her feet. She lifted a forkful of dinner—cheese and mushroom omelette, made from two of Emily's whopping eggs—and gazed out towards the darkening trees.

As she chewed, she thought of Arwyn, of the air of loneliness, obsession, and stagnated dreams that clung to the woman like stale cigarette smoke. Bess might be a crazy spinster out here, with her chooks and her knitting and her bicycle. But how much better to be this way than to be like Arwyn, so desperate for affirmation that she'd created a fake life and exploded into a rage when confronted with reality.

She finished her dinner, summoned the chickens inside, and took herself off to bed. Snuggled under the quilt, she found her mind drifting back to Margaret. To Margaret's sardonic manner and her flashes of wry humour. Her long, tapered fingers, her scent, the slashes of silver at her temples. The obvious strength in her arms. She had lifted those big books as if they were pamphlets.

Bess rolled over restlessly. She shouldn't be having these thoughts. Shouldn't have come over all flirty in Margaret's office. It wasn't that she thought Margaret guilty; she didn't any longer. But still, this wasn't right. Bess didn't even *like* Margaret.

Do you want it? That voice—so rich and crisp, each word so perfectly enunciated—went gliding through her. She gave a soft groan and rolled over, her thighs squeezing together. She thought of Margaret's long legs in her high leather boots, the way her coat swung around her, the dark gleam of her gloved fingers.

Do you think I don't know what I've got my hands on? That chuckle did things to her insides. Despite the chill in the tiny house, Bess's cheeks were growing warm. She turned onto her stomach and felt her hard nipples being pushed back into their cushioning orbs, the fabric chafing them pleasurably.

"Oh, God..." Giving in, she slid her hand beneath the waistband of her pyjamas, her fingers skittering across warm skin and springing curls, in search of hot, moist flesh.

Hands off... The touch of one wet fingertip set her clit throbbing. She pushed her face into the pillow and rubbed herself hard and fast, as if to get this forbidden interlude over as quickly as possible. *Yes, I want it. Oh, yes.*

Chapter 9

IT WAS AN HOUR BEFORE opening time at the Maritime Museum. Margaret was refreshing the display in the foyer when a knock sounded at the front door.

The morning had been quiet so far, and the security guard had wandered off to fetch coffee. Margaret was adjusting one of her favourite items: the tooth of a sperm whale, circa 1840. It was engraved with a picture of a ship drifting into the mouth of a breeching giant of the deep. These images had been carved by sailors and convicts to while away the hours below deck. The pictures—whittled with blades, then coloured with tobacco juice, lamp soot and blood—were delicate, painstaking, and exquisitely pretty.

So distracted was she by this beloved item that she failed to notice Kelly opening the door with her key pass, until it was too late to stop her.

"Here to see Miss Gale." A visitor lumbered into the vestibule, almost filling it with his bulk and shadow.

Margaret fancied she'd seen him before—ushering Georgina Harper around town, perhaps? With his dark suit, shaved head, and bodybuilder's physique, he looked like a caricature of a thug. It would have been funny, if he had been standing in someone else's doorway.

"Ms Gale's not available at the moment," Kelly tried to say, edging away as he loomed closer.

Dismissing her from his notice, he strolled over to where Margaret was standing. His arms were too bulky to hang normally by his sides.

"Miss Gale?" His cologne was eye-watering.

"I'm afraid we're not open yet." She drew herself up to her full height. It wasn't easy to look down her nose at this giant, but by tilting her head back she managed it. "If you're here for the shell-necklace workshop, it's scheduled for ten. The café next door is open in the meantime. I'm told they do a rather good babyccino."

"Funny." He didn't smile. Moving faster than his bulk would have suggested possible, the man dipped into the open cabinet and plucked out the whale tooth scrimshaw. "That's something I've noticed about this town." He glanced around, turning the precious item carelessly between his fingers. "Everyone's a stand-up comedian. For a bunch of inbred fucken hicks, you lot sure do like to think you're clever."

A muscle twitched in Margaret's cheek. Her hands quivered, longing to snatch the item back and knowing such a sign of desperation was just what he was hoping for.

"Nice." He glanced at it. "You've got some pretty things in here."

"And one breathtakingly ugly thing." Margaret kept her voice icy, her posture unflinching. She darted a gaze at the door—where the hell was that guard? "Well, you seem to want something. What can we do for you?"

"Actually, Miss Gale, it's more a question of what we might do for you." He held the tooth up to the light. "This stuff can't come cheap," he mused. "But I haven't seen a whole lot of people heading through these doors. You must be feeling the pinch."

"Perhaps you could recommend the place to all your friends." Margaret folded her arms.

Her guest gave a nasty smile. "Not sure you'd want to meet my friends, Miss Gale." He tossed the precious tooth from one hand to the other, making Margaret jolt with alarm. "Yeah, the upkeep must get pricey," he concluded. "Especially now. From what we see on the news, looks like you'll have some hefty lawyers' fees soon. Not to mention PR, security…" He looked around, taking in the absence of the latter. "Don't you think it might be time to economise, Miss Gale?"

"You're from Incursium Estate." She had suspected that from the start. "I see you've moved a step up from petty vandalism."

"Dunno what you mean." He used the whale's tooth to scratch his crotch. "But it sure does look like Incursium is offering a good deal." He leaned in until she could smell his breath. "Even for snooty fucken bitches who think they're too good to come to the phone. If you need a bit of help to pack up all this dusty old shit and move it someplace else, I reckon they'd kick in a few bucks. If not…" His smile widened. One of his teeth was yellowish and looked dead.

"I would have thought with Mr Powell gone, your bosses might stop and think about their next move," Margaret said. "You've just lost your biggest drawcard."

"That wanker?" Her visitor gave a humourless chuckle. "Sorry to disappoint, love, but it makes fuck-all difference whether Leon Powell's around to cut the ribbon. Matter of fact, we'll be able to do things properly now."

Without warning, he dropped the precious artefact. Margaret surged forward and grabbed it before it could hit the ground.

Kelly gave a muffled scream.

The intruder laughed. "Nice instincts there, Miss Gale. You might want to listen to them." He turned and sauntered out the front door, nodding to the returning security guard as he left.

Margaret laid the tooth back in the cabinet, slammed the lid, and turned the lock. She was humiliated to realise that her hands were trembling.

She strode to the doorway as fast as she could without breaking into a run. His car was pulling out; she memorised the numberplate.

A moment later she heard: "Margaret! Hey, Margaret!" A young man was racing towards her, his phone held up to catch her reaction. "Did you do it? Did you kill Leon Powell?"

She waited just inside the doorway, until he was close enough to touch. Then she reached swiftly to one side and hit the button to close the sliding doors. They shut with a whoosh; the intruder hit them with a meaty thump. Margaret found it deeply satisfying.

As he ricocheted backwards, swearing, and yelling about assault, she turned on her heel and strode away.

Kelly called after her in a helpless voice, "Ms Gale, should I ring the police?"

"Don't bother." Then Margaret added under her breath, "I'll call someone better."

As Bess rode to work, she found her thoughts drifting back to last night.

What was wrong with her? Was it just a Pavlovian response to meeting another lesbian—a rare event in Port Bannir? She ground her teeth. No, she refused to get stuck on this. She would make herself return to the moment: to the whisper of leaves above her, the birdsong, the distant slap, and sigh of the waves.

It was something else that distracted her, though. At the bottom of the drive that led up to the Cabinet of Curiosities, stood a familiar sight.

In scuffed court shoes, with laddered stockings on her spindly legs, her coat dusty, the cabbage rose in her lapel drooping lower than ever, Hermione Morris cut a forlorn figure. Not quite a bag lady, Bess decided, but getting close. Hermione's *FAITH* sign was the only thing about her that looked clean and new. Did she make a fresh one every day? Bess wondered if she should ask the old woman in for a cup of tea.

Oh, except for the fact that Hermione Morris might have murdered Leon.

Bess didn't believe it. Hermione's hands, wrapped around the edges of the sign, were knobbly and red, and swollen with arthritis. There was no way she could have overpowered a healthy man in his prime.

Except there was that intervention order that Leon had taken out against her. And Bess, recalling Arwyn's attack on the Maritime Museum, knew that small people could surprise you when they got into a temper.

She coasted to a halt beside Ms Morris.

"Morning."

"Good morning." The elderly woman's voice was slow, clear, and plummy, like someone who'd once taught elocution classes. She calmly returned Bess's gaze.

"We're not open for another half hour," Bess said. "Is there something I can help you with?"

"Oh, I doubt that, dear." Up close, she saw that Hermione had soft, pale skin beneath her layers of powder and paint. Her features were neat and slim; she might have been pretty once. "But thank you for asking."

Bess hesitated. Who knew that talking to possible murderers would feel so awkward? "Listen, I've noticed you here before with your sign. Nice calligraphy, by the way."

"Thank you, dear. I used to be an English teacher."

"That's...great." Bess fidgeted. "I wondered if we'd done something to offend you. I mean, *FAITH*..." She nodded at the sign and waited for a reply.

Hermione Morris said nothing.

"Did one of our exhibits upset you?" Bess prompted. "The *Star Trek* nativity scene, maybe? Or the foetus preserved in amber? You know that was made of plastic, right?"

Hermione Morris just gazed back at her, her face impassive above her sign.

With no idea what else to do, Bess was forced to mutter, "Well, goodbye then", and ride on.

As she chained up her bike outside the gallery, she heard her phone beep. She found a message from Margaret, which said: *Find out what you can about Incursium Estate. Possible their relationship with Leon Powell not as rosy as we thought. Report back. M.*

"Report back!" Bess glowered. As if she was some kind of intern. She stuffed her phone back into her bag. Who the hell did Margaret think she was?

Still, Bess had questions of her own she wanted answered. She bided her time through the morning rush, dealing with the invoices that had piled up, and replying to sympathy cards. She tried to tune out Irene's complaining, which seemed shriller and more incessant than ever.

"Hey, did you see that woman protesting by the entrance?" Bess asked her at one point. She wondered if Irene might have some sympathy for a holy roller, if that was what Hermione was.

"Disgraceful!" Irene's snort nearly blew Bess's head off. "There ought to be a law against it."

"Public protesting?" Bess blinked. "But she's not hassling anyone. She doesn't even speak much."

"She's a menace." Irene's lips tightened until they nearly disappeared. "She's lowering the tone of the gallery and blocking egress to the drive. What if someone ran her over? We could be liable!"

Bess stared, but Irene was dealing with a new group of tourists now, snatching their money and tearing off tickets with more force than necessary.

When Irene stamped off to the kitchen, Bess slipped out. She found Christos at his station by the front door.

"Hey, Christos, can I ask you about something? The night Leon died…I've been wondering about the CCTV footage."

"Margaret Gale on candid camera?" He grunted. "That was a bloody disgrace. There she was, clear as day, and the cops still let her go!"

"Actually, I meant the camera over the back door. I wondered if that camera picked up anything, and why no one will say. I know the tapes are with the police, but…"

"Don't need the tapes." Christos shrugged. "That footage won't tell you anything."

"Did you see it?"

"No need." He heaved himself up from his leather stool and waved to his colleague. "Anton, take over, will you? Smoke o'clock."

He led Bess around to the back of the gallery.

"I haven't touched anything," he said. "In case the cops come back, you know." He scratched his belly. "I come in through the back each morning, remember? Well, when I came in that morning, I saw this." Christos pointed up at the camera above the gallery's back door.

It had been turned around to face the wall.

That afternoon, as Bess went about her tasks, she thought about that sabotaged camera. And she turned Margaret's message over in her mind. Was it possible that Incursium Estate were involved in Leon's death? She couldn't see how; surely they stood to gain from Leon being alive and successful? If she had to pick a killer, Bess's money would have been on Arwyn.

Still, there were other reasons to kill a person besides romantic obsession. There was money, ideology, wounded pride… And family.

She waited until Steven Powell left the building in search of lunch. Then she crept into Leon's newly renovated office and fired up his computer.

What was she looking for? She wasn't certain beyond evidence of a fight, a grudge, a disagreement with *someone*… She inserted a USB thumb drive and began to copy Leon's files across. This was probably against the rules, but it was for a good cause. And besides, she couldn't imagine Leon objecting to a spot of outlawry.

She wouldn't get anything from his emails, though. She opened Leon's account to discover that every single message had been wiped.

"Jesus…" Bess stared. She didn't believe Arwyn Ross could have done that.

She glanced quickly around her. The corridor outside was empty. She retrieved the USB drive, tucked it into her pocket, and shut the computer down. Then she stared at Leon's filing cabinets. The contents, she knew, were a huge mess.

No way could she look through all that stuff before Steven returned. Still, she tugged open a few drawers, glancing at the file tabs. Where to start? *Finance*, maybe, or *Legal*? She opened a folder marked *Complaints* and flipped through it. There were angry letters from artists who felt their work had been appropriated, threats from various interest groups offended by this exhibit or that—and a photograph of Hermione Morris. It was clipped to some kind of police paperwork. A sticky label attached said in Leon's handwriting *Poor old biddy. Shouldn't have come to this, but no option. Couldn't handle the drama.*

Bess was lifting the note to read the police statement when she heard a raised voice in the corridor outside.

"No, I will not bloody well calm down!" It was Steven Powell. "What you're suggesting is way over the line!"

Bess's chest clenched in panic. She thrust the paper back into the file and yanked the drawer open to replace it—but she wasn't fast enough. As Steven barked, "I don't care—I never agreed to this!" he flung open the door and froze at the sight of her, his phone still clamped to his ear.

Caught fossicking in her late boss's files, she expected trouble. But she did not expect the dark red rage that flooded Steven Powell's face, until his bald head glowed like a traffic light.

"What the hell do you think you're doing?" He strode towards her and ripped the file from her hand. "Snooping through my records? How bloody *dare* you?"

Bess flinched backwards, her arms flying up in self-defence. Her eyes darted down to Steven's phone. She could hear a faint voice on the line calling his name. The caller ID read *Georgina*.

"I was checking up on a visitor," Bess heard herself say. Her voice was high with alarm. "That woman who's been hanging around the gate. I wanted to see if she had a record for harassment or damage."

"What?" Steven flipped the file open and tossed paper after paper onto the floor. When he came to Hermione's photo, he halted and glanced between the picture and Bess.

Then his shoulders relaxed. The heat seemed to leave his face.

"Oh, that mad old bitch. I've been meaning to speak to security about her." Steven dropped the rest of the file onto his desk. "Well. All right, then. But don't go messing around in here again, do you hear me?" He gave a smile that didn't reach his eyes. "Next time you might make me cross."

She hesitated, then picked her way around him towards the door. As she reached it, she heard Steven pick up his phone again and say, "You still there?"

This time, Bess did not hang around to eavesdrop. She hurried down the corridor as fast as her unsteady legs could carry her. When she reached the outside world, she kept walking into the scrubland behind the gallery, to her hiding place beneath the ghost gum. Once safely alone there, she pulled out her phone and punched in Margaret's number.

～

Margaret pulled her car up to the kerb in Peacock Avenue. The street was dotted with potholes and patches of gravelly mud. There was no footpath, just overgrown grass and bindii prickles straggling all the way down to the gutter. Burly dogs paced back and forth behind wire fences; rusted cars sat up on blocks; tattered Australian flags hung in front windows. A letterbox had been lying on the ground for so long that dandelions had grown up through the slot. Peacock Avenue was ten minutes' drive from Leon Powell's Cabinet of Curiosities, but it seemed to Margaret like another country—weary by day and dangerous by night.

She turned off the engine, switched her phone from speaker to regular, and leaned back in her seat. "Don't apologise, Ms Campbell," she said for the third time. The voice on the other end was still breathless and agitated. "You were quite right to call."

The second Mr Powell, it seemed, had demonstrated a nasty streak. And he didn't want people going through his brother's records. Interesting. With some admiration, Margaret said, "It was bold of you to check his documents. Evidently there is something in there you weren't meant to see."

"No kidding." Bess breathed out hard. "But I don't want to search his office again. For a moment there, I was sure I'd get sacked or worse."

"Fair enough. No sense in you being excluded from the building. That wouldn't benefit anyone."

"Why hasn't Steven just destroyed it, though?" Bess asked. "Whatever the dangerous record is, I mean. Why would he hang onto it?"

"Perhaps he hasn't found it himself yet. He hasn't been in the office long, and you said the late Mr Powell's record-keeping was…eccentric." She struggled to keep the disdain from her voice. Anyone sorting through Margaret's own records would find them in faultless order. Assuming they could crack her various passwords and break into her safe deposit boxes, of course.

"Thanks for listening," Bess mumbled. "I hope I didn't interrupt anything." A smile entered her voice. "You're not busy at a conference about maritime history or something? Hearing some ground-breaking research about bosun's calls?"

"You may mock, Ms Campbell, but the fact you've been researching bosun's calls shows you are starting to develop an appreciation for the finer things in life." A snort of laughter erupted from the other end, and Margaret was surprised by how much it pleased her. Talking with Bess Campbell was not so disagreeable, after all. "Actually, I'm out of the office this afternoon," Margaret explained. "A meeting with some consulting experts."

She said goodbye and removed all items of value from her car before climbing out. She locked the vehicle with greater care than usual, then pushed open the gate to number thirteen.

Her footsteps along the cracked concrete path provoked a volley of deep, explosive barks. The front door had been left ajar, and out of the house charged a Peacock Avenue dog—bowlegged and muscular, with no council tags and a street reputation to maintain. Growling and bristling, it bounded in her direction.

Margaret had already been threatened and humiliated once today; she had no intention of making it twice. She stood unmoving until her assailant was almost upon her. Then she shrugged out of her long black coat, swirled it outwards like a billowing sail, and wrapped it in one quick motion around the dog's head and shoulders, entangling it as if in a net. To the sound of struggling and bewildered yelping, she hurried through to the back of the property.

The caravan was rusted in places and had sunk deep into the yellowing grass. It was spray-painted with an image of Ripley facing the Alien. Margaret knocked at the door.

Music had been playing inside; now it was switched off. An adolescent voice called out "Password?"

Margaret rolled her eyes. Really, this was undignified. But she could hear her coat being savaged and slobbered on; it was only a matter of time before the dog dropped it and went after a larger target. She said, "Jersey Devil."

The door opened an inch. From the shadowy interior, a pair of eyes squinted at her. "M? That you?"

"Zan," Margaret said. "Mind if I come in? It seems to be feeding time at the zoo."

"Black Shuck?" Zan glanced over Margaret's shoulder. "She's a good judge of character."

"I've got a job for you." Margaret reached into her pocket and eased out a roll of cash, just far enough to show the yellow gleam of many fifties.

Her host paused, then moved aside at last. "Step into my office."

The floor of the caravan was piled with beanbags and mattresses. There were abandoned coffee mugs, Tolkien paperbacks, and bags of junk food. All these things looked cheap, battered and old, even the junk food, but the tech equipment everywhere looked suspiciously new. The caravan smelled of Doritos, weed, and teenagers' socks.

Margaret shut the door behind her and nodded to her three hosts.

The Midnight Hags.

There was Zan: swarthy and plump, with caterpillar eyebrows, a wisp of moustache, and Agent Scully's face tattooed on her forearm. There was Tammy: brown, wiry, and pierced through every available bit of skin. And there was Squid: large, soft, and shapeless, a beanie pulled down to her eyebrows, squinting at Margaret through Coke-bottle lenses that made her eyes look huge.

Margaret had asked them once why they'd named themselves after the three witches in *Macbeth*.

"Cos they've got the first magic superpowers in modern storytelling," Zan had said. "Shakespeare, like, invented the trope. They control the whole story by predicting it. Like the Oracle in *The Matrix*." When Margaret looked surprised, Zan said, "We watch things online, you know. Do you think we're stupid or something?"

Margaret did not think that.

Now the three of them grimaced at the flash of daylight, and relaxed when Margaret closed the door. Dark, enclosed spaces were the Hags' natural habitat. They didn't belong in this seaside town.

"Shouldn't you be in school?" was Margaret's opening.

"Shouldn't you be in prison?" was Zan's reply. "Hey, did you kill Leon? Cos if you did, Tammy's really pissed off with you."

Tammy scowled at Margaret over her bag of Cheezels. "Leon was okay," she said. "He told me he'd give me a job if I did a TAFE course and promised not to steal any more animal skulls from his gallery."

"On the plus side," Zan said, "if you did kill him, Squid wants to interview you for her blog."

Squid gave a solemn nod. She removed the Chupa Chup lollipop from her mouth and said, "Serial killers are my hobby."

"Well, I'm awfully sorry to disappoint you," Margaret said. "But I didn't kill anyone."

Tammy looked suspicious; Squid, mournful. Zan said, "Well, what can we do for you?"

"The usual," Margaret said. "Information." Handing over the records, she said, "I need someone to go through these security tapes from my museum and log all the movements in and out the doors over a two-week period. I've tried to do it myself but I don't have time. I also need more information on these two." She showed the photographs from her HR files.

"Kelly Petrovich and Kenneth O'Neill?" Zan frowned as she read them out. "Hey, Kenneth used to go to our school."

"A friend of yours?" asked Margaret.

Zan snorted. "Nup."

The Midnight Hags didn't have friends. That seemed to be how they preferred it.

"There's something else." Margaret took out the piece of paper where she'd scribbled down the numberplate of her threatening visitor. "I need anything you can find on the owner and drivers of this vehicle."

"You don't want much, do you?" Tammy rolled her eyes.

"My apologies if I'm interrupting a scintillating piece of fan fiction," Margaret said. "But I saw you right last time, didn't I?"

"Last time was a piece of piss," Tammy sneered. "The mayor's credit card records? Please."

"Who knew he'd be buying so many ladies' shoes when his wife's been dead for two years?" Zan pondered.

"But this new job sounds like a pain in the arse," said Tammy. "Like I want to spend the rest of the week staring at a screen."

Margaret didn't reply. Far too obvious, she decided.

Instead she turned back to Zan, who was asking, "What's this about, M?"

"You might have heard I had some property vandalised."

"What, the mystery brick-thrower or the chick with the baseball bat?"

Margaret sniffed. "The former."

"Yeah, we heard about it," Zan said. "We didn't like the sound of that town hall meeting. Every time there's a crime around here, it's always the young people who get blamed, no need for evidence. It's discrimination." She moved a brand new laptop and state-of-the-art noise-blocker headphones to one side and plopped down on the mattress. "No offence, M, but don't you need to get your priorities sorted? I mean, everyone thinks you're a murderer and you're worried about a busted door?" She scratched a fresh tattoo on her ankle. "And what have Kenneth and this Kelly chick done wrong?"

"I'm not hiring you to interview me; I'm hiring you to get me information." Margaret was growing testy. The Hags weren't completely ghastly, but would a little respect for an elder be too much to ask?

Tammy sneered. "You think we're so hard up? We've got other clients, you know."

"Yes, I know." She had never cared to ask the Hags too many questions about who paid for their smart phones, tablets, drones, monitors, and Maltesers. She knew they "cleaned up" old laptops for their neighbours (who had acquired the computers by means fair or foul) and gave canny advice on data protection to everyone from the local librarian to the local ice dealer. Rumour had it the Hags also made a few extra dollars by entrapping and blackmailing internet paedophiles.

In town, the Hags were called weirdos, nerds, queers, and freaks; they were ostracised but also feared. No other kids were game to bully them outright; it wasn't worth the risk of having your social media hacked or your home electronics sabotaged.

"Very well," Margaret said. "I'll explain it to you. My property has been attacked; the whole town knows it, and they know that no one was brought to justice. I cannot afford that. It makes me look weak. Meanwhile the driver of that car saw fit to force his way into my museum and threaten me in front of witnesses. I cannot afford that either. Now my staff are creeping around like frightened mice, more so than usual, and that makes me suspicious. If they know something and are hiding it from me, that is unacceptable. I require loyalty from the people I employ." Her eyes narrowed. "All of them."

Tammy looked unimpressed.

Squid said, "Museums should be in virtual reality. That way none of your stuff could ever get broken and people wouldn't have to go out to look at it."

Zan asked, "Do you think your broken door was linked to Leon being murdered?"

Margaret hesitated. "Perhaps."

It was the right thing to say. Zan gave a soft whistle and Tammy seemed to perk up.

Squid said, "I like true crime. I'm reading this book about Yvonne Fletcher; she killed her two husbands with thallium in the 1950s. There were, like, hundreds of men getting rat-poisoned by their wives in Sydney at that time."

Margaret couldn't think of anything to say to that. So she waited while Zan glanced at the other two. They appeared to come to a telepathic agreement.

Zan said, "All right, then. Half now, half on delivery?"

"A pleasure doing business with you." Margaret peeled off the relevant notes. "I'll come by Thursday."

"You'll come when we text you," Tammy said. "Unless you want to lose another fancy coat."

Zan held the door open. "On your way out, bang on the window and see if Nanna's awake, eh? She was going to make scones."

Margaret turned to leave. As she climbed down the caravan's wonky steps, she heard Tammy call out "And M? If it turns out there's anything in these records you wouldn't want people to see…" There was a chuckle, then the hiss of a can of Coke being opened. "Just remember, we will have already seen it."

Chapter 10

PORT BANNIR TURNED OUT A clear, sunny morning for Leon's funeral. Bess leaned her bike against the churchyard fence and gazed into the milling crowd. She recognised celebrity chefs, critics, actors, and a former premier. She counted four different news crews. She saw Christos looking awkward in a suit, Hilda wearing a black twinset that might have been in mothballs since 1970, and Irene craning her neck to watch the celebrities.

And there was Hermione Morris, standing outside the church gate. Perhaps out of a sense of occasion, she had swapped the cabbage rose in her lapel for a clump of velvety black pansies. She tilted her *FAITH* sign towards the crowd.

Bess's pity for the old woman evaporated on the spot. Picketing a funeral? That was sick. What had Leon done to deserve that?

Of course, Leon would have been delighted to know he'd caused such offence.

Bess grabbed her phone and snapped a picture of Hermione, intending to pass it on to the police, along with a formal complaint. But before she could storm over and confront the protester in person, she saw Constable Jacs approach Hermione, speak quietly to her, and usher her gently away.

Bess straightened her dark coat and headed inside.

The church was an old sandstone edifice from Port Bannir's boom days. The benches were packed; Bess had to squeeze onto the end of a row that was already full. The organ came to life with a jangling, booming chord, and the mourners scrambled to their feet. She caught a glimpse of the coffin, piled with native wattle, gum leaves, and banksia blooms. Her throat constricted.

"Welcome, friends, on this sad day…" The minister spoke gravely of the shock and sorrow the community was feeling. He described Leon's great achievements over the course of his shortened life, and of the need for faith, kindness, and gratitude in the face of horror, anger, and loss.

As the congregation rose for the first hymn—*Lift High the Cross, the Love of Christ Proclaim*—Bess found herself wondering what sort of funeral Leon would have chosen for himself. Would he have organised a New Orleans jazz band to lead his cortege? Would he have wanted a post-mortem photograph, like a dead Victorian, propped up in a chair with his eyes taped creepily open? Or would he have had his ashes fired out of a cannon? Whatever he would have chosen, Bess doubted it would have been this Anglican service—respectful, polite, and dull. It made her very sad.

Steven Powell stepped into the pulpit and began to read out an address. A list of his brother's professional achievements, it was devoid of warmth or personal stories. His face was grim.

"…and at this sad time," he concluded in a monotone, "let us not grieve Leon's passing, but rather focus on how best to continue his legacy." As Steven stepped down and resumed his seat in the front row, Georgina Harper leaned over to speak to him. She murmured in Steven's ear and rested one manicured hand on his shoulder. He stiffened, then shook it off without glancing her way.

Bess stared, before the congregation stood for the final hymn and blocked her view.

As the crowd straggled out again into the sunlight, Bess noticed two familiar faces. There was Deirdre, Margaret's sister who Bess had seen at the police station. She was wearing an ill-fitting black skirt and blouse. Holding her arm was Paul Baker, the shire council youth worker. Bess blinked in surprise. Were they a couple?

Approaching them, she said to Paul, "I recognise you from the town hall meeting. You spoke really well there. I'm Bess Campbell. I used to work for Leon."

"Thank you, Ms Campbell." Paul's lean, weather-beaten face creased into a smile as he reached out to shake her hand. His grip was firm and warm. "That town hall meeting was a bit odd—if I'd known it would turn into a promo for the Incursium apartments, I would have stayed away. Still, that's how it goes. Sorry we had to meet again on such a sad day; Leon was a good bloke, very supportive of our youth club. He'll be missed."

"I loved him, you know." That was Deirdre. She'd been gazing off across the churchyard before, but now she surged forward to grasp Bess by the wrist. "He was such a gentle soul."

Deirdre's blouse was buttoned in the wrong holes, her coarse hair unbrushed at the back. Gazing at Bess, Deirdre said, "It was an accident, you know, a pure accident. But no one will believe me."

"All right, love, let Ms Campbell go." Paul reached over to prise his wife's fingers loose. Deirdre's nails were bitten down to the quick. "Don't pay any attention, Ms Campbell. She's just having one of her dotty days." He pulled a weary, humorous face at Bess, like the parent of a squalling toddler. "We're all at sixes and sevens today, aren't we, love?" With a roll of his eyes, he led Deirdre away.

Bess stared after them. Surely poor, batty Deirdre had not even known Leon, let alone... And yet there was something about that exchange that had not felt right at all.

She was distracted, however, by another familiar face. Arwyn was stumbling out of the church in a black mini-dress, a floating black chiffon scarf, and a little black hat. She was sniffling into a handkerchief and clutching someone's arm for support. Bess recognised Arwyn's escort—the editor of the *Port Bannir Advertiser*.

Trying to look casual, Bess edged over to them. Across the lawn, she saw Paul, still holding Deirdre's arm, glancing in her direction with a frown of concern.

"There's..." Arwyn gulped, struggling for breath. "There's nothing left now! Without him, I'm just...I'm useless. I'm nothing!"

"Now, now." The editor's voice was hushed. "That's not true, is it? You've still got things to share. You've got to tell Leon's story, Arwyn, to keep his memory alive." He patted her arm with one hand, while grasping it firmly with the other. "But you've got to make sure you tell it to the *right* people, to people who will understand."

Arwyn nodded vaguely, mopping her eyes. Her gaze wandered over towards the dishevelled Deirdre, who was bending by the fence to pick a handful of flowering weeds while Paul waited beside her.

"They shouldn't let women in dressed like that." Arwyn pointed and grimaced, as if at a fresh dog dropping. "Leon deserved a beautiful service, not one with dirty old bag ladies hanging around." Then she noticed Bess standing nearby and her wet face hardened even more. She said loudly, "And I don't think they should let prostitutes in here either, do you?"

That was enough for Bess. Had any of these people even known Leon? The sight of the hearse parked by the chapel made her stomach tie itself in knots. She hated this. Hated all of it.

She hurried out of the churchyard, intending to unchain her bike and get out of here. Then she heard a voice calling her name.

Looking up, she saw a gleaming sedan parked a safe distance down the street. And leaning against it, in a black suit and dark glasses like a mistress banned from showing her face at the funeral, was Margaret.

"Ms Campbell. I thought you might want a lift home."

⌒◞

Margaret had vacuumed the car that morning. The floor was immaculate, the dashboard gleaming. Bess's bike, loaded into the capacious boot, had been far too dusty for Margaret's liking, but she'd gritted her teeth and said nothing.

Bess leaned back in her seat and let out a sigh. She was perspiring a little and one tendril of red hair was stuck to her throat.

Margaret felt an urge to reach over and peel it loose.

"Thanks for the lift."

"My pleasure." Margaret started the engine and took off, weaving with ease between the parked and idling cars, and changing gear smoothly as they took off out of town. Margaret recognised the address Bess provided; she knew most of the properties around here. In her rear-view mirror, the church spire receded and vanished.

"How was the funeral?"

Bess shook her head. "Well attended. Boring. Sterile."

"Mr Powell would have approved of the first aspect, at least." Margaret eyed her passenger.

Bess looked weary but deep in thought. "Makes you wonder what the point is," she said. "I don't mean to be negative, but... You do your best to live a vivid, distinctive, meaningful life, and what do you end up with?

A chorus of *The Lord's My Shepherd*, tea and biscuits in the church hall, and people making up nice, polite lies." She let out a wobbly sigh. "I hate funerals."

"I avoid them myself." The last one Margaret had been to was her father's. The minister had described her dad as a "colourful local character", which everyone knew was code for "mad bastard". The turnout was small. Margaret had read the eulogy, glaring back at every suspicious face in the church. Deirdre, loaded up with tranquilisers, had dozed off in the front row.

"Arwyn was there," Bess said. "Arm in arm with the editor of the *Port Bannir Advertiser*. I hate to think what sort of lies she'll be urging him to publish about her 'great love affair' with Leon." She shook her head. "Hey, I saw your sister there, too. Was she a friend of Leon's?"

Margaret's gaze slid sideways. Her stomach tightened with nerves at the thought of Deirdre speaking to people. "A friend? No, Deirdre's not one for friends." Margaret wondered if Bess would make some crack about it running in the family, but she didn't.

Instead Bess said, "She was talking as if she knew Leon. Could she have visited the Cabinet of Curiosities?"

Margaret's breath escaped in a harsh burst of laughter. "Deirdre's lucky if she can visit the supermarket nowadays." She cleared her throat; she shouldn't speak like that. Margaret was trying to think of a compassionate way to describe Deirdre's situation, when Bess's phone rang.

"Excuse me." Bess fished it out of her bag. "Oh, sorry, I need to take this."

Margaret nodded, approving of her manners. Most people thought nothing of yabbering loudly on their phones in front of everyone. Bess was proving more civilised than Margaret had first thought.

"Hi, Mum."

"Bess." The voice on the other end was loud and forceful enough for Margaret to hear without straining. "Nice of you to pick up the phone at last. Too busy embarrassing yourself on TV, I suppose."

"How is everything, Mum?" Bess's tone was subdued.

"Is that meant to be a joke?" shrilled the voice on the other end of Bess's phone. From the corner of her eye, Margaret saw Bess flinch. "Bess, I'm not getting upset with you, because I've got my mascara on, and quite honestly

107

there are enough other things on my plate right now. But if you don't call your sister and apologise *today,* you may as well forget about coming to the wedding. Melanie is devastated. I hope you're pleased with yourself."

The woman seemed to be holding several other conversations at the same time. Margaret could hear her snapping "I don't know, Adrian, find it yourself!", "Mellie, darling, no more sweet biscuits before the wedding, remember?" and "Yasmin, *down girl!* Mummy will smack!"

"Mum, what's the problem?"

When they'd met before, Margaret had thought of Bess as far too cheerful, but had to revise her opinion after hearing her on the phone for twenty seconds with her mother. Now Bess sounded tired and wary.

"The problem?" A furious snort sounded from the phone's speaker. "You get yourself all over the news and the internet, brawling in the street and dressing like a mad hippie, and you wonder what the problem is? Do you have any idea what this has been like for us?"

"Mum—"

"I've had cousins I hadn't heard from in twenty years calling all the way from Rockhampton to find out what's going on with you, Bess. Your old school principal rang to ask if you'd be needing a character witness! Do you think I've got time for this? I'm meant to be interviewing Melanie's short-list of bridesmaids today!"

"Sorry, Mum." Bess slumped, her face blank as she gazed out the window.

The voice on the other end of the phone began hollering, "Mellie, darling, leave my cottage-cheese snacks alone!"

"Mum? I said I'm sorry."

"Story of your life, isn't it, Bess?" The voice sounded disdainful now. "You ran away to the back of beyond to escape your problems, and you're still making excuses. Working at that silly gallery and living in a caravan like some toothless unfortunate... Don't you think it's time you grew up?"

Bess didn't reply.

Her mother began shouting, "Look in the dryer, then, Adrian!" and "Yasmin, *no peeing*!" before she hung up.

Bess slid her phone back into her bag, and rested her temple against the window.

Margaret sensed the tiredness emanating from her.

At last, Bess said, "Sorry about that."

Margaret took care to fix her eyes on the road. "Why apologise? If your relatives can't accept your career as an ultimate fighting champion, that's their problem."

Bess managed a chuckle. "They've never approved of me."

"Surely someone as proudly unconventional as you wouldn't care about the approval of others?" Margaret teased her. "People can surprise you, can't they?" Then she relented a little, and said, "Never mind. You should have heard my father when I told him I'd become a *museologist*. He spluttered, 'That's not even a word!' When I was growing up, he told me I could be a teacher, a nurse, or a doctor's receptionist. The only other female career in Port Bannir was hairdressing, and according to Malcolm that was for tarts."

Margaret stole a glance sideways in time to catch a smile from Bess. Then she swung the car into the property where Bess lived and proceeded up the bumpy dirt track.

"Watch out for chickens," Bess cautioned her. "They're part of the family."

Margaret raised an eyebrow. "Of course they are."

They pulled up in front of the tiny house, and Margaret got out to have a look. She took in Bess's set-up: the canopies, chicken feeders, water tank, and solar panel, the washing line strung between the trees.

Why do people from the city fantasise about coming out here to live like refugees? she pondered. She didn't glance back, but could sense that Bess had climbed out of the car and was standing behind her. "Don't tell me you've got a long-drop toilet, dug in the dirt, too?"

"No, I had to draw the line somewhere," Bess said. "But please, go ahead and tell me what a waste it is for a woman with a university degree to be living like a mad feral. It's nothing Mum hasn't said already."

"I wouldn't go that far." Margaret contemplated asking what Bess's degree had been in—postmodern window dressing? Digital haiku?—but for some reason she didn't feel her usual urge to pick and disparage. She surveyed the scene instead. "Living off the grid does have a certain appeal. Not being beholden to anyone…"

"It actually takes discipline. No long showers, no Wi-Fi, no hoarding mountains of crap you don't need. But it's worth it, if you want to live mindfully. To really own your life and feel good about the choices you've made."

"To be in control…" Margaret murmured. She turned around at last.

Bess had taken a step closer; now they were standing at arm's length from each other. Bess's eyes were bloodshot. Had she really been weeping over that tedious Leon Powell?

Margaret felt a surge of frustration. What a waste of a woman's energy. But there was an intelligence there in Bess's face, a sharpness in spite of her self-help babble, which made Margaret draw closer. Bess Campbell had potential; there was no denying that. Bright but isolated, falsely accused, browbeaten by family… Margaret turned those elements over in her mind.

It was Bess who spoke first. "Want to stay for a cuppa?"

❦

The cup of tea turned into a full pot, with a plate of Bess's homemade bran and apricot biscuits. Margaret gave them a dubious look, but nibbled one. They sat outside on folding chairs with the chooks squabbling around their feet.

Bess was glad of the company. The thought of being alone after the funeral had filled her with dread. And to her surprise, Margaret proved a good guest, complimenting Bess on her book collection, helping with the tea things, even letting Genghis the rooster inspect her ankles for hidden weapons.

She asked Bess what it was like to build a tiny house, to work at the Cabinet of Curiosities, to get settled in Port Bannir. In return, Margaret offered snippets from her own experience: her favourite sources of artefacts, the difficulties of accessing grant money, the strangest comments she'd received from museum visitors.

Bess was enjoying the conversation, maybe too much. Margaret's sarcastic jibes made her chuckle, and Margaret's quixotic views on what the world needed—classes for schoolchildren in the lost arts of blacksmithing and nautical navigation, prison sentences for movie directors who produced historically inaccurate films—were entertaining, at least.

"If you'll forgive me for being forward," Margaret said, "it seems to me you would benefit from a mentor. You're clearly talented and hard-working, but you're flying by the seat of your pants in that job, aren't you?"

She softened the sting by taking another of Bess's biscuits. "Oh, don't misunderstand me; it's not your fault. Mr Powell's leadership style was clearly spontaneous, not strategic. He had such *fun* running that gallery; it was his little kingdom. But it's not your kingdom; it's your career. He should have fostered your wider potential, and he didn't."

"I can't believe you're getting stuck into him on the day of his funeral." Bess shook her head, but she couldn't summon up any real anger. After that church service, so full of conventional lies, Margaret's frank criticism of Leon came as a relief. "Anyway, I've seen the way your poor staff creep around like they're working for Countess Dracula. Don't tell me you're a supportive boss."

"My staff..." Margaret paused. For a moment, it seemed that she was about to reveal something serious. Then she shrugged and said, "My staff were born without brains or spines. They work for me because there were no other jobs available. You can't expect me to nurture talent that is non-existent."

"I hope they're stealing from your petty cash tin right now." Bess took another sip of tea. She kicked off her shoes and wriggled her toes in the sunshine. Across the paddock, she could see the grey shapes of three kangaroos, bent over and nibbling the greenery. For a second, she felt oddly content.

Then Margaret asked, "What did your mother mean, when she said you ran away from your problems?"

Bess winced. "You heard that?"

"The volume was...generous. I think I heard Yasmin urinating on the floor."

Bess smiled a little. How long since she had had anyone to complain to about her relatives? Then she thought about Margaret's question. To answer, or not to answer?

She hadn't told a soul in Port Bannir what had driven to her to move here. She'd been so determined to live a grateful and upbeat life, to focus only on the things that brought her joy. But today, with Leon's funeral on replay in her mind and Mum's call leaving a miserable, scooped-out feeling in her chest...

She sighed. "When I was living back in Melbourne, I had this friend. Angela." Bess's breath caught as she spoke the name. "We'd been through high school and uni together. We studied together, went to gigs together, got high together, flat-shared together. Came out together…" Bess swallowed. "Best mates, you know?"

Margaret was silent.

Bess didn't look at her, but she felt the intensity of the other woman's attention. "We'd gone out dancing one night. A new place called the Boleyn. We left the club pretty late and, as we were walking out, this group of guys across the road started yelling stuff at us. *Hey, lezzos, why don't you kiss for us?* All that stuff. Angela shouted back at them to get stuffed, gave them the finger, and we kept walking. I didn't think much about it, to be honest. We got in the car. I was sober, more or less, so I was driving. We pulled out of the street and took the turn-off onto the freeway. It was a good five minutes or so before I clocked the car that was following us." Bess paused for breath. Suddenly it felt too hot out here.

"They started tailgating us," she said. "Flashing their lights. At first I thought it was just some impatient idiot trying to get past. It didn't occur to me that someone would threaten a woman's life just for telling him to go away."

Margaret gave a faint snort, but made no other comment.

"They zoomed up beside us, cut in front, and then slammed on their brakes so I nearly hit them. I sounded the horn, tried to get around them, and next thing they were zigzagging, blocking my car." Bess shook her head. Her palms and armpits were clammy. "It was surreal. There was no one else nearby, just the empty road and this car with its stereo pounding, swooping all over the place to stop us escaping. Angela was telling me to pull over, but I was furious by then. How dare they do that to us? The road widened and I managed to get around them, but then they came screaming up behind us again, so close I could see their faces in the rear-view mirror. There were four of them. They were laughing."

Bess looked down at her hands, balled up in her lap. "We were about to pass the turn-off to the western suburbs. I had this idea—it all happened so fast, you know—but I got this notion that if I turned off really suddenly we would lose them. So I gunned it, waited until the last second, then swung the wheel." She swallowed. "I lost control, felt the car go into a skid. And we started to spin. We spun all the way around, and I remember the radio playing and the blur of the lights, like a carnival ride. Angela called my name. Then we hit a wall."

Bess moistened her dry lips. The chickens were pecking around her feet, making gentle grumbling sounds. A breeze rustled the leaves. All around her was tranquillity, the very opposite of the memories now pressing on her heart with suffocating force.

"It was a passing truck driver who called triple zero. Not the men who'd been chasing us. They just drove off. Emergency services had to cut us out of the car; the metal had crumpled up like paper. I got whiplash and bashed-up shins; you should have seen my bruises, they were all the colours of the rainbow. But I walked out of the hospital a few hours later. Angela… Angela died."

Bess fell silent. She concentrated on her own breathing, her ribcage expanding and deflating, the puffs of air leaving her nostrils. The processes which took no effort at all, but which could stop at any moment.

"I wasn't charged," she made herself continue. "Angela's family never blamed me to my face, but it was made clear that I shouldn't go to the funeral. They'd always thought I was a bad influence, apparently. According to them, it was my fault she'd turned out gay." She took a shuddering breath. "And our friends… I don't know what they said when I wasn't around, but nothing was right after that. Awkward silences, people making excuses not to catch up. I heard there was gossip going around that I'd been wasted that night, that I'd taken ecstasy, that I started the fight with those guys, that they were actually friends of mine…"

She grimaced. "Well, I'm sure people were hurt by her death; they weren't being their best selves. Or maybe some of them had never liked me much in the first place. Angela was always the popular one…" She trailed off, staring out across the paddock. On the fencepost nearby was perched a huge crow.

"Everything fell apart after that. I couldn't work, couldn't craft, couldn't care less about anything. I'm sure my family were worried, but often they just seemed irritated. I overheard Mum and Melanie talking once. Mum said 'It's all this talk about mental health nowadays. People have a bad day, they diagnose themselves with depression, and bingo! They're depressed.' And Melanie said 'Not to be mean or anything, but she's always had to be the centre of attention'."

Bess had thought repeating those words would devastate her. Instead she thought about Melanie's $400-a-head hens' night and bridesmaid shortlists, and felt an urge to laugh. "My brother Owen encouraged me to get away and start again, and it was the best move I ever made. I took stock of everything and decided that if I'd got a second chance at life I'd better make the most of it. I would create my own life in Port Bannir and ensure it was beautiful and meaningful to me. I wouldn't allow any negative energy to drain my time or my spirit. And I would always greet other people with an outstretched hand."

She wondered if Margaret would make fun of her for that, but Margaret was silent, her eyes fixed on the distant trees.

At last, Margaret said, "So, you tried to escape to this town, and I tried to escape from it. Alas, neither of us were completely successful." Her tone was cool, reflective. It stung that she offered no sympathy—but in a strange way her lack of emotional reaction came as a relief.

Bess had had enough of managing other people's feelings about Angela's death. She wiped her nose and cleared her throat. "Why have you stayed here?" she asked Margaret. "If you hate the place so much?"

Margaret waited a while before answering. "It's not as simple as that. I have responsibilities in Port Bannir." Her gaze flickered sideways, landing on Bess. "And I don't hate everything here."

Something about her tone caused a warm sensation to steal through Bess.

In that same voice, confidential and strangely soft, Margaret went on, "I am sorry about your friend."

"Thanks," Bess mumbled. She rubbed her eyes hard for a moment, then pushed back her hair. "I hadn't told that story to anyone before."

"I'll keep it to myself," said Margaret. "Unlike most people here, I can respect a confidence. I hope…" She turned to study Bess's face. "I hope you will trust me."

Margaret's voice seemed to reverberate, to linger in the air. Bess felt the urge to reach out, to capture the sound and hold it close. But it was Margaret who reached out, to trace the line of Bess's jaw with fingers that smelled faintly of orange blossom.

Bess held her breath as those soft fingertips stroked the curve of her bottom lip. She should move away. It wasn't as if she really liked Margaret that much, she reminded herself. But the scent and the closeness of her filled Bess's consciousness, until everything else—the funeral, Mum's phone call, the loss of Angela—seemed to retreat, to fade back into the shadows.

Margaret leaned closer, bridging the gap between their chairs, and kissed her.

The press of her mouth was firm, her lips warm and supple. Bess's own lips parted automatically, welcoming the flicker of Margaret's breath, the teasing sweep of her tongue. Bess tilted closer, drawn to the heat of the other woman's skin. Her eyes closed, her thoughts stilled, suspended in the moment.

Then Margaret moved away. "I should get going." She stood up and pulled the hem of her jacket, straightening it with a quick, fastidious gesture. "Thank you for your hospitality."

"That's...that's all right." Bess's voice came out in a whisper. It took her a moment to stand, by which time Margaret had already stepped away.

"I hope to see you again soon, Bess." Margaret walked back to her car, got in, and retreated down the drive with a brief wave.

Bess watched her go, her heart pounding.

Chapter 11

MARGARET TOOK THE UNPAVED TRACK quickly this time, juddering and bouncing away from Bess's place. A muscle twitched in her cheek.

She should not have done all that. Gone looking for Bess Campbell, wasted the day talking, revealed things about herself. Kissed her. It had been impulsive and foolish. Emotional.

But Bess wasn't like the people around here. She was interesting, and passionate about things. She was tender. Couldn't Margaret connect with her—get close to her?

Margaret clenched her jaw. Connection was dangerous. It was one thing to stay on good terms with Bess—under the circumstances, she could scarcely afford not to—but she mustn't let herself get entangled.

She had other things she must deal with, and Bess could not know about them. It was impossible. She tightened her lips and drove on.

❧

Bess sat on the steps of the tiny house with Genghis nestled in her lap, stroking his feathers as she tried to get her head around what had just happened here. Margaret—haughty, sarcastic Margaret—had kissed her.

Why had Margaret done it? Was she for real, or just lonely, despite all her posturing? Or was this some weird little game?

God, it had felt so right, though. So soft and quiet and intimate. Bess couldn't even remember the last time someone had made her feel like that.

She rubbed her closed eyes. Of all the times to be falling for some woman. Now, when she was already fretting over Leon's death, Angela's death, Steven's takeover, not knowing if she still had a career, and not knowing who was behind it all. It was enough to drive a person crazy.

Crazy... She shook her head, distracted from the thought of Margaret by the memory of that funeral. She thought of Arwyn tottering around playing the widow, of Hermione with her *FAITH* sign, of Deirdre talking about love and accidents while gathering a bouquet of weeds. Jacs had said that Leon's murder had been savage. Did any of those women have it in them to kill like that?

People can surprise you. Once again, she heard Margaret's velvety voice and felt those fingers trailing along her cheek and down her throat. Her flesh tingled at the memory. God, why Margaret? And why now?

Bess breathed out hard. She shifted Genghis down to the ground, got up, and dusted off her dress.

"Stuff it." She wasn't going to stay here, getting tangled up in her own thoughts. The funeral may have been a farce, but she could try to do *something* for Leon. She shooed the chickens into their pen, picked up her bike, climbed aboard, and pushed off down the drive.

❧

Was there any point in confronting Arwyn again? The police must have questioned her. Still, the young woman's bursts of rage and treacly sentiment had left Bess suspicious. Arwyn had been at the Cabinet of Curiosities when Leon died. And she wouldn't be the first fan to react badly when an adored celebrity didn't welcome the attention.

Surely it was worth another shot. Arwyn liked to talk, that much was clear, and while she didn't like Bess, perhaps Bess could turn that to her advantage. If she could pester Arwyn a little, make her petulant enough to let her guard down, trick her into letting something slip... Bess muttered possible questions and prompts as she cycled down Buckley Avenue towards the Port Bannir Motor Inn.

But when she arrived, she found Arwyn's little blue hatchback missing from the car park. The motel—a squat, brown-brick eighties block—was livelier than usual with guests in town for Leon's funeral. Affecting an aimless manner, Bess found she could wander about without attracting anyone's attention. She glanced through windows and doorways, peered

117

between the net curtains into the reception area, but caught no glimpse of Arwyn.

She sauntered the length of the block to the last unit: 12B. The blinds had been left open and she noticed a familiar baby-pink cardigan slung over a chair. The lights were off and no one answered Bess's knock.

She looked over her shoulder, then risked another peek through the window. It seemed like a standard rural motel room: worn carpet, exposed brick, ancient air conditioner, and complimentary teabags. Not many places to hide a weapon.

Surely the police must have looked there? And surely no murderer would be silly enough to stash a large knife (or whatever had killed Leon; she didn't like to dwell on it) in a country motel in between the ironing board and the minibar? Still…

Bess looked around again. No one was close enough to watch her properly. She reached into her bag for a hairpin.

Thank goodness for dodgy old motel doors. And thank goodness for Leon's Australia Day Experience last year, when children visiting the Cabinet of Curiosities had got to dress up in nineteenth-century rags and learn the authentic convict arts of busting locks, pickpocketing, and swearing at the police. A few parents had looked askance, but the kids had enjoyed it, and Bess had found it informative too. She eased the door open and slipped inside.

Arwyn, it seemed, travelled light. The dresser held a couple of blouses, a blue fluffy sweater, skimpy nylon underwear, and a stack of women's magazines. There was a business card on top, from the editor of the *Port Bannir Advertiser*. The bathroom cabinet held soap and shampoo, a tube of Better Than Sex mascara, a spinach and green tea age-prevention cleanser, and something called a Babyfacial. The drawers beside the bed were empty. There was nothing under the bed except proof that the cleaners weren't very committed to their job.

Bess sighed with disappointment. She checked for loose tiles; she looked under the bathroom sink, beneath the mattress, even in the kettle, but she found nothing. She wondered what Arwyn did alone here every night, without books, newspapers, crafts, or even cable TV. How did she spend those hours? Posting doctored photos and furious rantings on social media would be Bess's guess. She made sure everything was left where she'd found it, and departed quietly.

She was fairly sure no one noticed her leaving, as there was a good distraction coming from the motel's caravan park out the back. Someone was screaming her head off.

Not Arwyn; the voice was older and rougher than hers. She edged around the side of the building, craning her neck to see.

The caravan park had a dozen tiny cabins and a shared toilet and shower block. Bess knew some people there were semi-permanent residents. Port Bannir could seem like a refuge to people from the city who needed a cheap place to start again, or to hide. But she hadn't realised Hermione Morris was one of them.

Hermione stood out in front of her cabin. Her shoes and coat looked dusty and she was still clutching her *FAITH* sign—upside down now. Her powdered face was crumpled as she mouthed words Bess couldn't make out. Pleas or excuses? The shouting was being done by someone Bess recognised with astonishment: Irene, from the Cabinet of Curiosities.

"I've bloody had it!" she was hollering. Irene was taller and chunkier than Hermione, and she loomed over her, jabbing a finger in the old lady's face. "You are ruining everything, you crazy witch!" Irene's funeral clothes strained at the seams as she gestured wildly. "Do you even care what you've done? You could have lost me my job, made me tainted by—by association! But no, none of that matters, does it? As long as you've made your point!" She ripped the sign from Hermione's trembling hands, hurled it to the ground, and stamped on it.

Bess stared. She was used to Irene complaining and passing judgement, but she'd never guessed the woman was capable of raging like this.

Irene stepped closer, almost pinning Hermione to the cabin door. "You get out of here," she snarled. "I want you to pack all your ugly, cheap junk and leave this town tonight, you hear me? Or so help me, I will go to the police myself!"

Bess edged closer to hear a little of what Hermione was saying.

"All I ask…" her voice quavered "…is that you let me explain why. Why I had to do it, why it was the right thing to do."

"The right thing?" Irene's voice rose to a screech. "You disgusting old—" She lashed out, slapping Hermione across the face.

"Hey, that's enough!" Bess bolted over. "What's going on here?"

Irene wheeled around. Her face was red, her mascara caked around her pouchy eyes. "What the hell are you doing here?" she snapped at Bess. "This is private property."

"What the hell are *you* doing here, attacking old ladies?" Bess's chest was thumping with alarm. She turned to Hermione, who held one knobbly hand to her cheek. "Are you all right?"

"She's fine," Irene jeered. "The old bag's tougher than she looks."

"What's all this about?" Bess stepped between them. "How do you two know each other?"

"Don't you say a bloody word, you miserable old bat!" Irene pointed an accusatory finger at Hermione.

"She can say whatever she likes." Bess turned back to Hermione. For a moment, she almost forgot about Hermione picketing Leon's funeral, about the police report from the gallery, about her own suspicions of the woman. Hermione's lips were quivering, a tear leaving a clear trail through the powder on her face. "Ms Morris, would you like me to call the police?"

"Oh, yeah!" Irene hooted. "She'd like that! Wouldn't you, *Miss* Morris?"

"I think that's enough out of you," said Bess, but Hermione was shaking her head.

In a voice like the crackle of tissue paper, she said, "No police, dear. I'm—I'm quite well. I'd like to go inside now."

"I'll come in with you," Bess said. She eyed Irene, who was breathing hard, her fists clenched. "How about a cup of tea?"

"You're not going anywhere with her!" Irene stepped forward, making Hermione flinch. "You've done enough damage already, you rotten old bitch. Just get inside, pack your bags, and go!"

"Right, that's it. I'm calling the cops." Bess reached for her phone, but Hermione's hand shot out and seized her wrist with surprising force. Up close, Bess could see the old woman's fingers were thick. The backs of her hands were alive with throbbing blue veins, her nails tough and filed square.

"Really, my dear, there's no need." Hermione held on tight until Bess dropped her phone back into her bag. "You've been awfully kind, but you can pop off home now. I've got a few little jobs to do here."

"Like packing," Irene insisted. "I'm not leaving until I see Jim's cab pull up, you hear me?"

Bess protested, but Irene was already retreating as far as the gate, where she stood with her arms folded, apparently ready to wait as long as necessary.

Hermione tiptoed into her cabin and shut the door.

Glancing between them in bewilderment, Bess wondered what to do now. No sound came from inside the cabin, and Irene looked grimly prepared to stay at her post all night.

After a minute, Bess shook her head in frustration and left via the front office, where she told the clerk to keep an eye out for trouble in the caravan park. As she climbed aboard her bike to ride away, she glanced over her shoulder and saw Irene still standing there.

❧

Where would you hide a weapon in Port Bannir?

That was the question that stuck in Bess's mind as she rode away. Whoever killed Leon had taken the implement with them, and the police must have been looking for it ever since. If the killer was Arwyn, Bess doubted the weapon was in her car; surely the cops would have poked around in there after the fight at the Maritime Museum. So, where else could it be?

Tossing it into a garbage bin seemed an obvious option—but hadn't Leon been killed on a Thursday? Rubbish collection in Port Bannir didn't happen until Tuesday. The shops and cafes locked their skip bins overnight, and in this nosy town, a person dumping rubbish in a neighbour's bin might easily attract the cranky attention of the neighbour in question.

Where else, then? Of course, if the killer was not Arwyn, they could easily have the object in their house, car, or garden, right now. What would that feel like, to have a bloodied piece of evidence stashed in the garage or buried under the geraniums? Did the killer picture it there all the time; did their heart stop whenever a family member wandered too close to the spot, or when someone knocked on their door? The thought made Bess's skin creep. If it was her, she would not have been able to keep that thing in the house.

Outdoors, then? Port Bannir had no shortage of fields, creek beds, and scrubby picnic areas. Good neutral spaces to get rid of something—but with the combination of police and milling tourists, wouldn't the thing have turned up by now? Maybe, maybe not.

Puffing, she put on a burst of frustrated speed. This was stupid; they were surrounded by hundreds of kilometres of farms, highways, and beaches. Not the mention a wild and endless expanse of sea. The weapon, and the person who had wielded it, could be anywhere. She should forget this, let the police grapple with it. Except she couldn't do that to Leon… Or Margaret.

If this crime was left unsolved, plenty of people would continue to assume Margaret Gale was the killer. How long could Margaret continue to live in this town with that hanging over her? The thought troubled Bess, maybe more than it should. Helping Margaret wasn't the point, she reminded herself sternly. This was about Leon.

Without thinking about it, she had cycled all the way to the Cabinet of Curiosities. The great dark building stood out against the cloudless sky, the white beach, and the glittering ocean. It was framed by several kilometres of bushland and thick scrub.

If you had killed someone here and were desperate to dump the weapon fast, what would you do? Throw it in the sea and risk it being washed right back up again? Or hide it somewhere?

This was probably a waste of time, she reminded herself, as she chained her bike to a fence post and set off along the beach. The police must have searched the area already. Still, there was no harm in looking, and it felt better than sitting at home.

It was a weekday and too cool for swimming, so the beach was quiet. Bess counted two dog walkers, a cluster of elderly tourists, and half a dozen surfers braving the chilly waters. The afternoon was glorious, though: crisp but sunny, with a light breeze lifting her hair out behind her. Holiday weather.

Angela would have stripped off and run squealing into the surf. Bess heaved a sigh, fished her sunscreen from her bag, and slathered her pale, freckly skin, before making her way along the edge of the scrub that served as a barrier between the beach and the road. She turned from the sparkling sea towards the shadowy tangle of banksia, long grass, and pines.

She imagined bolting away from the gallery in the dead of night, stumbling across the wet sand, skidding on seaweed and treacherous rocks.

Ducking down below the shrubbery to hide from the lights of a passing car, desperate to get rid of something. And beneath the gusts of sea air, the dark stink of blood.

But the ground here was hard, rocky, and riddled with tree roots. Unless the killer came equipped with a shovel, they would have found it hard to conceal anything. She peered into the gloom, looking for signs of disturbed earth or dumped rubbish, but it seemed untouched.

Bess tramped for an hour along the coastline, poking the bushes with a stick, turning over rocks, wrestling with branches. She walked until the Cabinet of Curiosities became a black spot on the horizon, but she found nothing.

As she turned around and trudged back, the sun burning a red streak along the part in her hair, Bess found herself thinking about what Margaret had said earlier today. Was she flying blind in relation to her career? Did she need a mentor, a résumé, new skills, a five-year plan? It seemed so conventional to fret about that stuff, not to mention callous when she was meant to be thinking about Leon's death. Still, the idea of working for Steven Powell did not appeal. Maybe it was time to reassess things.

People can surprise you. That low, abrasive voice of Margaret's, the way she'd kissed her with just the right blend of hesitancy and force. It had been good. Perfect. Still, thinking back now, it made Bess a bit angry, too. Margaret had some nerve, really, hitting on someone she'd been rude to in the past, someone who was upset at the time.

If only Angela was around to talk to. But if she had been around, Bess wouldn't be here, and all of this—Leon's horrible end, Margaret's confounding behaviour, the weirdness of Arwyn, Deirdre, Hermione, Irene—would be nothing to do with her. She'd wanted to live a vivid life, but this was getting too vivid.

The Cabinet of Curiosities was closed today for Leon's funeral; even the café was locked up and silent. Without the usual crowds, the big, featureless building struck Bess as creepy, like the sort of place a government would test weapons or conduct illegal experiments. She walked around the scrubby perimeter of the car park, finding nothing but drifts of litter from the tourists. Then she ducked under the branches and stepped deeper into the bushland.

The police must have searched here, too, but still Bess poked around for an hour, peering into hollow trees, kicking over fallen branches and ant nests, clambering down into the dry creek. Her shoes grew muddy and her feet hurt. Birds sang. She was starting to feel very silly.

Walking towards the gallery once more, she found herself in the shaded area behind the sculpture garden; the place where she'd often retreated to eat lunch in peace under the ghost gum. Plenty of people must have strolled through this space since the murder, including Bess. Still, she'd come this far; she might as well finish the job. Perspiring in the strong sun, she took a look around the sculpture garden, then sidled through the wattle bushes towards the ghost gum and the back wall, where the cartoon portrait of Leon still graced the brickwork.

She paused, gazing at Leon's quirky picture, resting her palm against the trunk of the ghost gum. Such a tranquil spot. Absently, she stroked the bark, comforted by its familiar texture. But something was off; her fingers found a scratch in the smooth trunk, then another. She turned her head and saw gouges and rips in the bark, a strip torn halfway off the tree. And across the pinkish-white surface were little smears of red.

Her breathing stopped. She froze, listening hard. Drawing her hand back from the tree, Bess very slowly stepped around it.

Lying in the grass was a black high-heeled shoe. It must have fallen off, or been wrenched off, when the woman who'd worn it had lost her footing.

That woman lay crumpled beneath the flowering wattle, her black funeral dress dirty, her fingertips bloody and torn, her throat mottled with bruises. Her pale eyes bulged in a face now distorted by death, staring up at Bess as if in amazement.

Bess covered her mouth, fighting an urge to scream, to be sick, to run away and pretend she'd never seen this.

With an effort, she lowered her shaking hand.

"Arwyn."

Chapter 12

IT WAS THE NEXT MORNING by the time Bess walked out of the police station. Her head was spinning from too much instant coffee and too little sleep. She blinked in the dawn light; the streets were quiet and empty. As silent as the bushland around the Cabinet of Curiosities, where she'd made her dreadful discovery.

Constable Jacs's spare jeans chafed around her hips; her football shirt reached almost to Bess's knees. Bess had handed over her own clothes for closer inspection. A lot of trouble to go to for someone who'd just found a body—except they obviously wondered if she'd done more than that.

She was halfway down the street before she remembered to go back for her bike. Was she alert enough to ride home? Her toe caught in a crack in the pavement and she stumbled to a halt, her heart racing.

Concentrate, she told herself. *Feel your breath, the earth beneath you, the soles of your feet…* But her feet throbbed from yesterday's hike, and that reminded her of what she'd found at the end of it.

She should head home. The police must have finished searching her tiny house by now, and she needed to check on the chooks. But somehow she couldn't face it: her kooky little refuge invaded and trampled over by the forces of the outside world. Bess imagined her books, cushions, and aromatherapy candles tossed around, covered in a dark film of fingerprint powder.

Fingerprints… She would have left them around Arwyn's motel room. She'd volunteered that information to the police, knowing they would find it out anyhow. She'd left out the part about picking the lock, making it sound like the room had been left open and she'd wandered in innocently, hoping to find Arwyn for a chat, and was doubtful that they believed her.

Bess swallowed hard at the memory of sterile white walls, of being examined by gloved hands and sharp, impersonal eyes. Hands, nails, hair, skin. She thought of what the police must have been looking for: bruises, scrapes, defensive marks from Arwyn's clawing fingers and desperate bared teeth. The image turned her stomach.

She paused for breath, leaning on her handlebars, as the detective Gavin's questions spun her head in nauseating circles: *Why did you go to her room? How did you know where she was staying? So, you'd rung around looking for her before? Why did you attack her at the Maritime Museum? It didn't look like a "peaceful intervention" to me. Is it true you two had an argument in the bakery? She told you she'd seen Leon's killer? No? What did she tell you, then? How did you know to go to the gallery to find her today? Is it true she provoked you at the funeral? You and Leon were close, weren't you? You must have been very upset by his death. Very angry.* And when Bess had finished babbling out her answers, sounding more bewildered and guiltier by the minute, Gavin had said, "Tell me about your relationship with Margaret Gale."

Bess took another gulping breath and forced herself to keep walking, as if a dozen officers would drag her back to the cells if she stayed out here too long.

In between making veiled accusations, the police had gone over and over her movements after Leon's funeral. *When did Margaret Gale drive you home? Did you go anywhere else? What time did you arrive? Can anyone verify that?* She was wondering if they'd ask exactly how many cups of tea she'd drunk—until the penny dropped.

"Was that when Arwyn died?" Bess had asked. "Right after the funeral?" No one answered her, but the looks on their faces—guarded, suspicious, frustrated—made Bess realise that Margaret Gale must be her alibi. And that she must be Margaret's.

"Bess."

She blinked, convinced for a second that the tall, black-clad figure calling to her from the steps of the Maritime Museum was a figment of her exhausted brain. It took the light touch of Margaret's hand on her shoulder to convince her otherwise.

"Good to see you at last. Would you like to come inside?" Margaret looked Bess up and down, and seemed to realise she was in no state to make decisions now. Gently, she removed the handlebars from Bess's grip and wheeled the bike away, summoning Bess after her with a jerk of her head and a promise too good to resist: "I have real coffee."

"Wow." Bess slumped back against the sofa in Margaret's office. It was too firm for her liking and its smell of leather was morally unacceptable—but Bess had never been more relieved to sit down anywhere. She wrapped her hands around the warm white china mug, breathing in the sharp aroma of Margaret's coffee. She took a sip and let out a groan of relief. "How did you know I needed this?"

"Because you looked like you were about to walk sideways into a wall." Margaret leaned against her spotless desk and lifted her own coffee cup to her lips. "Besides, I've tasted the instant swill they serve at that station. Remember?" She studied Bess's collapsed figure and red-rimmed eyes. "Although they let me out a lot earlier."

"You were questioned, too?" Bess blinked blearily.

"Certainly. They seemed very interested in my movements after Mr Powell's funeral." Margaret shrugged. "But they didn't keep me long. I had the sense to bring a solicitor, which I'm guessing you neglected to do." She sipped her coffee, her smooth throat moving as she swallowed. "I was also intelligent enough not to break into the victim's room or discover her body."

"How did you know I'd done those things?"

"I have my sources." Margaret clicked her tongue. "Really, Bess, you do make yourself an easy target. Why didn't you just write them out a confession in triplicate?"

Bess let out a hiccup of despairing laughter, which quickly turned into sobbing. Her shoulders shook, her coffee slopping onto the tiled floor. She expected Margaret to make some caustic remark about her clumsiness, but Margaret just wiped it up, before laying a hand on Bess's shoulder in a brief gesture of comfort.

"Now, now. We mustn't give way; that's just what our enemies want."

"Enemies?" With an effort, Bess got herself under control. She was very aware of the slight pressure of Margaret's hand. "Who do you mean?"

"I wish I knew." Margaret moved away. "But don't you get the teeniest feeling someone would like to pin this whole fiasco on us?"

"I think the police would." Bess sniffed, then clutched at Margaret's proffered box of tissues. "They asked so many questions I thought I was going nuts. And I don't think they believed anything I said."

"Hm. You weren't charged, though?"

Bess shook her head. "I think Arwyn was killed while you and I were… hanging out at my place." She wondered if she should bring up the kiss, but this didn't seem the time. Not with her face all blotched and swollen and the image of poor dead Arwyn jammed in her brain. The killer had just left her where she fell, like rubbish thrown from a car window.

Taking another sip of coffee, Bess gazed past Margaret into the museum. It was too early for guests, but the displays were lit up already. On a screen played ancient, jerky footage taken aboard a whaling ship a century before. The huge, intelligent creatures were hauled onto a deck sloshing with seawater and blood, their bodies hacked to bits. Bess shut her eyes against a fresh wave of dizziness.

"How can you look at that stuff?" She gestured. "Doesn't it…bother you?"

"This from a woman who works in a gallery famous for its display of celebrity stool samples." Margaret raised an eyebrow. "Yes, it bothers me. But I don't believe in sanitising history. People deserve the truth."

Bess wondered if Margaret meant that in the same way that people deserved water and oxygen, or in the way that criminals deserved prison. She drained her coffee and let her head fall back against the cushions. "Well," she said at last. "At least we know now that Arwyn didn't kill Leon."

"Do we?" Margaret frowned.

"Come on." Slowly, Bess collected her thoughts. "I don't think Port Bannir could be home to two vicious murderers at once."

"Perhaps not. It would be like trying to run two local museums." Margaret finished her own coffee and positioned the mug squarely in the centre of its coaster. "Well, let's assume it's the same killer. Why target the hysterical Miss Ross?"

"Obvious, isn't it?" Bess got the feeling Margaret was only prompting her because she enjoyed the exchange. Should she find that flattering? "Arwyn was nearby when Leon was killed. Either she saw the killer, or the killer was worried she might have. And she was a blabbermouth."

"Hmm." Margaret nodded. "Not the sort of person one could bribe or threaten into silence."

"I don't reckon it would have been hard to lure her somewhere," said Bess. "All you had to do was mention Leon's name and she came running." Bess shook her head. "She thought… She really seemed to think she was nothing without him."

"Unfortunate," Margaret said in a brisk, pitiless tone. "Especially since she was never actually *with* him."

"I don't—" Bess chewed her lip. "Maybe it's dumb, but I don't want to go home. I keep thinking of the police in there, snooping around."

"You don't keep 'special' pot plants in your garden, do you? No offence intended, but you do look the type."

Bess rolled her eyes

"Well, then, you've nothing much to fear," Margaret said. "They turned over my house after they saw that footage of me leaving Mr Powell's gallery. Naturally I resented it, and my solicitor invoiced them for the spilled coffee beans and the muddy doormat—but they didn't cause too much chaos. I'm sure you'll put things right in your home quickly enough."

"It's not the mess." Bess slid lower. Her body felt like lead. "It's… It's like nowhere is safe. And I'm thinking…"

"What?" Margaret leaned closer.

Bess took a deep breath and said, "I keep thinking if Arwyn was murdered because someone was afraid of what she might say, well, how safe am I? She spoke to me; people saw us together."

"You said she told you nothing useful."

"Yes, but does the killer know that?"

Margaret hummed to herself. She gazed up at a portrait on the wall, of Felicity Aston crossing Antarctica alone on her skis. She seemed to be turning the problem over in her head. Then she said, "I don't think you've much to worry about, Ms Campbell. You've been questioned twice by the police due to your entanglement with Miss Ross, and you've achieved infamy on social media as an unhinged amateur wrestler."

"*How* is this meant to reassure me?" Bess glared, distracted from her own fears by how truly annoying Margaret Gale could be.

"You are not a credible witness, Bess," Margaret explained patiently. "If you tried to repeat any conversation you'd had with the late Ms Ross, it would be hearsay at best. And it's doubtful people would believe you."

"Right." Bess wondered whether to be relieved or offended, but she was too tired for either. After a moment, she lifted her head and asked Margaret, "What about you?"

"Do I believe you?" Margaret arched an eyebrow. "You don't strike me as a competent criminal, and I daresay first degree murder would get in the way of your cosmic journey to lifelong positivity."

Bess scowled. "Can't you give the sarcasm a rest, just for a minute? I wasn't asking if you believed me. I meant: what about you? If the killer went after Arwyn because she was nearby when Leon was killed, what if they decide you're a risk for the same reason?"

"I never saw Mr Powell's killer." Margaret ground her jaw, apparently in frustration.

"They don't know that," Bess insisted. "Sure, it looks like they lured you there, setting you up to take the rap. But if they get nervous, change their mind…"

"I appreciate your concern, Bess, but I'm not worried about my safety." Margaret paused. "I would have some concerns about yours, though, if you attempted to cycle home in your present condition."

"I've had coffee," Bess protested. But when she gestured towards her empty mug, she misjudged and swept it off the arm of the sofa. Margaret swooped forward and caught it before it could shatter across the tiles.

"We're opening soon," she said. "Why don't you rest in here for a while? Just until you stop seeing double."

"I don't want to be a nuisance…" Bess broke off into a huge yawn. God, this sofa looked so inviting.

Moving swiftly, Margaret pulled the blinds and switched off the light. "Make yourself at home," she said from the doorway. Her tone was abrupt, awkward, but there was warmth there too.

"I… Thanks." Bess surrendered to her body's tiredness, kicking off her shoes and drawing her legs up beneath her.

"Don't mention it," Margaret said. As she pulled the door closed, she added, "And don't touch anything on my desk."

⁓

Margaret unlocked the doors to the museum and positioned the sandwich board out front. As she did so, she saw a grey Audi parked down the end of the street, and a pockmarked face sneering at her over the wheel.

"He was out there yesterday, too." Kelly clutched her handbag tighter as she hastened inside. "He's a bit creepy. You don't think he'll...do anything?"

"Probably not to you." Margaret followed her inside, switched on the computers and began setting up the till. "I'll have a word to our alleged security guard, once he's back from breakfast."

In the meantime, she would call someone more competent.

The museum would not open for another twenty minutes. Margaret took her phone into one of the quiet rooms down the back, the one that showed artefacts from the Tasmanian sealing trade. She punched in Zan's number.

"M. Hey, I was just about to text you."

"Really? Is that why I can hear *Jessica Jones* playing in the background?"

Zan yawned into the phone. "You want my info or not?"

"I want it."

"The car's registered to Georgina Harper," Zan said. "Multiple parking tickets and three speeding fines in the past year. No wonder she decided to employ a driver. Most of the fines successfully contested in court."

"Nice to know Ms Harper's sense of entitlement extends to the road laws," Margaret said. "Who's the sidekick?"

"The big Frankenstein-looking guy is Vince Polat. Georgina's driver. Before she hired him, he worked as a personal trainer, nightclub security, and debt counsellor."

"You amaze me."

"He's had two community services orders and six months inside after an incident with a truck driver and a crowbar."

"Scarcely an appropriate employee for a leader of the business community."

"Yeah. Maybe she took him on as part of some charity gig, hey?"

"Something like that." Margaret bit her lip and glanced around her. On a nearby plaque outlining the life story of Woretemoeteyenner—dispossessed woman, prisoner, matriarch, and world traveller—there was a speck of dust. Margaret wiped the plaque carefully. "Tell me more about Ms Harper and the Victoria Development Initiative."

"Well, they had a fight with the building union last year. Questions have been raised about their donations to political parties. They've been to court against environmentalists and residents' action groups. One time, a group of ornithologists dressed up as hooded plovers and chained themselves to the bulldozers at a beach where Ms Harper's company was going to build apartments."

"Standard stuff." Margaret clicked her tongue. "Nothing more... unusual?"

"Not really. What's a hooded plover?"

"Zan, focus."

"I dunno, M. Your Ms Harper is used to winning, that's all. Oh, and there was a story about her in the Melbourne papers six months ago. I'll send you the link." There was a pause, then it popped up on Margaret's phone. "She was at some fancy cocktail party at the Eureka Skydeck," Zan explained. "See her in the picture? Next to that bloke with the stupid hair?"

"Zan, that's the Premier."

"Is it?"

Margaret rolled her eyes. "How can you young people be so clever and so stupefyingly ignorant?"

"Our generation doesn't need to memorise useless facts, Margaret. The point is, we know how to *find* them."

"Zan, the story?"

"Oh, yeah. Well, evidently some crazy guy crashed the party and started yelling about business ethics and 'running stuff by the lawyers'. Then he grabbed a snack tray and threw it; it nearly hit Ms Harper. And before anyone could call the cops or security, she just snapped her fingers and Vince and some other bloke took the intruder away. And he was never seen again."

"Zan, did you add that last part?"

"Maybe. I don't know what happened to him. But it's pretty cool, hey? I bet you wish you had staff like that."

Margaret glanced through the door to where Kelly was filing her nails and the security guard was inspecting a breakfast stain on his shirt.

"Perhaps."

"Ah, speaking of which…" Zan hesitated.

"What?"

"You know how you asked us to check up on Kelly and Kenneth for you?"

"The matter has not slipped my mind." Margaret lowered her voice, backing further into the display room. "What have you found?"

"Well, nothing much on Kenneth. When he's not slaving away for you, he stacks shelves at the supermarket and looks after his mum and his little brother. He seems decent, Margaret. It wouldn't kill you to be a bit nicer to him."

"I didn't call you for interpersonal advice, Zan." Margaret's tone was peevish "What about Kelly?"

"Yeah," Zan said. "That's the interesting bit. I'll send you something now."

"Fine, but—"

"Text you when we know more, M." The line went dead.

Margaret glared down at her phone in time to see a new message pop up. She opened the attachment, and stared.

There were three photographs, evidently taken on three different days, but all by the same security camera. Based on the angle, Margaret guessed the camera was installed at the electronics shop across the road from her museum; how the Hags had gotten their hands on that footage she would rather not know. The grey imagery showed Kelly standing in the car park, leaning close to a man, apparently deep in conversation. Margaret recognised the hulking build and shaved head of Vince Polat.

Her phone rang before she could decide what to do. Confront Kelly now, or wait for more information? For once unable to make up her mind, she took the call instead.

"Margaret?" the voice quavered.

"Deirdre. I heard you had an outing yesterday."

"Yesterday…" Deirdre sounded frazzled, more so than usual. There was a tapping sound. She pictured her sister's fingers pattering against the kitchen counter, over and over. "That's what I have to talk to you about! Yesterday."

"What is it, Deirdre?" Margaret shut her eyes, wondering what the problem would be this time. The neighbour's dog, the postman, a helicopter overhead? And she wondered what would happen if Deirdre ever spoke her real problems out loud.

"Margaret, I had one of my funny turns. I went to the church and it was lovely, very tasteful, and the music was beautiful. And then I just... I just found myself in the lounge room and it was night time!" Deirdre's voice rose to a yelp of panic, which she muffled quickly. "I don't know... When I get like that, I don't know what's happened, Margaret. I don't know where I've been, or..."

"Deirdre, is Paul there?"

"No, he's at work." Deirdre's tone grew flat. "He says we came back here from the funeral, and he went out to the shed, and I went to bed for a sleep."

"Well, that's probably what happened." Margaret gazed ahead, at a diorama showing runaway convicts in the islands of Bass Strait, dressed in ragged animal skins and clubbing seals to death.

"But what if he's wrong, Margaret? Or what if he's just saying that to be kind?" The emotion rushed back into Deirdre's voice; she was almost panting now. "He's so good to me, Margaret. It's not his fault I'm so much trouble. What if I *did* something, Margaret?"

"Deirdre, you never do anything." Margaret spoke firmly, but she felt a brief flash of guilt. She remembered Deirdre at the age of seven, weeping inconsolably over a snail she'd trodden on in the garden. And herself, a callous nine-year-old, bewildered by Deirdre's grief but patting her heaving shoulders anyway, because no one else was going to. Sisters.

"Listen," Margaret said. "I'm sure there's nothing to worry about. If you're still upset tonight, get Paul to give me a ring. Now, why don't you go and get that bird feeder set up in the yard? You were looking forward to watching the birds, remember?"

Deirdre hung up, still murmuring anxiously, and Margaret glanced around the room in consternation, hardly seeing her precious artefacts at all.

By the time Bess woke, it was midday and a school group was destroying the museum. She could hear Kelly bawling plaintively "Put the oar *down*, please!" and "Don't do that to Sir Douglas Mawson!" Then she heard the sound of a door opening; there was a soft snarl from Margaret, and the gallery fell into a fearful silence. Bess smiled.

She reached up to find that someone had covered her with a blanket. Judging from the hospital corners, she guessed this was Margaret's handiwork too. She dragged herself into a seated position, fumbled for her coffee cup, and remembered too late it was empty. Lucky this was her rostered day off from work. Her colleagues must have found out about Arwyn's death by now and perhaps about her own role in finding the body. Would Steven Powell try to get rid of her for bringing the gallery into disrepute again?

She sighed. For now, she needed something to eat to give her the stamina to ride home and deal with whatever the police had done to her tiny house. As she sat up, she noticed a note on the desk with her name on it in precise, spiky handwriting.

Feel free to wait around if you still feel uneasy going home. I recommend our tours; you might learn something. And watch out for a man called Vince Polat, Georgina Harper's driver. He looks like a refrigerator in a suit, and he has a nasty streak. Perhaps you could train your chickens to attack? Regards, Margaret.

In spite of everything, Bess smiled again. She slipped the note into her pocket, unable to resist hanging onto this token from Margaret. She put on her shoes and slipped out of the Maritime Museum.

McKenzie's Bakery was her usual stop for lunch, but she couldn't face it today, knowing how much gossip must be flying around about Arwyn's death. And she wondered which person from McKenzie's had been speaking to the police about her own meeting with Arwyn. No, a salad from the supermarket would have to do. As Bess cycled slowly along High Street, she became conscious of the purr of a car engine behind her.

She flapped one hand, gesturing for the vehicle to overtake; there was plenty of room. Why were drivers so aggressive towards cyclists? But whoever it was stayed right on her tail, slowing when she braked, accelerating smoothly when she tried putting on speed.

"Pain in the—" Bess grunted crossly to herself and turned at the roundabout. She would take Batman Drive, then. But from the corner of her eye, she saw the car make a smooth left and keep following her.

"What the hell?" Was she being paranoid? There was no beeping or revving from the car. Just a quiet persistence as it trundled along in her wake.

Bess's heart was starting to pound, her grip on the handlebars growing slippery, as she recalled the night Angela had died. She steered close to the gutter, ensuring the driver could definitely overtake if they wanted to.

They didn't. They were less than two metres behind her.

Her face was hot now, her breath coming fast. This was crazy. She couldn't be about to be hunted, terrorised, run down, here in broad daylight in Port Bannir! Although that must have been more or less what had happened to Arwyn.

She pumped her strong legs harder, putting on speed. That paved alleyway between Robinson and Truganina Streets—there was her chance! It was too narrow and bumpy for a car to enter. She swung hard to the left and put on a desperate burst of speed, the bike jolting and bouncing over the uneven stones. Behind her, the sound of the car engine faded, then vanished.

The rough surface forced her to slow. The alley smelled of drains and garbage bins. Her cheeks flushed, her pulse thumping, she risked a look over her shoulder. No one was there. Had she shaken them? Or had the whole pursuit only happened in her own imagination?

Her legs felt weak. She made herself push off again, wondering if she should have asked Margaret for a lift. Obviously she was still upset after yesterday; she wasn't thinking straight. She frowned to herself. Then she nearly screamed, as she turned out of the alley and missed a dove-grey Audi by inches. It swung directly across the exit, blocking her way.

Bess stumbled to a halt, one pedal scraping the skin off her ankle.

Behind the wheel of the car sat the man she'd met at the police station: Vince, the human fridge. His battered face wore a smile of satisfaction.

She should turn the bike around. Try to escape the way she'd come. But already the back window of the Audi was gliding down with a kind of smooth menace. And frightened though she was, Bess couldn't resist leaning closer.

She heard Georgina Harper say, "Bess Campbell. I think it's time we were properly introduced."

⌒〜♀

The Victoria Development Initiative had set up headquarters in a spacious, elegant office behind the bank. There was a billboard out front, advertising the Incursium Estate; Bess saw two men in overalls scrubbing graffiti genitals off it.

"I'm not happy about leaving my bike back at the chemist." Much against her better judgement, Bess had gotten into the car. She was too curious to say no.

"Vince will drop you there afterwards." Georgina waved the problem away. "Now, do come inside; I've been rushing around like a madwoman all morning and I'm absolutely dying to put my feet up. Have you eaten?"

"Um…"

"Vince, go grab us a couple of sushi platters, there's a darling."

"Vegetarian," Bess managed to stipulate. It was hard not to be intimidated into silence in Georgina's car. The vehicle was roomy enough to seat several sumo wrestlers, and there seemed to be a cup holder or touch screen on every available surface. It smelled brand new.

Vince parked the car, lurched out of his seat, and lumbered out to hold open Georgina's door. She alighted as if stepping onto a red carpet.

Bess, her grazed ankle throbbing, clambered out without assistance. Feeling scruffy and conspicuous in Jacs's old clothes, she followed Georgina inside.

Georgina paused by the desk of her haughty-looking receptionist—"No calls for the next hour, please, Madeline"—before leading Bess through to her corner office.

"Oh, that's a relief!" Georgina sank down into one of the white leather seats behind her spotless glass-topped desk, and waved Bess towards the other. "What a morning!" She patted her silvery blonde French roll, although Bess thought it already looked so neat it could have been lacquered. "And I hear you've had quite a morning too, eh, Bess? Like *CSI Port Bannir!*" Georgina seemed to find this reference to Arwyn's death amusing.

"I'm not sure why you've…invited me here." The word Bess wanted to use was "summoned". She stifled the urge to cough; Georgina's office smelled of floral air freshener. "Have I offended you somehow?"

"Offended?" Georgina tittered. "Aren't you adorable? No, Bess, if I were cross I would have served our tea in the Fortum & Mason china. Nasty, tacky stuff." Perfectly on cue, Madeline appeared bearing a tea try. "Milk with none, isn't it?" Georgina prompted.

"How did you know?" Bess reached gingerly for a cup that looked like it was worth a week of her wages.

Georgina smiled. "I've had my eye on you, Bess. You're getting quite the reputation."

"Look, I didn't do anything!" Bess burst out. "I know I've been questioned, and every second idiot on Twitter thinks I'm Jill the Ripper, but Leon was my friend! And poor, stupid Arwyn—I never wanted her to get hurt either." Her voice was too loud; she could see Madeline peering back over her shoulder.

"I was referring," said Georgina delicately, "to your reputation as a curator."

"Oh." Flummoxed, Bess took a swig of tea and burned her tongue.

"I knew you were responsible for at least half the displays in the Cabinet of Curiosities, including several award-winning ones."

"Who told you that?" Bess croaked, wincing in pain.

"Oh, Steven Powell. He was eager to make it clear that those exhibits were nothing to do with him." Georgina smirked. "He's frightfully conservative, isn't he? But Leon used to mention you, too."

"Well, that's…nice." Bess still had no idea what Georgina wanted from her. She wished she'd had more than a couple hours' sleep and that she wasn't wearing an oversized football jersey emblazoned with *South Coast Eels*.

"Did you know I'm on your Board?" Georgina was studying Bess with a cool, appraising look. "I thought you might like to do a presentation to us next month about the curatorial side to your work. Many of us Board members are just philistines, I'm afraid, used to the rough-and-tumble of the business world. It would be delightful to learn more about the immense cultural contribution our gallery is making, and the personal talents of our staff."

"I—I've never been asked to meet the Board before."

"Oh, but you must!" Georgina purred. "So many young women are far too shy about putting themselves forward; they think working hard should be enough to get them recognised." She rolled her eyes at such naivety. "And assuming you wish to apply for the CEO role one day…"

"Me?" Bess stared.

"Why ever not? You've clearly been doing most of the work. Aren't you ambitious?"

"I… Yes. But—"

"Although you'll need to pay a teensy bit more attention to your appearance." Georgina eyed Jacs's jeans and battered old sneakers.

"Ms Harper." Bess made an effort to focus. "This is flattering, but I'm not sure why I'm here. You can't think I'm about to take over Leon's role now."

"Well, not *right* now, obviously." Georgina took a thoughtful sip of tea. "Tell me, Bess, how likely is it you'll be found guilty of murder?"

Bess goggled at her. "I didn't kill anyone!"

"Not what I asked." Georgina replaced her teacup in its Wedgewood saucer. "I'm sure you're far too dedicated to your career to take a silly risk like that. Well, two silly risks now." Georgina gave a kind smile. "That was what I told Steven this morning, when I persuaded him not to sack you on the spot."

Bess's stomach flipped over. "You did?"

"Yes, he's been quite unnerved by all this murder business. I don't suppose his old job prepared him for it." Georgina winked. "Did you know he used to run a business selling orthotic shoes?"

"Um, no."

"Chalk and cheese, those brothers. Although they both had quite a knack for getting on my tits." Georgina looked up, towards the doorway. "Vince! Aren't you a sweetheart? Just pop them down here." She gave a languid wave, and two plates of colourful sushi appeared on the desk.

Bess had never even realised you could buy sushi in Port Bannir. Did Georgina have a private chef hidden away in here?

Vince glowered down at Bess, as if his catering duties were all her fault.

Georgina beamed. "Tuck in! I'm absolutely famished." Still, she ate delicately, popping each miniature creation into her mouth with skilful swoops of her chopsticks and chewing without making a sound.

Bess nibbled at an avocado roll. "Leon annoyed you?"

"Oh, he was marvellous, obviously." Georgina waved a hand, her sapphire rings glinting. "A genius. But a little too socialist in his mindset. You understand me." It wasn't a question so much as a command.

"Not exactly…"

"And Steven is so backwards." Georgina snorted. "He has the mind of a small businessman—no entrepreneurial spirit at all! He should be running a newsagent in the suburbs, not an internationally recognised gallery. Don't you think?"

"I haven't worked very closely with him." Bess wriggled in discomfort. Why was Georgina doing this, trying to make her speak badly of her boss? Was it some kind of trap?

"But you…" Georgina paused and ate a spicy tuna roll with relish. "Divine!" She laid down her chopsticks. "Yes, you've clearly got talent in curation, bidding, communications, and design. And you're a passionate public speaker. I haven't forgotten how you took me to task at that town hall meeting." She wagged a finger. "Compelling stuff. If you can manage to stay out of prison, Bess, I'd be interested in supporting your future career."

"Thank you," Bess fumbled. "But I don't understand why you'd want to help someone who doesn't like your estate plans."

"Pff! Bess, I employ hundreds of people who can't *stand* me. Better inside the tent pissing out, dear, than outside pissing in. Assuming we girls can manage that, of course." Georgina pushed her plate away. Her manner had become brisk. "Now, to keep our shareholders happy, Incursium Estate needs two things: for the Cabinet of Curiosities to go on being a splendid success and for this wretched murder business to go away. After all, no one wants to buy a retirement property in a town where there might be a mad axe-man living next door, do they?"

"I guess not."

"Correct." Georgina raised her eyebrows. "Any ideas?"

"About…the murders?"

"If anyone's looking likely for it, I can always make a call. Hurry things along. The Attorney-General's not a bad sort, really, even if he is with the other side. You should see him in his bike shorts!" Georgina winked. "I heard that woman from the Maritime Museum was in the frame for a while there."

"Margaret didn't do it." Bess blurted out the words, then wished she'd been cooler about it. Georgina seemed to be waiting for her to suggest some other culprit, but all she could do was shrug. "I'm sorry. I wish I knew."

"Well, that's disappointing." Georgina sighed. "But to return to the other matter: the success of the Cabinet of Curiosities. Now, before Leon died, I understand he was designing a new headline exhibit."

"Yes." Bess wrinkled her brow, remembering. "Blood is Thicker."

"That's the one. Steven has been thoroughly unhelpful; claims he can't find any record of it and wants to drop the whole thing. But on reflection, I don't think that's adequate. Imagine: Leon Powell's final exhibit, released after his death! Think of the crowds it would draw." Georgina's eyes were alight. Then she seemed to notice Bess's appalled expression, and quickly modified her manner. "It would be a beautiful opportunity to honour his legacy."

"Well, Leon didn't tell me anything about it apart from the title."

"No, and there were no clues at his house either." Georgina didn't explain how she'd managed to look around there. "But you must have access to Leon's old records…?"

Bess hesitated, thinking of that USB drive which she'd filled with Leon's files, without Steven's knowledge. She had no particular wish to help Georgina Harper—but this was a woman who might hold Bess's career in her exquisitely manicured hands. "I might be able to find something…"

"Oh, I would appreciate that." Georgina beamed. "Along with anything I might need to know about Steven's management of the gallery." She pulled a face as if inviting Bess's sympathy. "So hard to get a real sense of what's going on, when one is on the outside. And if you *could* manage to help me out, Bess, there are some rather unflattering photographs of you leaving the police station this morning that I'm sure I could persuade the newspapers not to print."

She pressed a discreetly placed buzzer, and Bess turned around to see Vince looming in the doorway.

"He'll drop you back to your bicycle." Georgina thrust out a hand until Bess thought it best to shake it. "When you find those exhibit items, bring them straight to me, won't you? No need to bother Steven when he's probably still struggling to work his car park pass." She wiggled her fingers in farewell. "Thanks so much for your time, Bess. Have a lovely afternoon."

Chapter 13

BESS CHECKED HER PHONE, AND instantly wished she hadn't.

The news of a second unsolved murder at the Cabinet of Curiosities had spread like wildfire.

LEON POWELL'S FIANCÉE FOUND DEAD.
POWELL MURDER CASE: HORRIFIC NEW TWIST.
BIZARRE SECOND DEATH AT SITE OF POWELL MURDER.

Arwyn's name wasn't big enough to sell newspapers, evidently, although her picture on the front page next to Leon's might have pleased her, Bess thought. The papers were behind the times, though; several bloggers had already sussed that Arwyn's pictures with Leon had been faked. *Heartbroken fiancée or suicidal crazy?* tweeted someone, as if Arwyn had throttled herself to death in that garden. Bess winced and put her phone away.

When she got to the newsagent, though, she stepped inside to glance at the cover of the *Port Bannir Advertiser*. It read: *Grisly discovery: A town in shock.* But there was nothing new beyond the bare facts of Arwyn's death and a description of her "weeping" and "devastated" at Leon's funeral. The rest of the piece was padded with the details of Leon's own murder and comments from appalled locals. There was no fresh testimony from Arwyn herself; it seemed she'd died before she could give her promised interview to this newspaper. The murderer had timed things well. If Arwyn knew anything more about Leon's death, no one would hear it now.

Bess's own name had been kept out of things, at least. The footage of that fight at the Maritime Museum was being shared yet again, and a few people were tagging her to comment, but there was no sign they knew about her finding Arwyn's body or that she had been questioned by police. The tension in her shoulders loosened a little.

She unchained her bike and made reluctantly towards home, before it occurred to her she'd left something back at the Cabinet of Curiosities: her kit for cleaning out places troubled by bad energy. She'd been planning to rejuvenate her office after Leon's death. But maybe the candle, the mirror, the sweetgrass, and the cedar and sage smudge sticks should come home with her. Bess could use them to fix up her tiny house after the police search. Besides, if she left them at the gallery, Steven might easily throw them out. Yes, she would swing by and pick them up.

If she'd been less exhausted, it might have occurred to her that this was an even worse idea than checking her news feed. When she reached the grounds of the Cabinet of Curiosities, she found them roped off with police tape and guarded by a very cross-looking Constable Jacs. The gallery was closed, but either word hadn't got out, or the tourists were determined to try their luck anyway. There were two coaches out front, their passengers gawking through the windows and elbowing each other out of the way to take photos.

Christos was talking with the two drivers in raised voices, explaining that yes, the gallery was closed; no, he couldn't make an exception; and no, he didn't give a stuff how far they'd come: "Nothing to do with me, mate, now bloody well hop it!"

A few hopeful souls had driven in from town, too; they were standing around their cars, chattering avidly.

"I heard the chick who was killed was Leon's coke dealer; they both tried to cheat their supplier and..."

"Bullshit—I heard it was a terrorist thing."

"Well, *I* heard the cops are looking for a serial killer..."

Bess winced and kept walking. She was conscious of a few stares and whispers, but nothing different to what she'd experienced since that fight at the Maritime Museum. She wasn't suspect number one then—not yet. Her phone sounded; she glanced down to find a text signed "Georgina". How had Ms Harper found Bess's private number?

Don't forget that exhibit, will you? Dying to find out more!

"Hi, Christos."

"Oh, g'day, Bess." He wiped his sweating face on his sleeve. "Some bloody news, eh?"

"Horrible."

"Reckon it's true, that there's a psycho on the loose?" He leaned closer. "And do you reckon it's Miss Gale?"

"I don't know, and no. In that order." Bess could feel a tiredness headache beginning to pound behind her eyes.

"Poor girl, eh." Christos glanced around. "And poor us. The new Mr Powell was looking sick as a dog when I saw him. Reckon he's not too keen to keep running the place now."

"Bess," Jacs barked behind her. "Haven't you and I spent enough time together lately?" She eyed Bess suspiciously, and a miserable weight dropped into Bess's stomach. She used to consider Jacs a friend. Did Jacs think she was a murderer now?

She cleared her throat. "Sorry to be a pain, Jacs, but I left some belongings in my office. Could I nip inside and grab them?"

"Not a great time, Bess." Jacs folded her arms.

"Please? It would only take a moment, and they're essential items." Bess hated to think that she'd made this trip for nothing. She explained where she'd left the items, and Jacs gave a grumpy sigh.

"Well, we've finished with that part of the building. Hurry up about it." She nodded Bess through.

Many pairs of eyes were on Bess as she hurried past uniformed and plain-clothes officers. The constable on the door gave the items a final once-over before she could collect them. As she went to leave the building, she heard Steven's voice protesting "No, I haven't the faintest idea what's in there! But please be careful; there might be something valuable."

Bess peered through the doorway into Leon's old office. One detective was pulling drawers out of Leon's filing cabinets, while another was riffling through his cavernous cupboard.

"What's going on?"

"Oh, it's you." Steven Powell looked grey and crumpled. His gaze darted anxiously between the two officers and the items they were retrieving:

letters, files, photographs, trinkets. "Completely unacceptable," Steven muttered. "The police searched this whole building after my brother died; they told me! Why do they need to do it all again?"

"Because someone else was murdered nearby?" Bess hazarded.

Steven let out a snort. "Rubbish! The gallery was locked up at the time; neither that stupid girl nor whoever killed her could have got in here. This—" he waved at the police investigation "—is just another way of wasting taxpayers' money."

Bess saw the two detectives exchange a look.

Then Steven surged closer and seized her arm. "What did my brother have in here?" he hissed, this time making sure his tone was too low for the police to overhear. He glanced back into the room, scanning the objects being pulled from storage. "I haven't had time to go through it all. Had Leon brought in any new items recently? Was he hiding anything... awkward? You must know, Bess!"

Look at that—you remembered my name! she felt like replying. Instead, she took a closer look at Steven. He was fidgeting, his face shiny with sweat.

She shook off his hand. "What are you worried about them finding?"

"Well, what if—?" Steven hesitated. He composed himself, then said in a voice that tried to be casual, "I've no way of knowing what dangerous or illegal rubbish my brother could have been hoarding in here. But what if he stashed something that gets us into trouble? You know: drugs, stolen artefacts, human remains..." He attempted a sarcastic laugh. It came out sounding more like a whimper.

Bess narrowed her eyes. Were those really the sorts of items Steven was worried about the police finding here? Or was it possible he was worried about something more specific: about that *Blood is Thicker* exhibit, which, according to Georgina, Steven was trying to erase from the record?

She looked around at the mess of papers and mementoes scattered across Leon's floor. It would be easier if she had a clue what the proposed exhibit was about, but nothing in here looked worthy of display.

Her phone sounded again. She opened another text from Georgina Harper—to find several photographs of herself. In the pictures, Bess was slouching down the steps of the police station this morning. Her tired face was pasty, her hair lank; her expression looked dull, heavy-lidded and sullen. Bess swallowed. The woman in these photographs looked guilty. She read Georgina's text.

Managed to keep these out of the wrong hands! Don't worry they're safe with me. ☺

Bess turned back to Steven. "I don't know what Leon was keeping in here."

"Well, didn't you tidy his office?" Steven rolled his eyes. "Obviously you didn't do it very well; the place is a tip!"

"That wasn't my job." Bess folded her arms.

"No, your job is to land us in trouble with the police, apparently!" Steven's eyes were growing wide, his voice rising. "Yes, they told me who found that silly little tart in our garden. I got woken up at dawn by officers on my doorstep. Do you think I found that convenient, Bess?"

"I don't suppose Arwyn found it convenient, either." Bess couldn't help herself.

Steven's snort sent a wet spray across her face. "That hysterical bint—she's causing us more trouble now than when she was alive. Trust my brother to attract psychotic fans. He probably encouraged them—probably thought it was 'ironic'! Well, I don't mind if you want to kill off a few of them, Bess, but in the future please be kind enough not to do it on my property!" He swung away and returned to berating the police.

Bess stared at him. She picked up her phone and tapped out a text to Georgina.

I'll do it.

⚊⚬

Bess was wheeling her bike down the gallery drive and contemplating the long trip back home, when her phone rang.

"Where did you disappear to?" Was it Bess's imagination or did Margaret sound hurt? "I returned to my office and found no sign of you. Apart from a sloppily folded blanket and a mug-ring on my desk."

"Sorry about that. I figured I'd imposed enough on you for one day." Bess had intended to sound considerate, but the silence on the other end of the line felt frosty. "Thanks for being such a good host."

"No need for thanks. I buy my coffee in bulk and the couch wasn't being used." Margaret's tone was definitely cool.

Had she been hoping Bess would stick around? Had she been disappointed when Bess left? The thought of hurting Margaret's feeling caused Bess a strange jolt of concern.

Keen to keep Margaret on the line, she glanced around to make sure the crowds were out of earshot, and offered, "I've just had a strange afternoon. Steven Powell is freaking out that the police might discover something weird in his brother's collection—what, I've no idea. And Georgina Harper just offered to boost my career if I would spy on Steven for her, and if I could find Leon's lost collection."

"His what?" Margaret's tone was interested now.

That caused Bess to perk up, too. "Oh, the last exhibit he was planning before he died. I've no idea what it was about, but Georgina Harper thinks it's a licence to print money, and Steven maybe wants to kill it."

"If it's anything like Leon Powell's previous works, he has my sympathy," Margaret sniffed. "Still, it would be interesting to know more."

"Yeah." Bess glanced up the drive towards the crowds still milling in the car park. "Especially since Georgina is threatening to expose me to the media as the chief suspect in Arwyn's murder, if I don't keep her happy."

"How Machiavellian." Margaret sounded rather admiring.

"Yeah, she doesn't mind getting her hands dirty."

"Mm." Margaret hummed to herself. "How dirty, I wonder?" Then she asked, "And how is your house? Still standing?"

"I haven't left the gallery yet. Trying to psych myself up for the ride home." Bess sighed. God, her legs felt like concrete.

To her surprise, Margaret said, "If you come back here, I can give you a lift. I'm about to leave, anyhow."

"Really?" Perhaps it was impolite to sound so eager, but Bess couldn't help it. What a relief, to skip the journey out to the paddock. Not to mention the prospect of being alone with Margaret again, which caused a funny little flutter in her belly. She imagined them sitting side by side in Margaret's car, close enough for their hands to touch, close enough to hear each other's breathing. "That would be so nice of you."

"Just be back here by quarter past." Margaret's voice had grown curt, as if she were already regretting reaching out. She'd hung up before Bess could thank her.

⌒〜⌒

Margaret's car felt deliciously comfortable as Bess sank down into the padded seat. She gave a groan of relief and let her head loll back.

"I'd say make yourself comfortable, but you already have." Margaret started the engine.

"Thanks for this." Bess opened her eyes. "Really."

"It's nothing." Margaret gave a stiff little shrug, then pulled out of the Maritime Museum's car park. "I've been keeping an eye on the news. No sign of an arrest yet—and no mention of your name. Ms Harper seems to be holding her fire."

"For now." Bess sighed. "I told her I'd look for Leon's missing exhibit."

"You did?" Margaret frowned.

"I can't have my name dragged through the mud again." Bess knew she sounded defensive. "For one thing, Mum would have a stroke, and my sister would take out a contract on me for ruining her wedding."

"I see."

"Besides, I don't trust Steven, and he clearly wants to get rid of me. Why should I cover things up for him? Maybe Leon wanted his final work shown."

"Hm." Margaret raised an eyebrow. "Well, if his final exhibit turns out to be anything like the urinal fountain or the inflatable guillotine, please don't invite me to the launch."

"You know," Bess said, "for someone who claims to despise the Cabinet of Curiosities, you seem to know a lot about our exhibits. What did you do—sneak in wearing a disguise?"

Margaret's lips quivered. She might have been suppressing a smile. "My spies are everywhere, Bess."

She turned the corner, exiting High Street. Then, to Bess's surprise, she pulled over.

"Why are we stopping?"

"Apologies; this won't take ten minutes." Margaret was craning her neck, looking back towards the museum. "I'm checking something."

148

"What?" Bess tried not to sound cross, since Margaret was doing her a favour, but her scraped leg was bruised and aching, and her headache was threatening to get worse. She longed to be home in bed.

"My staff are due to finish their shifts now." Margaret's eyes were trained on the museum. "I want to see whether Kelly heads home in her usual direction, or whether she has other plans."

"Why?" Bess stifled another yawn.

"I've reason to suspect her loyalty." Margaret scowled. "She's been caught on camera talking to Ms Harper's bodyguard." Her eyes narrowed as she stared at the museum doors, apparently willing Kelly to step through them and reveal her treachery.

"Weird," Bess conceded. "Still, maybe Kelly's comfortable talking to scary people, since working for you." She paused. "No offence."

"Oh, none taken." Margaret's voice was brittle with sarcasm. "I'm 'scary', am I?"

"To some people, yes." Bess found the question surprising. "Isn't that the effect you're going for?"

"I would have preferred 'authoritative'," Margaret said. "I don't see what I've done to deserve such disloyalty; she hasn't been with me six months. When I think of my earliest jobs and how we were managed: no minimum wages, unpaid overtime, customers leering at us, bosses asking when we were going to leave and have babies… Nowadays these young people all cry injustice if they don't get made CEO within the year."

"I'm not sure that's fair."

"Neither is moonlighting for the enemy," Margaret snapped. "Ungrateful brats."

"You do seem a bit hard on them."

"I set an example." Margaret folded her arms, angling her body away from Bess. "They could have learned from me, if they'd shown any real interest."

"Well, I'd like to learn from you," Bess said, rather to her own surprise.

Margaret glanced sideways, suspiciously. "Would you, indeed?"

"When this madness is over, yes. I don't know enough about caring for nineteenth-century artefacts, for example." Bess kept her tone light; somehow it seemed important not to overwhelm Margaret with enthusiasm.

She got the feeling that now was not the time to mention that kiss. "I'm not asking for anything; I know you're busy. But—"

"Perhaps." Margaret's tone was brusque. "That is…I'm sure I could find some time. Let's talk later."

"Thanks." Bess pretended to watch the museum, too, but she was really looking sideways at Margaret. She was noticing the sharp, decisive lines around Margaret's eyes and mouth, the way her tongue flicked over her teeth. She found herself wanting to coax Margaret's attention away, to persuade Margaret to look back at her again. "Hey, I didn't even tell you about the big bust-up in the caravan park yesterday."

As she'd hoped, this seemed to tickle Margaret's attention.

She looked sideways, returning Bess's gaze. "Really? What happened?"

As Bess described Irene attacking Hermione, she realised how much she enjoyed this. When Margaret Gale listened to you, she really seemed to listen, with an attention and focus that felt absolute.

"A strange tale," Margaret said. "You don't see this Hermione Morris as a suspect in Leon's death?"

"She can't be, surely." Bess reached for her phone and brought up the photo she'd taken of Hermione at Leon's funeral. "Look at her—she's a bag of bones in a weird hat."

"And yet your colleague Irene seemed to consider her very dangerous indeed." Margaret chewed her lip, looking down at the photo. "What's the meaning of that sign she's holding?"

"I never found out."

FAITH. Margaret seemed to ponder it. "A firm belief in something for which there is no proof."

"Like the value of museums and galleries, maybe." A note of gloom crept into Bess's voice. "Doesn't all this make you wonder? I mean, Leon wanted to be known as a patron of the arts and a grand impresario, but now he'll probably just be remembered as part of a *True Crime* special."

"Tch, don't be so morbid, Bess." Margaret hesitated, then gave her shoulder a light pat. Her movements were awkward.

Bess didn't know whether to find this frustrating or adorable.

"I've no doubt Mr Powell will be remembered for his unique ability to irritate and offend, and to make a fortune out of displaying items better suited to a lunatic's garage sale, long after his tragic death has faded from view."

This caused Bess to laugh a little. "You're all heart." She glimpsed something over Margaret's shoulder. "Hey, someone's leaving your museum."

Margaret swung around, then relaxed. "It's only Kenneth." The lanky, pimply kid shut the doors behind him, and began walking in the direction of Margaret's parked car.

"Quick, he'll see us!" Bess hissed, sliding down lower in her seat.

Margaret stared at her. "Good heavens. Where did Bess Campbell go?" She shook her head. "We're not doing anything amiss, and it's not Kenneth we're looking for. What does it matter if he sees us?"

But Kenneth's mind seemed to be on other things. He walked right past the car, stopped four doors down, and climbed the steps to a peeling-white weatherboard cottage. He dumped his bag on the veranda and fumbled for his key.

"That's convenient," Bess said, as Kenneth let himself in.

Margaret had dismissed him from her notice and was watching the museum again for a sign of Kelly. "What's that?" She turned her head.

"Living right around the corner from work. Think of the sleep-ins…" Bess pointed at the house.

The door was opening again, and out came Kenneth, pulling on the uniform shirt for the local supermarket. He got into a dented old Toyota parked out front, and drove away. "Wow, a double shift? That's brutal. He must be a hard-working kid."

"Since when does he live here?" Margaret tapped a finger against her lips. "He told me he'd moved from the house on Ivy Street, but he never gave me his new address…"

"So?"

Margaret didn't answer. She was staring at the house. There was a neat row of shoes lined up beside the doormat, next to a cat's food bowl and a child's bike. The garden was overgrown and neglected, but there were roses blooming by the letterbox and a possum feeder in the tree. At last, Margaret said, "This house is just around the corner from the museum."

"Duh…"

"By my calculations, it must be one of the properties which Incursium Estate is planning to seize and demolish."

151

Bess squinted at her. "So what?"

"I'm not sure. But Mr Powell was Incursium's biggest investor..."

"What—you think that kid broke into our gallery and murdered Leon, so that his family wouldn't have to move?" Bess snorted. "Come off it, Margaret! For one thing, half the homeowners in this street would have the same motive. And have you seen Kenneth? He wouldn't say boo to a goose."

"Well, there's a rock-solid alibi." Margaret rolled her eyes. "I'm not accusing anyone. I'm just wondering why Kenneth wouldn't tell me his new address."

"He probably just didn't want you grabbing him for extra shifts, if you knew he lived nearby. Some bosses are jerks like that." Bess massaged her temples. "Margaret, I don't mean to be rude, but you did say you'd drop me home."

"In a minute." Margaret looked back to the museum, where another figure was emerging and climbing into a car. "Right, it looks like Kelly is headed for home."

"Half her luck." Bess yawned.

"So, I'll just go and see if Kenneth's household can tell us anything."

"*Margaret...*" But Bess's companion was already sliding out of the car. Bess thought about staying where she was and taking a nap. However Margaret was striding towards the house and beckoning to Bess over one shoulder. And while the imperious gesture annoyed the heck out of Bess, she found it strangely hard to resist.

Grumbling under her breath, she hauled herself out of the car and followed. "Why are we claiming to be here?" she hissed, as Margaret rapped smartly on the door.

Margaret shushed her, then said, "Good evening", as the door cracked open to reveal the curly head and wary eyes of a kid aged about eleven. "I'm your brother, Kenneth's, employer. Is your mother home?"

The boy dashed away from the door, leaving Bess and Margaret standing on the porch and listening to a mumbled conversation somewhere inside the house. Then he came edging back and beckoned to them, keeping his distance as he pointed the way down the hall.

Kenneth's family home was shabby but clean. The walls were decorated with football posters and kids' drawings. A voice called "In here."

Margaret and Bess walked into the kitchen, where a woman was sitting at the table rolling meatballs for a stew.

"You must be Kenneth's mother." Margaret gave a formal smile, began to hold out her hand, then eyed the meatball mix between the woman's palms and thought the better of it. "I'm Margaret Gale, and this is my associate, Bess Campbell."

"Jean." The woman didn't get up, but nodded them towards the seats. "What's going on? Has Kenneth done something wrong? I've warned him about getting to work late—"

"No, nothing like that," Margaret reassured her. "I just wanted to let him know we'll be giving him the morning off, paid, next Tuesday, as we've got some tradesmen coming in to fix the bathrooms. Since he lives so close by, I figured I'd drop by and tell him in person."

"Oh, that's nice of you. But he's already off to his other job."

"What a pity. Well, perhaps you'll tell him?"

"Course." Jean finished the meatballs and wiped her hands on some paper towel. "'Scuse me, I've just got to pop these in the oven." She reached for a walking stick, which Bess had not noticed before, propped beside the table. It seemed to take some effort to haul herself up.

Bess made to pick up the baking dish for her, but Jean waved her away and managed it herself with one hand, before making her way slowly into the kitchen.

"You have a very agreeable home, Mrs O'Neill," Margaret called after her. She pinched Bess's elbow and pointed towards something else Bess had not noticed: a letter rack on the windowsill. Poking up from between the bills was an envelope with the distinctive silver and black logo of the Victoria Development Initiative.

"Aw, thanks. We love it. Only bought it last year." Jean leaned heavily on the kitchen counter while she eased open the oven door and slid the baking dish inside. "Couldn't really afford it, but we were so sick of renting and I'd just got a little inheritance from my mum's estate. And the boys are at the age when they need separate rooms, you know?"

"Oh, yes," Margaret said, although Bess doubted she'd ever given much thought to the problems of raising teenagers. "It's clear you're very fond of this place."

Bess rolled her eyes at her, but Margaret lowered her voice and murmured, "Well, look around. How do you think this family feels about being pressured to leave?"

She took in the room, with its pot plants, cat basket, and awkward oil painting of Kenneth and his brother. Bess shrugged. "So, they like the house. It doesn't mean—"

"Can I get you ladies a cup of tea?" Jean called.

Bess said, "Oh no, we've got to keep moving—"

But Margaret raised her voice louder: "That would be lovely, thank you."

"You are being mental," Bess whispered. She got up to help, but Jean shooed her out of the kitchen, grumbling, "Sit down, I'm not completely useless."

She moved around her kitchen with slow, deliberate movements, one hand braced against the benchtop as she reached for the kettle, teabags, and milk.

Margaret called out, "I do hope this business with Incursium Estate hasn't caused any problems for your family."

"Problems? No, no." Jean gripped the bench as she poured boiling water into their mugs. Her arms were muscular. Making her way back with a mug in one hand and her stick in the other, she said, "No problems here." She put the mug down in front of Margaret and went back for her own.

"That's good—"

"We're delighted to sell."

Margaret blinked. "Excuse me? I thought—"

"Well, of course we'll be gutted to leave the place. But the reality is, they offered us a really good price, and…" She dropped into her seat with a thump. "Well, I'm not sure we could have stayed much longer anyway. Since last year, my health's gone downhill. Soon I'm going to need a newer place: one storey, wide doorways, no stairs." She shrugged. "Pain in the bum, but there it is." Her face brightened as she added, "And Nathan, my youngest, has just been accepted into the gifted and talented program at a school in Warrnambool."

Her smile faded as she added, "But I can't drive him there and you know what the buses are like: rarer than rocking-horse shit. So, we'll sell up and find a unit near Nathan's new school."

"Really?" Bess raised her eyebrows in Margaret's direction. "So, your family's actually quite happy with the Incursium situation?"

"Well, we will be." Jean sipped her tea and sighed. "If it would just hurry up and get sorted. It's dragging on so long, and I'm worried about this terrible murder business." She glanced anxiously at Margaret. "You don't think it would scare people off buying here, do you?"

"I'm sure it will be resolved very soon," Margaret said.

Bess thought she looked miffed at being proven wrong, although why she'd been so suspicious of Kenneth in the first place, Bess could not understand.

She glanced back towards the kitchen. Jean's fridge was decorated with so many school report cards, sports ribbons and photos that it was hard to see the door. Bess craned her neck to study the pictures, and noticed something unexpected.

"Hey, that man in the photo next to Kenneth?" She pointed. "Is that…?"

Jean glanced over.

"Oh yeah, that's Paul from youth club." She smiled. "Kenneth goes every Thursday. Paul's a lovely bloke, so good with the boys. He's really tried to build up Kenneth's confidence, you know? And what with Kenneth not having a dad around…"

"That's great," Bess said. "But I meant the other man." In the photo, Kenneth was grinning and striking a silly pose, in between Paul and another figure in a purple corduroy suit and cowboy boots. "That's Leon Powell."

"Hm? Oh, yeah." Jean nodded. "That's right—Kenneth got to meet him at a career expo that Paul organised at the town hall a couple of months back. For the young people, you know, to tell them about all the opportunities out there. Leon gave a speech and hung out with the kids afterwards. Funny bloke. That was awful, what happened to him. He really impressed Kenneth—even offered to get Kenneth some work experience at his gallery." Jean beamed. "A proper gallery like that! Wasn't that nice of him?"

The look on Margaret's face would have curdled milk.

Bess rushed in: "Well, you've been so hospitable, Jean, but we really have to get going." Her tone grew pointed. "Don't we, Margaret?"

As Margaret stamped back out to her car, Bess said, "So, I'm your associate, am I?"

There was no reply.

"Well, can we at least agree that young Kenneth is probably not our psycho killer? I don't know why you were so suspicious of him and Kelly in the first place. He didn't update his address, she spoke to Vince—so what?"

Margaret just shrugged as she opened Bess's car door for her.

They drove back to Bess's place in silence. Bess watched Margaret out the corner of her eye; her long, elegant hands wrapped lightly around the wheel, the gleam of her dark eyes as she scanned the road ahead.

She pulled into Bess's drive, saying at last, "Here we are, then."

"Thanks." Bess paused, looking over at Margaret. Last time they'd said goodbye here, they'd just finished kissing. Bess hesitated, wondering if she should say something about that at last. If she should lean closer…

"Well, good night, Ms Campbell." Margaret flashed her a brief smile, then glanced towards the car door, apparently wondering what was keeping Bess so long in here.

Bess flinched and mumbled, "Good night." By the time she had climbed out and shut the door behind her, Margaret was staring straight ahead once more, deep in some thought she evidently felt no need to share with Bess.

After retrieving her bike from the boot, Bess stepped back and waved.

Margaret accelerated off down the drive.

Bess knew she should go inside, check on the chooks, clean up, and crawl into bed. But instead she stood there, watching the tail lights of Margaret's car vanish into the distance. All of a sudden, she'd forgotten her tiredness and bruises. She was too busy feeling humiliated and painfully disappointed.

Chapter 14

EARLY MORNINGS WERE QUIET IN Port Bannir. The streets were empty, and there was a faint rumble of trucks from the distant highway. The air smelled of grass clippings. The dog that lived at the school trotted past on some private mission. It was Margaret's favourite time, when everything was tranquil and in good order, before people came along to mess it up.

Still, as she turned into the car park at the Maritime Museum, she was frowning. She needed to get to the bottom of things, including the issue of her employees and their dubious loyalty. She held suspicions about both Kenneth and Kelly, but were they correct?

The thing that really troubled her, though, was how hard it was to focus. Her mind—usually so disciplined and tidy—kept drifting away and landing on the memory of Bess. Bess rolling her eyes at Margaret's attempts at intrigue, Bess laughing at her, asking "I'm your associate now?" That irritating good humour of hers, even in the face of violence and loss. Her refusal to be afraid of Margaret. The shape of her pink lips, their plump, satiny texture.

Margaret slammed her car door and strode up to the back door of the Maritime Museum. She was so deep in thought that she'd reached the doorstep before she noticed the woman waiting for her there, huddled in a shapeless coat that seemed to blend into the brickwork.

The woman stepped forward. The morning sunlight showed with harsh clarity the grey shade of her face, the weight she'd lost recently, the way her skin seemed to sag. She looked truly ill. How had Margaret not noticed before?

"Hello, Margaret," Deirdre ventured. "I hope I'm not being a nuisance."

⁓

It was an unnerved Margaret who got Deirdre settled in her office before she hurried off to the kitchen to fetch them some coffee. How long had Deirdre been like this, with her own sister oblivious to how badly she had faded?

"I don't want to get in your way," Deirdre had fluttered, darting glances around Margaret's office and clutching her handbag in her lap, as if to avoid taking up any more space. "But I've got a doctor's appointment at nine and Paul had a work meeting. He told me I'd be fine to go by myself, but I wondered…"

"Of course I'll come with you." Margaret knew this was a time when a normal person would offer hugs and comfort, but her voice came out stiff. She left the room as quickly as she could, guilt and fear snapping at her heels.

She flung coffee into the plunger with wild flicks of the spoon. It spilled across her disinfected kitchen bench. She threw the spoon down. Damn Paul for not calling her about this! But no, she couldn't blame Paul for her own inattention, the way she'd dismissed Deirdre's hypochondria, dodged her pleas for attention, and left Deirdre alone with her demons. Margaret spread her hands against the bench, let her head hang down, and swore savagely under her breath.

Her eyes drooped shut, and it all came flooding back: the barren yard of the old Gale property, the mad gouges of tyre tracks in the dust. The darkness, the intense heat, the gritty damp in the palms of her hands. The foul reek of beer, piss, and vomit.

"But we can't—" Deirdre's voice had been high, choked with panic. "We have to tell. We have to get help!"

And her own voice, flat with mingled shock and certainty, as she replied, "No. If this gets out, we'll both be finished."

Had Deirdre argued with her? Margaret thought so, but not for long. It had been easy, far too easy, to assume the leader's role as she had always done. To hustle her trembling sister indoors, assuring her, "It's over now. Nothing we can do. It's all done."

Had she patted Deirdre's shoulder? Offered some semblance of comfort, as she ordered her to "Go inside and keep your mouth shut"? Margaret hoped she'd shown Deirdre kindness as she'd blighted her sister's life by trying to save it. But she couldn't remember.

She walked back to her office. When she crossed the threshold, Deirdre turned in her seat, and her face lit up with childlike happiness.

"Oh, Margaret," she beamed, reaching for her hot drink, "it's so nice to hang around together again. You're very good to me."

Margaret couldn't meet her eye. She gripped her own coffee cup until the tips of her fingers seared with pressure and heat.

"This doctor's appointment." Margaret spoke curtly. "What are you seeing Dr Patel about?"

"Dr Patel?" Deirdre frowned. "Oh, no, I'm not seeing him again. Last time he kept wanting me to go and see people in Melbourne, and that got me all confused. Besides, I could hardly understand his accent!" She gave a hopeful smile, inviting Margaret to agree with her.

Margaret stared. "What do you mean? Who did Dr Patel want you to see in Melbourne? And who are you seeing today? Not—"

"Just Duncan, of course." Deirdre clicked her tongue at Margaret's expression. "Oh, Margaret, I know you don't like him, but you have to learn to let bygones be bygones. He's a nice man these days, and he does a lot for this town. Look at all those fundraiser barbecues he hosts for the school!"

"I don't care if he auctions off his kidneys for the Scouts." Margaret scowled. "He's still garbage."

"Now, Margaret—"

"What does he think is wrong with you, anyway?" She forced herself to focus, although her insides were knotted up with anger. Bad enough that Duncan Mather still lived in this town; now Margaret's own sister was using him as her doctor? But of course, Duncan's father had been the local GP before him, and small-town dynasties had a way of enduring.

"He's very understanding." Deirdre touched her arm to reassure her. "He knows how silly and nervous I get, but he's really kind about it. I'm sure he can give me something to calm me down." Deirdre looked at her watch. "Oops, we'd better hurry." She put her cup aside, stood up and toppled over, clutching the desk for support.

Margaret grabbed her and eased her back into the seat, appalled by how little Deirdre weighed now and the knobbly feeling of her protruding joints.

"Deirdre, what is this?"

"Oh, don't get all worried, Margaret." Deirdre, who went into conniptions over a car backfiring or a neighbour's cat getting into her yard, was laughing breathlessly as she struggled back to her feet. "It's nothing; just one of my dizzy turns. Happens all the time now."

Margaret stared into her sister's shrunken face, and felt her anger give way to an icy, clutching fear.

Panting, her face hot, Bess swung her old badminton racket for the tenth time and battered the rug over the clothesline. It released another puff of dust, making her cough. Her place must have been overdue for a spring clean. Maybe the police had done her a favour by turning it over. She hit the rug again, harder.

Her thoughts drifted back to Margaret. Bess recalled their teasing banter last night, how Margaret had seemed to want her around—only to drop her off here with scarcely a goodbye. The memory made her insides squirm with frustration. Why had Margaret kissed her that time, only to act later as if it had never happened? Had the kiss disappointed her—was she having second thoughts about Bess? What was Margaret's game?

Whatever it was, there was nothing Bess could do about it now. She lowered the racket, shut her eyes, and forced herself to breathe slowly, to pay attention to the sounds of whispering leaves and squabbling chickens, and the sun's warmth. She took another calming breath, got rug-dust up her nose, and retreated, sneezing.

The clean-up was nearly done. She'd woken before dawn from dreams of Arwyn's swollen dead face trying to form words, to tell her something. The image had sent her racing for the lights. Even now, in this quiet, wide-open space, she could not help glancing over her shoulder.

She'd kept busy, at least. Her bedding and cushion covers were in a bag by the door, ready for a trip to the laundromat. The floor of the tiny house was freshly swept and mopped, every surface wiped down, the doors and windows flung open to let in the air. The chickens, outraged by their long imprisonment, had been freed into the yard and soothed with treats of chopped banana and sunflower seeds.

As she wandered inside to fix herself some breakfast, she wondered how to spend the rest of the day. A text had arrived from the gallery telling her not to bother coming in; they were still closed for the police investigation. The Cabinet of Curiosities must be losing profits because of this.

Bess stirred her eggs in the frying pan with more force than necessary. How were the people in charge feeling now? Steven with his rudeness and unspoken fears; smug Georgina who assumed that everyone around her could be threatened or bought. Why should either of them get to control Leon's legacy? Bess glowered and spooned eggs onto her plate with an angry splat. She would look for Leon's lost exhibit—she didn't have much choice—but what would she do if she found it?

She sat down on the steps of the tiny house, chewing thoughtfully. Once she was finished, she should perform that cleansing ritual, wafting sage, cedar, and sweetgrass around all parts of her home. It would be an affirming gesture, and it might keep the nightmares at bay.

But her gaze kept sliding back to the kitchen, where a USB thumb drive lay on the bench. She'd buried it, wrapped in plastic, down the other end of the paddock days before, and retrieved it first thing this morning. On that stick were all of Leon's personal files, the ones Steven didn't know she'd stolen.

Bess looked at her sage sticks and the other implements of healing. She swallowed her last mouthful of eggs, and put the plate aside. Then she climbed the steps into the tiny house, shut the door and curtains, and booted up her laptop.

⟡

"Deirdre!" Duncan greeted Margaret's sister with a kiss on the cheek and a hearty voice that reminded Margaret of a department store Santa Claus. "Good to see you! You're looking foxy as always."

Margaret stared at him, but Deirdre just gave an uncomfortable giggle and said, "Oh, Duncan, you're dreadful."

He looked past Deirdre and forced a follow-up smile. "Margaret. I heard you were back."

"For ten years now." Margaret stood ramrod straight, not offering a hand. "Dr Mather." There was a way of pronouncing the word "doctor" that made it sound like the person you were addressing had obtained their qualification online in crystal healing. Margaret took pride in getting that pronunciation just right for Duncan.

Back in the day, Duncan had been the star of the local football team: broad, tanned, and muscular. Girls had lined up to accompany him to the school dance. But some time during the past thirty years, that tan had turned pink and leathery, Duncan's hair had migrated to his neckline and the backs of his hands, and new flesh had gathered around his waist and beneath his jaw.

Margaret knew it was petty, but she couldn't help comparing their reflections in the surgery window and feeling a surge of satisfaction. *Who's the ugly dog now, Duncan?*

Still, as she was ushered into his room, she sensed a lurking danger. Margaret took in the sporting trophies on the window ledge, the family photo on the desk, the framed memberships of Rotary and the Country Fire Authority, the photographs taken during his term on the shire council. Whatever else Duncan might be, he belonged to this town. She must not forget that.

"Now, Deirdre." Duncan seated himself behind his desk. "Tell me what's been on your mind."

"Well…" Deirdre looked flustered, as if she hadn't expected that question in a doctor's office. "Well, it's nothing really. Just my usual…" Her description of tiredness, dizzy spells, a struggle to catch her breath, a bleeding she was too embarrassed to describe, was broken up by so many apologies and equivocations—"I can't remember", "I'm not sure", "it really wasn't that bad"—that Margaret could barely follow it. The parts she did understand made her stare at her sister, riveted by dismay and fear.

"I'm sure it's nothing to worry about," Duncan soothed her. "But let's have a look at you, just to be sure." As they disappeared behind the white curtain into the examination area, Margaret felt a bubble of nausea rising in her chest. And she hoped against her own judgement that Duncan would turn out to be rigorous, knowledgeable, careful; the sort of doctor Deirdre deserved.

"As we suspected, nothing to fret about." Duncan's voice was hearty as he washed his hands, seated himself again, and opened Deirdre's file.

Deirdre was slow in emerging; when she did, she was white-faced and fumbling with the buttons on her cardigan. Margaret reached over to help her.

"Yes, just haemorrhoids—a bit uncomfortable, but quite normal," Duncan said. "None of us are getting any younger, are we?"

Deirdre forced a titter in response.

However, Margaret stared. "Aren't you going to do further tests? A colonoscopy, or—"

"Now, let's not get dramatic." Duncan smiled and Margaret longed to send her fist pounding into his bulbous pink nose. "There's nothing really wrong here, apart from a bit of discomfort and all the usual nervous collywobbles. Eh, Deirdre?"

"I'm...I'm sure you're right." Deirdre summoned a smile. Her hands were trembling.

"I'll write you out a script. This new anxiety medication's meant to be amazing—a mate of mine even gives it to his dog!" Duncan winked. "She hasn't bitten anyone since. And I'll arrange a follow-up appointment to treat the other, uh, little problem. In the meantime, I suggest hot baths, lots of fluids, and this cream from the chemist; it works wonders."

"Thank you, Duncan." Deirdre clasped the script to her chest and got up to leave.

"Is this a joke?" Margaret stared between them. "Deirdre, this is completely unsatisfactory. You need to see a specialist, get a scope done—"

"Uh-oh!" Duncan was still grinning. "I think someone's been watching too many episodes of *Grey's Anatomy*!"

"My sister—" Margaret's breath caught. "My sister appears to be seriously unwell, and you've not even investigated the cause. I hadn't expected much, *Dr* Mather, but your negligence astonishes even me. She should be referred—"

"No offence, Margaret, but I think I know Deirdre's symptoms a little better than you do." Duncan folded his hands over his belly. "I don't recall you ever popping along to any of her appointments in the past..."

Margaret flinched, and his smile broadened as if to say *Gotcha*.

163

"Now, Margaret, don't make a fuss." Deirdre touched her wrist and gave a gentle tug, imploring Margaret to follow her out of the room.

Margaret's stomach lurched as she remembered that other occasion, all those years before. The white sun scorching the top of her head, reflecting off the school windows. That knife stolen from the art room clutched in her perspiring grip while Deirdre dragged her backwards, sobbing in a whisper "Stop it, you'll get in trouble again, don't be so crazy, Margaret!" And Duncan Mather, flanked by that pack of chortling boys, Margaret's letter to Amy crumped in his huge hand, her words of desire and shame and adoration smeared by his sweat. His teeth showed as he grinned at her in triumph.

"Freak."

Now, Margaret shook off Deirdre's hand, but opened the door and held it for her sister. Her eyes narrowed as she regarded Duncan, still smirking and seated so comfortably among his trophies of expertise and belonging. "I'll be getting a second opinion."

⁓

Bess sat hunched over her laptop, a mug of raspberry tea turning cold at her side as she worked her way through Leon's files. She'd known he was disorganised (a "creative anarchist", he would have said), but these folders were a bigger mess than she'd expected.

Some files she could scarcely understand. One was especially frustrating; it was a scan of a whiteboard brainstorming session headed *Incursium*. In Leon's large, swirling handwriting it said:

Vet bills est. $1000 per quarter. Buy feed in bulk. Geriatric nurse on call. Ornamental cave cash discount!

Bess chewed the end of her pen. What was she meant to make of this?

She rubbed her eyes and opened the next file, marked *Invoices*. It was full of old fees for the costs of transportation, storage, and insurance for exhibits that had closed ages ago. Still, it wasn't hard to place them. In her anxious early months in her job, Bess had swotted to memorise the details of every piece ever shown at the Cabinet of Curiosities, just in case.

So she was surprised to find half a dozen recent invoices to an artist whose name meant nothing to her at all.

Taking off her glasses, she wiped them, and studied the screen. Billy Bower was the artist's name, and for the first three months of this year he'd sent Leon invoices for art supplies, rent on a studio in Daylesford, and a truly ridiculous consultation fee for what was described as *a blue-sky vertical turbo-planning session*. If Bess had known about it, she would not have let Leon spend that kind of money on what was clearly just a meeting.

She brought up Leon's calendar. The date in question, he'd been away from the gallery. He'd told her he had a conference in Adelaide.

Billy Bower. Bess found a number on one of his invoices and dialled it. Then she hung up before anyone could answer. What was she going to say to him? *"Um, why did my boss pay you ten grand without telling anyone?"* She searched for him online instead.

Billy Bower's website was curtly mysterious, with no personal photos and very little text. The artist claimed to have graduated top of his class at Victorian College of the Arts, and to have become known for *my confronting but playful installations*.

A further search revealed that someone with the same name had claimed responsibility for two acts of vandalism in Melbourne last year: once for installing human-sized Lego soldiers outside the Watsonia RSL before the dawn service on Anzac Day (as a comment, apparently, on how generic and superficial the public's memory of war had become), and once for fitting public statues of Captain Cook, Burke and Wills, and Queen Victoria with the taxidermy heads of a pig, a dog, a rabbit, and a goat.

According to a tweet by the artist, the aim was to remind people that introduced feral animals had spread through the landscape faster and more efficiently than pioneering Europeans. The Watsonia RSL and Melbourne City Council had not enjoyed Bower's historical commentary and announced they would be installing new security measures.

Bess found his style interesting, and was not surprised Leon had liked it. But what had Leon hired Billy Bower *for*?

After a bit more searching, she found that someone called B. Bower ran art classes for seniors and pre-schoolers at a community centre in Daylesford. He'd left that information off his official website, but Bess didn't blame him; even an art revolutionary had to eat.

Should she email him? But any communication from her work address seemed risky. What if he rang the gallery to check up on her and someone else answered? Instead she called from her personal phone and was half-relieved when she got a digital voicemail: "The person you have called is unavailable…" She left a message for him to call her back, giving no information except her first name.

Then she leaned back in her chair and stared up at the ceiling of the tiny house. What did all of this add up to? Nothing much, maybe. Leon had hired some outrageous junior artist to do something unknown, as well as taking peculiar cryptic notes that had something to do with the Incursium Estate. How likely was it that any of that would prove relevant, though? Would someone really commit murder over controversial artworks or expensive real estate?

Bess gazed around her, not seeing anything.

⁓

"Don't look like that, Margaret."

Margaret and Deirdre sat in the tiny park between the doctor's surgery and the library. There was one picnic table and three shaggy gum trees. Sparrows hopped around their feet. The sun was strong but the breeze carried a touch of ice.

Deirdre—anxious, hypochondriac Deirdre—seemed calm as she patted Margaret's hand. She said, "Don't take it so hard. I'm all right, aren't I?"

"*All right?*" Margaret struggled not to shout the words. She had refused to leave the surgery until Dr Patel found time to see them—but when he'd ushered them in straight away, it had filled her with fear. He had been cautious, softly spoken; referrals had been discussed and arranged. But the underlying message was impossible to miss, or so Margaret had thought.

"Deirdre." Was it cruel to say it out loud? But Deirdre had been encouraged to believe untruths too many times in the past. "Deirdre, Dr Patel thinks this may be bowel cancer. That's why he's sending you to Ballarat to see a specialist. Do you understand that?"

"Of course I understand, Margaret. I'm not completely stupid." Deirdre gave a self-deprecating smile, but her gaze was unusually direct. "But there's no point in getting all upset."

"I want you to come and stay at my house." Margaret's mind, numb with shock, kicked into gear as she considered the practicalities. "I can take time off work, get a temporary manager from somewhere…"

"What have you done with Margaret?" Deirdre chuckled in surprise. "I thought you never took a day off from the museum of yours."

"Don't be silly." Margaret's voice came out harsher than she'd intended. Shouldn't she be comforting Deirdre? But she'd never been much good at that. She tried to soften her tone: "It's no trouble."

"I don't know, Margaret." Deirdre picked at the skin around her nails. Her cuticles were ragged and raw-pink from what must have been regular injury. "Listen, Margaret, please don't tell Paul about this. Not yet."

"What? Why not?"

Deirdre shook her head, nervousness stealing back into her tone as she said, "It's just… It would cause so much trouble, Margaret, and I've caused him so many problems already. He's sensitive; he takes things to heart…" Margaret could barely restrain a snort, but Deirdre pressed on, "I just don't have the energy for it right now, Margaret. Can't you understand that?"

At the sight of her imploring expression, Margaret's shoulders slumped. "I suppose so. Well, tell him you're staying with me for a while, so we can sort through all the junk from Dad's estate. Say I'm threatening to sell the lot unless you come over and make some decisions at last." Margaret raised an eyebrow. "Say I'm being a nuisance about it. He'll believe that, I daresay."

Deirdre seemed about to protest, but instead she gave a little smile. For a moment, she left off tearing at her ravaged fingers. "You wouldn't really sell Dad's things, would you?"

"No." Margaret looked away. "If it wasn't for you, I would have taken them straight to the dump." She thought Deirdre would object to that, but her sister's mind seemed to have drifted off elsewhere.

After staring up at the sky and the rippling leaves, Deirdre asked, "Will you come with me to Ballarat, Margaret? To see the doctors?"

"Of course."

"It's good to have you here for this." But Deirdre was frowning as she explained, "You understand, Margaret. You understand why this is happening. Why I deserve it."

"Deserve—?" Margaret gaped at her.

Deirdre just gave a sad smile. "After what happened, I knew I'd have to make amends one day."

"Are you crazy?" Margaret's voice burst out impatient and furious.

For once Deirdre didn't flinch. "It's time I made amends, Margaret." Her lips quivered. "Jacob didn't deserve to die."

Deirdre sat holding her cheap handbag calmly in her lap while Margaret gazed back at her, appalled.

⟞⟝

"Ms Harper is out, I'm afraid." Madeline, the receptionist, seemed to take deep pleasure in saying those words.

Bess already knew Georgina Harper was out; she'd waited outside until she saw the car leave. Now she smiled and adjusted her accent a little. After years of working in galleries, she could impersonate a posh background quite well if she put her mind to it.

"So sorry to bother you," Bess drawled. "I promised Georgina I'd drop off some files from poor Leon's estate—things they'd been working on together." She held up a new flash drive, onto which she'd copied a bunch of items, most of them pretty well useless. Notes from planning meetings where Leon worked out his *broad conceptual directions* for exhibits over the next three years. Bess doubted Georgina would find anything helpful there, but she needed a friendly gesture—and an excuse to talk to Madeline. "I don't suppose I could be really rude and leave this with you?" She nodded at Madeline's funky bracelet. "*Gorgeous.* Is that from Felicity At Large?"

Madeline relented enough to give a tight smile. "Yes, it is. And you can leave things with me; I'll make sure Ms Harper gets them."

"You're a star. Thank you *so* much." Bess took a quick glance around the office, confirming what she'd already suspected; very few other people seemed to be based here, and it looked like Madeline was the only one with administration duties. For all her snooty airs, she probably had to empty the bins at night. And Bess would hazard a guess it was Madeline who took the minutes at meetings here.

"Breaks my heart that Leon won't get to finish his work with your team," Bess said. "Mind you…" she gave a significant smile and lowered her voice confidentially "he could be a bit difficult in a meeting, bless him. All that leaping around, drawing diagrams all over the place, changing his mind every five minutes, and getting all impatient if people didn't get on board with his ideas straight away. Try writing up those minutes afterwards!"

Madeline rolled her eyes in recognition. She glanced around, checking they were alone, then murmured, "Tell me about it."

Bess pressed on, "Well, he was a genius, obviously. But it's all very well to have brilliant ideas if you're not the one who has to run around doing the actual work. Am I right?"

Madeline gave a heartfelt nod.

Casually, as if she knew exactly what she was talking about, Bess went on, "I mean—ornamental caves, for goodness sake?"

The phrase clearly struck a chord with Madeline, who shut her eyes, apparently at some distasteful memory, and whispered, "Ridiculous."

Repressing a grin of triumph, Bess pushed on, "Not to mention vet bills and a geriatric nurse on call!" She gave a rueful chuckle.

Madeline looked less amused. She leaned forward and hissed, "That was insane. Did he seriously think we were going to do all that?"

"I know." Bess rolled her eyes in solidarity. "Crazy."

"I tried to say so at the time," Madeline huffed. "Those old pensioners were probably perfectly happy at home, and he wanted to dump them in the hotel bar at Incursium and fill them with free drinks and meals every night? Did he think we were made of money?" She snorted. "A 'human library'! No offence, but did he really think our guests would want to hang out with a bunch of old dears, listening to their war stories and what have you? If I wanted that, I'd visit my grandparents, right?" She tittered.

Bess blinked, trying to take this in, but decided it was more important to keep Madeline on her roll. She prompted, "And as for the vet thing..."

"*That*," Madeline said, "was downright dangerous! Taking all those mangy animals from the shelter and sticking them in the hotel rooms and grounds at Incursium. Jesus!" She shook her head, incredulous.

Hiding her confusion, Bess said, "I bet he looked pretty pleased with himself when he announced that plan, right?" That was usually a safe bet with Leon.

Madeline growled, "Oh, he thought it was genius! 'Pets make a house a home', he reckoned, 'so imagine how they could transform a sterile, boring hotel into a warm and welcoming place. It'll be like Turkey or Cuba, where the community animals wander freely and are cared for by everyone...'" Her lipsticked mouth curled in disdain. "As if people come to our elite hotels looking to catch fleas and rabies! Talk about unhygienic."

"And who would have had to give all those animals their worm tablets, right?" Bess pointed meaningfully at Madeline, who harrumphed in agreement.

Feeling daring, Bess added, "I never understood the whole cave thing, though. I mean, that was *weird*. Where did he come up with that stuff?"

"Ugh, that. That was the silliest idea of all." Madeline shook her head. "Leon reckoned that centuries ago, rich people in England or wherever used to build little caves or hovels on their estates and hire some old beggar to live there as a hermit, dressed up in animal skins." She sniffed. "I don't remember that in *Downton Abbey*, do you?"

"Hermits hired to live in caves at Incursium?" *Dear God.* Had she heard that right? Bess plastered on a bright grin. "What a concept!"

"He reckoned it would give the place 'character'. You know that smelly old guy who sleeps on the bench outside the supermarket here?"

"He calls himself The Professor," Bess said. "I've chatted to him a couple of times; I'd say he used to be quite an educated man once." She stopped when she saw Madeline's good opinion of her sliding. "Leon wanted to hire *him* to live at Incursium?"

"Yeah, cos every gated community needs a resident hobo, apparently." Madeline grimaced. "And you know he would have had plumbing and heating in that cave, and free meals, and goodness knows what else. Totally crazy."

"Crazy," Bess echoed, turning over all this new information. So, Leon had wanted to make a place at Incursium for a homeless bloke, some stray animals, and some lonely old people? She bit her lip, surprised to feel tears rising. Leon had been greedy and self-centred and superficial, but at times he had been really rather kind. He had not deserved to die the way he did.

Madeline's phone rang, and as she turned away to answer it, she emphasised her point one more time. "*Crazy*. But Ms Harper wasn't going to stand for his nonsense. I can tell you that."

⁓

The sun was setting by the time Margaret got Deirdre settled in her spare room. Deirdre had declined dinner, insisting she just wanted to rest. Margaret considered having something to eat herself, but rejected the idea. Her stomach was in knots.

She cleaned the kitchen instead: vacuuming, mopping, scrubbing out the microwave, working over the benchtops until her arms hurt and the steel fittings gleamed.

Deirdre. How had this happened, without her noticing?

She flung open the pantry and began yanking items from the shelves. She rubbed each one with disinfectant wipes, then filled a bucket with hot water and vinegar and set about scouring the shelves with all her might. What if there were moths nesting in here? Parasites burrowing into her home, nibbling away at her belongings and befouling everything she thought she'd kept pristine? Her breath came out in bursts.

"It's time I made amends. Jacob didn't deserve to die."

Did Deirdre really believe that—that her illness was some great cosmic judgement? Margaret puffed with frustration and worked her cloth harder into the door hinges. Justice? In her experience, there was precious little of that around.

The smell of vinegar and cleaning products was making her eyes water. Her back ached from craning over; her hands were wrinkled with moisture. Every light was glaring in her kitchen, but the rest of the house lay in darkness. Her phone rang. She considered ignoring it; if it was Paul, she did not want to talk now. She glanced at the screen, then peeled off her gloves, and grabbed it.

"Bess?"

"Hi." Bess sounded oddly subdued. "Am I interrupting anything?"

"Nothing of importance." Margaret heard her own voice; she sounded dazed.

"Um, how is everything?" Bess's reception was cutting in and out. Margaret pictured her wandering around that paddock of hers, looking for the right spot to connect.

"Worse than usual," Margaret managed to say. "You?"

"Not so great." Bess paused. "Nothing's happened, but I just...I just found out about some things Leon was planning to do, before he died. Quite nice things, really."

"Truly?" Margaret wiped her brow. She couldn't summon the energy to be sarcastic.

"It hit me all over again," Bess said. "The cruelty of it. The stupid bloody waste. You know?"

Margaret shut her eyes. "Yes. I know."

"Sorry about this." Bess sighed. "Calling you to complain."

"I don't mind."

Bess hesitated. "I'm not sure why I'm calling."

The silence lengthened between them. Margaret looked around at her half-tidied kitchen, her darkened house. Down the hallway, Deirdre's room was silent.

Margaret asked, "Would you…like to meet up somewhere?"

On the other end of the line, she could hear Bess let out a breath. "I'd love to."

◦ ～ ๑

"I thought beach walks were meant to be romantic," Bess yelled above the wind. Her hair whipped and tangled around her face. She fumbled for an elastic band to pull it back. The sea before them looked black, almost indistinguishable from the night sky, although she could discern the gleaming movement of cresting waves and the white wash of foam.

"It's invigorating." Margaret strode along, her hands plunged deep into the pockets of her coat. "Blows the cobwebs away."

"It just blew my scarf away." Bess gave chase, her feet sinking unsteadily into the sand. By the time she caught up with her companion, Margaret had found a calmer spot, a little inlet surrounded on three sides by rocks heaped with kelp.

"It's something, isn't it?" Bess clambered up to stand beside her. In the darkness, the seafront looked primordial, wild. "Makes you wonder if people stood here a thousand years ago and saw the same view."

Margaret pointed between two spots on the horizon. "In the nineteenth century, there were twelve shipwrecks just between those points. Most of them are still down there. It's surprising what can be lost without leaving a trace."

Bess turned to look at her. Above her black-clad figure, Margaret's pale face seemed to float in the darkness.

"Margaret? I'm sorry about your sister."

Margaret had broken the news of Deirdre's situation when she'd picked Bess up, specifying she would speak no more about it.

That didn't seem healthy to Bess. "Look, you don't have a diagnosis yet; it's important not to jump to pessimistic conclusions." When Margaret didn't reply, Bess added, "If your sister would like a pick-me-up, I've got a recipe for goji berry and coconut milk smoothies which are meant to be very high in antioxidants..." She subsided helplessly. "I am sorry, Margaret."

"If I'd been more vigilant, I might have caught it early." Margaret's tone was harsh. "If I'd done my job."

"I read a book that said self-blame is just another ego trap." Bess paused. "Well, it doesn't help, anyway. Are you confident she's got good doctors?"

Margaret let out a short snap of laughter. "Deirdre's doctor is a lazy, arrogant lout called Duncan Mather. I had the misfortune to go to school with him. I wouldn't trust him to keep a pot plant alive." She tugged her coat straight. "I'll find Deirdre someone else."

"You know this Duncan Mather well, then?" Bess squinted, trying to get a closer look at Margaret's expression in the shadows.

"Better than I wish to, certainly."

The wind whistled around them, stinging Bess's eyes. After a while, she ventured, "Is there anything you want to share?"

"I didn't realise I was on a talk show," Margaret sneered. Then she held up a hand in apology. "I'm sorry, I've no business taking it out on you. But I'm surprised no one's told you the story already."

"What story?"

Margaret fell silent, her hands clasped behind her back. At last she said, "You may as well know. Probably that nosy woman at the bakery will enlighten you at some point anyway. When I was at the local high school, Duncan Mather was in my class. He didn't like me very much." She shrugged. "Tormenting the unconventional girls was part of the curriculum back then. I daresay he was affronted by my high marks and refusal to fake an interest in football or footballers—but it may have been my relationship with his sister that really offended him." Margaret glanced sideways at Bess.

"Was that..." Bess hesitated "Amy?"

"So, you did hear about it."

"Not really."

Margaret shrugged again. "I don't care. Yes, that was Amy. We were infatuated with each other—you know what teenagers are like. I wrote to her every day in between classes, slipped the letters into her locker. We thought we were keeping it a secret." Margaret sniffed. "We were wrong, of course. Duncan spread rumours about us. Then he searched Amy's room, found a stack of my letters, and handed them around the school. I couldn't stay on after that." She cast a sharp glance at Bess. "Do you know what it was like in the eighties? In a country town?"

"I can imagine…"

"There was another girl like us in Warracktown, the next stop on the bus route," said Margaret. "The story went that a group of boys tried to set her on fire."

Bess touched her sleeve. "I'm sorry, Margaret." For a second, she thought of asking about Jacob, the dead kid, the one people said had been Amy's boyfriend. But she feared doing anything to sabotage this impulse of Margaret's to confide. Instead, she asked, "What happened to Amy? Do you know where she is now?"

"Now?" Margaret sounded surprised. "Oh, she's married now."

"Oh." Bess tried not to slump.

Margaret added "To a woman who digs up dinosaur remains in China. Last I heard, they'd bought a flat in Chengdu and spent their days happily dusting and labelling old fossils."

"I see." Bess couldn't hold back a smirk. "So, Amy had a type, then?"

Margaret arched an eyebrow.

Bess rushed on, "Hey, thanks for telling me about it. And thanks for bringing me out here. Once you get used to the screaming Arctic gale—"

"Antarctic," Margaret corrected her.

"…it's actually kind of magnificent." Bess smiled, and warmth spread through her chest as Margaret smiled back.

"When I was young, I used to walk out here all the time," Margaret said. "I'd get dinner on the table for Deirdre and Dad, then catch the eight o'clock bus to the surf club, and hike all the way out to the peninsula and back again."

"After dark?"

"It was peaceful. No one saw me."

"Right." The wind was gathering strength, making Bess's clothing billow out behind her. "Must have been a bit too cold for a swim, though."

Margaret's mouth twitched. She hesitated, then said, "May I tell you a secret?"

Bess's stomach gave a flip of excitement.

"I can't swim," Margaret said.

"No!" Bess could not hold back a yelp of laughter. "Really?"

"Not a stroke. I skipped the lessons at school, and Dad never bothered to teach us."

"And you, with all that maritime stuff..." Bess was laughing helplessly. But when she sensed Margaret starting to close up again in self-defence, she reached out and touched her arm. "Never mind." On impulse, Bess leaned closer, until she could smell Margaret's perfume, like cardamom and musk. "I'll teach you."

Margaret stared back at her, before covering Bess's hand with her own. Despite the gale that buffeted them both, her hand was steady. Soft fingertips pattered up Bess's wrist, making her shiver. But when Margaret bent her head and brushed her lips against Bess's, it didn't feel strange or surprising at all.

Margaret's skin was cold to the touch, the soft brush of her nose and forehead chilled from the sea air. But her breath and the inside of her mouth were irresistibly warm, making Bess draw closer still.

Could her touch melt the hardness there, the armour that had grown up around Margaret during those years of isolation and cruelty? Through their layers of clothing, Bess felt the rough rise and fall of Margaret's chest, the gripping strength of her hands. And everywhere, the smell of the sea, the taste of salt.

Chapter 15

THE BUS DOORS SNAPPED OPEN and shut with a whoosh, jolting Bess out of her daze. She glanced at her watch; still half an hour to go before they reached Daylesford. She should focus on what to do when she arrived there, but instead she had been daydreaming about Margaret and that kiss.

They'd left the beach soon after, speaking little more to each other. Bess had longed to ask questions, to delve into what Margaret was really feeling. But Margaret's silence, and the cloud that seemed to hang over her since the discovery of Deirdre's illness, had intimidated Bess into holding back. She regretted that now.

Chicken, she scowled to herself, then apologised mentally to her own beloved birds, which were plucky little things, unlike their owner.

She reached for her phone and texted Margaret.

What are you up to?

Twelve seconds later—not that she was counting—she received a reply.

Ballarat. Taking Deirdre for tests. You?

The bus hit a pothole; the sleeping man in front of her awakened with a grunt and toppled halfway into the aisle.

Bus to Daylesford. Following up a mystery artist. Heard of Billy Bower?

She leaned her forehead against the window, waiting for Margaret to reply.

Safe to assume I've not heard of any of the people you have, Bess.

Then a moment later came a follow-up.

Who is this Mr Bower?

Bess yawned and stretched as well as she could manage in her narrow seat.

> *Radical installation artist. Leon hired him for something mysterious. Georgina Harper wants to know what. Steven maybe wants to stop it. Seems to live in Daylesford. Going to find out more.*

Don't hipsters use telephones now?

Bess narrowed her eyes; was this Margaret flirting? She wrote back.

> *Gosh, that never occurred to me. Left messages, no reply. Tracking him down in person.*

Giving chase on a regional bus? At least he won't be able to evade you.

Smart arse.

Bess then felt bad for being so cavalier, so texted again.

How's Deirdre?

> *Calm. Waiting for doctor. Good luck with the mystery of the missing installationist.*

A squeal of brakes got Bess's attention; they'd arrived at last. She struggled down the aisle, and stepped, blinking, into the sunlight. The details of the artist's studio were in her bag. She could only hope Leon had paid the rent to the end of the month.

❧

After messaging Bess, Margaret stood for a while, gazing out across the hospital's flower beds, her phone still in her hand. It wasn't like her to get distracted. Text messages were for business and administrative matters, she'd always thought. Not for frivolous banter. Not for…fun.

It was a few moments before she realised that Deirdre, whom she'd left in the waiting area, had disappeared.

The receptionist hadn't seen her. She wasn't in the bathroom, or the gift shop, or in the forecourt outside. Surely she wasn't unstable enough to wander off?

Margaret hurried down the corridor, peering as discreetly as she could into the specialists' offices, but there was no sign. Would she have to head upstairs to the patients' rooms, or ask the nurses if they'd seen her? How would she describe Deirdre, anyway? *A middle-aged woman, looking ill—may have seemed confused or disoriented?* Margaret winced. How humiliating.

At the very end of the corridor, a sign pointed to the hospital chapel. In there, she found Deirdre.

"You were right, you were quite right…" Deirdre was seated on one of the chairs up the front, near the altar.

Margaret glanced around the quiet blue room, at the framed black-and-white photographs of pioneering sisters and the statuette of the Blessed Virgin. Deirdre's head was bent as if she were praying, but Margaret saw she was leaning in to talk to an older woman seated beside her. The woman's gnarled fingers were twined in a rosary.

"You did the right thing," Deirdre repeated in an urgent whisper. "The truth—that's what matters! When you're gone, you want to be sure someone knows what really happened. In my case—"

"Deirdre, there you are," Margaret cut in loudly. Who knew what Deirdre might be about to disclose to this stranger? Margaret did not trust her to be sensible right now. "You shouldn't have wandered off; the specialist will be ready for us soon."

"Not till half past." Deirdre's occasional moments of clarity could be quite irritating. "And I've been having such a good chat with Hermione here."

Deirdre's companion had painted herself brightly for her hospital visit, the crepe-paper skin of her face adorned with rouge, blue eye shadow, and coral lipstick. A fabric chrysanthemum was pinned to her lapel. Despite this, Margaret thought the old woman looked tired, bowed over in her chair as she held her rosary in a limp grasp.

"Have we met before?" Margaret frowned.

"I don't think so, dear. But I'm always in and out of here." The woman's voice seemed affected to Margaret, as if she was trying to sound like a BBC announcer from fifty years ago. But her shoulders slumped as she added, "More in than out, nowadays."

Deirdre patted her hand as though they'd been friends for years instead of ten minutes, and explained to Margaret in a stage whisper, "It's in her lymph nodes now."

"I'm…very sorry."

"Oh, nothing to fret about, dear." The woman forced a smile. "I'm a tough old bird—as someone recently reminded me." Her expression clouded over.

Suddenly Margaret realised where she'd seen this Hermione before: in that photograph Bess had shown her, from Leon Powell's funeral. "You've been to Port Bannir, haven't you?" Margaret blurted.

Deirdre frowned at her rudeness. "Yes, Margaret, we were just talking about it. How there's no proper hospital there, so people like us have to drive for ages to see the right doctors. I'm one of the lucky ones, to have you ferrying me around. Poor Hermione had to take two buses."

"Can we give you a lift back this evening?" Margaret felt obliged to ask, inwardly groaning at Deirdre's knack for making things difficult.

"That's kind of you, dear, but I'm being admitted today." Hermione gestured around her. "I just came in here to…"

"Of course. We'll leave you alone." Margaret gave Deirdre a look and began moving towards the door, but Deirdre seemed oblivious.

"It's a terribly sad situation, Margaret. Hermione is all by herself here."

"Perhaps it's no more than I deserve." Hermione shook her head.

Desperate to wrap this up before they missed their appointment, Margaret said briskly, "Well, perhaps you would have more well-wishers if you hadn't taken it upon yourself to picket the funeral of a popular murder victim." She arched an eyebrow. "It's all one and the same to me, you understand, but I gather your little display caused offence."

Deirdre gave an appalled "Margaret!"

Hermione looked merely surprised. "Why would that cause offence?" She furrowed her brow. "The dead travel on a different celestial plane to the rest of us, my dear. They are not troubled by the quarrels of the living."

Hermione explained this to Margaret as if reminding her of how to tell the time. Then she faltered and added in a different tone, subdued and mournful, "And I do have plenty of troubles. My word, I do."

The artist's studio turned out to be a large converted shed out the back of a petrol station. Bess thumped on the door, waited, then inched it open.

"Billy? Hello?"

The place was empty of people but stacked with canvasses, half-finished metal work, a blowtorch, a stepladder, and a lathe. The light was strong enough to make her squint, thanks to a massive skylight in the ceiling. The place reeked of paints, glue, and turpentine. Bess looked behind her. The street was deserted. She sidled inside and shut the door.

Billy Bower's unfinished works were all around. Bess wasn't sure which to look at first. Her eye was drawn to two giant screen prints, which appeared to be photographs transferred onto canvas. One showed an elderly woman scowling at the camera, a colourful party hat on her head, held under her chin by elastic which looked uncomfortably tight. She was seated, but her chair had been removed from the picture, making it seem like she was poised in blank white space, her wrinkled hands claw-like as they clutched at chair-arms that weren't there.

On the next canvas, a long-haired young woman was reclining, stretched out nude on a picnic blanket. An equally naked baby was suckling at her breast as she stared intently into the camera's lens. The image was in grainy black-and-white. Here, too, the background had been removed, this time replaced by a night sky sprinkled with stars.

Were these pictures what she'd come for? Pulling out her phone, Bess took a few quick snaps. Then she straightened her glasses and stepped in for a closer look.

"What the bloody hell are you doing?"

The voice echoed off the tin walls, making Bess leap with alarm. She spun around, staring at the figure in the doorway.

It hadn't occurred to her that Billy Bower might be a woman, or that Billy might be only four feet tall. Or that she might be armed with a very large spear.

Margaret frowned as she looked between her sister and this woman whom Deirdre seemed to have taken under her feeble wing. Deirdre said, "Poor Hermione! Did you know she has a daughter?"

"Deirdre, I don't know anything about your new acquaintance, apart from the trouble she caused back home." Margaret glanced longingly towards the door.

Oblivious, Deirdre went on, "And her daughter refuses to visit her. Can you believe that? She won't even phone!"

"Well, that's very—"

"I brought it on myself." The old woman ignored Margaret, confiding softly in Deirdre instead. "I was fifteen when she was born, and, well, those days were not like today." Her shoulders tensed, as if in memory of some ancient wound. "I gave her up, and I wanted to believe it was for the best. I moved to Brisbane to start again. Thankfully I still had a few relatives who would speak to me." She managed a smile. "It was twenty years before she found me. I'm afraid it was not a happy reunion." Her voice caught.

Deirdre reached out to clasp her hand.

Margaret watched her sister's gestures of comfort with surprise. When was the last time she'd seen Deirdre look after somebody else?

Hermione continued, "My daughter had been adopted by a couple whose marriage was already troubled. Her mother pinned all her hopes and regrets on the little girl, while her father considered the adoption an insult to his manhood, and blamed the child for her origins." Hermione's mouth tightened. "It's no surprise she ran away from them, but I couldn't give this angry young woman what she wanted: a stable home, a perfect family… This was thirty-five years ago, and, well, I had my own problems. I told her I would like us to be friends, equals, but I couldn't promise any more than that."

Hermione shuddered, apparently at an ugly memory. "She took it hard. That was the last I saw or heard of her, until two years ago, when I got my diagnosis."

"Hermione tracked her daughter down, all those years later!" Deirdre looked rather thrilled. Perhaps she enjoyed having a ringside seat for someone else's family dysfunction.

"When I knew what was happening to me, I was forced to take stock of my life," Hermione said. "I regretted never making things right with my daughter. I had to find her, to explain everything at last."

"What did you do?" Deirdre pressed, wide-eyed.

"Well, she made it clear that I was never to come near her house or contact her directly." Hermione nodded. "I respected that. Instead, I decided to place myself where I would be visible and available to her if she ever wanted me. To stand in the sun or rain all day, day after day, if that was what it took to prove that I could change. That this time she could rely on me to be there, not to abandon her again. I'd hoped she might come to trust me a little, believe in me..." Hermione heaved a defeated sigh. "But she was not persuaded."

Deirdre seemed moved by this.

Margaret thought it sounded more invasive than loving, but she decided that telling off an elderly cancer patient might seem graceless. Instead she asked, "Does your daughter spend a lot of time at the Cabinet of Curiosities, by any chance?"

"Yes, she works there." Hermione blinked. "Why, do you know her?"

"Not personally. I may know a colleague of hers."

Deirdre said, "Well, I think she's lucky to have a mother who came back for her, even if it was years later."

But Hermione seemed to have stopped listening. Gazing at Margaret, she said, "If you do know a colleague of my daughter's... My dear, I don't suppose I could trouble you for a very great favour?"

Margaret was about to say that she should certainly not suppose anything—but Deirdre was quicker.

"We'd love to help."

Hermione fossicked around in her handbag and drew out a small padded postal sack. She said, "I'd been hoping to give this to her myself, but..." She managed a smile. "Perhaps you could pass it on?"

"Of course." Deirdre reached for it, but Hermione stalled her, hunting around for a pen and taking a long time to write the name "Irene Callahan" in small, precise letters on the envelope.

"Thank you." But she hesitated for several seconds before handing it over. Her fingers twitched, as if fighting the urge to snatch it back.

Deirdre placed the parcel with great care in her own bag.

Margaret frowned, confounded by this whole exchange. Since when did anyone confide their troubles in Deirdre, or trust her to fix them?

Thirty years ago, when Margaret had been bullied and needed help, Deirdre had been no use whatsoever. And although she knew how irrational and weak it was to fixate on that memory, Margaret could not deny the anger that stirred inside her.

Perhaps that was what made her snap at Hermione. "Out of interest, are you aware there are people who suspect you of impaling Leon Powell on a sharp object, then hiding the evidence?"

"Margaret!" Deirdre's voice rose in outrage.

But Hermione took the question quite calmly. "Then those people are mistaken, my dear. I'd met Mr Powell when I was waiting outside his gallery for my daughter, hoping she could come out and speak to me. He explained he was taking out an order to make me stand further away. He said he had to keep his staff happy, but he was really very nice about it. I remember he brought me out a cup of tea."

Hermione gave a wistful smile, gazing at Deirdre's handbag where the memento of her daughter was hidden. "I thought him a very nice young man. He told me he understood. You know, about difficult families."

❦

"Who the fuck are you?" bellowed Billy Bower, her spear jabbing the air inches away from Bess's midriff.

"Sorry about this." Bess's voice came out squeaky with alarm. "But I did knock."

"I don't care if you sent a messenger on fuckin' horseback—this is my place and it's my work!" Billy stomped forward, her stocky, muscular legs braced wide apart, the spear grasped firmly in her small hands. Her head was barely on level with Bess's ribcage, but the look on her face was alarming. "You bunch of fascists think you can hassle me into silence? There's such a thing as freedom of fuckin' speech, you know! I've got lawyers!"

"I don't know what you're talking about." Bess darted back as the spear shot unexpectedly upwards, just missing her nose. "I left a message on your phone." She waved her hands, as if that could placate an assailant. "I'm Bess Cam—" Her retreating foot caught in Billy's stepladder. Losing her balance, Bess tumbled sideways, landing with a dreadful crash right through one of Billy's canvases.

"Oh, I'm so sorry!" Bess fought to disentangle herself. The frame was twisted beneath her, and she'd put her arm through the fabric.

Billy was standing above her, her eyes wide, her spear poised.

"I'm a friend of Leon Powell's!" Bess called desperately. "I'm trying to find out how he died—"

"Shut up." Billy motioned with her spear, making Bess crawl away. Billy leaned closer, staring at the mangled canvas with the intensity of a cat watching a bird. "Oh, yes," she murmured, lowering the spear. She seized the canvas, stood it up, and examined it from every angle.

It had been painted with swirls of chilly Arctic blue and white, now dented and ripped from Bess's crash landing. "Oh, *yes!*" Billy laughed in delight. "I'll call it *Fat Girl Breaks the Ice*. Perfect! What do you think?"

"I think I could admire it more if you put that spear down." Bess also thought she'd had enough of this rudeness, but maybe it was wise not to say so. She dragged herself up, rubbing her aching hip.

"Oh, right." Billy glanced over and seemed surprised to find Bess still there. "Hey, what did you say your name was?"

"Bess Campbell." She dusted down her clothing.

Billy eyed her with interest. "Not Leon's assistant?"

"I worked for him, yes."

"Got any proof of that?"

"For goodness sake…" Bess fumbled in her bag until she found her staff ID from the Cabinet of Curiosities. "Here. You didn't get my message?"

"Well, yeah, but you didn't say you were *that* Bess." Billy shrugged. "Sorry about the spear." She leaned it against the wall. "But I've had a bit of aggro about my work, you know. Especially this bloody exhibit." She waved towards the portraits of the two women. "Pain in the arse. If Leon wasn't a mate…"

"What *is* the exhibit?" Bess was running out of patience. "Who are the women in those pictures?"

"Leon didn't tell you?" Billy frowned. "Then I dunno…"

"Listen." Bess planted her hands on her hips. "I've had enough of this. Someone murdered Leon and I've no idea why, but if it had anything to do with your stupid mystery exhibit, I am going to work it out one way or another, you hear me?" Her voice rang off the metal walls, making Billy stare at her. "If you know *anything* about what happened to him, you'll tell me now, or so help me I will put my fist through all your other artworks too and see how much you like that!"

"All right, all right." Billy flapped her hands. "Settle. Of course, I don't know who killed poor bloody Leon. If I did, I'd have told the cops. Although it's usually against my principles to collaborate with the militarist police state..." Catching the look on Bess's face, she repeated, "I don't know anything, all right? Leon just hired me to do a bunch of pieces. I was meant to keep them a secret, because he wanted the exhibit to be a revelation—and because he said some people might not be happy about it."

She pointed around the studio at various half-finished works. "There's the beanbag with the safety rail. Over there, a hospital screen. I'm going to project psychedelic goannas and cassowaries onto it. And the *Female Eunuch* torso with incontinence pants. And there's the portraits—"

"Who are they?" Bess repeated. "Who are those two women?"

"One woman." Billy corrected her. "That's Sybil. Didn't you know? She's Leon's mum."

⟡

Margaret had imagined that an oncologist's rooms would be all white, scrubbed and sterile, the lights reflecting off shimmering steel. But Dr Tran's rooms were like the rest of the hospital—painted pinkish beige and decorated with the sort of landscape paintings you forgot about as soon as you looked away.

She felt vaguely affronted by that. If their lives must be shattered here today, would a proper dramatic setting be too much to ask?

The news wasn't good. And although Margaret had suspected the truth before they stepped into this room, sensed it deep in her clenching gut, yet still she had not been ready to hear it.

Dr Tran was kind but pragmatic, outlining Deirdre's recommended treatment using monoclonal antibodies. Margaret knew she should be taking notes, but it was hard to move. This seemed oddly offensive, too, this discussion of her little sister's body parts: rectum, colon, abdominal cavity. Liver.

"Failing that," Dr Tran said, "there may be the option of a clinical trial. And of course there are always palliative steps we can take. To manage the symptoms and improve your quality of life."

Margaret remembered Dad's doctor saying much the same thing, and how Malcolm had snorted that he would have settled for a bit more bloody quantity. Her fists were clamped shut; they ached as if they had been forced into snow.

Deirdre reached over, coaxed her fingers open, and gave them a squeeze. "Don't worry," Deirdre mouthed, as though as she wasn't shocked by this at all.

❧

"Yeah, they seemed like an interesting family." Billy tapped the portrait of Sybil Powell lounging on her picnic rug, breastfeeding her baby. Bess wondered if the naked little boy was Leon. If it was Steven Powell, she couldn't imagine him being happy about being put on display.

"Did Leon give you these photographs?"

"Yeah. I've got other ones in there." Billy gestured to a battered old suitcase in the corner. "Framed shots, loose prints, negatives—I'm still working my way through them. I'll make some sort of giant collage when I'm done." Seeing Bess's questioning look, she explained, "Leon's mum used to be a pretty amazing photographer back in the day. See that old 35mm camera? That was hers."

"Really?"

"Yeah. She was published in underground magazines, held an exhibit or two—there are review clippings in the suitcase. Not sure why she never took it further. Maybe having kids slowed her down, or maybe she was too busy with her open marriage and her guru and her experimental share houses." Billy shrugged. "Must have been a lot of work, trying to transform the family unit."

"And she wanted you and Leon to exhibit her pictures?" Bess glanced around Billy's studio. "Along with your works?"

"Bit of a mash-up," Billy said. "But I'm not sure whose idea it was, originally. I only met Sybil once, and we didn't exactly get time to chat."

Bess looked around at the art. Half-finished, it was hard for her to tell how good it was. But there was no doubt the concept was marketable:

Leon's famous, unsolved murder, and a bohemian artist mother who'd been very pretty, and willing to be photographed nude… "You know how to get in touch with Leon's mother, then? I don't remember seeing her at his funeral."

"Yeah, I went to visit her." Billy frowned. "But listen, I can't just give you her address. I probably shouldn't have told you any of this. I've got my career to think of—"

"Yes, you do." Bess folded her arms. "Leon's brother, Steven, is running his gallery now, and he wants to stop this exhibition going ahead. But a powerful local developer wants it to happen, and she's not too scrupulous. And I've got her direct number." Bess raised her eyebrows, trying to imagine how Margaret might have handled this. "From what I've seen, Leon only covered your initial costs, Billy. If you want the Cabinet of Curiosities to take possession of your finished works, and pay you for them, you'll need to work with me. Of course, if artists still enjoy starving…"

"All right, all right. Cool it with the supervillain act." Billy hunted around and pulled out an address book covered in wood shavings. "I'll write it down for you." She glanced back at Bess and added, "You'd better watch your back, though, when you visit."

"Why?"

Billy handed over a scrap of paper bearing a street address in Melbourne. Narrowing her eyes, she said, "Why do you think certain people aren't happy about this exhibit?"

"Well…" Bess looked around. "Some of the items are a bit confrontational. And I can't imagine Steven wanting the public to look at naked pictures of his mum."

Billy snorted. "Trust me, a bit of hippie sexting was the least of it." Seeing she'd got Bess's full attention, she preened a little.

Billy Bower, Bess decided, was nothing if not theatrical.

Billy righted her stepladder and climbed up to sit on the top rung. "Leon was crazy about his mum," she explained. "He said she'd inspired his love of art and taught him to be spontaneous and to live incandescently." Billy waggled her eyebrows. "That was the problem. Sybil Powell was a pretty wild lady back in the day. According to Leon, she once threw a bucket of pig entrails at the US Ambassador."

"Why?"

"Why not? The point is, she was daring, passionate, and a little bit crazy. One too many acid trips back in the day, who knows?" Billy inserted an anticipatory pause.

Bess felt an impulse to strangle her, but breathed through it.

"Leon told me that one night, back when he had his fancy restaurant in Sydney, his mum came for a visit," Billy continued. "It was his birthday, so they'd shut the restaurant for the night and Sybil wanted to cook for him. Trouble was, she was a bloody awful cook and Leon wasn't shy about saying so. Well, one thing leads to another, they have words, he storms out for a walk to cool off..." Billy leaned forward. "And he comes back twenty minutes later to find the place lit up like a bloody Christmas tree. The most expensive restaurant in Sydney, and his dear old mum had set fire to it!"

"My God." Bess stared. "Are you sure that's true? Leon told me the fire was an accident."

"Yeah, well I'm pretty bloody sure he never said anything to the cops or the insurance company either." Billy snorted. "But he swore to me it was true. And—this is the tricky bit—he wanted to talk about it in the exhibit."

"You're joking."

"I know, bloody stupid idea. I told him he'd get into trouble, or the old lady would, but he kept saying a tribute to someone's life should be warts and all. He reckoned we could hint at the truth without admitting anything that would stand up in court." Billy looked dubious. "Usually I don't need to talk to lawyers until *after* my stuff gets displayed, but he had them there at our planning meeting."

"His mum was really okay with this?"

"She never objected, far as I know."

"I don't understand." Bess stared at the photograph of Leon's mother as an old woman. The frown on her face seemed to have grown deeper, bordering on rage. "You said Leon loved his mum. But this feels weird."

"Yeah, well, families are weird." Billy climbed down, her tone turning businesslike. Bess got the feeling she was being encouraged to leave. "If you can get me paid for all this, I'd be grateful. Sorry again about the spear. It was part of an old exhibit of mine and it comes in handy."

"I'll bet." Bess tucked the piece of paper in her wallet. "Thanks for the address."

"Yeah, well. You be careful over there." Billy wasn't smiling. "Like I say, my visit didn't go so well."

"Why? What did she do?"

"Nothing," Billy said. "I'd just come in and said hello. The old lady was really quiet. I had to get to work, so I started setting up my first shot. And I'd just given her the box of matches to hold—"

"You what?"

"Don't complain to me; it was Leon's idea, and the old bird didn't seem to mind. Like I say, I was just setting up when this bloke I'd never seen before comes barrelling in like a Rottweiler, screaming for blood! Calls me every name under the sun, chucks my camera clear across the room—Leon still owes me for the repairs, by the way—and says I've got ten seconds to get out before he calls the cops. Well, I wasn't hanging around for that." Billy shook her head. "I'm already on a good behaviour bond, just because a few boring bourgeois ballsacks don't understand public art."

"Yeah, I read about that."

"So, off I fucked. The bloke threw that box of matches at my head as I was leaving. And since then, I've had anonymous phone calls, threatening messages... Nasty stuff."

"This man." Bess leaned in. "What did he look like?"

Billy thought back.

"Another boring bourgeois ballsack, I'd say. Bald. Middle-aged. Bit of a belly on him. Fancy suit that looked cheap."

"Was it Steven Powell?"

"Well, he didn't give me his bloody business card." Billy rolled her eyes. "But if it was, you'd better tread carefully. 'Cos he didn't seem too happy at all."

⁙

The light was fading and the hospital car park was emptying out by the time Margaret and Deirdre emerged. Margaret got Deirdre settled in her seat, noticing the thinness of her sister's wrists, the fragile lines of her throat, the flesh withered. Margaret climbed into the car after her and sat staring ahead. A light rain had begun to fall.

"Margaret," Deirdre sounded tentative, as if afraid Margaret would be angry with her. "It will be all right."

"Of course." Margaret did want to sound comforting, but her tone came out mechanical. Devoid of emotion. "Dr Tran seems competent, and we have a regime to follow. I can drive you out here, or to Melbourne. Or I could organise accommodation onsite. Yes, perhaps that would be better—"

"Margaret." Deirdre—anxious, stammering Deirdre—sat composed with her hands in her lap. "I'm dying."

"Don't be stupid." Margaret sneered at the words, quite terrified.

"It'll be all right," Deirdre repeated. "I'm not really frightened, and I'm not surprised."

"No, why would you be?" Margaret's voice rose. "You told me a hundred times that you were feeling sick, only I wouldn't listen." Her voice cracked. She clenched her jaw until pain rang through her skull.

Deirdre laid a hand on her shoulder. "Margaret, there are things I need to do."

"Yes." Margaret swiped angrily at her watering eyes. "Of course. But I can't face dealing with Paul tonight. Can't we—?"

"Oh, not him." Deirdre waved that away, to Margaret's surprise. "I mean, I have to tell people what happened to Jacob."

"To…?" Margaret gaped. "Are you mad?"

"Not really." Deirdre ventured a smile. "Not any more. Margaret, I wasn't surprised to learn I was dying because I always suspected some punishment would catch up with me, one day."

"Not this again." Margaret jammed the key into the slot and started the car with an angry twist.

"Margaret—"

"I'm not listening to this." Margaret stamped down on the accelerator. The engine roared.

"Margaret, Jacob's death was my fault and you know it!" Deirdre tightened her grip on her sister's shoulder until Margaret was forced to turn and look at her. "And I'm not going to my grave lying about it. It's time to make things right."

"For the love of…" Margaret clutched the wheel until her knuckles bulged. Forcing her temper under control, she said, "Deirdre, this is not just about you. If you start telling people the *truth*—" her face twisted into a snarl "—have you thought about what it will mean for me?"

"Of course I have! But we've run from this for thirty years."

"Correction: I ran. You holed up in Port Bannir like a scared little rabbit." Margaret thumped the wheel, then hated herself as Deirdre flinched from the violence of the gesture.

But Deirdre's voice barely trembled as she said, "Jacob was my friend, Margaret. Ever since we were little kids, he was good to me. He must have family left somewhere. I'm doing this."

Margaret stared at her sister in desperation, but the look on Deirdre's face was set—determined, as Margaret had never seen it before. "Don't do it right now." Margaret found herself almost pleading. "Wait a bit. We have to…" She searched desperately for a pretext. "We have to think of the most sensitive approach. We mustn't cause pain to anyone."

"I know that." Deirdre patted her. "And Margaret, I'm very sorry. I know this will make things hard for you. But I'm the one who's dying."

"For God's sake." Margaret bit her lip. "I suppose you think that's a winning argument?"

"It's not a bad one." Deirdre smiled. Her eyes were wet. "Let me have this, Margaret. It's not often I get the last word."

⌒〜⌒

It was late when the bus crawled back into Port Bannir, and almost midnight by the time Bess had cycled home from the station. The sky was clouded over, no moonlight to guide her way. The unlit road was dangerous; her eyes strained from watching out for potholes, rocks, or a kangaroo hurtling by.

Today's discoveries played over again in her mind: Billy with her spear, Sybil with her exotic past, Leon planning to expose his own mother as an arsonist… How Bess longed to tell someone the whole story and then ask what they thought. Who was waiting to hear it, though? Her chickens?

But parked in front of her tiny house was the sleek metal shape of Margaret's car. Margaret was leaning against it.

Bess propped her bike against a tree, hesitated, then stepped towards her.

"What's happened?" She tried to make out her visitor's expression. Margaret wasn't moving. "Are you all right?"

"Not…" Margaret's voice was hoarse. "Not really."

Bess hurried forward. Her flesh, warm from the long bike ride, throbbed where the cold night air brushed it. "Is it your sister?"

Margaret gave a brief, strangled laugh. "You don't know the half of it." She sniffed and Bess caught a glint of tears in her eyes. "It's been a trying day, Ms Campbell."

Bess reached out to touch the dense, smooth wool of Margaret's jacket sleeve.

Margaret looked down at her stroking fingers.

Up close, Bess could see the intensity of her expression, the tremor of her lips.

"I realise this is an imposition..."

"No." Bess's breath caught. "I mean...I've had a weird day, too. But you're welcome to...impose."

The last word seemed to hover on her lips, before Margaret leaned forward and captured them with her own.

Chapter 16

BESS STRUGGLED TO CATCH HER breath. The cold air made her face smart, made her flesh feel startled and wide awake. Every inch of it. She touched the tip of her tongue to a stinging spot on her lip, where Margaret's teeth had nipped her.

"Wait," Bess tried to say, but she was tired of waiting. Her hands were still clutching the lapels of Margaret's coat. Bess drew her close again, opening her mouth to the pressure of Margaret's lips, their rhythmic movements, and the rush of her breath.

She had not had a kiss like this before. Bess had always thought of herself as a generous, affectionate lover, but not, she realised, a passionate one. Where had this come from?

Her bottom lip caught between Margaret's teeth, and Bess let out a groan. The pinch increased until she teetered on the edge of pain while from between her thighs came a throb of delight. Straining forward against the tug of Margaret's hand in her hair, Bess's scalp was burning as she drove deeper into the kiss. Her tongue extended to tease the sleek underside of Margaret's lip, the sensitive roof of her mouth, and she felt Margaret twitch in response.

Margaret drew back a little, forcing Bess's head to the side. She captured one earlobe, teasing it with a dextrous tongue, before her mouth travelled down the curve of Bess's neck, leaving a trail of sucking bites in her wake. Bess felt each hot mark throb and thrill as the night breeze tickled the wet traces left by Margaret's lips.

Feeling bolder, Bess wound her arms around Margaret's neck and pushed her hips up hard, seeking the hidden heat of the other woman's body. She whispered, "Shall we go inside?"

Margaret drew back and shook her head. Her voice was hoarse as she replied, "Not in there, Bess, please. I can't be in anyone's home tonight."

Bess nodded, sensing Margaret's anguish, if not understanding it. She stepped backwards, drawing Margaret with her, until her back rested against the side of Margaret's car. The metal door handle and the window's glass raised goosebumps across her skin as Margaret slid her hands under Bess's sweater and blouse and drew the fabric higher.

"I can't believe I'm doing this…" Bess's words were swallowed up at once into the night. There was no one else to hear them, no walls or fences out here, just miles of open darkness, the shivering sound of her wind chimes, and the tree boughs creaking above them.

When had she ever known such secrecy, such freedom? She permitted her sweater to be hauled up over her head, her blouse unbuttoned and shooed off her shoulders, her bra popped open to accommodate Margaret's caressing palms and plucking fingers.

Moving by instinct, she let her hands glide down to grip and squeeze the muscular shape of Margaret's behind, wanting her closer. Margaret's knee nudged its way between Bess's legs, until Bess shifted to permit it. Then she guided Margaret's hand down to the zipper of her skirt, determined to be free of that too.

Bess's kicked-off shoes lay in the grass by her feet. Thanks to Margaret, her other clothes were kept clean, piled on the spotless bonnet of Margaret's car. Thin cotton tickled the length of her legs as her underwear was peeled down, damp and scented from where Margaret's thrusting thigh had rubbed it against her.

Naked, she winced at the chill of metal against her hips, her ribs, her shoulder blades, and she dragged Margaret up to her, a shield against the night air. She'd sensed that Margaret would not want to be undressed in turn, not tonight. Instead, Bess wriggled back just far enough to welcome the hot shape of Margaret's hand. It glided down her belly to cup the modest mound there, to scrape those short nails gently through Bess's curls, then stroke her swelling clit and slide one questing finger between her wet folds and up inside.

"*Oh...*" Bess's tone was one of amazement.

Then Margaret kissed her again, and it seemed there was nothing more to be said.

Layers of clothing, some abrasive, some smooth, rubbed Bess's body, chafing her taut nipples and brushing between her open knees. She leaned back further, pinned between the car and Margaret's weight, and lifted one bare foot to run it up and down Margaret's boot, relishing the ridges of metal buckles, and the smooth, flexible leather.

Her hands, hanging on tight to Margaret's buttocks, slipped lower, inward. Through the fabric, she sensed a smouldering heat.

Margaret's breath released with a growl. Her movements stilled, and Bess wondered if she had gone too far—then Margaret resumed her slow, deliberate thrusts, the heel of her hand rocking against Bess's mound with a skill that made Bess whimper with pleasure.

Desperate for more—more heat, more closeness—Bess snuck one arm around the front and let her fingers creep nearer to their target, tracing the seam of Margaret's trousers until she felt through the material a seeping moisture and sweetly responsive flesh. She explored it with a sense of wonder—had she really had this effect on Margaret? She rubbed lightly, tentatively...and was unprepared for the result.

Margaret's breath caught, her hands shook. Then a spasm seized her, her fingers giving a searing twist in Bess's hair, her face contorting in a silent cry.

Bess stared. "Margaret? Did you...?"

But before she could finish speaking, before she could name what Margaret probably saw as weakness, Margaret had pulled herself free. She was breathing hard.

Bess feared she would withdraw, go away, and leave her like this—then without a word, Margaret dropped to her knees instead.

The sight as Bess looked down made her mouth part, her breath growing shallow with wonder. Her white flesh glowed in the shadows, the brightest thing for miles around, while between her open thighs there crouched a black-clad shape, dark as the earth below them.

Margaret's touch was deft as she massaged the plump outer lips, then spread them apart so Bess could feel her sultry breath, followed by the slow, luxuriant sweep of her tongue.

Bess gazed down in amazement, watching the pale star-shape of her own hand as she stroked Margaret's thick, short hair, the perfect oval shape of her skull. The other woman's face was buried between Bess's thighs, each flick of her tongue causing jolts of bliss so intense that soon the darkness was filled with Bess's murmurs and cries.

God, this wasn't like her. This was surely too fast, too exposed. Margaret's free hand grasped one fleshy buttock, digging her fingers in deep, making Bess gasp as the sharp sensation transmuted into a fresh surge of pleasure. Still, she opened her mouth to protest that she couldn't, not out here, not with her knees shaking so much that she would surely fall... But as she struggled to form the words, she felt that tell-tale flutter beneath her belly, that sweet tension clenching, stirring, gathering itself there, before exploding into a million points of light, like cascading diamonds.

She slumped against the car, her head lolling back to stare at the drifting speckles of the Milky Way. At the shape of a beautiful, catastrophic thing that had already happened.

～

Margaret leaned back into the heat and roar of the shower and closed her eyes. Her house had been silent when she'd crept home, but there was no chance of her getting to sleep. Not now, when it was almost dawn.

Water pounded the top of her head, plastering her hair to her brow, blocking her ears, sticking her eyelashes together in wet clumps. Her skin flushed pink, steam filling her lungs.

How could she have done this?

For years, she had avoided...entanglements. She had kept things together, answered to no one but herself. Years of being avoided, suspected, deferred to, tiptoed around. She'd preferred it that way.

But now, with Bess... To have found someone like that, a woman so bursting with life and vitality and that sturdy, sensuous energy of hers. To have someone like that expose herself so willingly, offer herself to Margaret—*touch* Margaret, without a hint of hesitation or fear... It made Margaret's legs weaken, made her brace one hand against the streaming tiles, afraid she might fall. It had been so very sweet, and that terrified her. Could a thing that wonderful ever last?

Reluctantly, she turned off the water and stepped out of the stall. She rubbed her short hair vigorously and blotted the water from her face. And although she hated marks on her mirror, she reached out and wiped away the steam, contemplating her reflection for a second before the glass misted over again. The ridges of her collarbones, gleaming with water, her hair standing out in wet black spikes. The long muscles in her limbs, the extra flesh gathering at her hips and buttocks, the bounce of her breasts as she towelled herself dry. It was rare she bothered to look at herself undressed these days, rarer still that she wondered what another woman would think.

God knows what Bess would expect from her now. The woman was so…enthusiastic.

The memory of Bess's passion, the sound and scent and taste of it, made Margaret catch her breath. She'd already known she enjoyed Bess's company: her brightness, her wit, her dedication to the things she loved. Her unabashed relish of her own pleasure had been a surprise and a delight. Still, anxiety fluttered in Margaret's chest. Was she too old for someone like Bess, too unfashionable and set in her ways? Could the night have been a mistake? As if she didn't have enough to worry about, with the police harassing her and the Incursium Estate after her museum, to say nothing of Deirdre's illness.

Deirdre… Margaret frowned as she dried the soles of her feet and between her toes. Attention to detail: that was critical. A pity Deirdre's doctor, that born-to-rule creep Duncan Mather, could not have remembered that.

She was dry now, but she worked herself over with the rough towel one more time, her skin hot from the friction. How could anyone be so useless? So inept and lazy as to miss the most obvious signs that something was amiss?

Stiffening, she clutched the towel in front of her body as she straightened. Despite the steam still fogging the mirror, a sudden chill ran through her.

No. No, surely she was wrong.

Margaret Gale didn't scare easily, but the possibility that had just occurred to her made her swallow hard, forcing down a wave of nausea. She dressed herself as fast as her trembling hands could manage.

She cracked open the door of the spare room. Deirdre was asleep. Still, Margaret took care to step outdoors and shut the house up before taking out her phone. Dawn was breaking in layers of grey, pink and gold when she called.

"Zan?"

"Piss off, M," came the groggy teenage voice. Before she could hang up, Margaret rushed in: "I know it's early, but I'll make this worth your while. Double your usual rate—how about that?"

The answer sounded like "Mmph", but Zan hadn't rung off.

Margaret took a deep breath. "I've got a new job for you. And it needs to go at the top of the list."

⟿

Around the corner from the Maritime Museum, Bess halted, steadying herself on her bike with one foot on the ground. What was she going to say when she saw Margaret again? What would she do? She drew in a breath, her grip tightening around the handlebars.

She had woken up alone with her muscles sore and her thoughts racing. Bess's past relationships had been fun, usually, and affectionate, sometimes, but they had not been passionate. They had not prepared her for last night.

She chained up her bike and headed this time for the museum's back entrance, where she glimpsed Margaret's car parked. Rounding the corner of the building, she found the woman in question unlocking the door.

"Bess." Margaret breathed her name, her face lighting up with a small, uncertain smile. The keys slipped from her hand.

"Oh! Here, let me—" Bess crouched down to help her and they just missed cracking heads. "Sorry..."

"My fault, I think." As Margaret gathered up her belongings, she shot Bess a glance. It looked tentative, almost shy. "I wasn't sure if I would see you."

"I..." Bess was not used to feeling so tongue-tied. "I hope this is all right?"

"Yes." The word came out loud with need, but Margaret's expression remained uncertain.

"Because we should probably talk." Bess watched Margaret's face working with some suppressed emotion. "You ran off pretty fast last night."

"I... My apologies." Margaret's voice was husky. "I had thinking to do." Her hand ventured out to pluck at Bess's sleeve. "But I never meant to

198

insult you. You don't know..." She swallowed. "You can't imagine what a difference your company has made to me, Bess." She pronounced the last word in a whisper.

Bess's lips twitched into a smile. Was this the closest Margaret would come to saying what she really wanted? But the intensity of Margaret's gaze spoke for her, and when Margaret asked, "Can you stay a while?" Bess nodded.

Bess followed Margaret as she unlocked the museum door and made her way down the corridor to her office. She watched Margaret from behind: the glossy darkness of her hair, the hint of rounded, muscular buttocks moving beneath her well-cut trousers, her spine perfectly straight.

"Coffee?" Margaret asked.

"That'd be nice." Bess paused. "I didn't get much sleep last night." And she could have sworn Margaret blushed before hurrying away to the kitchen.

When she returned, Margaret seemed composed again. As she handed Bess her cup, she said, "We never got to speak about what we discovered yesterday."

Bess raised her eyebrows, and Margaret looked flustered again before she clarified "During our travels to Ballarat and Daylesford."

"Oh." Bess looked hard at Margaret. "We can talk about that. But for the record, the main thing I discovered is how incredibly annoying you are, Margaret."

"I beg your pardon?" Margaret's eyebrows shot up, a little of her old hauteur returning.

Bess narrowed her eyes. "You gave me one of the most memorable nights of my life, then you want to talk about my bus trip?" She wondered if she was taking her teasing a little too far—but watching Margaret's face turn from ivory to diamond-pink made it worthwhile.

When it was clear Margaret was struggling to find a reply, Bess relented and touched her hand. "Okay. Let's talk about our travels."

⸙

They sat together, on Margaret's impeccable leather couch, sipped their coffee, and talked. Bess described her curious meeting with Billy Bower, and the revelations about Leon and his mother.

"Honestly, was there nothing that man wouldn't turn into an exhibit?" Margaret clicked her tongue. She related her own tale of meeting Hermione Morris in the hospital chapel, and the truth behind the old woman's public protests.

"She's sick?" Bess asked.

"Very, by the sound of it."

"I suppose that explains why she doesn't care what people think of her." Bess chewed her lip. "Still, picketing her daughter's workplace—I'm not sure that was okay."

"Don't tell me you're feeling sorry for Irene? I thought she was your least favourite colleague."

"She is." Bess sighed. "But I know what it's like to have a mother who won't leave you alone."

"Yes, I remember." Margaret gave another smile, and Bess returned it. "But Ms Morris did pester me into giving you this." She produced a padded envelope with Irene's name on it. "I don't know what it is. Would you be too uncomfortable, handing it to Irene?"

"I suppose that's all right." Bess shrugged and slipped it into her bag. "She can always bin it."

"Quite."

Bess hesitated, then reminded herself to seize the moment. "Listen, about last night."

"Yes." Margaret's voice was hushed.

Bess slid her hand closer, across the cool leather, until their fingers linked. "Your company has made a difference to me, too."

Margaret caught her breath. Holding Bess's gaze, she leaned closer. But before either of them could find another word, there was a knock at the door.

"What is it?" Margaret snapped, as Kelly cracked the door open.

"I'm sorry, Ms Gale. But the rep. from our security company is out front. You'd complained our guard was, um, 'as much use as a cardboard cut-out', and they're here to discuss a change?"

"Oh." With an exasperated look, Margaret got to her feet. "My apologies for the intrusion, Ms Campbell. If you need to leave, I understand."

"I'll hang around." Bess got up, too, but she was not willing to leave, to distance herself from whatever was growing, slowly, with Margaret. Instead, she said, "I might have a wander around the museum, if that's all right?"

"Be my guest." Margaret managed a small smile for Bess before she followed Kelly away towards the reception area and out of Bess's line of sight.

Bess strolled through the displays and in and out of the alcoves, where the smaller items were lit up. There was always something special about the peace and quiet of a gallery before its doors opened She examined an early-model life jacket and ship's surgical kit, before her feet led her back to the whaling tableau.

By anyone's standards, it was horrible, she decided, as she studied the dummies in their oilskins brandishing their harpoons and knives above the whale's fibreglass body. Stodgy and gruesome at the same time. If only she could persuade Margaret to make some of these displays less literal, less bloodthirsty, less…Victorian era.

In the distance, she heard Margaret's office door close; Margaret must have finished dealing with that matter at the front desk and returned to her inner sanctum. Bess should return to her, but on impulse she leaned in for a moment to take a closer look at the display.

The whale and the human figures looked about thirty years old. The whale's body had been heavily daubed with fake blood, but the dummies were clean. Bess rolled her eyes; the display wasn't even consistent.

The knife, held in mid-air between the dummy's hands, looked like it could be an original. Bess glanced at the explanatory blurb. It was called a leaning knife, apparently, made of steel and around fifteen inches long. Once, that weapon had been part of one of the most lucrative industries on earth.

And although she knew Margaret would be horrified (or perhaps because of that), Bess couldn't resist craning in to look at the blade up close, from its hilt to its sharp point. She should really move away. But what was the point of museums, if they didn't get you close to history?

Then she saw something, up there near the hilt. A tiny trace of brownish red.

Bess glanced down at the model whale, but the daubs of paint there were bright scarlet, and they must have been dry for three decades now.

Rust, then? But Margaret would never permit that to happen to one of her artefacts. Wildly, she wondered if this could be the last trace of some poor whale, hacked to death a century before.

Strange. She wasn't conscious of alarm, but somehow her feet were carrying her back to Margaret's office, her hand on the doorknob pushing the door open, her voice calling out, "Margaret? The whaling display—there's something wrong—there's something on that knife…"

But even as the words tumbled out, Bess was taking in the scene before her.

Margaret had not returned alone to her office. That detective, Gavin, was beside her, accompanied by a uniformed officer. The sight of them made Bess freeze in shock.

The officer, wearing latex gloves, was sifting through the drawer of Margaret's desk. Then, like a magician, he pulled out a length of scarf. A black chiffon scarf, like the one Arwyn had worn to Leon's funeral. The one that had been missing afterwards from her strangled body, because the killer had taken it with them.

Bess's lips trembled. She shook her head, fighting to summon the right words. Like "No", and "Mistake".

But the detective spoke first. "Margaret Gale, I'm arresting you for the murder of Arwyn Ross…"

Margaret wasn't arguing now; she wasn't even looking at the damning evidence. She was looking at Bess, her eyes wide and desperate.

The detective was still speaking, "And maybe now you'd like to be more forthcoming about what happened to Leon Powell, too…"

Bess stared back, willing Margaret with all her might to explain this away, to prove it was a set-up, a ruse. To make fools of these men like she always did.

Instead, Margaret's eyes darted, for the briefest moment, over Bess's shoulder. And the second policeman suddenly turned to Bess and said, "Miss Campbell? What was that you were saying about a knife?"

Bess's stomach lurched. Suddenly, she knew which display Margaret was looking at.

Where would you hide a weapon in Port Bannir?

The object that had caused Leon's death had never been found, had it?

Bess's left hand flew to her mouth, pressing it shut against the memory: that smear of Leon's blood.

She recalled Jacs saying, "Whatever the killer used, it went clean through his ribcage and out the other side…"

"Bess, it's not what it looks like." Margaret's words echoed, as if from down a long corridor. "I didn't do it, Bess. Please, you have to trust me."

Her voice faded out, drowned by the rush of blood to Bess's ears.

Chapter 17

BESS SAT IN THE INTERVIEW room and wondered if things could get worse. Disinfectant filled her nostrils, not quite covering the smell of old vomit.

If the police had been suspicious last time, now they were openly hostile. Her eyes grew wide with disbelief as question after question was fired at her:

What's the nature of your relationship with Margaret Gale? Why did you help her assault Arwyn Ross at the Maritime Museum? Well, we're asking again, aren't we? Where did you go with Margaret Gale after Leon Powell's funeral? What were the two of you doing all afternoon? Anyone else see you? Did you and Margaret Gale arrange to meet with Arwyn after the funeral? Arwyn insulted you, didn't she? Was that why you hated her? Did you help Margaret strangle Arwyn? Where were you at 2 p.m. after the funeral? Who else can verify that? When did Margaret Gale ask you to lie for her, to give her an alibi? How did you know exactly where to find Arwyn's body, then? Do you expect people to believe that? And again: What is the nature of your relationship with Margaret Gale?

This time Bess recalled Margaret's words and insisted on a solicitor. She tried hard not to wonder if this sensible advice had come from a killer.

It was hours before she made it home. She sank down on the steps of her tiny house and let her forehead rest on her knees. The ride home had drained her remaining energy. Even staggering inside and climbing the ladder into the loft bed seemed beyond her.

They hadn't been able to hold her. As the solicitor had pointed out, there were no incriminating forensics and no witnesses to Bess's involvement. No one could place her at the scene of any crime. When he'd asked the police whether Margaret Gale had named Bess as an accomplice, there was no reply, which Bess assumed must mean she had not. Did that make Margaret an honest murderer?

Bess cushioned her head on her arms and felt a tear squeeze out. Her ribcage ached from trying not to sob. Was she insane for believing, even now, that Margaret could have been set up?

No. No, Bess did not believe she was a murderer, *still* did not believe it, in spite of everything that had happened today.

Besides, she got the sense Arwyn had died while Margaret was at Bess's house. As she had said to Margaret earlier, it was hard to imagine this little town as a hideout for two killers at once. And anyway, whether there was one culprit or a hundred, she refused to see Margaret as a murderer.

Everyone else did, though. And she had to admit, circumstantially, at least, they had grounds.

Back at the museum, it had taken the police all of about ten seconds to figure out which knife Bess had been talking about, and to decide it was worth a closer inspection. Perhaps it had something to do with the direction of Bess's gaze, the look of horror on her face.

She'd heard the news before cycling home: Margaret had been charged, but so far only with the murder of Leon Powell. Well, Margaret had been caught on tape leaving the crime scene, and now the weapon had been hidden in plain sight on her premises. And she had good reason to want Leon gone.

But it also looked like the police were finding Arwyn's murder harder to pin on Margaret. The time of death would have proved a problem. How inconvenient for them Margaret had Bess as an alibi. Bess tightened her lips; yes, there was that in Margaret's favour. That was something, wasn't it? For now, all the police really seemed to have was the weapon—the scarf pulled from Margaret's office. Anyone could have planted that there.

Bess sniffed and swiped at her watering eyes. Except that Margaret would have kept that office locked when she wasn't in it—Bess felt sure of that.

Jess Lea

She heaved herself to her feet. No, she would not let herself be crushed by this. She didn't believe the killer was Margaret, she *didn't*—and she would not give up on discovering what had really happened to Leon.

Still, every step was an effort as she hauled herself over to the hutch to change the chickens' water and straw and scatter their grain. The news must be out by now. Perhaps it had hit the airways before she'd even made it out of town; as she'd unchained her bike to go home, she'd noticed a couple of teenagers huddled outside the youth club, staring at her and whispering to each other.

God, what if Georgina Harper had lost patience with her and released those photos? If she had, Bess would be out of a job, for sure. She'd be lucky not to be run out of town.

Watching the hens wandering placidly around in the dirt, Bess was hit by a wave of misery. She'd been happy here; she'd made a home. Could she bear to pack up and leave all over again? As she thought about that, she heard the hum of a car engine.

Straightening up, Bess squinted in the glare, as a glimmering shape appeared at the end of her long drive. Slowly, it purred its way down the track, coming closer until she recognised Georgina Harper's Audi. It braked ten metres away and sat there, engine throbbing. No one got out. They were waiting for her to walk over.

Anger stirred inside her. She was tempted to go inside the house and shut the door. Call that woman's bluff. But there were those photos to think about and the influence Georgina seemed to wield over Steven Powell.

Bess put down the sack of grain and approached the car. Georgina waited until she was right there before sliding the window down. In the front seat, Bess glimpsed the gigantic figure of Vince Polat, watching her in his rear-view mirror.

"Bess, dear." Georgina gave a lazy smile. "Aren't you going to invite me in?"

Georgina picked her way through Bess's yard and into her house like a queen inspecting an orphanage. Her smile was fixed and she remarked on how "charming" everything was while watching carefully where she put her feet.

Genghis made threatening noises and darted at her several times, until Bess had to lock him, protesting, in his hutch. She came back to find

206

Georgina standing in the centre of her homemade rug. Georgina's arms were folded; her immoveable hair gleamed like a silvery blonde helmet. Her blue suit was neat, understated, and appeared to have been tailored just for her.

"Please, have a seat." Bess was annoyed to realise her mouth had gone dry. "Can I get you a drink? I've got some lavender tea…"

"Oh, that's sweet, but I couldn't possibly." Georgina shooed the idea away, as if Bess's income couldn't stretch to hot water and plant clippings. "I just wanted to check in." She scrutinised the cushioned bench, before resting her well-sculpted behind on the very edge. She crossed her legs, folded her hands, and watched Bess for a full five seconds, before saying, "Well. Your friend is in a bit of a pickle, isn't she?"

Bess swallowed. She wished she could take a seat too, instead of fidgeting in front of Georgina like a kid in the principal's office. But the only other spot was the bench beside her visitor, and Bess was not about to sit there.

"If you mean Margaret Gale, she is innocent until proven guilty." Bess tried to sound fearless, but she didn't quite succeed.

Georgina seemed to find her remark quaint. "And I hear you've been helping the police with their inquiries again." Georgina's smile grew wider at the look of alarm on Bess's face. "Oh, don't worry. It's not public knowledge."

There was no need for her to add *"not yet"*.

"You haven't released those photos."

"Oh, I've been far too busy." Georgina flicked an imaginary speck of dust from her sleeve. "Sorting out the acquisition of land for Incursium Estate. Thanks to Margaret Gale's dreadful deeds, I don't suppose there will be any further difficulties with that museum site, at least." Her smile grew saccharine. "Perhaps that was Leon's last gift to us."

Before Bess could protest about that comment, Georgina drawled, "It must be just *awful* for you. But tell me, Bess, before you get into any more trouble, did you find out about Leon's final exhibit?"

Bess bit her lip, struggling to make a decision. Steven Powell already wanted her gone. Once people knew she'd been questioned in relation to Margaret's crimes, how long would she last at the Cabinet of Curiosities? The gallery she'd helped to *build*, goddammit? The situation was so unfair.

If anyone could pull rank on Steven and enable Bess to stay, it was Georgina Harper.

Still, there was something about that last exhibit of Leon's that made Bess uneasy.

She swallowed. "I did find out about it, yes. I've met the artist, and seen some of the exhibits."

Georgina raised one flawless eyebrow. "And?"

"It's…very interesting. Controversial. Likely to draw crowds."

"Bess, dear." Georgina's eyes narrowed. "Dramatic build-up is for the paying public. I require the facts."

"I…" Bess closed her eyes briefly for courage. "I can't disclose any more information yet." She met Georgina's reptilian stare, and explained, "There is another person involved in this exhibit. A sort of…co-creator." Was that the right way to describe the elderly Sybil Powell? "I'll need to speak with this person, to get their permission, before I pass anything on to you."

"Bess…" Georgina glanced around the tiny house, seeming to catalogue every one of Bess's handmade possessions. "Don't think I'm being impatient, but you seem to be holding out on me. Perhaps even lying." Her smile didn't budge. "People generally learn not to do that."

"I'm not playing games." Bess wished her voice wouldn't wobble. "I just need to do this ethically."

"Ethically?" Georgina seemed delighted by the word. "Tell me, Bess, was it ethical of you to provide a false alibi for a murderer?"

"I…" God, how Bess wished she could release Genghis to attack this woman's ankles. "I never did anything like that."

"If you say so, dear." Georgina got to her feet, dusting down her suit as if Bess's cushions might have grubbied it. "Now." She stepped forward, right into Bess's space. In her heels, she could look down at Bess, as she said, "For the last time, what do you know about Leon's final exhibit?"

Bess's heart fluttered. She steeled herself not to step back. "I'll tell you everything, if the other person consents. Give me a week."

Georgina's hand shot up to seize Bess by her chin. Her grip was hard, her skin smelled of rose-scented lotion. Her manicure bit into Bess's flesh.

"You've got three days." Just as abruptly, Georgina released her. The marks of her nails stung in Bess's skin. As she stalked to the doorway to let herself out, Georgina said conversationally, "It's a very pretty block of land you've rented here. I'm really quite jealous." She glanced out across the paddocks. "So peaceful. Not another person for miles and miles…" Georgina flashed a final smile over her shoulder, before climbing into her spotless car. She gave Bess a little wave as Vince drove her away.

Bess stared as the Audi became a shining dot on the horizon, then vanished. She let Genghis out of the hutch, scooped him up and held him. Her phone buzzed in her pocket.

It was a blocked number. The message read: *M didn't do it. Meet supermarket freezer section 1 hr.*

Bess gazed at the screen. She stroked Genghis behind his comb, and wondered if the only sane, trustworthy person in her life was a rooster.

Bess learned one thing that day: there was only so long you could stand in front of the freezer section at the supermarket in Port Bannir.

After five minutes, she was shivering in her yellow checked dress. She studied the ingredients on an ice-cream punnet. She checked the prices on frozen peas. She was examining the allergy warnings on a packet of fish fingers and wondering if this was some weird practical joke, when a voice beside her said, "Don't look around. Look at the fish fingers."

Bess kept still, but glanced sideways at the reflections in the glass door. Standing next to her was a large, pear-shaped girl in tracksuit pants, a *Black Panther* sweatshirt, and a beanie pulled down to the top of her thick glasses. She was scowling in furious concentration. She hissed, "Don't look at me, I said."

Bess returned her focus to the thawing fish fingers.

"Recognised you from that YouTube clip," the girl said. "Are you alone?"

"Yes." Growing impatient, Bess risked a glance to the left, where two other teenage girls in ratty black clothing and Doc Martens were pretending to be engrossed by the frozen dim sims. "You're not, though."

"Security measure." The kid shuffled to and fro, sneaking looks around. "Where's your phone?"

"In my bag." Bess was growing incredulous—was she about to be the victim of Port Bannir's silliest mugging?

"Put it in the freezer and shut the door."

"You've got to be kidding!" Bess's voice rose.

The girl hissed a frantic "Shuddup!" But the aisle was deserted, the only other sounds the jangle of music and the hum of freezer engines.

Bess replaced the fish fingers and rubbed her numb fingertips.

The kid jittered from foot to foot. Would she run off if Bess didn't cooperate? Was there a tiny chance she might have something real to confide?

Rolling her eyes, Bess pulled out her phone and slipped it between the hamburger patties and the party pies. She closed the door and said, "Whatever this is, make it quick. My phone didn't come with iceberg insurance."

Out the side of her mouth, the kid said, "No names, all right? We're associates of M."

"Who?"

"Margaret Gale."

"Right..."

"We think she's been falsely accused," the girl whispered. "Also, she owes us, like, a shit-ton of money, and I already put my name down for the new iPad."

"Okay..." Bess tried to imagine why Margaret might owe money to a bunch of teenagers. One of the other girls, a solid, swarthy kid, moved closer and said in a more normal voice "What Squid here is trying to say—"

"No names, dickhead!"

"—is that she's got something to confess."

"I see." Bess tried to sound like this made sense. Despite her instructions, she turned to look properly at Squid. "What?"

Squid bounced on the spot, as if she needed to pee. "Okay, a while ago I found this note stuck in our letterbox, right? I always get our mail; Mum doesn't like to go outside much. She's...not feeling good." Squid pushed her smudged glasses up her nose. One arm was held on with gaffer tape. "And the note offered me money if I would sort of hack into a security camera. At the Cabinet of Curiosities."

Bess stared at her.

Squid explained, "The one over the back door. It's okay, they just wanted me to turn it around to face the wall. It wasn't pervy or anything."

"*You* turned that camera around?"

"Easy." Squid shrugged. "No offence, but your security's shit. You should get it looked at; there's creeps out there."

"Why did you do that?" Bess hissed, helplessly, not daring to raise her voice in case she scared the girls off.

"For money, duh." Squid seemed to find it a remarkably stupid question. "I figured it was a break-in, but come on. That guy who ran the gallery was, like, a millionaire. Like he wouldn't have insurance."

"'That guy' was called Leon, and he was murdered in there the night you turned that camera around!" Bess was shaking with anger and shock.

Margaret had entered and left the Cabinet of Curiosities by the front door, where she'd been caught on tape. If someone else had managed to slip in undetected through the back... Bess whispered frantically, "Why didn't you come forward when he was killed?"

"And shop myself?" Squid frowned through her thick lenses and fiddled with her necklace. It was a tiny model of the Millennium Falcon. "I don't think I would thrive in a prison environment."

Bess ran her hands through her hair, struggling not to scream with frustration. "And this person who hired you—you don't think it was Margaret Gale?"

"Nup." Squid traced a pattern on the fridge door. "They left the cash in an envelope in the letterbox the next day. And it was all in Kermits."

Bess took a second to interpret that. "Hundred dollar notes?"

"Yeah. M always pays in fifties or lower. What sort of dodgy fuckwit uses the green ones? No shop'll change them." Squid scowled, apparently still feeling hard done by. "And check out the letter." She fished it out of the pocket of her sagging tracksuit bottoms.

Bess leaned across to look; she wasn't about to put her prints on evidence. The note was typed in a standard font on an ordinary sheet of paper. She read it:

turn round camera over back door cabinet curiosities tues night 7. theres 500 4 u. its confidential

Squid shot her a meaningful look. "See? That never came from M."

"It's a bit awkward," Bess said. "Could it be an adult trying to sound young?"

"No caps," Squid observed. "And isn't that 'its' meant to have a little thingy?"

"Apostrophe?" Bess frowned. "Well, Margaret could have misspelled the word on purpose, to disguise herself."

Squid's round face scrunched up in disbelief. "Come on. It's *Margaret.*"

Which was a fair point. For the first time since that awful scene at the museum, Bess felt a flicker of hope. "So." She rubbed her eyes. "The police station is around the corner. You want me to come with you?"

"What?" Squid started. "Fuck, no." She stuffed the letter away, looking ready to bolt.

"Well, why did you call me here, then? Why show me that thing at all?"

"Well, cos…" Squid frowned. "Cos now you know. M didn't do it."

"I never believed she did." Frustration was thrumming through Bess's body. "But what's your point?"

"Well, now you can do something, can't you?" Bess must have looked bewildered, because Squid urged, "You work at that fancy gallery, don't you? You must be cashed up. And you're a—" She hesitated.

Bess smacked the fridge door in frustration. "I'm a *what?*"

In a small voice, Squid said, "A grown-up."

Bess stared back at her, and then at her two friends, who were already backing away, heading for the door. They might be her only allies. But despite their tech savvy and their big mouths, she realised, they were just kids. She wondered how to tell them that right now she didn't feel very capable, strong, or grown up at all.

⌇

Margaret sat on the edge of the bed. It was bolted to the floor. Above her, a fluorescent light throbbed inside protective mesh. The linoleum showed the streaks of a recent mopping; the toilet was a few feet from the bed. She lifted her aching head to stare at the wall.

Someone had painted this place a pallid shade that wasn't ready to commit to being green. Possibly it was meant to be soothing. It made her think of the pastel walls of that hospital, where she'd found out Deirdre was dying.

A sudden flash of memory: a dusty front yard, an endless hot blue sky, and herself and Deirdre sweating in knee socks, patent-leather shoes, and new black dresses. Dad's frown accusatory, somehow, as he announced, "Mum's gone. Margaret, you're in charge of your sister now."

At eight, she'd resented that. Maybe she'd never stopped resenting it. But she'd done what seemed appropriate, which was to take Deirdre inside, order her to wash her hands, and made her a sandwich. It was just two bits of bread, because Margaret couldn't think of what to put between them, but Deirdre ate it without complaint.

Obligation.

She leaned her weight forward and heard a plastic cover rustle across the mattress. How many women had wept, sweated, or vomited over this bed down the years? She turned to look out the window; the small patch of sky was gun-metal grey.

Someone had put her in here.

Someone had known about the knife; someone had planted the scarf and pointed the police towards it, too. Someone had been playing her.

Her muscles were cramping. She leapt to her feet, paced the tiny space, fists held stiffly at her sides lest she give in to temptation and smash them against the mirror, the door, the empty walls. Tension seared across her shoulders; she fought to slow her breathing.

What was wrong with the police? Did they believe Bess had lied about them both being together when Arwyn died? What were they playing at? She paced some more.

That task she'd given Zan. Had the Hags done it yet?

Margaret clutched at her temples. What if those feckless girls had dropped the job, believing she couldn't pay them now? Or had simply given up on her?

What if Bess had given up on her?

The thought caused her a twist of pain. Halting her pacing, she glanced into the mirror and was alarmed by what she saw. An ageing woman, her skin pasty and lined, her hair tousled, her eyes surrounded by shadows. Would Bess trust a face like that, let alone love it?

Swinging away, Margaret breathed out hard as she stamped the two paces back to the door and braced her hands against it. *Love.* That was where the trouble had started. Deirdre had always needed love, clutching with desperate gratitude at any semblance of the stuff, and look where it had got her. Look at the stupid, terrible, innocent choices she had made.

Where was Deirdre now? Back home with Paul? Was he taking care of her?

The police had moved Margaret out of Port Bannir's tiny lockup, "for capacity reasons", shifting her two hundred kilometres down the highway. The distance felt immense.

Frustration tore at her muscles, hammered inside her head. She was needed at home, damn it, and she wanted to be there, with Bess and Deirdre. And here she was, miles away and penned up like a battery hen. And about as voiceless as one, too. No one believed her denials, and even if somebody did show willingness to listen, how could Margaret possibly tell the truth?

From outside came a jangle of metal; the door swung open.

"Gale." The guard looked Margaret up and down. "Visitor for you."

When Margaret stepped into the visitors' room and saw Bess, the first thing she said was, "You shouldn't have come."

Bess stared. If it hadn't taken her three hours to get here, she might have got up and walked out. As it was, she was tempted to snap back with a sarcastic retort—but her guilt stopped her. After all, Margaret wouldn't be in here, sounding so ferocious and prickly, if it hadn't been for Bess's big mouth yammering on about the knife. So she waited, seated at the cheap plastic table.

Margaret looked like she hadn't slept since Port Bannir, but she appeared unharmed and her gait was upright and purposeful as ever, as she strode over.

Instead of leaping up to embrace her (as she might have done a moment before), Bess leaned back in her chair and crossed her arms. "A bus *and* a train to get here, and this is the thanks I get?"

Margaret seemed to catch herself. She gave a wild shake of her head. "I didn't mean—" She bit her lip. Pulling out the other chair, she sank down opposite Bess, and whispered, "The police will find out you've been here. People will talk."

With a shrug, Bess held the gaze of the woman in front of her. "Let them."

"Bess, I don't..." Margaret glanced around, her face taut with distress. Her hands were clenched at her sides. She couldn't seem to meet Bess's eye. In a whisper, she said, "I don't want you to see me like this."

Bess gazed at her. Then she reached slowly across the table, extending both arms with her palms facing up. Margaret looked at them. Bess caught a glimpse a glint of tears in her eyes, before Margaret lifted her own arms, unfolding her fists with some effort, and clasping Bess's hands in hers.

They sat in silence for a while. Then Margaret cleared her throat.

"We don't have much time. I need you to do something for me. I need you to contact a girl called Zan." She recited a phone number, evidently from memory, and waited for Bess to scrawl it down. "She and two of her friends are supposed to be doing a job for me—actually, several jobs—and I need to know that they're doing it. Promise them I'm still good for the money."

"Three girls?" Bess frowned. "I think I met them. They told me you were innocent."

"Did they?" The relief in Margaret's voice was unmistakable.

Her reaction gave Bess the urge to slap her. She tugged her hands away. In a tone as frosty as anything Margaret herself might have managed, she said, "Well, I'm glad that's a weight off your mind. Things haven't been easy at my end, what with the police interrogation and you being hauled off to the watch house and all, but as long as some teenage nerds with bad personal hygiene are happy to keep working with you, I guess that's the main thing"

"Wait." A note of pleading crept into Margaret's voice. "Let me explain."

So *now* she cared what Bess thought? Bess ground her jaw and glanced around the room. There were posters about the dangers of smoking, and about treatments for hepatitis, interspersed with reminders that they were being filmed at all times. The air conditioning tasted stale. She wriggled her toes inside her shoes, ordering herself, to remember her own life force and stay grounded.

Apparently with some effort, Margaret uttered, "Please…"

That voice of hers. Bess had always found it hard to resist, but now it sounded pained. Shutting her eyes, Bess tried to breathe through the sense of being utterly overwhelmed. The circumstances were too bewildering, too much.

But when she opened her eyes again and saw the anxious need in Margaret's expression, she said, "All right. Tell me what happened, then." She narrowed her eyes. "All of it."

Margaret let out a breath. "Thank you, Bess." She paused, apparently gathering her thoughts. "Most of what I told you was true. I just...left something out."

Bess's stomach twisted.

"I did receive that text from Mr Powell—or from his phone, at least—inviting me to the gallery," Margaret said. "I did go to the Cabinet of Curiosities intending to meet with him, and I did find the front doors open. Well, you've seen the security tapes."

"Uh-huh."

"But there was something I didn't disclose. When I walked into the lobby, I saw a light on down the staff corridor...and the security door leading to that section wasn't locked. It was open."

"You lied," Bess said.

"If you insist." Margaret clicked her tongue. "I assumed that was where Mr Powell must be, so I made my way down the corridor. I was not impressed that he hadn't bothered to come to the front door, but I can't say I was surprised."

"And?" Bess's shoulders ached, tensed for impact.

"I reached his office," Margaret cleared her throat. "The light was on inside; the door was ajar. I pushed it open, and..." Her breath caught. But when she spoke again, her tone was tart, almost mocking. "I remember thinking: *that's a remarkably ugly pattern for a carpet, even by Mr Powell's standards.* Then I realised it wasn't a pattern."

"Jesus." Bess looked away. She forced herself to breathe deeply. "So, you're saying he was already dead when you got there."

"Rather flamboyantly dead, I'm afraid."

Margaret's sarcasm gave Bess another urge to slap her. But then again, what would it be like to walk into a room expecting a work quarrel, and discover something like that?

Continuing, Margaret said, "He'd made a dreadful mess of the floor, but the furniture was all still standing, and I didn't see any cuts on his hands. I'd wager whoever did it took him by surprise."

"I see." Bess rubbed her eyes. Margaret's words swirled inside her head. She breathed slowly, struggling to take this in. "So, you found him dead, and instead of calling the police, you decided to steal the weapon, hide it, and tell no one?"

"I didn't 'steal' anything, Bess; that knife was the property of my museum." Margaret paused. "Not that I'd realised it was missing; it had been in storage. But I recognised it at once, and yes, I retrieved it." At Bess's appalled silence, she said, "Oh, not from between Mr Powell's ribs, if that's what you're worried about. It was on the floor. I wrapped it in paper from his desk, hid it under my coat, and got myself out of there."

Bess's head pounded. "Why? Why would you do any of that? Why not call for help?"

"What would be the point?" Margaret sounded impatient. "He was thoroughly dead, Bess, I can promise you that. And what with the mystery text message, the unlocked doors, and my own weapon used to kill the man—well, it was obvious I'd been set up to take the fall. I admit I experienced a momentary...alarm."

"You mean you panicked?"

"I don't care for that word." Margaret's tone stiffened. "I'd say I took a reasonable course of action, based on the limited information available to me at that time."

"A reasonable course of action?" Bess's words came out in a squawk.

Across the room, a guard turned to stare.

Margaret gestured at her to lower her voice.

"By displaying a murder weapon in your own museum?"

"Well, I couldn't destroy it or throw it away, could I? It's a valuable artefact." Margaret paused, then seemed to remember something else. "And I knew it might have the killer's prints or DNA on it."

"I'm glad that occurred to you." Bess snorted. "But it didn't have those things, did it?"

"According to my lawyer, sadly no. The only biological evidence on the weapon comes from Mr Powell himself."

"I can't believe you put it in that horrible whaling display." Bess dropped her head into her hands.

"It was a perfectly sound decision," Margaret sniffed. "I simply replaced the replica knife in the display with the real one. It was safer there than in the storage area, where my staff or visiting restorers might go poking about and handling things."

Bess took a deep breath and said, "And the scarf? Arwyn's scarf? How do you explain that?"

"I can't." Margaret's tone turned curt. "I never put it in my desk, never even saw it before the police came."

"You're saying someone planted it?" Bess leaned forward. "In your private office? Really?"

Margaret held Bess's eye, unflinchingly.

Bess bit her lip. "I would have to be mad to believe that."

"Well, you don't mind a little madness, do you? Look at the life you lead." But the mockery vanished from Margaret's tone as she reached across the table, stretching her right hand out once more. "Can't you be mad enough to listen to me? Bess, I didn't kill anyone."

Bess looked at the pale and elegant hand lying open in front of her. Hesitating, she inched closer, reached out, and took it. She did believe the story, although it was no surprise that nobody else did. To believe it, they would have to know Margaret, and Margaret rarely permitted that.

Bess looked down at Margaret's fingers. They were cold, their grip bordering on desperate. "If you didn't kill Leon and Arwyn, who did?"

"I can't answer that." Margaret let out an exhausted breath. "But I have wondered…"

"What?"

"Well, I assumed that someone wanted Mr Powell and Ms Ross gone, so they killed them and set me up to take the blame." She faltered. "But…"

"But?"

"But I'm starting to wonder if it may have been the other way around."

Bess frowned. "What do you mean?"

"Gale!"

In the tense silence, the guard's bark made Bess jump. She whirled around to look, and by the time she turned back to her companion, Margaret was getting to her feet. Her expression had closed up again.

Leaning closer, she whispered, "Bess, I have to go. You will find Zan, won't you?" The sarcasm had gone from Margaret's voice; suddenly she sounded urgent. Frightened.

Bess had never heard that tone from Margaret before, and it alarmed her.

"Make sure she's doing her job, Bess, please—"

The guard had seized Margaret's elbow and hustled her away before Bess could touch her again, before she could say goodbye.

Chapter 18

THE SIGNALS CLANGED AS THE country train hooted and rattled its way over the crossing. From her window, Bess saw a man with two little kids and a family dog, lined up in their backyard, waiting to wave to the train. The man held the dog up, making its paw wave too, while the children grinned and bounced on the spot. Did they do this every day? She waved back, wishing she could trade places.

By her calculations, she should reach her new destination in Melbourne this afternoon. She was going to see Sybil Powell.

Leaning back in her seat, she glanced around the carriage. Was this really the right thing to do? But that kid Zan wasn't answering Bess's calls, and the visit from Georgina and Vince had spooked her. She couldn't just sit around waiting for some fresh disaster to happen; she needed to investigate, to act. Tracking down Leon's mystery mother might shake something loose.

Bess leaned her head against the cool glass, watching fields and highways flashing by. Would this trip help Margaret?

"Idiot," she whispered. She wasn't sure if she meant the woman who'd hidden a murder weapon in plain sight because it was a "valuable artefact", or herself for believing that woman. But there was no way she could accept that Margaret was a killer. She thought back to her visit: the grip of Margaret's hands, how alone she seemed. Bess would not abandon her in there.

And if Margaret was innocent, then it meant someone else had slaughtered both Leon and Arwyn. Someone who killed at close range, using muscle and guile. She recalled Billy Bower's tale of Steven finding her in his mother's home and flying into a rage, threatening and throwing things around, and she wondered.

Her phone rang. The two old ladies sitting opposite her glared at the intrusive sound.

"Bess," Georgina Harper drawled. "I'm waiting, darling. Tick-tock."

"I'm on my way to Melbourne," Bess said. "I'm going to see the other party, to talk to her about the exhibit."

"Day trip? That's lovely. Hope you're not doing it on company time." She could picture Georgina's mannequin smile. "Meanwhile, I've got Steven on the line telling me about the portrait exhibit he's organising for the Christmas holiday season." Georgina's sniff of contempt echoed all the way from Port Bannir. "Pictures of retired politicians, Australian poets, and the sort of art dealers I'm always avoiding at cocktail parties. Do you think that will get the punters in, Bess?"

"Not really."

"No. And have you seen the Melbourne papers this morning? They're calling Port Bannir a *Murder Town*. Who do you think wants to buy property in a murder town, Bess? Undertakers?" Georgina's voice was rising. "We need to take back control of the narrative. We need a distraction." There was a meaningful pause. "You said you would help me with that, Bess."

"I am helping."

"And yet I have seen no sign of it." Was Georgina seated at her beautiful desk, Bess wondered, firing someone by email as she spoke? Or was she in the back of her Audi, gazing out the tinted windows while Vince smirked in the front seat?

"Just wait another day or two…"

"I'll be speaking to the local councillors and the Heritage Board today about acquiring the Maritime Museum. My legal team have advised me there shouldn't be too many obstacles, once Ms Gale is…fully appraised of her position."

"Wait!" Bess almost shouted, then blushed as half the carriage turned to stare. Rising from her seat, she stumbled down the rocking train, looking for a private place in which to plead. The toilet was her only option. She hauled open the folding door and locked herself in.

"Are you still there?" she called above the jolting, clanking rhythm of the train.

"Ten seconds, Bess."

"Leave the museum alone. Please." The carriage swayed; Bess toppled and grabbed the door handle. Her hip banged against the sink; her foot slipped in a puddle. "Leon's final exhibit will be worth it, I promise."

"Five seconds and counting…"

She took a deep breath, then said in a rush, "Look, the exhibit was about Leon's mother. She was evidently a pretty wild artist back in the day, very talented, very beautiful, took lots of lovers, and threw pigs' intestines at politicians. Nowadays she's old and angry—and she may have torched his famous restaurant. And Leon arranged a scandalous young artist with a criminal record to create the exhibit about her." Silence. "Georgina? Are you listening?"

"Two seconds and holding." Scepticism dripped from every syllable.

"Hang on. I'll text you some of the artworks." Bess fumbled with her phone, praying the reception would hold, trying to breathe through her mouth as she located the pictures she'd snapped in Billy Bower's studio. She forwarded them through. Then she waited.

"Well." After a long pause, Georgina's voice came through loud and clear. "I don't pretend to know anything about art, thank Christ. But these pictures catch the eye. Crazy naked women sell, as long as they're photogenic, and that's not a bad story. Our PR team could spin it into something passable. As long as it's true." She paused. "And by 'true', I mean legally permissible."

"I'm going to see Sybil Powell now," Bess said. "To ask for her consent."

"Aren't you sweet?" Georgina chuckled. "You track her down; my lawyers will see to any 'consent'." She paused. "All right, Bess. Off you trot."

"But this is confidential, right?" Bess urged. "You won't say anything yet? And you won't touch the Maritime Museum?"

"You have my word as a leader of the Australian business community, Bess." Georgina hung up.

Bess was left to wrestle her way out of the smelly metal cubicle, wondering what Georgina Harper's word was worth. And wondering whether life was always this difficult when you got too tangled up with Margaret Gale.

Four hours and two delayed train services later, Bess was feeling less and less sure about this. She looked around the steep, tree-lined streets of one of Melbourne's most exclusive old neighbourhoods, and tried to get her bearings.

From behind a high wall, she heard the *pock* of balls on a tennis court. Above her head, a security camera swivelled around to watch her. A Bentley glided by. Did the hippie artist Sybil Powell really live out here?

She found the street number that Billy Bower had given her, and checked it twice. It belonged to a handsome sandstone building, surrounded by ten-foot gates. Elegant wrought-iron gates, but locked ones nonetheless. A small plaque read *Barton House*.

Bess pressed the buzzer.

"Barton House, how may I help you?" a voice sang.

"I—May I see Sybil Powell, please?"

A pause, then to Bess's surprise, the gate swung open. The voice said, "Please report to reception on your way in."

As she crunched her way up the white-gravelled drive, she glanced around at the gardens. The paths that wound through them looked smooth, laid with some material softer than concrete. Ramps led up to the door. She pressed another buzzer to be admitted, stepped inside, and found herself standing in front of a reception desk. There were pumps of hand sanitiser on every wall, and folding wheelchairs stacked in the corner. Was this a nursing home?

A cheery woman in a blue uniform greeted her from behind the desk. "Hello there! First visit?"

"Yes, I'm Bess Campbell." She was too surprised to lie. "I'm here to see Sybil Powell."

"Lovely." The nurse waved her towards a clipboard. "Are you a family member?"

"I'm a friend of Steven's." Bess guessed this would attract less suspicion than using Leon's famous name.

"Right. Well, just sign in here, and I'll put a call through." Bess's heart sank; would that call reveal that she had no right to be here? But as she began to write her name, a phone rang in the office behind them. The nurse excused herself and ducked in to answer it. Bess hesitated, then took her chance and sidled past the desk. She slipped off down the corridor in search of Sybil.

Barton House was a cut above any nursing home Bess had visited before. The rooms were spacious and nicely furnished; the air freshener smelled expensive. Each room had a plaque on the door. She hurried along, trying to seem like a regular visitor, as she looked for a plaque reading "Powell". At the end of the hall, she found it.

"Excuse me?" Bess didn't dare raise her voice. She knocked on the frame of the open door. "Syb—Mrs Powell? May I come in?"

"What do you want?" The woman's voice was surprisingly full and forceful for someone in her seventies. She wore a tracksuit clearly chosen for comfort rather than looks, and her hair had been styled in the manner of a much older woman. She sat at a desk beneath the window.

"My private physio comes on Monday," Sybil Powell snapped, eyeing Bess with disapproval. A newspaper was open in front of Sybil; she was doing the crossword. "So you can nick off."

"Sorry to disturb you…"

"Then don't. I'm busy."

"But I'm not a physio. My name's Bess Campbell. I work for your son, Steven. And I used to work for Leon."

"Leon?" Sybil's face cracked into a smile. Her blue eyes crinkled wickedly.

For a second, Bess caught a glimpse of the young woman from those photographs.

"What's that boy been up to now?"

"I—" Bess faltered.

Sybil let out a cackle. "Darling, if he's stolen your copyright, or knocked you up, or given you food poisoning at that bloody silly restaurant of his, there's no use crying to me about it. He's been a bad egg all his life; nothing I can do now." Her tone was warm, as if Leon's badness was a source of pride and delight.

Bess stared. Did Leon's mother not know that he was dead? "Um, Mrs Powell?"

"It's *Ms*, darling. What century do you think this is?"

"When did you last see Leon?"

"What?" Sybil huffed. "How should I know? Yesterday, maybe." She leaned in confidentially. "They hide the clocks in here, so you can't tell."

Bess glanced down at the newspaper in front of Sybil. Half the squares of the crossword were filled out—but not with letters. She had coloured them black.

She opened her mouth, with no idea of what she would say next. But she was spared the trouble, as a voice sounded behind her, making her heart clench with shock.

"What the hell are you doing here?" Steven Powell spoke in a hiss, his eyes popping with outrage. "*Get away from my mother!*"

⌘

"Gale."

Margaret looked up. She had been thinking of Bess, visiting her here. How astonished Margaret had been to see her—gobsmacked, really, that Bess still believed her, still…cared. Margaret had bungled that visit dreadfully, being so awkward and rude, and yet still Bess had stayed, and listened, and pledged to help. No one had given Margaret the benefit of the doubt before, or cared for her like that. It felt so strange, almost as strange as the circumstances that had landed her in here.

She was forced back to the present moment as the guard said, "Letter for you." She flicked an envelope through the air.

Margaret shot out a hand and caught it.

"Nice." The woman raised her eyebrows, before walking on.

Margaret glanced down. There was no return address, but from the ungainly purple writing on the envelope, she was sure it was from Zan. She waited a feverish five seconds, ensuring she was alone, before tearing the letter out and reading it.

We had a look. They call each other every couple of weeks, starting 4 months ago. No calls before that. First call was right after an appointment.

Margaret stared. Her grip tightened, the paper scrunching between her fingers. She read on.

So what? Don't you have other things to worry about?

Perhaps to soften it, Zan had added a smiley face.

Margaret sat down heavily. Her mouth was dry. Yes, she had many other things to worry about. But this had just gone to the top of her list.

Steven's suit was rumpled and speckled with food crumbs; his remaining hair stuck out at wild angles. He smelled of sweat and petrol-station coffee. Had he driven all the way from Port Bannir this afternoon? He advanced on Bess, forcing her back into his mother's room.

"You bloody little bitch!" He kept his voice low, so as not to draw attention from the outside. He yanked the door shut behind him. "I know what you've done!"

"What are you talking about?" Bess stammered, wondering if she should hit the panic button on Sybil's wall. But if she did, the staff would throw her out and she'd be no closer to finding anything.

Sybil was staring in bewilderment at the intruder. "Who are you?" she demanded. "Get out of my house!" Then, "Oh, Steven. You look *dreadful.*"

Ignoring her, Steven fumbled for his phone, then thrust it in Bess's face. In an explosive whisper, he said, "I'm talking about *this*!"

Bess flinched, then focused on the screen. Someone had sent Steven an email with a picture attachment.

It seemed to be some sort of flyer. She recognised the black-and-white shot of a young Sybil Powell, nude and nursing her baby. Someone had merged it with a shot of the adult Leon, looking handsomely tortured. The edges of the image were burned, so that Leon and Sybil were surrounded by charred blackness and crumbling ash. The tagline read: *Leon Powell: Forget everything you've heard.* Then, in smaller letters, *November 30 – February 28, only at the Cabinet of Curiosities.*

Bess shook her head. "I don't know what this is. Did it come from Georgina Harper?"

"So, you admit it!" Steven growled.

His mother had risen from her seat and was tugging at his sleeve, but he didn't look at her. "I got hold of that bloody Billy Bower on the phone. She admitted you'd been around snooping."

"I told Georgina not to do anything like this," Bess protested.

"Well, she's done it anyway, hasn't she?" Heat seemed to be rising in Steven's face, turning his ears red and making a vein rise in his temple. "The bitch rang me at lunchtime. I'd emailed her about the portrait exhibit, to confirm sponsorship by Incursium Estate, and this was her reply. 'Never mind your boring little pictures, Steven. I've found something people will really pay to see.'"

"She's already had a poster designed?" Bess blinked. By her calculations, Georgina must have done all this within an hour of putting down the phone to her.

"Oh, she doesn't sit around!" Steven shook his head. "She said she'd already sent someone to track down Sybil Powell and persuade her to agree to this. And when I told her that under no circumstances would I agree to my mother being exploited—*prostituted*—like this, the bitch told me it was out of my hands! Turns out two of the other shareholders in the Cabinet of Curiosities got spooked by all this *Murder Town* business, and were persuaded to sell their entire interest to a company that the Harper woman controls. Making her the majority owner. Her first act was to get rid of me as acting CEO. 'You've been ever so helpful, Steven, but I've found someone more suited.' Now I know who!"

"What are you talking about?" Bess didn't know whether to make a run for it, or burst out laughing. "You think she offered the CEO job to me?"

"You should be ashamed of yourself! I realise no protégé of my brother could be expected to show integrity, but this—"

"No one has offered me any new job." Bess glanced with concern at Sybil.

The elderly woman had snatched a cushion off the bed and was holding it anxiously to her breast, her face a mask of bewilderment.

Lowering her voice, Bess explained, "You've got the wrong idea. I didn't know your mother was…unwell. And I told Georgina not to do anything until we got your mother's consent—"

"Consent?" Steven let out a snort. "You've seen her! She's away with the fairies, and you took advantage, just like bloody Leon always did!"

"Leon?" Sybil's voice quavered. She clutched at the word. "Is Leon here? Has he come to see me?"

"Oh, that'd be right." Steven ground his jaw. "Always the favourite, wasn't he, Mum? Always the blue-eyed boy, no matter how much stupid, selfish shit he caused!" He turned to glare at Sybil. "Who organised this place for you, Mum? Who manages your money? Who visits every week, even when half the time you can't bloody recognise me?"

She flinched away, whispering to Bess, "What's happening?"

Steven turned his back on her, apparently in dismissal. "I tried, you know," he told Bess, as if to justify himself. "I tried to protect her. When Leon sent that so-called artist in here to steal pictures of her, I sent her packing! And I let her know never to try it again."

"Hey, I don't think Billy Bower realised your mother's condition—"

Not listening, Steven went on, "And I did my best to destroy all my brother's records of this disgraceful 'project'. I wiped his emails, guarded his files…" Steven shook his head. "I know Leon was a selfish little bastard, but even I didn't think he'd go for this. Naked photographs and Alzheimer's jokes? Criminal accusations?"

"You mean the restaurant fire?"

"Of course!" Steven glanced at his mother.

Sybil's expression had closed up; she was still gripping the pillow. Her lips moved again, silently.

Steven waved a hand. "It wasn't her fault. She was already starting to lose her marbles by then. But if the story got out—Jesus, you can imagine what people would say about us? About my family?" His face twisted with revulsion. "I did my best to talk my brother out of it, you know, when I realised what he was up to. I tracked him down at a cocktail party, poncing about with all his fashionable friends, and I tried to have it out with him. And you know what he said?"

Steven leaned in close, forcing Bess to take another step back. "He told me not to worry about it. He said Mum would have enjoyed the scandal, that it was 'what she would have wanted'!" His breath came out in a silent bark, half-laughter, half-fury. "And he told me the arson accusations weren't a problem, because he'd run it past his lawyers!" Steven glanced up, incredulous, as if inviting the heavens to witness this. "And now you come in here, working for that Harper woman, and thinking you can do the same thing? Thinking you can make your fortune by dragging my family's name through the muck?"

He glanced down at the phone in his hand, at the pictures of his mother and her favourite son. "Sick!" he hissed. "You're all sick!" He lifted the phone and flung it at Bess's head.

She ducked. There was a crunch, then a clatter as the phone hit the plaster and skittered across the floor. Bess looked up into Steven's bloodshot eyes, reached out, and slammed the panic button.

She'd hoped that a siren would go screaming through the building. But all she heard was a polite "beep" at some nurse's station far away.

Steven laughed at this effort, and advanced upon her. But before he could lift his hand again, his mother had swooped forward with a burst of speed that amazed Bess and placed herself in between them.

"That's enough out of you!" Her pitch was almost theatrical.

Bess wished she could have met Sybil when she was young.

"I won't have fighting in this house! I've told you before!" Raising herself on tiptoe, she smacked him across the back of the head.

The blow couldn't have hurt more than swatting a mosquito, but it made Steven stagger to a halt. Forgetting Bess, he rounded on his mother. "What is—*wrong* with you?" he spluttered, clutching at the air. "After everything I've done for you!"

Seeing her attacker stopped short by an old lady gave Bess an urge to laugh. Instead, she stepped forward, her fears forgotten, as she demanded, "What else did you do for her, Steven? Besides the nursing home and the visits and wiping your brother's emails?" She stared into his sweating, frustrated face. "Did you try to shut Leon up for good? Did you kill him?"

The room fell so quiet that Bess could hear the clock ticking on the wall. Steven stared at her.

Sybil clawed at his arm. "What's she saying?" She glared at Bess. "She's talking about my Leon, isn't she?"

Bess glanced at Steven. "You haven't told her?"

"Told me what?" Sybil glowered. "She's a rude little piece. Who is she?"

Steven's reply to Bess came from between clenched teeth, "Just shut up, for Christ's sake. You want to make things worse?"

When Bess stared at him, he said, "You've got no idea, all right? There's no point in telling her anything…"

"Telling me what?" Sybil's voice was growing shrill.

Behind her, the door swung open. "Now, Sybil, dear, what's all this kerfuffle?" The nurse was wearing an exasperated smile. "You've gone and pressed your button again. You haven't had another squabble with the chaplain, have you?"

Sybil blinked; the arrival of a new person seemed to have confounded her.

Steven straightened his tie and smoothed down his residual hair, trying, it seemed, to look normal.

"Oh, Mr Powell!" The nurse's smile faltered, before she hitched it up again. "Nice to see you."

From her forced welcome, Bess gathered that Steven was indeed a regular visitor, but probably not a popular one with the staff.

"What brings you here on a weekday?"

"Concern for my mother." The look he shot Bess was pure loathing.

Oblivious, the nurse checked Sybil's pulse and said with forced cheer, "Since you're here, Mr Powell, we've had those photos printed out. They've come up nicely—would you like a copy?"

"No, I—" Steven caught himself. The heat seemed to leave his face. He gave Bess an unpleasant smile, and said, "Actually, nurse, that's a good idea. I'd love to see those photos." She turned to leave, but he caught her elbow, startling her. "No need to trouble yourself looking for the prints, nurse. The ones on your phone will do nicely. My *former* employee here would love to see them."

"Would I?" Bess frowned. What photos was he even talking about?

"Oh, yes. I think they'll be of interest." Steven slid his hands into his pockets and leaned back in a satisfied pose, as the nurse, now frowning in confusion, scrolled through her files.

The nurse handed over her phone.

Bess peered down at the screen. The pictures had been taken in a dining room where the furnishings and paint matched those she'd seen so far in Barton House. There was Sybil Powell, wearing a pink floral dress that hung awkwardly on her narrow frame. Crumpled wrapping paper lay on the table. Steven was sitting beside her, his finger pointed, encouraging her to blow out the candle on a cake. A couple of nursing staff stood around, applauding. Everyone in the picture wore a fixed smile, except Sybil herself, who stared at the photographer with a kind of baffled anger.

Bess glanced up and saw the same look on Sybil's face now. Tears of frustration glinted in the old woman's eyes. What was life like for her? Bess had a horrible suspicion it might feel like being trapped in some never-ending "Gotcha" television show, where strangers leap out to play pranks on you, then roll their eyes when you don't understand.

Looking back at the photo, Bess noticed what Steven must have been talking about. In the corner of the screen was the date the picture was taken.

"But that was the day Leon—" Bess caught herself before she could say "died", remembering Sybil's presence. "The day Leon stopped being my boss," she finished.

"Well spotted." Steven's smirk had grown triumphant. "And if you look at the windows, you'll notice it was dark outside. I'd come over for dinner. Hadn't I, nurse?" He turned to her for confirmation. "I stayed for a while, too."

"Yes, Mr Powell. You had a few…concerns you wanted to raise with us."

Bess let out a breath. Leon had died before ten that night; the police had said so. If Steven had been here at Barton House in the evening, he couldn't have made it back to Port Bannir in time.

"Mum's birthday," Steven said. "Leon couldn't be there, of course. He told me he had a very important meeting to attend, about some new real estate. Pity. He might have had a better night if he'd joined us here." There was a bitter satisfaction in Steven's voice.

Sybil prodded him. "What you are saying about Leon?"

"Nothing, Mum. Just a joke." He grabbed Bess's elbow and steered her away from Sybil, before hissing, "Sorry to disappoint you, you nosy little bint, but you've got it all wrong. I never laid a hand on my parasite of a brother, no matter how much I—"

He glanced at Sybil, who was asking the nurse, "What's he saying?"

Turning back to Bess, Steven added in a whisper, "I did tell her about Leon's death, by the way. I broke it to her as nicely as I could." He shrugged. "What a waste of time that was. Now, when I visit, she just asks about him more than ever! 'When's Leon coming? Where's Leon?'"

Bess twisted away from him. "You're disgusting."

"You're one to talk. Doing that Harper woman's dirty work. Anyway, if she was hoping for more filth to throw at my family, you'll have to go back and tell her the bad news. I didn't kill bloody Leon." Steven was staring at his mother now, a mingled contempt and hunger in his expression. "Since no one here even remembers he's dead, there would have been little satisfaction to be had."

"Tell me, then." Bess longed to get away from here, but she felt the need to ask, "If it wasn't you, who do you think did it?"

Steven snorted. "Listen, I've just lost my job. I've got my brother's will to deal with, astronomical fees on this place, not to mention child maintenance and an ex-wife who wants what's left of my balls—and now my family's reputation is about to get flushed down the toilet. So forgive me if this sounds heartless, but I don't especially care." He tried again to smooth the wrinkles out of his suit jacket. "But here's a tip: think about who stands to gain the most from this fiasco." He glanced meaningfully at his phone, where the flyer for the upcoming exhibit was stored.

"Georgina?" Bess blinked. "Why would she? She's always complaining about what a nuisance those deaths have been."

Steven sniffed. "In the short term, sure. But in the long run, look at what she's gained. Complete control over one of the biggest tourist attractions in the country. A blockbuster new exhibit—let's face it, shows about dead celebrities always sell. And a prime piece of real estate with no more interference from my brother, with all his zany 'concepts' and his do-gooding little schemes."

Steven paused, then added, "And isn't Incursium Estate going to take over that Gale woman's museum?" He raised his eyebrows. "Two birds, one stone."

"I don't buy it." But Bess's voice wavered. "Georgina's a businesswoman. She wouldn't get involved in something like that."

Still, even as she spoke, Bess was struck by a memory: herself at the police station, telling Constable Jacs how Arwyn Ross had been at the Cabinet of Curiosities when Leon died. And Vince Polat lumbering up behind her without making a sound.

Steven shrugged. "Well, maybe you're right. Why would millions of dollars and a God complex make a person capable of killing?" He paused a moment. "She was the one who approached me, you know. Georgina." He grimaced. "She was at that cocktail party, when I tried to have it out with Leon. It was her goon who marched me outside—and demanded my ID!"

Steven shook his head. "That should have told me what I was dealing with. You could have knocked me down with a feather when she called me a week later, offering to get me a spot on the Board. When I told her I didn't know the first thing about art, and that my brother and I didn't get on, she laughed. 'Don't you worry, Steven. I'll hold your hand.'"

He chewed his lip at the memory. "I suppose my brother must have been starting to piss her off even then. Or maybe she just undermines everybody, as a point of principle."

Bess frowned.

"It's how she works; she plays people off against each other," Steven explained. "I suppose I knew I was being used, but I was so desperate to stop that bloody exhibit and to cause Leon a few of the hassles he was always causing me, that I agreed."

He glanced back at Bess and managed a sneer. "Well, you have fun working for Incursium Estate. Be sure to keep Georgina happy, eh? And when she gets sick of you, you'd better pray she lets you down the way she did me." He raised his eyebrows. "Not the way she did my brother."

Bess had no answer to that. But she needed none, for Sybil was walking stiffly towards them.

"What are you doing in here?" she demanded of them both. "Get out of my studio! I can't think with all your bloody noise and whingeing. I just want one hour to myself, to create, all right?"

The nurse stepped in: "I think we should end this visit now…"

"Where's my camera?" Sybil yanked at the nurse's arm. "I told Leon I'd show him how to use it. He always loved it. When I die, it's going to him…"

The nurse hustled Bess and Steven out the door, then ushered Sybil back to her chair and slipped the crossword in front of her

Sybil was saying, "Get them out of here; I never asked for them. And find my red dress and my silver earrings. My Leon's coming to see me soon, and I want to look my best…"

Turning to Bess, Steven said, "You stay the hell away from here. I'll be telling security." Then he stamped off down the corridor.

Bess looked back one last time, and saw Sybil Powell sitting tall, gripping the arms of her chair, and gazing out the window, waiting. Despite her frumpy clothes, she reminded Bess of a queen in exile.

Quietly, Bess closed the door.

Chapter 19

BESS SPENT A MISERABLE TRAIN ride back to Port Bannir thinking of Margaret. She'd hoped—stupidly, perhaps—that Sybil would help her get to the bottom of Leon's death, prove Margaret innocent of that crime, at least. But what had she come home with? Nothing except proof that Leon's death hadn't been a family affair, after all. Plus a vague accusation against Georgina Harper that seemed to be totally baseless. For now.

She thought of Margaret—Margaret, who was always in charge, always in control—locked up behind metal doors, wire, and concrete. Being ordered about, crammed in with other people, unable to decide even the most basic things for herself. Was she thinking of Bess now? Did she trust that Bess was fixing everything, or did she doubt that Bess was capable? Bess groaned and shut her eyes. She wasn't sure which was worse.

As she stepped out at the station, she mulled over what she could do right now, to try to help Margaret.

First, she tried calling the Victoria Development Initiative, but Madeline the receptionist insisted that Ms Harper was in meetings for the foreseeable future. Perhaps Bess could put whatever it was into an email to their inquiries desk?

Bess decided to stake out the company's car park instead.

At five minutes past the hour, the Audi swung into the parking space nearest the door. Bess, peeking around the side of the building, waited for Georgina to get out. Instead, Vince emerged from the front seat and strode into the building. He left the engine running. Through the glass door, Bess saw him speak to the receptionist, who ducked out, apparently to fetch something. Aware of how silly she would look if the car turned out to be empty, Bess decided to risk it. She trotted over to the Audi and knocked hard on the back window.

Nothing happened. Bess raised her fist to knock again, then clumsily whacked her knuckles on the edge of the glass as it slid down.

"Bess!" Georgina sounded amused as Bess clutched her throbbing hand and tried not to swear. "What a nice surprise!" Georgina was dressed in emerald-green today with a single strand of pearls. She finished typing a message into her phone, pressed Send, then glanced back up at Bess. "Thanks for those pictures; they were perfect. Did Steven show you the mock-ups?"

"He...yes, he did," Bess spluttered. "Right before he threw his phone at me! You told me you wouldn't do anything like that until I gave you the word."

"Oh, Bess." Georgina waved that away. "Can't I have a surge of artistic inspiration now and then?" She leaned closer, as if in confidence. "Tell me, how was Steven? Did he burst a blood vessel?"

"Just about." Bess shook her head, incredulous. "He won't give his consent, you know. And his mother can't give hers; she has dementia pretty badly."

Georgina tutted. "Sad. Must be hard on the family. But don't you worry about the consent angle, Bess. Awfully sorry to have sent you on a wild goose chase, but it turns out consent won't be a problem."

She made no effort to get out of the car so Bess was obliged to keep craning uncomfortably through the window, her neck twisted and her bottom sticking out.

"My solicitors tracked down Billy Bower first thing this morning," Georgina continued. "She confirmed the art is mostly her own work, and that the photographs taken by Sybil Powell were purchased officially by the Cabinet of Curiosities months ago. So we've every right to go ahead with the display."

"But..." Bess's eyes widened. "But we're talking about intimate photographs here—family stories..." She lowered her voice. "And criminal allegations."

"Don't you fret about that, Bess; that's what lawyers are for." Georgina's smile hardened. "And mine could eat Steven Powell for breakfast."

"This is…" Bess leaned closer, searching for any sign of guilt in the other woman's features. But Georgina's expression was as smooth as cream. "You can't be serious. We are talking about a vulnerable elderly woman who's lost her memory."

"Well, she won't mind that we're doing this, then, will she?" Georgina glanced down as a new message flashed on her phone.

"That's disgraceful! It's completely unethical."

"It's an art show, Bess, not organ harvesting." Georgina rolled her eyes.

"And you're exploiting Leon's death, too." Bess wondered again about what Steven had said, that Georgina might have found Leon more valuable dead than alive. Looking into Georgina's ice-blue eyes, she couldn't find the nerve to repeat it. She contented herself with declaring, "This isn't right."

"Well, Bess, as your new employer, I'd be happy to arrange some career counselling for you, if you're no longer happy in your role."

How did Georgina manage to sound threatening and coolly bored at the same time?

Partly to dodge that suggestion, Bess demanded, "And how did you find Billy Bower, anyway? I never told you the artist's name."

"No, but when I broke the news about the exhibit to Steven, he started frothing at the mouth about some 'bloody dwarf painter who's really just a vandal' and 'why haven't the police kept her locked up where she belongs?' I figured there couldn't be many women who fit that description, so I had my people do a ring around." Georgina frowned in carefully simulated disapproval. "He's not very *inclusive*, is he? Not very good at keeping secrets, either. Rather a relief to see the back of him, quite honestly." She tapped out another text message.

"I hear you've found us a new CEO."

"Yes, but no clues, I'm afraid, Bess." Georgina shook her finger. "You'll find out at the end of the month, like everyone else."

"You know…" Bess fumbled for the right words. How could you argue with someone who had no shame? "Steven was extremely aggressive, and you effectively sent him after me. I could have been hurt!"

"And yet here you are, whole and healthy." Georgina smiled. "You obviously handled him well."

"No thanks to you!" Bess's fists balled up in frustration.

Georgina glanced away, as if calculating the more lucrative ways she could be spending this time. "Well, Bess, if that's all—"

"No, it is not all. That's not even what I came to ask you about. What about the Maritime Museum? Did you keep your word about that? You said you would hold off meeting with the Heritage Board."

"Hm?" Georgina frowned. "Oh, yes. Well, it turned out there was no need to meet with them after all."

Bess began to relax. So Georgina had kept her word about one thing, at least, and Margaret's beloved museum was safe for now.

Then she jolted forward as Georgina said, "The Heritage Board rang me. Turns out the Board have done an audit of the building, and it's absolutely riddled with safety hazards. Termites, dry rot, concrete cancer— amazing it hasn't come tumbling down already. Clearly Ms Gale has been very negligent." Georgina examined one fingernail. "So once Ms Gale agrees to sell—and really, at this stage, she can hardly afford to refuse—the Heritage Board will need to find a company that can make the necessary refurbishments."

"Really?" Bess blurted. "And would this company happen to be yours, by any chance? And will the 'refurbishments' involve turning the building into a hotel?"

"Now, really, Bess." Georgina gave a tolerant smile.

"Margaret would never neglect anything in that museum." Bess's face grew hot with anger. "The building looked fine to me. And she never mentioned a safety audit."

"Visiting her in prison, are you?" Georgina leaned back in her leather seat. "I'd keep that to yourself if I were you."

"Did you bribe someone to declare that building unsafe?"

"Bess, this is bordering on offensive…"

"What about Margaret?" Bess was almost shouting. "This is totally unfair on her!" She gasped as someone seized her arm and flung her backwards, sending her staggering.

Vince Polat wiped his huge hand on his trousers, as if Bess's skin had been dirty.

She steadied herself, clutching at the painful spots on her arm left by his grip, her heart thudding with shock.

He curled his lip. "Don't touch my paintwork."

Wrenching open the door, Vince squeezed his vast body into the front seat and put the car into gear.

Georgina craned over the window's edge to catch Bess's eye. "Your concern for Margaret Gale does you credit, Bess. But I think she might have other things on her mind just now than her pointless old wreck of a museum."

The window glided up again. The car pulled away.

Bess stared after it, wondering if she had been speaking with a killer.

~

The Cabinet of Curiosities was open again, but it wasn't the same. The crowds stayed away; the staff crept around, avoiding each other's gaze. In his office, Steven Powell was packing up his things.

As she led a small group of visitors through a lacklustre tour, Bess glanced around at the displays and thought about the man who'd brought all this together. Leon had been a fun boss who'd taught her a lot, but she couldn't feel easy about his decision to exhibit his mother's past when she was in no state to agree.

"Excuse me?" A man in a faded Marvel T-shirt pointed his phone towards the staff corridor and took a photo. "Is that where the murder happened?"

Bess replied with her frostiest "No comment".

That didn't stop him snapping a picture of her, too, and whispering to his neighbour, "That's the one from the video…"

Trudging back to her office, Bess realised Georgina had been right about one thing: they needed something fresh in here to take minds off all these ugly events.

"Nice of you to stop by." Irene glanced up from her desk. "You've taken so much time off lately that I wasn't sure if you were still working here."

"For now." Bess sighed. "Oh. I was given something to pass on to you." She unzipped her bag, drew out the padded envelope, and handed it to Irene.

Irene wriggled her reading glasses into place and squinted at it. "What's this?" She tore it open, peered inside, and froze. Glowering at Bess, she demanded, "Who gave you this?"

"Long story, but it came from Hermione Morris."

Irene wrenched her glasses off her face and sent them clattering across the desk. She thrust her chair out, got up, and pushed it away so hard it nearly toppled over. Then she stormed across the room, pausing only to dump the envelope in the rubbish bin on the way out.

"Hey, I didn't mean to upset you." Bess hurried after her.

Irene was in the staff kitchen now, unloading the dishwasher with a slamming of plates and jangling of glassware. Without looking up, she said to Bess, "I suppose she blabbed the whole story to you, did she?" Irene shut the cutlery drawer so hard its contents rattled. "Our little family secret. My mother was a teenage tart!"

Bess edged nearer. "You know she's dying?"

Irene seized a clean mug and began scouring it with a tea towel. "I heard. Not interested."

"Look." Bess tried to catch Irene's eye, but Irene's attention was focused on the mug. She was rubbing it hard enough to take the pattern off. "I know her behaviour here was…invasive. Pushy." Bess cleared her throat. "But it sounds like she's had a hard life, and…and once she's gone, you'll have lost your chance. You'll never get to speak to her again."

"Good!" Irene shoved the mug into the cupboard with such force that several items toppled over. Cursing under her breath, Irene reached in to straighten them. "When I needed that woman, she let me down." Irene's voice echoed inside the cupboard. "Some things, you don't forgive or forget."

Irene closed the cupboard door with forced calm, then turned to face Bess. "Now, mind your own business and sort out your own problems. From what people are saying, it sounds like you've got plenty." She left before Bess could think of a reply. From down the hall, the bathroom door slammed.

Bess sidled back to the office and lifted the envelope out of the bin. She slipped her hand inside, and her fingers closed around some kind of sturdy plastic loop.

It was a hospital wristband. A very small one.

The print on the tag had faded over what must have been many years. She held it up to the light, and read the name.

"Faith Morris."

Bess paused, looking at it for a while. Then she placed the baby's name bracelet gently on Irene's desk, before heading back to the gallery.

⁓

Bess stopped by the supermarket after work to buy milk, bread, and feed for the chickens. She was strapping it into the panniers on her bike when she heard a whistle from across the car park. The three girls who'd accosted her in the supermarket were leaning against a distant wall, sharing a cigarette.

"Late-night shopping?" Bess asked.

"Youth club," said one, jerking her chin towards the wall, freshly decorated with graffiti designs.

Through an open door, Bess could see Paul Baker reasoning with a bunch of yelping twelve-year-olds: "Now, you guys remember the list of rules we all agreed on? It's pinned up there. Number one: we all treat each other with respect here. No matter which footy team someone supports, or how 'totally gaybo' you think they are…"

"Looks welcoming," Bess said.

"It's all right," said the swarthy girl. "My name's Zan, by the way. How was your trip to Melbourne?"

"How did you know…?"

"You said hello to some friends on Messenger, and you liked a café in the city." Zan retrieved the cigarette from her friend with the piercings, and took a quick drag. "Seriously, you should check your privacy settings."

"Thanks. That's…very creepy of you."

"What about the trip, though?" Zan glanced around, checking no one was in earshot. When her friend snatched the cigarette back, she added, "This is Tammy, and you know Squid."

Squid glanced up from her phone for a microsecond. "Salutations."

"Hello." A cold breeze stirred Bess's clothing; the sun was sinking. If she didn't head home soon, she would be riding on potholed roads after dark. Hurriedly, she said, "The trip was pretty frustrating, actually. There was a man I'd been wondering about, but I discovered there was no way he could have killed Leon."

"That blows." Zan frowned. "Hey, this man—was it Vince the Golum?"

"How did you know about Vince?" Bess decided there wasn't time for that. "No, it was someone else. But why do you ask?"

"Well, he looks a bit murder-y," was Zan's assessment. She took back the cigarette, pinched the filter long enough for one final drag, before grinding it out beneath her Doc Marten. "And he hangs around that Maritime Museum, doesn't he?" When Bess looked at her in confusion, Zan said, "Here." She whipped out her phone, retrieved an image, and held it up to Bess's face.

Bess took in the unmistakeable sight of Vince Polat in a car park, deep in conversation with Margaret's nervous employee, Kelly. "He had someone on the inside?"

"It's a boat museum." The girl with the piercings rolled her eyes. "Not the Mafia."

"Ships," Squid said. "Not boats."

"Same difference."

"It's not."

"Bullshit."

"No one travels to Gallifrey in a spaceboat, do they?"

"You can't travel to Gallifrey; it was destroyed in the Time Wars, dickhead."

"No, it wasn't—"

"Will you two *shut up*?" Bess's voice rang out.

The girls blinked. Behind them, on the basketball court, a few kids looked over.

But Bess was busy staring at the photo. The photo showed Vince had a means of getting items out of, and into, the Maritime Museum. Suddenly Steven's accusations against Incursium Estate didn't seem so wild after all.

⁓

The handset slid around in Margaret's grasp, greasy from the palms of the dozen women who'd used the phone ahead of her. She grimaced; nothing felt clean in here. The guard at the desk was flicking through a newspaper. Margaret didn't want to talk to Bess here, like this, but she couldn't stand the silence either. She closed her left ear with one finger, blocking out the sounds of this place, and squeezed her eyes shut.

"Bess. How are you?"

"Fine." She sounded stilted—was someone else there? "What have you been up to?"

"Oh, you know. Training for the marathon. Visiting gourmet restaurants. Composing a light opera. You?"

"Not much." Bess paused. "Oh, but I did go to Melbourne and found that Steven Powell isn't our killer. Unfortunately."

"Mr Powell the Lesser?" Margaret sniffed. "I'm not here to talk about him."

Silence fell at the other end of the line. Then Bess asked, "What are you here to talk about?"

Margaret faltered. She held her breath, listening hard, and fancied she could hear Bess's own breathing down the line. Her eyes closed, she pictured the rise and fall of Bess's breasts, the faint flutter of her nostrils, the parting of her lips. Was that what she had called for?

Before she could begin to put this longing into words, Margaret was startled by a familiar voice somewhere behind Bess: "Give it here. I've got stuff to tell her too, you know."

"*Zan?*" Margaret's eyes popped open. She could hear the sounds of squabbling in the distance—"Excuse me, that is my phone and I was still talking!"

"You were being boring, and this phone's a museum piece. Must be four years old."

"What is going on there?" Margaret called down the line. Then she ground her teeth in frustration when Zan's voice came through loud and clear; evidently Bess had lost her struggle.

"So, I told your Bess we should talk," Zan said.

That sounded impertinent. Margaret almost blurted, "She's not my Bess"—but she didn't. Although she scarcely liked to admit it, there was something secretly appealing about the phrase.

Zan went on, "You two were so busy being mushy that you didn't even get to the interesting bit: your Bess reckons it could have been Georgina Harper's mob who set you up. You remember how we busted Kelly hanging out with Vince? And now the Heritage Board is getting ready to hand your museum over to those developers, soon as you agree to sell it. To cover your legal fees, I guess."

"I heard." A headache pulsed behind Margaret's right eye. Last night, she'd woken up every hour, fears, frustrations, and questions galloping madly through her head. "But you're saying Incursium Estate did all this? Just to get hold of a building?" Margaret shut her eyes tighter, pressing her fist to her forehead until patches of light drifted through the blackness. "I don't know, Zan. It's…possible, I suppose."

Margaret shook her head, trying to focus. There were two other women queuing behind her, and she could hear mutters of "Hurry up" and "People are waiting here."

Remembering the tasks she had given Zan, she said, "My museum's security tapes. Did you find anything?"

"There were zillions of hours to get through, M." Zan yawned. "The broken door didn't tell us much; the angle and quality of the footage was shit. Your door got smashed by someone in a black hoodie who kept their head down; that's about all I can tell you. And I've not yet seen anyone out of the ordinary going into your office to hide that scarf."

"Marvellous." Margaret's shoulders dropped.

"But—"

"But what?" Margaret gritted her teeth. Did Zan have to enjoy this so much?

"But there's something interesting about the footage from the main gallery," said Zan. "From that angle of the camera, you can see the door that leads to the staff corridor, where your archival stuff is stored. That was where that knife came from originally, yeah? Before it was used to kill Leon?"

"Yes."

"Well, there's a point in the footage where it looks like the camera shuts down. Just for six minutes, then it starts up again. No signs of disturbance in the gallery itself. Could be a glitch in the system, but—"

"Enough time for someone with a security card to let themselves in and grab that knife." Margaret nodded.

The woman behind her yanked at her elbow, whining, "Hey, I've got things to do, you know…"

Margaret swung around, drawing herself up to her full height, shooting a demonic black gaze as she thundered "Like what!"

The woman drew back, her mouth opening and shutting in silence.

Margaret turned back to the phone. "Zan. When did this happen?"

"Six-twenty p.m. After hours."

"The date, Zan."

"Oh." There was a pause.

Margaret's jaw clenched; she prayed the call would not cut out.

"Wednesday, seventeenth."

Bess's voice cut into the background, prompting Zan, "Ask if we can check the roster. Was Kelly on duty that night?"

But before Zan could relay this, Margaret was already replying slowly, "Last thing on Wednesday? No…No, that's Kenneth's shift."

There was a click and a dial tone; her time was up. No more updates from Zan today—and no more talking with Bess. Why hadn't Margaret said more, earlier, when she had had the chance? She looked down at the grimy handset and fought back frustrated tears.

⌒〜◌

A breeze gusted through the darkened car park out the back of the supermarket. It lifted the piles of dead leaves, litter, and plastic bags, swirled them through the air, then dumped them again. Most customers and staff had gone home hours ago. A sour smell drifted from the rubbish bins. Kenneth shivered in his cheap windcheater as he heaved a stack of trolleys into the bay. Another ten minutes and his shift would be done.

"Hello, Kenneth."

"Jesus!" The voice had come from the shadows deep inside the trolley bay. He saw the neon dot of a cigarette glowing in the darkness. Slowly, the intruder stepped forward. "What do you want?"

It was Squid, one of those weird girls who used to go to his school; the one who looked like a puffer fish in glasses.

She exhaled, sending a stream of acrid smoke straight up his nose. "We have business to discuss."

"What the fuck…?" He heard footsteps behind him and spun around. Squid's two friends had appeared from out of the alley, along with that red-headed woman who kept visiting the Maritime Museum.

The woman twiddled her fingers in a wave, and said, "Sorry to startle you, Kenneth. We wanted to speak to you about a sensitive topic, so we thought it would be more ethical to meet you somewhere quiet…"

"Bullshit—you said I could do the intro!" Squid brushed her out of the way. Then she peered at him through her enormous glasses and struck another pose with the cigarette. "Kenneth," she intoned. "We know what you've done."

⌒～⌒

To Bess's surprise, Squid's performance seemed to be having an impact. Instead of laughing or walking away, Kenneth stood rooted to the spot. His fingers clamped around the trolley handle, his knuckles white.

Keeping her voice low, Bess said, "Look, we understand your situation. Your mum's not well, right? She wants to sell her house to Incursium Estate, and send your little brother to a better school."

"So?" Kenneth tried to shrug, but his shoulders looked painfully tight.

"So, it must have been very upsetting when you found out one stroppy owner was getting in the way, holding up the sale of the whole street." Bess stepped closer. "And how much worse was it when that person turned out to be Ms Gale—your cranky boss, who was always snapping at you and complaining about your work." Bess shrugged. "I'm guessing it didn't take much persuading for you to turn against her. Did it, Kenneth?"

"Dunno what you mean." Under the trolley bay's cheap light fitting, his face looked deathly pale.

Squid stepped forward, flicking ash across his shoes.

"We have the security footage, Kenneth."

"Bullshit—you do not!" He bit his lip too late.

Squid gave a smirk of victory. "So, you do know what we're talking about, then."

"Nup." Kenneth's jaw jutted out. "Anyway, I don't care. That Incursium Estate bought our house yesterday. Mum's got the cheque and everything—she posted a selfie with it! So you can't stop us getting out of here!"

Bess looked at him closely. "That's important to you, isn't it, Kenneth?"

"Yeah!" Kenneth's voice had grown defiant. "You've seen our place; Mum can barely get around it any more. And Nathan deserves a chance. He's smarter than me; he'll finish school and go to Melbourne or Adelaide. He won't get stuck out here, begging for shitty jobs like this." Kenneth scowled and shoved the row of trolleys so they slammed into the wall, the crash of metal echoing around the car park.

"You love your family, we know that," Bess said. "But we're talking about being party to a serious crime. You could go to prison…"

"For a few broken windows!" Kenneth spluttered. "You're talking out your arse!" But he hesitated. "Listen, please don't tell. Mum would freak out if I had to go to court."

Tammy punched Zan on the arm, muttering, "The fuck's he on about…?"

But the words "broken windows" rang a bell for Bess. She stepped forward. "The vandalism." She pointed at Kenneth. "All those properties Incursium Estate was trying to buy—the ones that had their mail stolen, their bins torched, water damage. And there was the door to Margaret's museum…" Kenneth's eyes slid back and forth as Bess went on. "Scaring people, making it uncomfortable for them to keep living there. Giving Georgina Harper and her friends justification for saying we needed a war on crime in Port Bannir, and that the solution was a posh gated community—"

"Hey, I didn't hurt anyone! I always checked no one was around first…" Kenneth bounced from one sneakered foot to the other. "It wasn't a big deal."

"How did you get the idea to do all this?" Bess asked.

"Piss off. I'm not talking to you." He began to leave.

Zan and Tammy stepped in front of him. "You want us to tell your Mum?"

"Fuck's sake!" Kenneth ran a hand over his stringy hair. "It was nothing, all right? Just this bloke who came around our street. I heard him talking with our neighbour, Mr Santos. He said he was a real estate agent." Kenneth chewed the inside of his cheek. "I'm not sure he was, but those people from Port Bannir Real Estate are always really friendly, aren't they? And they drive those little cars. But this bloke's car was big, and he didn't seem all that friendly." Kenneth shook his head. "Anyways, Mr Santos told him to bugger off, and I said to Mr Santos that he should think about selling, that my mum was going to. And after Mr Santos had gone inside, that agent bloke pulled me aside and had a word with me. About how I could…you know. Help things along."

Bess and Zan exchanged looks. Zan held up her phone, with the picture of Vince Polat.

"Was this the agent? A man called Vince?"

"Yeah." Kenneth added hurriedly, "But I'm not telling the cops he made me break those windows. No way."

"And was Kelly in on this?" Bess prompted, recalling those pictures of Margaret's other employee in conversation with Georgina Harper's brute.

Kenneth blinked. "Don't think so. She doesn't talk to me much."

"Hm." Bess let that go for now. "And this real estate agent who encouraged you to make life difficult for your neighbours…did he also get you to steal something from your workplace?"

"Huh?" Kenneth glanced back towards the supermarket, apparently bewildered. "Nup, I haven't nicked stuff from here since I was a kid—"

"Not here—the museum!"

"Dunno what you mean."

"The knife, Kenneth." This was Squid's big moment. Her voice was a stage whisper; her eyes, behind their telescopic lenses, were enormous. "We know you took it."

"What are you talking about?" Kenneth's lips were quivering. "You've lost me."

Bess said, "We're talking about the knife that was used to kill Leon Powell. After he'd started to become a nuisance and the people behind Incursium Estate decided he might make them more money if he was dead."

Kenneth stared at her, shaking his head.

Bess pushed on: "The same knife that was used to frame Margaret Gale for murder, and get her out of that museum building for good."

"This is crazy!" Kenneth's voice cracked. "I don't know what the fuck you're talking about. I just broke some windows."

"Kenneth, the weapon was stolen from the museum by someone with access to the security system, someone working your shift after hours—"

"Someone—" Squid leaped in with relish "—who then plunged that knife through the victim's torso, leaving a blood-spatter pattern that clearly showed—"

"Squid!" Bess grimaced.

But Kenneth was already blurting, "Nah, that wasn't me! It was a different—"

"A different what?" Bess caught her breath. She leaned in.

Kenneth shook his head. "Nothing. Piss off."

"Clamming up now won't help you, Kenneth."

"Yeah," said Squid. "We've got the blood-spatter analysis."

"Squid, please stop talking." Bess focused on the cornered young man in front of her. "But we do have your admission of the vandalism and proof that you interfered with the museum's security cameras."

"It was a different knife, all right?" Kenneth kicked the trolleys. "Ms Gale killed that poor guy with a knife from our whaling display, Kelly told me! The knife I took came from storage. It wasn't the same one." Kenneth's hands shook. "It wasn't."

"Kenneth, Margaret took the murder weapon from the crime scene, and she put it in the display to hide it. It was the same knife you stole."

Under his threadbare windcheater, Kenneth's chest was rising and falling hard. He managed a breathless "Bullshit", but it came out terrified. "Look," he tried, "it wasn't like that. He thought our old weapons were cool, he said so. He just wanted to look at one of them up close, show it to a mate of his. That was all!"

"Who wanted to look at the knife, Kenneth?" Bess gestured to Zan, who held up the picture of Vince again. "Was it this guy?"

Kenneth's eyes were like saucers as he nodded.

Inside Zan's caravan, the temperature was only a degree or two warmer than outdoors. Bess kept her coat on. From outside, she could hear the wind whistling and Black Shuck baying at a possum.

"You three are really young," Bess said. "So I can't drag you into anything. But I'm not letting Margaret get framed for this."

"We're up for a bit of action," Zan said.

"And we want our money from your Margaret," Tammy added.

"Well, then." Bess swallowed. Hearing Margaret described that way was nerve-wracking. What would Margaret have said if she'd heard? Would she be startled, offended? Should Bess deny Margaret was "hers"? She shook herself, trying to focus. "We're going to set a trap for Vince and Georgina. We're going to blow their whole business out of the water."

Squid munched on a Caramello Koala. "What could possibly go wrong?"

Chapter 20

BESS SAT IN THE BACK corner of McKenzie's, watching as the café emptied out. She tried to focus on her breathing, but her anxious mind skittered away.

The afterschool rush was over and the sun was sinking. Kylie was wiping down the abandoned tables and shooting meaningful looks at Bess, the last customer, who sat hugging her cooling coffee. She'd ordered a decaf; she was tense enough already.

Was she taking too great a risk here? If Georgina Harper had ordered the death of someone as wealthy and highly regarded as Leon, surely she would not hesitate to do the same to a nonentity like Bess? And this plan had more holes in it than Bess's favourite bed socks.

Still, she had to try. Leon may not have been perfect, and Arwyn might have been a difficult person, but their murders should not go unsolved. And Margaret... Bess looked down into her coffee, at her own watery, distorted reflection. Margaret had been maligned and blamed for most of her life, just for being strange and "not nice". Bess knew what it was like to be falsely accused. She could not let it continue.

Shutting her eyes, Bess thought of Margaret's low, melodic voice, her sarcastic jibes, the pads of her fingers like white petals brushing between Bess's thighs. Was she thinking of Bess now? Was she counting on her?

Again she glanced at the doorway, but the plastic ribbons hung limp and undisturbed. Was anyone coming? She could feel Kylie glaring at her, so she raised her tepid coffee and took a tiny sip. She and the Hags had felt quite clever as they'd concocted this plan. Had they been fooling themselves?

"You'll need two things," Zan had said at their planning meeting in the Midnight Hags' caravan.

The girls had told Bess to call them that; she found it unsettlingly dark, but tried to respect their wishes. Squid and Tammy were crunching Twisties. Black Shuck was lying across Bess's feet, breathing loudly.

"Item one," Zan said. "Clear photographic evidence that Vince Polat put that envelope of cash in Squid's letterbox. Caught on a carefully concealed security camera in the roof of Squid's house." She handed over a grainy print that showed a man who looked very much like Vince, envelope in hand, half hidden by some shrubbery.

"You never said you caught him on camera!" Bess's eyes widened.

Tammy choked on a Twistie.

"Oh, Bess. Keep up." Zan sighed. "What do you think we've been doing today?" She eyed the printout critically. "It's not a great job, but it's passable."

"It's fake?" Bess took off her glasses for a closer look.

"Course. As if anyone would bother putting in security cameras at that hole where Squid lives." Zan paused. "No offence."

"None taken," came Squid's reply through a spray of Twistie crumbs.

"Well, it looks good," Bess said.

"Yeah," Tammy said, "and we're counting on that meathead Vince not knowing any more about technology than you do."

"You tell him we've got these, and others, saved on a hard drive," Zan told Bess. "He hands over ten grand, you'll hand over the files for him to destroy."

"But that's blackmail!"

"Fake blackmail. We're not going to *keep* the money."

"Well," Tammy began. "There could be a finder's fee—"

Zan silenced her with a look.

"I'm not sure how the police or the courts would react to this." Bess frowned. "And I'd feel disgusting, demanding money for covering up a murder. Even if it's just an act."

"Remind me again why we're mentoring this chick?" Tammy asked Zan.

Squid patted Bess's arm and said solemnly, "I understand; espionage is hell. Trusting no one. Betraying your original self. Burrowing deep under cover until your cover *becomes* your new reality—"

"Fuck's sake." Tammy's voice echoed inside her Coke can. "Let me talk to Vince."

"Shut up, both of you." Zan turned to Bess. "Listen, we're trying to catch Vince on tape admitting to the murders, okay? We reckon he's more likely to do that if he thinks you're a dodgy character yourself, not some crusader for justice. You need to ask for an amount that's big for a nobody like you—no offence—but small for people like him and Georgina. That way, hopefully, they'll take you seriously but not too seriously. They might decide it's easier to pay you off, rather than kill you like they did to Arwyn."

Bess chewed that over. "You really think they'd choose a non-violent solution?"

"Oh no," Tammy said. "They're going to kill you, princess." She twirled the steel tunnel in her left earlobe. "But this way, they might tell you stuff first."

"Which," Zan said, "is where our second item comes in."

She unlocked a drawer and reached inside, ignoring Bess, who was saying, "Sorry, could we get back to the part about them killing me...?"

"This," Zan said, "is something we've modified ourselves. We're pretty pleased with it." She held up a small item, the size of a watch face. "It's a stealth video camera. Records crystal-clear video and audio from right across the room, with five hours' battery life. And it looks awesome, right?"

Bess took it from her. It appeared to be some kind of lapel pin, in the shape of a grimacing skull decorated with crucifixes, spider webs and blooming black flowers. "What the heck is this?"

"It's a brooch," said Tammy. "Inspired by the Day of the Dead in Mexico, when all the souls come back to earth to visit their families."

"It's horrible."

"I made it."

"It's very nice." Bess coughed. "I'm just not sure it looks like something I would wear. I try to choose clothes that are mood-lifting and life-affirming—"

"Look, Vince isn't going to be an expert on ladies' fashions, is he?" Zan huffed. "Just find a dress that matches and pin it on. Then get him to admit it's him in the picture leaving that money for Squid, and tell him you're about to lose your job and you need the cash to get out of town. Try asking him why he did it, or why he let Margaret take the fall. Stuff like that. You're supposed to be good at getting along with people." She sounded dubious about that last point.

"Then what? I leave the café and he runs me over in his car?"

"No. You sneak out through the back door, where we'll be waiting." Zan beckoned her over, opened the caravan door a crack, and pointed outside.

"What am I looking at?"

"Our getaway vehicle!" It was a mustard-brown station wagon older than Bess, with no numberplates and a generous coating of rust. It crouched in Zan's yard, half-camouflaged by the weeds.

"It's my dad's," Zan said. "But he's not bothered about me driving it."

"Maybe because it's got no tyres." Bess frowned.

"And cos your dad's in Dubbo with his new family," Tammy added.

Zan waved those points away. "Wilko said he'd fix it up tomorrow. Don't worry about a thing." She gave Bess a morale-boosting punch on the shoulder. "Second you get out of that café, we'll be waiting to whisk you away to safety."

"None of you look old enough to have a licence." Bess chewed her lip. "I've got a few concerns about this plan—"

"Look, we've got Kenneth on the ropes, haven't we?" Zan prodded her. "A bit more pressure, and he'll tell the cops what he knows. All you need to do is get Vince to slip up a little. And we've got to do it fast, before they can start planting any more evidence against Margaret. Come on, Bess. Have a bit of courage."

Tammy lowered her Coke can and said, "Or do you want to spend your whole life at that gallery, doing fancy shit that doesn't mean anything?"

Bess was silent for a moment. She thought of Margaret, sitting in a cell, away from everything she loved. And she thought of Angela. "All right."

From the corner of her eye, she saw Squid punch the air.

Zan said, "Great. We'll get onto Kenneth, tell him you want a word with his boss."

"Show him the photo?" Squid suggested.

"Show it, but don't let him keep it," Zan said. "We don't want them getting a good look."

"*Wait.*" Bess rapped the table. "Before you do any of that, we're going to put all this stuff in an email and set it up to send to Constable Jacs the day after I meet Vince. In case all four of us go missing." She grimaced. "And if things go wrong between me and Vince, you three have to get out of town, okay? Lie low until after Margaret is convicted." She hated saying those words. "Don't let anyone know where you are. All right?"

"We can do that." Tammy sounded bored. "Chill. It's not like Vince'll do anything my stepdad hasn't."

Bess wanted to offer some supportive response to that, but she couldn't think of any. Instead she said, "You'll have to excuse me. I've got to call my colleague Christos and ask him to swing by my place the day after all of this."

"Why?"

Bess caught her breath. "Because if I don't come home, someone will have to take the chickens."

⁓

Now Bess shifted in her café seat and checked her watch again, feeling stupid. The camera pin was in place and recording, the incriminating photos lay on the chair beside her—and for what? There wasn't a soul in the street outside, and Kylie had begun mopping the floor.

She had thought there was a chance this might work. True to their word, the Hags had grabbed Kenneth again and reminded him of how he'd stolen the murder weapon for Vince. They'd shown him the photo and demanded he set up a meeting with Vince that very afternoon. Resentfully, fearfully, he had agreed to make the call. But Bess had been sitting here for a full hour and Leon's killer was nowhere to be seen.

Doubt and embarrassment gnawed at her stomach. Had Georgina ordered Vince not to respond? Had Vince simply laughed at Kenneth, with his story of a group of teenage girls and a bad photo? Now that Bess thought about it, it did sound pretty pitiful. Or had Kenneth lost his nerve and decided never to make the call?

She looked down into the dregs of her coffee. How she had wanted to help Margaret. To find out if the two of them might have a future. And to save the day, this time.

"Anything else I can get you, Bess?" Kylie's voice was loud, politely exasperated.

Bess heaved a sigh. "No." She pushed her chair back. "No, it looks like I'm done here."

⌒〜⌒

The horn of Zan's car sounded like the croak of a dying mastodon. Bess hurried over.

"Took you long enough!" Tammy kicked the back of her seat.

"Thanks for your patience," Bess snapped. "It didn't work. He never showed."

"Aw, yeah, we know." Zan pumped the accelerator until the engine wheezed into life, and steered their way out of the alley.

"What do you mean, you know?"

"Facebook." Tammy passed her phone forward. "We've been following the Victoria Development Initiative." A photograph showed Georgina Harper beaming as she snipped a red ribbon at some brand new shopping complex. Standing off to the right, looking pleased with his new suit and earpiece, was Vince. The caption showed it was taken two hours ago, in Sydney.

"Sydney?" Bess's voice came out in a groan.

"Must have flown up this morning," Squid said. "Hey, do you think she's got one of those chartered planes?"

"So, they're nowhere near Port Bannir." Bess almost threw the phone back to Tammy.

"'Fraid not." Zan sighed. "Tammy took a quick walk past their office here; it's all locked up. Looks like Kenneth lied to us."

"Or Vince didn't take him seriously." Bess slumped back in her car seat and felt three separate springs poke her in the back. "Why didn't you come in and tell me?"

In the rear-view mirror, she saw Squid frown in disapproval. "We couldn't break your cover."

"This is…" Bess shut her eyes in defeat. "This is pointless."

"What do we do now?"

"I don't know, all right, Zan?" Bess's voice burst out loud and angry. She wanted to think positive, but what the hell was positive about any

253

of this? "I'm sorry. If your car can survive the distance, would you mind dropping me home?"

She supposed she should offer to drive, rather than leave it to an unlicenced teenager, but this didn't feel like the time to start confronting her old nightmares. Not when she'd just failed so dismally again.

Leaning back in the seat, she closed her eyes. She felt the car jerking as Zan changed gear, then felt the smooth roads of the town give way to hills and gravel. She didn't open her eyes again until they jolted to a stop outside her gate.

"Thanks." Bess clambered out. "I'll call you tomorrow, okay? We'll think of something." All she could think of now was bed. With a screech and a smell of burning rubber, the car took off again and vanished over the darkening horizon, Zan tooting one last farewell.

As Bess trudged up the drive, the shadows were lengthening. Moulting pines flanked the entrance to the property, partially obscuring the view beyond. Her feet crunched through their aromatic needles, through dried grass and dead leaves. Somewhere out of sight, a farm dog barked.

In the distance, her tiny house looked strange. Alien. Its cheerful colours showed up garish, half hidden by the murky shapes of the washing line and the trees. Like a gingerbread house in a forest, she thought. A shadow moved, separating itself from the other shapes there.

Someone was waiting for her.

Chapter 21

Bᴇss's ꜰᴏᴏᴛsᴛᴇᴘs sʟᴏᴡᴇᴅ. Aʟʟ sʜᴇ could see was a tall human shape, half hidden by the sheets that flapped on the clothesline.

The evening breeze had whipped up, trailing cold fingertips across her cheeks, her bare legs. She glanced behind her towards the road, but no headlights or engines disturbed the evening calm. The Hags were long gone.

Should she stop? Back away? She thought of facing Vince alone, out here, and her hands shook with alarm. Surely he was still in Sydney with Georgina, but that didn't quell her unease. She had locked up her bike inside the little shed near the front gate, too tired to haul it all the way up the track. Could she get back to it in time, leap aboard, pedal all the way back to the safety of the town?

Her stomach tightened. Suppose she could do all those things—what would she miss finding out? Then she remembered how Margaret had turned up here that night, unannounced, unguarded. And although it must be impossible, her heart leapt at the thought: the thought of Margaret miraculously freed, hurrying here to tell her the good news...

"Bess Campbell, isn't it?"

She froze. Not Margaret's voice. Not Vince's, either.

"Sorry to startle you." The figure stepped forward, raised a friendly hand. It drew closer and she recognised the mild voice, the lanky, slouching walk, the worn jeans, muddy boots and woolly jumper. Reassuringly scruffy clothes, Bess thought. Trustworthy, somehow, in their lack of style.

Paul Baker explained, "My car broke down up the road. Bloody thing. And I've got a dozen punnets of ice-cream for Friday-night youth club melting in the boot." His lined face twitched into a smile. "Thought I'd see if anyone was around to lend me a phone; mine's dead."

While he was speaking, he'd ambled nearer. Bess was caught between the urge to step backwards and the fear that this would be impossibly rude. After all, what had Paul done wrong? Today's business had nothing to do with him. She reached into her bag and pulled out her phone.

"The reception's pretty bad here. You might have to walk around a bit."

"Thanks. You're a lifesaver." He glanced down at it. "Security code...?"

Bess shook her head. "I never got around to it."

"Right."

A scratching sound made Bess turn her head. Something was rifling through the long grass, crunching the twigs and crisp leaves. It was Emily, one of the chickens. But Bess had put the chickens in their tiny house before she went out. Their hutch needed repairs and she'd been worried about foxes. Holding still, she let her eyes slide towards the house. The door was ajar.

What was it that made her turn, as subtly as she could, to look behind her again? Inside the field, a hundred metres or so from the gate, there was a thick thatch of lemon myrtle, higher than Bess's head. In the last rays of the sinking sun, she could see that a car had been parked there behind the hedge, invisible from the road.

Bess looked back in time to see Paul Baker slide her phone into his pocket.

"So." That laconic smile again. "How are you liking Port Bannir?"

What the hell? Bess's breathing quickened. What was he doing? As normally as she could, she made herself say, "I love it. Although lately, of course, things have been difficult..."

"Of course." Paul's brow furrowed. "It's not usually like this, though. Normally you couldn't ask for a nicer, more peaceful place."

"Did you grow up here?" Bess's voice came out too high, her throat tight with tension. Keep him talking—had she read that advice in a self-defence article somewhere? She wished to God she could remember the rest of it. What was going on here?

"Born and bred." Paul grinned. "Course, Port Bannir was a rougher place back then. Geez, I got into my share of strife here, when I was growing up! We all did, us young blokes. Suppose that's why I became a youth worker. To give back, you see?"

Bess nodded, automatically. The sunlight was fading fast.

"Some of these kids around here," Paul said, "they've got so much potential. But there's people who would write them off, ruin their whole lives, just because of some stupid mischief they got into when they were in their teens." He puffed out a breath. "Doesn't seem fair, does it?"

"Um…"

"Take Kenneth O'Neill." Paul took a step closer. "I was having a chat to him earlier this evening. All the kids know they can contact me if they need a bit of support. Like today, Kenneth was feeling stressed—he'd told a fib to some other kids, and now those girls are hassling him." Paul gave an innocent shrug. "He wasn't sure what to do, so he came to me. You know Kenneth, don't you, Bess?"

Bess tried to form some answer, but her throat seemed to be full of sand.

Paul said, "Great kid. Heart of gold. Look at how he takes care of his poor mum. But just because he didn't do very well in school, people tagged him as a loser. They've taught him he's lucky to have any job at all." Paul shook his head. "The 'soft bigotry of low expectations.' It's a bloody shame. I've done a lot of work with Kenneth over the years, trying to build his self-esteem.

"Then a few months back, he turned up at youth club with a nasty great cut on his hand, and very adamant that I wasn't to call his mum." Paul gave a knowing grunt. "Well, I'm not a muppet; I knew there'd been houses vandalised, windows broken. I opened his bag, and there's two spray cans sitting right on top! He didn't even have the sense to hide them." Paul let out a rueful chuckle. "They're not criminals, see. They're just boys being boys. Now, I suppose I could have called the cops, turned him in. But what good would that have done? He was just experimenting, testing the boundaries a bit. Expressing himself. So, I fixed up his hand, took the cans off him, and we sat down and had a good talk instead."

"I see." And Bess thought she was beginning to. The wind was gathering force now, shaking the leaves above her and making the hairs stand up on her arms. "Did you ask Kenneth to do something for you? In return for keeping his secret?"

"Funny you should ask that, Bess. I did, as it happens." In the lengthening shadows, she thought she saw Paul smile again. "Youth work is all about building trusting relationships. I told Kenneth about an old mate from school who made a lot of money in the Middle East. He's a bit of a rough diamond, but I thought I might persuade him to kick in a few dollars to pay for an extension to the youth centre. He loves fishing and hunting, so I thought I'd remind him of what a great town this is for outdoor sports." Paul leaned back, hands in his pockets, apparently at ease as he reminisced. "A tranquillity garden—that was what I thought we could build. A place for the kids with autism and anxiety to chill out. Kenneth agreed that was a good idea; he wanted to help. Like I say, he's a nice kid."

"I walked past the youth club the other day," Bess said. "I didn't see any garden being built."

"No. Well, my mate has been a bit slow to get involved after all."

"Did you ask Kenneth to 'borrow' something for you?" Bess asked. "An antique hunting knife? Did you tell him it was a gift to impress your friend?"

Paul's only answer was another chuckle.

Bess's voice came out in a croak as she asked, "What did Leon ever do to you?"

"Leon?" Paul looked surprised by the question. "Not a thing. Lovely bloke. Helped out with our Careers Expo, and always happy to take work-experience kids. Wish we had ten more like him." The clouds across the rising moon drifted apart for a moment, affording Bess a clear glimpse of Paul's face. She saw his smile fade, the friendly wrinkles around his eyes slackening into something smoother, colder. "But when you're in a position of responsibility, sometimes you have to make a tough call. Margaret wouldn't be reasonable." His eyes narrowed, his jaw working against some private frustration. "She wouldn't shut up."

"Margaret..." Bess stared in bewilderment. Then she remembered Margaret's words: "*I assumed that someone had wanted Mr Powell and Ms Ross gone, so they killed them and set me up to take the blame. But I'm starting to wonder if it may have been the other way around...*"

Bess's skin prickled with cold. The muscles in her limbs twitched, primed for flight. "Did you kill Leon so you could set Margaret up for murder?"

"Hey, I didn't feel good about it." Paul's tone was defensive. "Like I say, Leon was a top bloke. But I had to move fast, and it had to be someone people would believe Margaret would kill." He snorted. "My bloody sister-in-law had pissed off plenty of people around here, but it's not quite the same thing, is it? But a rival gallery owner, pushing a new development that was about to shut down her precious Maritime Museum—oh yes, I'd heard who was backing the Incursium project…well, it was perfect."

Paul paused, as if distracted by some old irritation. "I never liked her museum, you know. So old-fashioned and inaccessible. It was like she didn't even *want* young people to visit." He gestured to Bess in an amicable fashion. "Whereas you guys at the Cabinet, you really make an effort to be youth-friendly. It's great."

"Why…?" Bess's heart was drumming, her body tensed for action. But where could she flee to? A possum rattled the tree boughs above her, the sound unnaturally loud in this dark, open space. From the road, she heard a truck sweep by, but it was gone before she could even contemplate running, waving, yelling for help. The driveway had never looked longer.

"Why did you want people to think Margaret was a murderer?"

"Well, it's not a big stretch is it?" Paul asked. "She's a bitter old bitch with no sense of humour, who'd rather die than be nice to anyone." He gave a slight laugh. "Never could understand women like that. Absolute killjoys. It's sort of sad." His tone hardened. "But she'd made threats against me. False accusations. She was trying to ruin my career, my reputation—even have me arrested!" His voice rose, growing incredulous. "Un-bloody-believable. Me!"

"What accusations? What did she threaten you with?" Every muscle in Bess's body was screaming for escape, but now, more than ever, she wanted to hear the truth.

She could no longer see Paul's expression, but his voice, when it came, sounded startled. "She didn't tell you?"

Bess stayed still, unwilling to give anything away, but her silence must have revealed the truth to Paul, and he let out a burst of laughter. "Oh, for Christ's sake, I thought…" He was still chortling, as if the joke was on him. "Jesus, I thought you lezzers told each other everything."

Bess stiffened, wondering how he knew about her.

Seeming to notice her shock, Paul said, "Oh, you can't scratch yourself in this town without someone noticing. Especially since you've been doing all those things for my lovely sister-in-law." A sneering edge had entered his voice. "Defending her to everyone, visiting her in prison, making up alibis for her—"

"I didn't—" Bess swallowed. "What are you talking about?"

"Oh, there are no secrets in this town." Paul paused. "It's a strength of rural communities; we know how to pull together, share information, work as a team. For example, as the town's youth worker, I've always had a very good relationship with the local police."

"Apart from not telling them about vandalism," Bess quipped, her mouth dry.

But Paul wasn't listening. "That's how we do things out here; we're not tied up in procedures and red tape. If we want to find out something, we just pick up the phone and give someone a call."

"Someone at the police station told you I was Margaret's alibi, when Arwyn died?" Bess swallowed. "Was it Jacs?"

"That dyke on the desk?" Paul snorted. "No, she wouldn't tell me the time. Mean as cat sick."

"You don't seem to like our people very much." It was probably a bad idea to provoke him, but Bess said it anyway.

"Hey." Paul sounded quite offended. "I run a highly inclusive youth service, I'll have you know. We were the first place in the region to set up a LGBTIQAP+ youth support program." His tone hardened. "But I'm sick and tired of you miserable bitches interfering in everything!" Composing himself, he went on, "But back to what I was saying. Gary, the sergeant, he's a good bloke. Went to the local high school together, as it happens; I used to be his Scout leader. He knows I only want what's best for this town."

"Gary told you I was Margaret's alibi." Bess stared. "Did he find out who'd been visiting Margaret, too, after she'd been locked up?" A nod from Paul prompted her to ask another question: "Did Gary also give you that security tape of Margaret leaving the crime scene? The one that got leaked to the press?" Paul's silence was answer enough. She whispered "Arwyn Ross. What about her?"

"Wow—there was a crazy one, right?" Paul whistled. "A total nut. I'm surprised Leon put up with her." He shook his shoulders lightly, as if dislodging a fly. "Yeah, that was a balls-up, all right. I'd messaged Leon, asking to meet at his office after the town meeting; I said I wanted to talk about how his Incursium Estate might provide jobs for our unemployed young people. He must have been feeling guilty after everyone at the meeting complained about the Estate, cos he agreed. I came to the back door of the gallery and he let me in. That place after dark—I figured there wouldn't be a soul around for miles. How was I to know there'd be a bunny-boiler hiding in the bushes?" Paul gave another self-deprecating laugh. "Just my luck."

"You strangled her." Bess took a step back.

Paul moved forward, matching her. She could smell him: an ordinary, harmless middle-aged bloke smell, like engine oil. Had Arwyn's last moments gone like this? She felt a sudden, fierce pity for that lost young woman.

"Arwyn wasn't reasonable. Come on, Bess; you met her." Paul's own manner was eminently reasonable, as if eager to reach a common-sense solution here. "She was unstable, and I couldn't be sure what she'd seen. The sergeant told me she'd been at the gallery when Leon died, according to you. And at the funeral, she looked right at me; she seemed to recognise me…"

"She was looking at Deirdre," Bess said. Tension seared along her jaw and down her neck and shoulders. "Was it difficult? Luring Arwyn away?"

Paul sniffed. "Hardly a genius, was she? All it took was a note about Leon on her windscreen. Once I'd got Deirdre settled at home with her medication, it was easy." He sighed. "Seriously, some women take no responsibility for their own safety, do they? But they're the first to complain when something goes wrong! Like I say, very unfortunate, but it couldn't be helped. And since Arwyn was another person Margaret had quarrelled with, I figured…"

"Arwyn's scarf?" Bess prompted. "You planted it in the museum?"

"Eh? No, Deirdre did that for me." He chuckled again, perhaps affectionately. "Poor old thing; she's a sweetheart, really. I gave it to her wrapped up, told her it was a surprise present for Margaret, to hide it somewhere and cheer her up later. Deirdre couldn't have been keener to help, bless her."

"Why—" Bess forced her voice to stay level. "Why did you want Margaret convicted of murder?"

Paul fell silent. Squinting in the moonlight, Bess could see him glancing out across the darkened fields. After a moment, he said, "I was actually pretty offended when Kenneth told me you thought Incursium Estate were behind all this. Of course they weren't; Kenneth just blamed that Vince bloke to get you off his back. Then Kenneth came straight to me about it. He's a loyal kid, and I've always been a good mate to him. I was gobsmacked when he told me your theory about Incursium and Vince. As if some slick outfit from the city would know how to manage things out here."

He laughed in disbelief. "Sure, they've got the cash, but do they have my local expertise and relationships? How would they have known to use Squid McCaffery to get past gallery security, for one thing?" He bounced back and forth on his toes, apparently at ease with the world. "I understand this town in ways that nasty Harper woman never could. I grew up here."

After a pause, Paul went on, "Although, like I say, back in my youth I wasn't always perfect. Back then, it was Deirdre who tried to keep me in line, if you can imagine that! Did you know we were high school sweethearts?" He didn't wait for a reply. "Yeah, they were fun times. Kids had more independence back then. Like one time, in our last year at school, my mate Duncan and I nicked his dad's car and drove all the way to Warrnambool to watch our footy team play the regional final. Everyone knew we were underage, but they let us into the bar anyway."

He chuckled. "Not that I'd condone that sort of thing nowadays, of course. Anyway, there was this other kid there from our school. Jacob." Paul hesitated. Then he went on in the same casual tone, "These days, I make all the young people feel welcome, naturally, but back then we didn't have today's inclusive values. Basically, we thought Jacob was a skinny little drip. At school, we did all the usual stuff: stacks-on at lunchtime, peeing in his schoolbag, locking him in the girls' dunnies... He was meant to be going out with Duncan's sister, Amy, although everyone knew that weird Margaret Gale was lezzing all over Amy. Maybe she had bigger balls than Jacob, eh?" He snorted at his own joke.

"So this particular evening, Duncan and I were sinking a few at the bar, having just watched our team get an absolute flogging. And Duncan was pretty dirty about that. So when he saw Jacob there, I could tell he was thinking about starting a bit of trouble. Deirdre was with us; she started whingeing that she was bored and wanted to go home. Duncan told her to shut it, and Jacob—he and Deirdre used to be friends in primary school or something—turned around and told Duncan off!"

Paul whistled. "Duncan didn't say anything right then. But later we were out in the car park getting ready to leave, and he saw Jacob heading out too—and then it was on! He jumped Jacob, gave him a smack, then we thought it'd be a laugh to chuck him in the boot of the car and take him for a ride." After a pause, he explained, "Of course, it's common for adolescent males to have very limited impulse control. So, we tossed him in. Deirdre wasn't happy, but I guess she didn't want to be left miles away from home, so she got in, and off we went! You should have heard all the thumping and slamming going on in that boot! Kids, you know?"

He seemed to be waiting for Bess to agree. "Well, I remember we stopped for more grog somewhere, then headed for home. Christ, it was a stinking hot night. We had the windows down the whole way. Deirdre was pissing me off by then, snivelling about Jacob, but Duncan wasn't bothered; he was gunning it, whooping, taking the corners like we were in the Formula One. Speed limits were more of a suggestion back in those days. We got to the Gale property—old Malcolm was away, thank Christ—and Deirdre jumped out, really bawling now, and said we had to let poor Jacob go. Duncan and I thought it'd be a bit of a laugh, actually. He started yelling for Margaret to come out and fight Jacob like a man..." Paul's cheerful memory seemed to trail off.

"See, we'd forgotten that Jacob had a problem with diabetes. And what with the heat and the grog and the shortage of air, and I guess not having his medication... well, when we opened the boot and pulled him out, we realised he'd, you know. Expired." Paul cleared his throat—a gruff, embarrassed noise. "Like I say, a total accident. We weren't criminals; we were just boys mucking around. When we saw him lying there, we shat ourselves. I thought Margaret would call the cops on us, but she just told us to get out, which we did. I spent all weekend tanning my jocks, expecting the sergeant to knock on my parents' door any minute...but he never did.

"Margaret kept it quiet; she pretended she'd just found Jacob out there. Well, she wasn't stupid, I guess. If she'd told the truth, Deirdre could have been charged, too. Deirdre had been with us the whole time, and she hadn't stopped us from doing it. It was equally her fault, if you think about it."

Paul rubbed his hands together, as if dusting something off. "And that was that. Jacob's death was put down to a weird accident, which it was, of course. I'm sure it was better for everyone that way. Deirdre and I got married a few years later. Duncan got his medical degree and moved back here, and he and I have been doing our bit for this town ever since."

"Margaret knew you'd killed someone." The words came out slowly. It was too dark to see, but Bess could sense Paul watching her.

"She had the nerve to take me aside on my own wedding day," he said. "Not that anyone wanted her there, but Deirdre insisted. Margaret came strutting back into town all dressed in black, like the bad guy in a Western, and she made it clear she'd rather I was dead in a ditch than married to her sister. She told me she'd respect Deirdre's wishes and keep quiet to protect her, but if anything ever happened to Deirdre, she'd sing like a lark. Even reckoned she'd tracked down a few witnesses, people who'd seen us with Jacob in the bar. Oh, and she added that in case I had any 'ideas', she'd put copies of all the statements in safe deposit boxes, to be sent to the 'appropriate people' in the event of anything happening to her!"

He gave a disbelieving laugh. "Like I was some sort of monster! Instead of an innocent kid who'd nearly had my life ruined by what happened. But that's how her mind works, I guess. Just plain hateful."

Bile was rising in Bess's throat. She forced it down. "Something did happen to Deirdre. She's dying."

Paul's tone, when he replied, was subdued. "Yeah. Poor old thing."

"Duncan is Dr Mather now, isn't he? Deirdre's doctor?" Bess glimpsed a nod from Paul. "Margaret said he was a useless doctor."

"Well, she never has a nice thing to say about anyone, does she? Duncan Mather is actually a very good GP who makes a fine contribution to this town." Paul said nothing more, but something in his tone made Bess take another step back.

"How long have you and Duncan known that Deirdre was dying?"

"Since late last year." Paul sounded irritable now, as if she were nit-picking. "We agreed there was no point in telling her; it would have just upset her, and there's nothing to be done, after all. Then bloody Margaret starts dragging her around to specialists—typical! I'll have you know, I tried to build bridges with that woman over the years. But all she ever did was interfere and try to turn my wife against me. I couldn't trust her to be reasonable after Deirdre had, well…"

"Died?" Bess blurted. "I think you kept Deirdre's illness a secret because you were making plans. Getting ready to make Margaret look so vicious and crazy that no one would believe her if she tried to expose you."

"She *is* vicious and crazy!" Paul snapped. "She's done her damnedest to poison my marriage—she actually blames me for Deirdre's mental health issues, can you believe that? After all I've done to take care of my wife. Spiteful bitch. You ask around this town—everyone thinks the same." He paused. "That's why it never occurred to me that someone would give Margaret an alibi, let alone charge around running errands for her and trying to convince people that she's innocent. Since when did my sister-in-law have a *friend*?"

"I will be speaking in Margaret's defence." Bess willed herself to sound fearless. But she could not stop a gasp of horror when Paul reached into his back pocket and she saw the flash of a knife.

"You won't be speaking to anyone."

Bess could feel the yielding softness of damp grass and soil beneath her feet, the crunch and crumble of leaves and seed pods as she began to edge sideways. She had no clear idea of what to do. But around the side of the tiny house was garden furniture: folding chairs, a birdbath. Could she place those objects between herself and Paul? Fighting to stay calm, she said, "You can't commit a third murder and blame it on Margaret. She's in prison, remember? And people know I've been looking into this; they'll figure it out."

"People?" Paul still sounded relaxed, conversational even. But she could smell some new odour drifting from him: an excited sweat. "What, you mean Zan Alexandris and her little crew? Yeah, I wouldn't worry too much about them. They're all NEETs."

"They're what?" Chest pounding, Bess tried to move smoothly, to not look like prey.

Paul followed after her at the same pace, as if they were out for a stroll together.

"Not Engaged in Education or Training", he explained. "What used to be called juvenile delinquents. Did you know Tammy never even went to high school? They're all Department of Human Services kids. Wouldn't talk to the police if their lives depended on it, and who'd believe them if they did?" Paul heaved a sigh. "Sad. I can deal with the usual teenage hijinks, but in cases like that we're dealing with entrenched intergenerational disadvantage. Well, I can't save everyone." His arms hung loose and easy, the knife held lightly in his right hand. The blade gleamed in a familiar shape; Bess recognised it from her own kitchen.

"And I'm not going to kill you," Paul said. "You're going to kill yourself."

He surged forward.

She felt the rush of air as his hand narrowly missed her face. She dodged sideways, began to run, before a hard shove sent her tripping across the uneven ground.

His full weight hit her, and pounded her into the dirt.

"I've been researching you." Paul's voice was panting, excited. His knee crushed her back, his elbow grinding savagely into her ribcage, forcing the breath out of her.

She smelled eucalyptus leaves, damp earth.

"Sad about your friend," he taunted. "The one you killed. Angela, wasn't it? But with a tragic background like that, and then getting tangled up with that evil Margaret Gale… The way Margaret manipulated you into giving her a fake alibi for one of the murders she committed—well, with all that guilt, it's no wonder your mental health collapsed, Bess. No wonder you couldn't go on—"

"Get off me!" She thrashed against his weight, clawed desperately through the dirt for anything: a rock, a stick.

A strangled scream was forced from her as Paul grabbed her left arm and twisted it viciously behind her. "Thanks for the phone," he said. "It'll make things simpler if your contacts get a farewell-cruel-world text." His grip loosened as one hand reached for the knife.

She tried desperately to wrest her arm free, then felt a howl burst from her chest as the blade sliced into her wrist. A fiery pain shot the length of her arm—then Paul's grip slackened.

Lights. There were white beams of light from somewhere nearby. Her heartbeat roared in her ears. Was she dying?

"What the fuck?" Paul's voice was a yelp.

The air moved, then Bess heard the beating of wings.

Paul was twisting around on top of her, slapping at something beyond Bess's eye line. His weight lifted a little, and she was able to turn her head.

In the weird half-light, she could make out frantic, darting movements, flashes of white. It was Genghis the rooster, defending his flock. Head down, he charged at Paul again and again, leaping up to gouge this enormous foe with his talons and slash at him with his long, pointed spurs.

Paul swore and kicked out at him, missed, then yelled with pain as Genghis scored a direct hit.

Bess managed to twist sideways, her wrist wet and burning. She looked up to see Tammy standing over them, Bess's granite tranquillity water feature lifted high in both hands.

She hit Paul over the head with it, and he dropped like a stone in the garden bed.

Heart pumping, Bess scrambled to her feet. She took off at a stumbling run, energy surging through her, her body screaming at her to get away. The cold air hit her lungs; she coughed, then forced in great gulps of it.

Her wrist hurt like hell. She gripped it hard, a warm stickiness oozing through her fingers.

She looked back at Tammy and Squid standing over their captive.

Paul was stretched out on the ground; Genghis was strutting and flapping around them.

A hysterical laugh began to bubble up in her chest. She staggered around the side of the tiny house, towards the blaze of headlights.

"What the fuck's going on?" The voice came from a mustard-brown station wagon parked in Bess's vegetable garden. The passenger doors were open; Zan was clambering out the driver's side. Zan's eyes widened as she caught a glimpse of Bess's arm.

"All right." Bess heard herself gabbling. "I'm all right. It's Paul. He killed Leon and Arwyn. He attacked me. He's back—back there—" She gestured, and a wave of dizziness sent her toppling sideways.

Zan propped Bess against the side of the car. Then she tugged and fiddled at the front of Bess's dress.

"What are you...?"

"Got it." Zan held up the lapel pin, examining it in the light of her phone's screen. "Let's hope you're as crap with technology as we thought...

Yes! You didn't turn it off!" She gave a whoop of triumph. "Looks like we got that evidence after all."

Bess focused her gaze on the object between Zan's finger and thumb: the grinning decorative skull to mark a day when the dead came back to visit the living.

She leaned against the car and shut her eyes for a while.

Chapter 22

SHE WAS STILL ALIVE.

Time passed in a haze. Bess slumped against the car and watched as it all went spinning by.

There was Squid yelling at Zan for binding up Bess's bleeding wrist with her Doctor Who scarf—"I knitted that myself from the BBC's original pattern, dickhead!"—before Zan shooed her off down the drive at a wheezing jog to find a phone signal and call the police.

There was Tammy slouching back to announce that Paul wasn't dead, just knocked out, and regretting that she hadn't brought along the Taser she'd bought illegally online from the States: "Shit, I've been waiting for ages to try that out."

There was Kenneth, lolling half-conscious in the station wagon's back seat, slurring things like, "Give it back, I'll get in trouble" and "Not the same knife, is it? The murder knife?"

"What's he doing here?" Bess peered in at him.

Zan explained, "We called him after we dropped you off. We were going to kick his arse for lying to us about setting up that meeting with Vince. But this lady answered his phone, sounding really panicked, and she kept saying he was dying and someone had to come and help her. Well—" Zan reached into the car, gave Kenneth a shove, and watched as he slumped in slow motion across the seat. "You can see he's not dying, just totally fucked. We thought at first he'd been drinking, but now I reckon someone slipped him something. There was a mug on the coffee table, come to think of it."

"Zan, what *happened?*"

"Well, we drove to the address the lady gave us. She said her name was Deirdre; I'd seen her around town. She let us in, sobbing that 'the poor boy' was dying and she didn't know what to do. She said he'd shown up there and had a big blue with her husband; she could hear them yelling about knives, so she was too scared to go in. Then she heard her husband calm him down, and the car driving off. She thought hubbie had gone to drop the kid home; she screamed the place down when she walked into the lounge room and found Kenneth face-planted on the rug. Anyway, we said we'd take Kenneth back to his mum's place, but it all seemed a bit suss, so we tried to call you, but I guess your pissweak phone wasn't getting any reception out here, so we thought we'd stop by in person, and…" Zan paused for breath. "Here we are." She stared around the paddock. "Bess, what's going on? I mean… Paul? From youth club?"

"He had secrets," Bess said. "He wanted to make sure Margaret couldn't tell."

And suddenly, there was Deirdre, bursting from the car, a blue towelling dressing gown flapping around her, one slipper missing, zigzagging across Bess's yard in a frantic search for something. "We had to bring her; she was carrying on so much," Zan said.

Reaching the tiny house, Deirdre discovered her husband's prone form and stopped dead. She pressed both hands to her mouth. She didn't touch him.

Backing blindly away, she just missed the bird bath. Bess, fearing she would fall, hurried towards her. In the blare of the headlights, Deirdre's face was white. The hem of her dressing gown was grimy; her eyes shone with tears. At the touch of Bess's hand on her shoulder, she turned away from Paul's limp form and seized Bess by her elbows.

In a frantic whisper, Deirdre said, "He's dead, poor boy, but don't worry. We won't tell. We'll think of something…" She flung her arms around Bess. Her clutching fingertips dug into Bess's skin; her cheek was hot against Bess's throat. "We'll be all right; we'll look after each other. We always look after each other, don't we, Margaret?"

Chapter 23

IT WAS A LONG JOURNEY back to Port Bannir. Margaret had refused the offer of a lift. The train travelled slowly, and she could only imagine how many strangers had left their germs over every surface. But after days of being forced to follow orders, she relished the independence and the silence.

Alighting at the station, she paused to look around her. Port Bannir seemed so innocuous: a quaint little town, a relaxing spot for a long weekend; the sort of place where nothing much ever happened. Hard to imagine it as a site of exile, or murder.

Years ago, Margaret had been enraged at being forced back here. Later, she'd been determined to stay out of sheer bloody-mindedness, to remind people of their past and be a thorn in the side of this place. But now… She gazed up at the station's crumbling red-brick façade, at the clock tower, and at the gum trees. It was all so ordinary. She exhaled, her shoulders loosening. In this moment, she didn't mind being here, and she also wouldn't mind leaving.

She flagged down the local cab driver, ignoring his shocked expression when he recognised her. Sliding into the back seat, Margaret wound the window down. She couldn't get enough of the cold, fresh air.

As they approached the old Gale property, she frowned through the open window. It had been years since she'd watched her own house appear on the horizon, as a passenger with nothing else to do but observe. A square, dark block of a place, she realised; neat and neutral, finished with concrete. Like a display home on an estate that had never been built. Strange to think that two people had died here, in this very driveway, and that their deaths had cemented Margaret's monstrous reputation.

She climbed out of the cab, slammed the door shut, and waited until it vanished over the horizon. Then she looked around her once more. Such a quiet spot.

Margaret Gale had never been a religious woman, and besides any restless spirits here would have no reason to bear a grudge against her. It was the memory of Paul and Duncan that made her grimace, as if at the sound of nails on a slate.

She shut her eyes, banishing the thought. When she opened them to look again at her house, she was surprised to see a movement, a flutter of colour against the concrete. A green dress in a shade that was both delicate and vivid, like a fern, its fronds unfurling.

Bess. The woman stepped forward and waved. She was smiling.

"This is a surprise," Margaret managed to say. She was smiling, too, for the first time in days.

Bess's wrist was bandaged and one knee looked grazed, but her expression was so open, so happy, that it made a bubble of hope rise in Margaret's chest.

"I wanted to bring you some zucchini bread and a plant from my garden." Bess paused. "To say welcome home."

"Well." Margaret's mouth was dry. "No one has done any of those things for me before." No one had looked at her like that before, either. The delight on Bess's face, the shape of her lips when she smiled, even her boldness in letting herself onto Margaret's property to wait for her—all these things set Margaret's heartbeat galloping.

Bess stepped forward, hesitating only a second, before wrapping her arms around Margaret's waist and pulling her in for a kiss. Her mouth was warm, her movements unafraid, and Margaret relished the plush texture of her lips, the surge of her breath. Bess had believed in her all this time, had not given up on her. Margaret clutched her, grateful for the solid weight of her, the heartbeat in the side of her throat when Margaret dropped her head to kiss her there.

"Come inside," Margaret said. They had hours of catching up to do—not all of it talking. She pictured Bess's red hair spread across white linen, sunlight warming her freckled skin. Their first time together had been too rushed, without the tenderness and exploration they both deserved. Time to make up for that now.

Bess nodded, the longing in her expression mirroring Margaret's own feelings, but they didn't move away just yet.

Shutting her eyes, Margaret inhaled the scent of Bess's hair and skin, listening to the breeze and the distant chirrup of birds. She flexed her feet inside her boots, anchoring them more firmly to the ground, and imagining the dark earth beneath the concrete. All the things that were buried, and the things still living.

Epilogue

Three months later

B*ess* s*watted* h*er* w*ay* t*hrough* the plastic ribbons and stepped into McKenzie's Bakery. It was a sunny Saturday morning and the place was buzzing. The air smelled sweetly of rising pastry and cooling cakes. In one quiet corner sat Margaret Gale.

The tables on either side of her were empty, but her coffee cup showed she'd not been refused service, and the glances people directed at her seemed less hostile now—more curious, confused, and wary. Today her long coat was vivid red with gold stitching around the cuffs and collar, like a victory banner. She saw Bess and raised her chin in greeting.

"Am I late?" Bess dropped her bag and sat down.

"Always, I suspect." But Margaret's eyes crinkled at the corners with something like warmth. "Still, I arrived early. We're packing up the last of Deirdre's things, and she wanted some time to say goodbye to her house."

"How is she?"

"Dying." Margaret spoke flatly, but without denial or anger now. "We think she may see in the New Year. She likes our new unit in Melbourne, with the tea rooms and parks nearby. Even I hadn't quite realised how much time she spent hiding in the house, when she lived here." A muscle worked in Margaret's face. Then she let out a deep breath, as if to expel the tension.

Lowering her voice, Bess said, "And…the police investigation?"

Margaret straightened her cuffs. "Well, Paul is on remand, as you know, awaiting trial." There was grim satisfaction in her tone. "With Kenneth's testimony, Deirdre's, and yours of course, I expect a satisfactory outcome. They haven't charged Deirdre over the scarf, but she may face historic charges concerning Jacob's death." Margaret sighed. "At the speed it's moving, I doubt she'll see the inside of a courtroom. But she's been calmer since it all came out. She's stopped jumping at shadows; she's even stopped apologising for everything." Margaret drained the last of her coffee and grimaced, as if at the bitter dregs. "Perhaps the end of her marriage helped with that, too."

"That's…good." Bess leaned forward. "But actually I was asking about you."

"Ah." Margaret lined up her coffee cup carefully on the saucer. "Making false statements to police. Failing to report an unexpected death. Don't worry, Ms Campbell, I've not been declared a law-abiding citizen just yet."

Bess glared; she wasn't ready for Margaret to make jokes about this stuff. "You're still at liberty, though."

"Ms Harper's legal team have proven most efficient," Margaret said. "I don't imagine they do much pro bono work, but I made free legal representation of me a condition of the sale."

Bess nodded, her shoulders slumping a little. If she glanced out the window and craned her neck, she could see the great white behemoth of Incursium Estate, already half built and dwarfing the rest of the street.

"It's horrible," Bess said.

"Hard to disagree."

"I can't believe you gave up your museum to them."

Margaret shrugged. "Ah, well." Her expression was solemn, but there was a looseness in her shoulders, a lightness in her tone, that Bess had not observed there before. "Deirdre and I needed the best legal representation, and I needed the money and time to care for Deirdre. Something had to give. And besides…" She glanced around the café, then up and down the street. "I was hanging in here, in this town, to spite them all. To make a point. But I'm not sure I need to do that any longer."

Bess watched her. Margaret's skin had darkened to a faint olive, as if she'd been spending more time outdoors since her release. It was strange to think of her ever being content without her rooms full of relics, explanations, evidence. "You're really going to sell off your collection?"

"Not all of it." Margaret didn't elaborate. "But I've found a few acceptable buyers. And a contact has offered me some part-time work at an auction house in Melbourne." She managed a smile. "Don't look so downcast, Bess. I'll still get to hunt, access, restore, and tell people what to do. And I'm thinking of writing a book, a history of seafaring in Bass Strait." Her eyes narrowed. "Go on, say it. You think that's the dullest topic imaginable."

"I think you may need some assistance to market it." Bess smirked. "But I'd be happy to help." She studied Margaret closely. "You're really all right with this?"

Margaret exhaled. "I am accepting what I can't change. Attempting to make the most of the here and now." She spoke the words suspiciously, as if afraid they might be trite. "Surely that aligns with your philosophy, Bess?"

"My philosophy?" Bess hesitated. An image flashed through her mind of Tammy clobbering Paul with the tranquillity fountain. She wasn't sure whether to shudder or laugh. "I need coffee."

Joining the queue at the counter, Bess gazed at the dark, moist fruit cakes, crisp sultana scones, and chocolate muffins overflowing their wrappers. Idly, she listened in to the conversations around her, before catching a familiar voice.

"Listen, I've told you before, no one wants pamphlets from your Spiritualist Society." The voice was nasal and irritable as usual, but softer than Bess had heard it previously.

Irene swapped the phone to her other ear and said, "I don't care what plane of existence you think they're on; just let the nurses do their job and look after you." She paused. "What about your blood test; have you got the results yet? All right, I'll see you Sunday." Hanging up, she caught Bess looking at her. "Take a picture, why don't you?" Irene snapped. Then, as if defending herself, she added, "It's not against the law to visit an old lady in hospital, is it?"

Bess, feeling certain it had been Hermione on the line, shook her head and turned away. She thought it best not to let Irene see her smiling.

Returning to their table with a coffee and a lavender macaron, Bess seated herself comfortably. She scooped the foam off her drink and licked the spoon. Then she fixed her eyes on Margaret and said, "So, are you going to explain now? Why you didn't tell me your suspicions about Paul and Duncan?"

Margaret took a sip of water.

Bess watched her throat as she swallowed, admiring the texture of her skin, the elegant hollow there that seemed to invite a kiss.

At last, Margaret said, "At first it was nothing but paranoia on my part. How would it have looked if I'd started accusing two respected pillars of the community?" She grimaced. "Then that scarf appeared in my office, and I was fairly sure the only person I'd left alone in there, who could have planted it, was Deirdre. But I couldn't bear to accuse her, and once they'd arrested me, I had no way of finding out how deeply implicated she might be."

The memory seemed to send a cloud across Margaret's countenance. "Deirdre would never deliberately harm anyone, but she was always easily led. I'd asked the Hags to hack into Duncan Mather's system to find out whom he'd been ringing and speaking with. They were able to confirm that he'd been in long conversations with Paul after Deirdre's appointments, going back months. The two of them allowed her to get sicker, while they plotted to protect themselves." Margaret's voice dropped to a rasp; her eyes darkening.

"Is Duncan really going to get away with it?" Bess shook her head, appalled. "I couldn't believe it when I heard he was still practising!"

"I've got the legal team on it." Margaret's jaw tightened. "Negligence might be the best lawful solution we can find, in relation to Deirdre. As for Jacob's death, well, you know charges haven't been laid yet."

"I can't believe some people are sticking up for him," Bess said. "The golf club even held a fundraiser! It's sick."

"A few minds have been changed." Margaret shrugged, as if she hadn't expected much more. "Some locals even contacted me privately saying they'd always suspected something like this."

Bess spluttered. "Where were they thirty years ago?"

"Quite." Margaret's mouth twisted up in one corner. "But, as with museums, you can only put the history out there as accurately as you can. Whether people choose to look at it is up to them."

"I suppose." Bess broke off a piece of macaron with her fork. "And you haven't answered my question yet. Why didn't you let me in on your suspicions?" After the dangers she'd faced, it stung to think that Margaret hadn't trusted her.

"I was ruminating on what to do," Margaret said. "I was afraid of putting Deirdre in more danger, especially as I'd no real proof of anything. I figured if Paul was the killer, he'd be content with my imprisonment and leave it there. I didn't think he would go after anyone else." She met Bess's gaze properly at last. "And I didn't dream you would go to such lengths to try to help me." Margaret hesitated. The fingers of her right hand gave a twitch. Then, moving stiffly, she reached over to cover Bess's hand with her own.

The warmth of her skin, the awkward caress of her thumb against Bess's wrist made Bess catch her breath.

"I'm sorry, Bess." Margaret swallowed. "And thank you."

Bess tightened her lips for a second. She still thought Margaret's habit of keeping secrets was dangerous and stupid. But she turned her hand over to clasp Margaret's fingers. Then she lifted a piece of macaron to her mouth and let the sugar, almond, and gooey nougat dissolve on her tongue.

Changing the subject, she asked in a conversational tone, "Have you been reading the papers?"

"Naturally." Margaret eyed her. "Perhaps you're referring to the news that someone is making a telemovie about the life and death of the unfortunate Arwyn Ross?"

Bess winced. "I did read that. Starring that blonde runner-up from *Kitchen Renovation*." She wondered if this was the final insult to Arwyn's strange, shattered life—or whether Arwyn might have been pleased by it.

Shaking her head, she said, "No, I wasn't thinking of that. I meant this." From her bag, she pulled the Saturday Arts and Lifestyle magazine from one of the Melbourne papers. She dropped it on the table and tapped the leading article. Narrowing her eyes, Bess said, "Don't pretend you didn't swallow your tongue when you saw this."

The article, rather predictably headed "Sisters are doing it for themselves", showed Georgina Harper wearing the Arctic-white pants suit of an unnaturally confident woman and a wide, smug smile. She had her arm around a woman whom the article breathlessly described as the youngest CEO of any gallery in Australia. The woman had a funky new haircut and a dazed look in her eyes, but there was no mistaking her. It was Margaret's old lackey, Kelly Petrovich.

"Yes. Well." That muscle worked again in Margaret's cheek. "I suppose it's a testament to how well I trained her."

"Bullshit!" Bess snorted. "You suspected her of plotting behind your back with Vince; now we know what they were really talking about. Pretending to be so meek and submissive—she played you."

"That's one way of looking at it."

"Is there another way?"

"I'd say your Ms Harper likes training up sweet young protégés." Margaret's left eyebrow arched almost to her hairline. "She's got herself a capable curator with strong local knowledge, who'll work like mad, do everything she's told, and be ever so grateful. Quite a bargain, really." Learning back in her chair, Margaret added, "A pity you turned out to be so ungovernable, Bess. It could have been you."

"I'm glad it's not." Bess realised they were still holding hands. She thought about drawing away, then realised there was no need to, not any more. "Still, maybe Kelly will do a reasonable job. She's been handling that exhibition about Leon and Sybil Powell okay. She persuaded Georgina to drop the most offensive Alzheimer's references and include a stronger focus on Sybil's great photography."

"Ah, yes, I heard that exhibition was going ahead. Despite Steven Powell giving angry interviews to the press about what an absolute bastard his brother was to design it."

"Yeah, I saw those interviews." Bess crunched her way through the rest of the macaron. "Georgina didn't mind them. No such thing as bad publicity."

"That's rich," Margaret said. "Coming from a woman whose company is now under fire for conspiring to bribe a senator."

"I saw that, too." Bess rolled her eyes. "Never mind, I'm sure she'll do another exclusive interview about how a busy superwoman unwinds at the end of a long day, and the whole thing will go away."

"Bulletproof." Margaret sounded envious.

"Maybe." But Bess didn't want to talk about Georgina now. She finished her coffee and said, "Fancy a walk?"

Margaret followed her out of the bakery. For a moment they stood and gazed at Incursium Estate. The front section had already been built: square, stark apartments like white cement cubes, looming over the preserved façade of the old Maritime Museum. Behind them were the skeletons of several new storeys, still swathed in scaffolding.

"Never in my life," Margaret said, "have I see ugliness on such a scale."

Bess touched her arm. "I'm sorry about your museum."

Margaret gave a brusque nod. "I gather they're converting the main gallery into some kind of five-star restaurant. I haven't been inside." Pain flickered across her face as she turned away.

Bess stroked her arm. "It's not fair."

"Ah, well." Margaret straightened her spine. "At least I was able to get something out of it in terms of legal representation. Quite a lot actually. Worse things happen at sea. And perhaps... perhaps a fresh start will not be the worst thing imaginable."

"Change is key to personal growth," Bess ventured.

Margaret grunted and beckoned her away, saying "Shall we walk past my car? I need to get something."

They set off down the road. Every second step, their elbows brushed together. Despite their layers of clothing, each accidental contact ignited a spark of excitement inside Bess.

Margaret glanced at her. "You haven't told me what you intend to do now."

"Me?" Bess took a deep breath. Feeling oddly shy, she announced, "I'm going on the road." When Margaret's eyes widened, she explained, "I had the idea of putting together a roadshow from the Cabinet of Curiosities, to take around the suburbs of Melbourne. You know: schools, local galleries, Neighbourhood Houses. And nursing homes," she added firmly.

"You'll have to choose your exhibits with care, then." Margaret was watching her closely. "But if you're going travelling, won't that mean...?"

"I've been taking driving lessons." Bess gulped and tried to sound normal about it. "I'm going to get my licence back."

"I see. And how are you—" Margaret seemed to find the next word faintly distasteful "—*feeling* about that?"

Beneath the obligatory sarcasm, Bess caught a soft note of concern.

"Scared," was her reply. "But I want to do it. I can't hide here forever." Bess nodded to herself. "Plus, a retired couple just moved in down the road from me; I've got neighbours! They're happy to chicken-sit sometimes."

"So… On with your next adventure?"

"I guess so. Travel nurtures the spirit."

"I'll take your word for it."

"Plus…" Bess brightened. "I've got a notion to start looking around at all the places I visit. You know, junk shops, artists' retreats, garage sales. I've been thinking about starting my own collection." She said it quietly, with some embarrassment.

"Very good."

Bess was taken aback. "You think so?"

"Of course. I'm sure you'll pick the most ghastly items, but still it's a smart idea. You have nerve and ingenuity, and you don't present too badly."

"Aw, shucks." Bess hesitated. "You really think it's a workable idea?"

"I had a premonition you'd do something like it," Margaret said. "I couldn't imagine you working for the avaricious Ms Harper for very long."

Bess shuddered. "God, no. I need something to look forward to, that's for sure."

They reached Margaret's immaculate car. She pulled out her keys and popped the boot open. "On that note…" Margaret lifted several layers of what looked like drop-sheets, which were carefully concealing the boot's contents. Then she pulled out a small wooden crate and passed it to Bess.

"What's…?" Bess lifted the lid, shooed aside the packing material, and gaped at the sight of the leather travelling case with its glass panel and silk lining of midnight blue. "Margaret!"

Her companion shuffled, as if unnerved by Bess's enthusiasm. "Just something to help start your collection."

"You're giving me that antique dildo?" Bess tried not to come over misty-eyed, but it was impossible. She caught Margaret's look. "Sorry. I mean, faux-Roman fertility symbol."

"Indeed." Margaret's eyes were narrowed. "Even long-dead women deserve a little privacy, to keep their secrets intact." She pronounced the last word with exaggerated crispness and a significant glance. "Don't make me regret this, Bess."

"I won't." Reverentially, Bess closed the lid. "Thank you."

Margaret looked away. "Least I could do."

Taking great care not to scratch the paintwork, Bess lowered the crate onto the boot of Margaret's car, and turned to face her properly. "Margaret."

"Still here."

"We—we haven't spent very much time together in an ordinary way." Bess searched for the right words. "Without a murder hanging over us, I mean."

"That's true."

"I'm…" Bess bit her lip. "I'm not completely sure what that would be like."

"Also true." Margaret's face had become rigid with expectation.

Bess steeled herself to be brave, to seize the moment—but it was Margaret who spoke first.

"But I would very much like to find out, *Ms Campbell*." She pronounced the last words with a mischievous gleam in her eye.

The tension left Bess's muscles in a warm rush of relief. In the back windscreen of Margaret's car, she glimpsed her own reflection, a smile spreading across her face. "I'd like that, too."

Silence settled between them. Bess followed Margaret's gaze towards the very end of the street. On the horizon was a sparkling streak of blue, where the hill sloped down towards the ocean.

"I have to get back to Melbourne tonight," Margaret said. "Deirdre can't be away from her specialists for long." She cleared her throat. "But is there any chance—I mean, if your new job is taking you to Melbourne on a regular basis, I don't suppose…"

Bess's face ached from smiling. "I can't wait to see you there. You can show me around where you live, take me to the auction houses. Stop me from buying anything unfortunate."

Margaret muttered something like "I'll certainly try…"

"You'll be sick of the sight of me."

Margaret's lips twitched. "I very much doubt that."

Then something occurred to Bess, and she added "Actually…look, you won't thank me for this, but my sister Melanie is getting married in Melbourne next week. I don't suppose…"

"Are you asking me on a—?" Margaret seemed to be striving to pronounce the word "—on a *date*, Ms Campbell?"

"You're right. Bad idea." Bess edged away. "It's too soon to make you hang out with my family; it's weird. And it'll be horrible. My mum will yell at everyone and burst into tears at least twice. My brother will be smoking weed in the toilets. My dad will get drunk and dance the Nutbush. All my right-wing relatives will be telling offensive jokes. There'll be long, cringeworthy speeches, and we'll all have to gather around and pretend to want to catch Mel's bouquet—"

She broke off then, because Margaret had leaned forward and kissed her. Her lips moved softly against Bess's, as if whispering her a secret.

Bess reached for her hands and held them.

"I'd love to," Margaret said.

Acknowledgements

Thanks, firstly, to my partner, Sam, for her wonderful support. I could never have finished my first novel without her! Thanks to my writing buddies Emma and Rachel for their encouragement and insights. And many thanks to Lee and Astrid for their smart and tactful editing and management—it's been a privilege to work together.

About Jess Lea

Jess Lea lives in Melbourne, Australia, where she started out as an academic before working in the community sector. She loves vintage crime fiction, the writings of funny women, and lesbian books of all sorts. Jess can be found writing in cafes, in parks, and in her pyjamas at home when she should be at work.

CONNECT WITH JESS
E-Mail: JessLeaContact@gmail.com

Other Books from Ylva Publishing

www.ylva-publishing.com

The Red Files
(On the Record Series – Book 1)
Lee Winter

ISBN: 978-3-95533-330-0
Length: 365 pages (103,000 words)

Ambitious journalist Lauren King is stuck reporting on the vapid LA social scene's gala events while sparring with her rival—icy ex-Washington correspondent Catherine Ayers. Then a curious story unfolds before their eyes, involving a business launch, thirty-four prostitutes, and a pallet of missing pink champagne. Can the warring pair join together to unravel an incredible story?

The Return
Ana Matics

ISBN: 978-3-95533-234-1
Length: 300 pages (85,000 words)

Near Haven is like any other fishing village dotting the Maine coastline—a crusty remnant of an industry long gone, mired in sadness and longing. Liza thought she'd gotten out, escaped on a basketball scholarship, but a series of bad decisions has her returning home after a decade. She struggles to accept her place in this small town, making amends to people she's wronged and rebuilding her life.

Driving Me Mad
L.T. Smith

ISBN: 978-3-95533-290-7
Length: 348 pages (107,000 words)

After becoming lost on her way to a works convention, Rebecca Gibson stops to ask for help at an isolated house. Progressively, her life becomes more entangled with the mysterious happenings of the house and its inhabitants.

With the help of Clare Davies, can Rebecca solve a mystery that has been haunting a family for over sixty years? Can she put the ghosts and the demons of the past to rest?

The Lavender List
Meg Harrington

ISBN: 978-3-95533-623-3
Length: 249 pages (62,000 words)

After the Second World War, Amelia Maldonado opts to live a quiet life bussing tables at a diner during the day and going out for auditions at night. The one bright spot is her friendship with the charming Laura Wright, a well-heeled woman with a mysterious war-related past.

When Laura shows up outside the diner, barely conscious and spitting lousy lies, Amelia takes it upon herself to figure out the truth. From mobsters to spies, Amelia quickly finds herself forced back into a world of shadows she thought she'd escaped long ago and thrust into partnership with the one person she's sure can ruin her—the enigmatic Laura Wright.

A Curious Woman
© 2019 by Jess Lea

ISBN: 978-3-96324-160-4

Also available as e-book.

Published by Ylva Publishing, legal entity of Ylva Verlag, e.Kfr.

Ylva Verlag, e.Kfr.
Owner: Astrid Ohletz
Am Kirschgarten 2
65830 Kriftel
Germany

www.ylva-publishing.com

First edition: 2019

Credits
Edited by Lee Winter and Amber Williams
Cover Design and Print Layout by Streetlight Graphics

.